BONE SHROUD

ANDREW MEREDITH

Games Afoot, LLC

For Bompa and Grandmother, Pop and Gramma,
The adventures we had, the work ethic taught,
and fond memories I have of you,
shall always define who I am.

Forward

Difficult circumstances reveal our true nature. For some, a jaw set against adversity is the path to success. For others, ignoring the problem until it goes away is their best tactic. But in the end, we all must face our problems. How we handle things under pressure is character changing. How we last under the constant drip of fate shows others who we really are.

If *Deathless Beast* was the autumnal path, with plagues of problems hounding the heels of our heroes, then *Bone Shroud* is the long, harsh winter. Having run from their past, the Clouws find themselves arriving full circle back at them, and must choose whether to run away or live up to the expectations they have for themselves. Jined Brazstein found the path he was called to only just beginning, thrust into a position of leadership he might not have chosen for himself, but knows failure would be a far worse option. Katiam bears the looming worry now that the Rotha has opened—to abandon it would be a greater failure than persevering and seeing what other secrets it holds. And now we have Seriah Yaledít, a woman happy to fulfill her duties. But difficulties can make even the simplest daily tasks hard to stomach. How Seriah— how any of them—will handle blunt adversity is as varied as they are.

Thank you for continuing past *Deathless Beast* and into this next step in the Kallattian Saga. The journey may have stopped to outlast the winter, but this volume is replete with deepening intrigue, hardship, and adventure. (And, possibly a new, smaller companion for one of our heroes.)

Thank you for joining me on this journey.

—Andrew D Meredith

Summary of Events Thus Far

DEATHLESS BEAST, VOLUME ONE OF THE KALLATTIAN SAGA

In *Deathless Beast*, we met Hanen and Rallia Clouw, Black Sentinel bodyguards with a caravan detail running north and south across the center of the continent of Ganthic. After one of their guards, Ghoré Dziony, is turned over to authorities for plaguing those under their protection with winged vermin, they return to their homebase in Edi, where Sentinel Captain Thadar Saliss extorts them for having saved their life. The man who introduced them to the job, Searn VeTurres, rolls into town with his new apprentice, Ophedia del Ishé, and an opportunity. The Clouws take it, if only to hoof it out of town and away from Thadar. Searn kills Thadar in a show of authority, and the Clouws soon arrive in the city of Birin, offering their services to the voluntarily blind monks of Nifara, who seek to travel north and meet with the heads of sister religious organizations. Before they can arrive at their destination, brigands attack, killing one monk, and poisoning the head of the monastic order.

In the far north, the entourage of Dorian Mür, the Prima Pater—head of the Church of Grissone and the Paladins of the Hammer—traverses the Northern Scapes, examining the Order's holdings, and arranging meetings with heads of state. Jined Brazstein, guard of the entourage is encouraged by a mysterious figure to seek out Deeper Faith, and discovers it to be a book by the same name. Even while he unravels this mystery, everything seems to go wrong, and none seem to expect the arrival of the Prima Pater. A mysterious group of paladins, heretics to the religion, seek to bring the Prima Pater and his order down from within.

Alongside the Prima Pater travels his wife, Maeda Mür, Matriarch Superioris, the head of the sister religion following Crysania, goddess of purity and oracles. Among the paladame guards is the physician Katiam Borreau, great-niece to the Matriarch Superioris. Katiam is given a mysterious seed pod, said to be unaffected by the centuries as it passed from hand to hand.

The entourage meets up with the monks and Sentinels traveling north, only to be attacked by a mysterious figure who commands all manners of winged creatures. He calls himself the Deathless Beast and it is revealed to be Ghoré Dziony, having given his soul to a dark god and made into a winged monster himself. He is only defeated when another equally dark figure assists the Clouws and Jined. The mysterious seed in Katiam's possession has also opened, only just beginning to reveal its secrets.

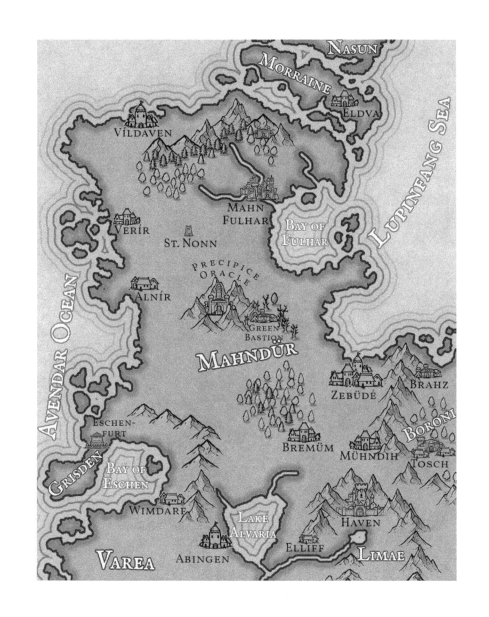

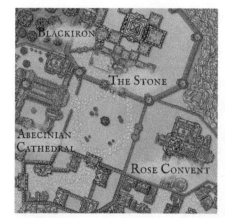

PART 1

Prologue

Pater Minoris Jakis Gladen stood upon the wall of the Aerie, Citadel of the Order of the Hammer, and the command center of Pariantür's northwestern domains on the continent of Ganthic. He could make out the line of Paladins riding through the southern gate of the city of Haven, their hammers at attention. They looked menacing—ready for a fight.

"It seems Bell did as he promised; the capricörs are coming to the butcher house," Pater Gladen said.

So we follow the plan? Primus Slate signed. He was a thin man. While he naturally stood shorter than Gladen, the boots he wore, which he fashioned himself in his leather shop, gave him several additional inches of height.

Gladen nodded. "Have the Portion brought to the courtyard, and have the Gauntlet and Brazier prepared."

As you command.

The three hundred Paladins arrived at the gate of the Aerie, which opened as they approached. They filed in and brought their six-legged sleipnir horses into formation, filling the courtyard with the smell of sweat, steel, and eagerness.

At the head of the platoon rode a Paladin with gold cordons upon his breastplate, denoting him a Pater Minoris. He had a severe face, and the ruddy skin of southern Morriego, perhaps even Hraldor.

"Greeting, Pater Minoris Koel of the Bulwark!" the Paladin atop the wall of the keep called.

"And greetings to you, Pater Minoris Gladen, by the Grace of Grissone. We have answered your call for aid."

What aid? Slate asked as Gladen took the ornate box from his hands.

"Bell has told them that we're under siege by vül. And the Bulwark's aid would be needed to push back the slavering horde."

"Is there time for my fellow brothers to wash and rest before we ride out against the foe?" Koel called up.

"There will be time," Gladen called, "but I'm afraid that the vül were a pretense. You have been deceived."

Pater Gladen opened the box and lifted out a black orb of twisted metal.

8

"What do you mean?"

"There are Paladins, Pater Koel, who have turned against the faith, and seek to found a kingdom and church of their own."

"What heresy is this?" Pater Koel asked. "Who would do such a thing? We are charged to defend humanity!"

"You will, Pater Koel," Gladen said. "You will join my vanguard. You have no choice."

He lifted the black metal orb up high and struck it with his hammer, then tossed the ball into the midst of the Paladins fifty feet below.

"Sometimes betrayal is more merciful if you don't take the time to explain yourself," Pater Gladen said under his breath to Slate. "We need soldiers, that is all."

A throbbing sound arose, filling the courtyard. Pater Koel stared at the orb a moment before his sleipnir whinnied and tried to buck.

"What is the meaning...?" His words were cut off as dust exploded around the orb.

The legs of every sleipnir buckled underneath them, and they collapsed to the ground. The riders fell, hollering as they did. The Paladins of the Aerie flooded out into the courtyard and fell upon the Paladins of the Bulwark with truncheons, knocking them senseless. Some resisted, but soon succumbed, bound with shackles, and held in place on their knees by those who betrayed them.

A pair of Paladins wearing black cloaks in semblance of wings pushed out a brazier on wheels as Gladen came out into the courtyard. Slate picked up the metal orb, put it back into its box, and gave it to someone to take it away.

"The Gauntlet?" Gladen asked.

Slate made a signal, and another Paladin came out from the citadel carrying an even larger lacquered black box.

"What are you doing?" Koel demanded from the ground as Gladen approached.

Gladen silently took the gauntlet and put it on his hand. It was the same black metal as the twisted orb, and bore intricate etchings over its entirety. The two attendants to the brazier emptied out a ceramic jar of steel coins into the heat of the fire, and waited.

Pater Koel continued to shout, demanding explanation. Gladen simply watched the fire glow, and when enough time had passed, nodded. The attendant took up tongs, and lifted a single coin out of the embers. Gladen held the gauntlet palm up, and the attendant dropped the red-hot coin onto it. Gladen gave no sign that the heat from the metal reached his own flesh. He walked over to Koel as Slate pulled off the man's gorget and breastplate, and tore open his under-robe to reveal his collar bone.

"This will hurt," Gladen said with an apologetic smile.

He pressed the coin in the palm of his gauntlet into the man's flesh, leaving the coin to cool in his skin. Koel screamed for only a moment before suddenly ceasing, although his eyes continued to scream as his body went rigid.

Gladen took his hand back. "Now, stand up."

The man did as he was commanded, even while his eyes protested in horror.

"Remove the breastplate and gorget from the next man."

Koel did as he commanded, as Gladen took another hot coin onto the gauntlet. He proceeded down the long line, prepared to do the harsh work long into the evening.

I

Mahn Fulhar

New vistas now sit open,
Climb on, the roads and wend.
Or sit in city unmoved,
    And harbor sloth and sin,
      The enemy of men.

-FROM *THE TRAVELER*, BY JUREN LIEFSEN

The late rising sun sat on the verge of cresting the horizon, showering the already bustling city of Mahn Fulhar with dull winter light. Carved from sandstone cliffs, pillared walkways overlooked Quayside where members of the upper crust walked. Meanwhile, the working class carefully navigated frost-encrusted streets, showered by the mist of the canal, a river flowing mostly unseen by the terraced streets, ever descending the city that grew up and around the channel.

Hanen Clouw sat at a window table, his black Sentinel cloak lying over the bench beside him, as disheveled as his thick black hair. He had not made an effort to tie it up on the back of his head. Rallia would insist on giving him a shave and trim soon, he didn't doubt.

His long, thin nose twitched at the smell of greasy ash being kicked up by the young soot girl as she returned to her work cleaning up the ashes, after offering him a bowl of the soup barely kept warm by the embers of the dying hearth. The Ship Tack Inn, known for harboring merchant captains and naval officers during their stay in the city, sat high above the harbor.

Quayside, to the south of the river channel, was visible and, while not high enough up the sloping north side of the city to see the tops of the sandstone cliffs, it afforded the view of carved windows and houses built into the cliff-face. Plumes could be seen rising off the plateau from the city's smokehouses. Their fires, along with the external torches that warmed and lit the Grotto Market, provided a glow that slowly diminished in the waxing light of the rising sun.

Beyond the plume of smoke, the tops of the castle complex could be seen; they were massive, but shorter than the complex's two neighbors —the Cathedral of Aben and the Rose Convent of the Crysalas. The Cathedral was topped by a gout of flame rising from a great iron arrow pointing toward the heavens. The rose-tinted windows of the tallest parapet of the Crysalas's own convent softened the harshness of her two counterparts.

"The city has been gossiping about the Church of Aben replacing the iron arrow with a mirrored one, lit with Bortali starblush," Rallia said, appearing from behind.

Hanen's little sister had freshly shaved the sides of her blonde head the night before, indicating to others that she was open for business as the company's barber. She was several inches short than Hanen, and just as many years younger. Where Hanen was lean, Rallia had strong arms, maintained by her early morning regimen and constant self-improvement.

"Why is that gossip?" Hanen asked.

"I heard a couple of cobblers in the Grotto. One said the flame burning in the iron arrow was a source of oppression. The other corrected him by offering that the flame scorches the iron. It was never meant to be black, but to symbolize prayers to Aben."

"I can see that," Hanen said, pushing his half-eaten bowl of soup across to Rallia, who took the offering and finished it off. "You've already been to the Grotto this morning?"

"The sun is just now rising," Rallia said, "but I've been up for hours."

"And had time to shave a few heads, it seems," Hanen said.

Ophedia del Ishé entered from a back room, the left side of her own head shaved. She ran her fingers through her hair, letting it fall over the shaved side, then approached, smiling.

"It feels so odd!" she said, throwing herself down on the bench next to Rallia. The girl was nineteen, but carried herself like someone five years older. She arched her eyebrow at Hanen as he gave her new hair-style a once-over.

"It suits you," Hanen said.

She lifted her chin and smiled. "It feels like zvolders are crawling along the side of my head."

"I warned you," Rallia said. "It'll take some getting used to."

She wore a soft leather vest over linen sleeves. The black wool of the vest was embroidered with deep, wine-purple patterns, fitting of the Mahndürian city.

"What are we talking about?" Ophedia asked as she took her hair in her hands and began pulling the locks into a braid over her shoulder.

"The iron arrow on the top of the Cathedral."

"Yeah, I wandered up there a couple of days ago. I wasn't that impressed."

"The top of the city is probably not the right place to look to set up an office," Hanen said.

"Why not?" the girl said, making a sour face.

"For one, it's just estates."

"Then you haven't been up there," she said.

"I was up there when we arrived, and escorted the Nifarans to the Abecinian complex. Making our way back into the city in the middle of the night, all we saw were the estates, along with their guards giving us the evil eye."

"Add to that," Rallia said, "Searn said there wasn't likely to be any places to do business up there. That's why we've been looking down here in the lower tiers."

"Since it was dark when we arrived," Ophedia said, "I wanted to see it in the light. You weren't looking close enough, or taking any risks, save what Searn told you, so I went off to look at it on my own. There is a whole market up there. Mostly for the servants of the estates to shop at without having to leave the comfort of their upper crust homes."

"So were there any places that might be willing to let us rent a space for a new Black Sentinel office?"

"Oh, definitely not," she said. "There were some bakeries with over-priced pastries, some tailors, a few goldsmiths. But Searn was right, there is nowhere to set up shop."

"Then why are we arguing?" Hanen sighed.

"Because you didn't think there was anything other than estates, and it felt like a good time to correct you, and make sure you knew you were wrong."

She rose with a smirk on her face.

"I'm going to walk the streets. I heard there is a whole street owned by the Salter's guild. I didn't know there were different kinds of salts. And the boy that was bragging about his master's wares was kind of cute."

Hanen rolled his eyes. "Just remember, we're looking for an aban-doned shop, or perhaps even a guildhall falling into disrepair that we can rent a portion of."

Ophedia walked over to the door and took up the cloak and staff she had left there. Where Rallia had affixed both of her clubs to either end of a slender quarterstaff, Ophedia had chosen a stout stick to attach her badge of office to, in imitation of Rallia.

She pulled her cloak over her frame, swung the staff heavily up onto her shoulder, and pushed her way out the door. She crossed the street to the banister looking out over the sea, nodding to herself as she turned and walked away. The sun had fully come up over the horizon, and lit her black hair with a tinge of red.

"She is going to continue to be trouble," Hanen said.

"What is that supposed to mean?" Rallia asked. "She's just a kid."

"She's not just a kid," Hanen said. "She's what, nineteen?"

"That's not my point," Rallia said. "I mean she's still young. And we've all gone through similar phases in life. Remember that first year with Master Taben? I was sullen, and looking for trouble. Remember that week in Nihn?"

"I'd rather not. You weren't at your best."

"No, I wasn't. I've matured. So have you."

"I suppose," Hanen said.

"And so has she, even in the short time since she and Searn met up with us in Edi. And she does a good job. She talks a lot about the trouble she wants to get into, but she's not actually trouble. She's all talk."

"Since the attack by Ghoré at the bastion, though, she's gone from cocky to outright brazen."

"Just like you've been even more sullen and morose," Rallia said with a smile. "But I don't complain."

"What?"

"You've had a lot on your mind," Rallia said. "We've been dragged north, with the promise of a bigger opportunity than what we had in Edi, or so Searn says. And as we actually neared Mahn Fulhar, you've been locked in your own mind, piecing together how we're actually going to do that. And during the two weeks we've been here, it's gotten worse."

"Doors have been barred to us. The city is treating us as unwelcomed, and our coin is running out. Of course I'm morose."

"You and I aren't the only ones who know this," Rallia said. "So all I'm saying is please be forgiving of a few personality quirks among the others, like Ophedia. We're all under a little stress."

Two Black Sentinels approached from the way Ophedia had walked. Both had their peaked hoods up over their head, but while their faces were mostly obscured, Hanen knew them both by sight. The waxed and curled mustache of Aurín Mateau couldn't be missed, and next to him the confident air of Searn VeTurres was obvious. They both walked around a merchant cart as it passed, and opened the door to the inn, stomping off the dampness on their boots.

"Ah," Searn smiled as he saw Hanen and Rallia, "I'm glad you're here."

Searn was twice Hanen's age, but moved through the world like a man barely forty. He took in the room with a quick side glance, and then devoted his attention to the Clouws.

The tavern's proprietor made an appearance and stood behind the bar, giving the counter a better cleaning in the light of day than the keep the night before had. Searn held up a hand, and he took the hint and began preparing drinks for the four of them.

"Been out early?" Hanen said as Searn came to sit next to him.

"Out late, actually," Searn said as he shook some of the dampness from his shorter black hair.

"We just came from the Plateau," Aurín said, in his tight Œronzi accent. He touched at his looped mustache, and flicked a crumb off the table.

"No need to get ahead of ourselves yet," Searn admonished the man jovially.

"Of course," Aurín said.

The proprietor approached with tankards of small ale, and placed them on the table.

"I've only just come down from the house," the man said, taking the empty bowl from in front of Rallia. "But if you're all here for a time, I can prepare something other than last night's soup."

The man had been very accommodating once Searn and the Clouws began spending good money.

"Do you recall the way I asked to have a morning cake prepared?" Aurín asked.

"Yes, Good Mateau."

"You added a spice of some sort yesterday."

"My sincerest apologies," the man said, bowing his head. "My wife added a bit of caraway, I believe."

"No need to apologize," Aurín said. "Whatever it was, do it again."

"Of course, sir."

"For each of us," Searn added.

The man shuffled away with a coin Searn had slipped him with his request.

"I take it you've had news," Hanen said.

"I'll get to that," Searn said. "However, first, tell me how your search has gone."

"It's been a futile chore," Hanen said. "Any doors we've found have been closed in our faces."

"Where have you been looking?" Searn asked.

"We chose not to look on Quayside, given our clientele are those who need to move by land, not sea," Hanen said.

"Most of our searching has been along the northern slope," Rallia added, "but because we're not a member of a guild, the craftsmen won't even speak to us, let alone consider traveling with us."

"They all fall back on Guild guards as their best means of protection on the roads," Hanen said. "As what one says is almost verbatim what everyone else says, I'm starting to question why we're here."

"Tell me," Searn said, "how is Mahn Fulhar any different than the merchants of Edi City?"

"For one, the guilds seem to control things very tightly here," Hanen said. "The guilds don't have much control in Edi City. The trade is controlled by the houses. The taxes flow uphill, rather than to inner-trade guilds."

"And did you go individually to each craftsman in Edi?"

"Well," Hanen said, "there were only a few merchants who were craftsmen themselves. Usually those were crafters who could travel during their off-season, or were looking to expand their markets."

"So who did you arrange to travel with?" Searn asked.

Aurín's plate arrived first, and a slice of a southern citrus fruit sat next to it. Aurín took it up and squeezed it over the cake before him. After taking a bite he smiled in satisfaction.

"We usually spoke to traveling merchants who were already negotiating to take products from local craftsmen," Rallia said.

"And are there no merchants like that here?"

"Most are sea captains," Hanen said. "And the others run general product stores to sell a few wares from cottage craftsmen. But that is the problem—there are no merchants traveling anywhere. Or at least no big merchants moving outside of guilds."

"If I had to guess," Rallia added, "in Mahndür, trade travels toward Mahn Fulhar. In Mahn Fulhar, trade goes out around the Lupinfang."

"So," Searn said, continuing to goad them toward his thinking, "would you say the guilds themselves might be the equivalent of the greater merchants?"

Rallia gawked at Hanen, who looked back dubiously.

"I supposed," Hanen said. "But they won't give us the time of day. And they're so insular that there is no way they'll tell outsiders like us if a particular guild is not doing well and might benefit from renting a portion of their hall to us."

"And they don't give you the time of day because you're not a guild member."

Hanen nodded.

"You're a member of the Black Sentinels, though."

"What are you getting at?"

"The Black Sentinels are built on the principles of a guild," Searn said. "And the Sentinel Charter in Mahn Fulhar in particular is built as such because of the guild control over politics here. The Sentinels are treated differently because we have no 'shop' nor guildhall."

"That makes sense," Rallia said.

"All of this is a round-about way for me to say that I solved most of that problem last night."

"How so?" Hanen asked.

"I went and visited the King. We have a mutual acquaintance, and he finally took time to see me."

"You met King Erdthal?" Rallia asked.

"Yes. The Sentinel Charter in Mahndür is an older charter than those of other countries and sorely needed an update. He agreed to speak to us about that. In the meantime, he agreed to loan us the use of a dilapidated metalworks in the castle complex as a guildhall."

Hanen pursed his lips. "An old smithy?"

"It's the smithy that used to arm the entire castle. That's all moved over to the control of the Guard Guild, who have their own means of armament."

"I imagine it'll take a lot of work to get something like that in working order," Rallia said.

"I imagine it will," Searn said.

"How..." Hanen said, then clamped his mouth shut.

"Is there a problem, Hanen?"

"The castle complex is a far cry from the city. How are we going to get clients from there?"

Searn smiled and sighed. "Hanen, you're good at planning. But I think you have trouble seeing farther than next week. If you were looking to make a contract with a caravan that will offer protection, and you found that the meeting would not be on Quayside, ruled by sea captains, nor in the middle of town under the auspices of the guards, but in the castle complex itself, in the shadow of two grandiose cathedrals, what would you think?"

Hanen looked over at his sister, who was staring at Searn and nodding to herself.

"I would think," Rallia offered, "that the caravan is running with the express permission of the King himself."

"Exactly," Searn said. "And if the clients who come and meet there are representatives of a guild?"

"The other guilds wouldn't be watching them while they entered or left the castle," Hanen said.

"And what kind of daily guard contracts could Sentinels hope to find if their offices are based there?" Searn asked.

"Upper crust," Aurín interjected.

"Now," Searn said, "do you see what I'm doing?"

Hanen nodded. "Yes. I'm sorry I doubted."

Searn's smile broadened. "No need for apologies, my young friend," Searn said. "I just want to see if I can adjust you to my way of thinking.

I think you have great potential, and I'd like to see that you fill that cup to overflowing."

Hanen forced a smile to cover up some of his embarrassment. "When can we go and see it?"

"I've already asked Aurín to stay here and see that everyone closes up their accounts with the proprietor and makes their way to the new hall. In the meantime, the three of us can head there now."

"You might be waiting a while," Rallia said to Aurín. "Ophedia just left."

"We ran into her on the way here," Aurín responded. "She already knows to meet us there."

Hanen and Rallia soon had their packs over their shoulders, walking toward the center of town with Searn between them. They came to the overpass that crossed over the canal, and walked by the entrance to the Grotto Market. Vendors in the half-covered grotto stood in long lines of temporary shelters, while a row of the nicest shops in the lower tiers were built into the sandstone walls of the massive amphitheater-shaped cave.

"I'm glad the three of us have a chance to walk together," Searn said. "As I said, I see a great deal of potential in you, and I'd like to develop that."

"What do you mean by that?" Hanen asked.

"The two of you are both naturally born leaders, and I think you owe it to yourselves to take advantage of that."

"I'm not a leader," Rallia said.

"You are," Searn replied. "You're up before dawn. I know a couple of the other Sentinels have made a habit of joining you in your morning routine. I think it's because of the trust you've built, keeping them safe under your blade as you shave them."

They came to the gate leading into the upper tier. A soldier in a gray uniform stood before them. The man held a crossbow with an axe blade mounted underneath.

"Business?" the man asked.

"If the message hasn't come down from the Stone yet, we're Black

Sentinels, and we have a signed charter from the king, regarding freedom to pass into the castle complex and the city, as our guildhall is located there."

"Guildhall?" the man said, taking the paper offered to him. "Only our Voktorra Guildhall is in the castle complex."

"As of last night, the Black Sentinels are taking over the old Blackiron smithy as a guildhall."

The guard laughed. "Blackiron? That must be a joke. The place is half collapsed."

Hanen and Rallia glanced at each other.

"Fine, go on through," the guard finally said, "but if you didn't personally speak to one of the Voktorra captains, to ensure the message is passed along, I doubt any of us will ever hear about your little guildhouse."

"I left a message for Captain Navien, so the message should be circulating over the next several days."

The guard saluted and let them through.

The upper gate let out into a small street of small shops. A few house-cörs roamed the alleys looking for vermin to exterminate, and a handful of housemaids walked with baskets along the side of the street. The smell of baking wafted across the place and followed them as they came out into one of the large parks that stood at the center of several estates. Gardeners raked away the last vestiges of autumn, and a house guard on a sleipnir rode out from a gatehouse to take a message to another.

Above all the buildings, as grandiose as they were, stood the complex of the three authorities they approached. The gray stones of the Abecinian Cathedral and the white stones of the Crysalas Temple stood out in harsh contrast to the blackness of the castle, known to most as The Stone.

It rose above the outlying buildings for a hundred feet into the sky—a testament to its own power. It loomed ever higher as the three Sentinels circled the last green toward its gates, where ten Voktorra guards stood outside, barring entrance.

"Names and business," one of them said as they approached.

"Captain Abenard Navien, I believe," Searn said as he let his hood fall back from his head.

The guard scowled.

"Searn VeTurres, is it?" he asked.

Captain Navien wore a short but thick black beard. The clasps on his dark gray uniform were a burnished gold, and the gray crested helmet on his head was polished to a mirror. Rather than the crossbow his soldiers carried, he held in both hands a short-handled glaive.

"Correct. Master and Commander of the Black Sentinels. And these two are Hanen and Rallia Clouw. As I mentioned in my letter, they act in my name, and in the name of our organization, which you're to treat with the same respect as you grant every guild in the city of Mahn Fulhar."

"My respect is earned, not ordered," Captain Navien said.

"Regardless," Searn said. "We'd like to pass. And you should expect many more Sentinels to be trickling up here over the day."

"You and I can have a discussion of the curfew the castle has," Navien said. "Until then, my men will be seeing you to and from the Blackiron."

"As long as they leave us to our privacy within the hall, I don't see any problem with that."

"Very well," Navien said. He made a hand gesture, and the gate boomed open.

They passed by and through the gate house into the first courtyard, where ten more Voktorra practiced their routine.

They passed a stable yard, and then passed a courtyard littered with broken furniture and equipment.

"There ought to be some things here we can use to furnish the hall," Searn said to himself.

They crossed the debris field and came to stand outside the entrance that led underneath a ruined portion of a castle arm.

"This?" Hanen asked.

"Yes," Searn said, "this is the Blackiron. Not much to look at right now, but if we took a week to clean up the space, we'd have a good thing going."

Inside the mortar had deteriorated around an old forge in the center. The rotten wood that once partitioned storage spaces lay where they fell years before.

Hanen shook his head.

"What's the trouble, Hanen?" Searn asked.

"We don't have the coin to clean this place up. And none of the Sentinels will work for nothing to see it is so."

"Don't worry about the coin. I'm in negotiations to see that taken care of."

"What does that mean?" Hanen asked.

"It means I brought additional coin from Limae when I rejoined the caravan, expressly for this reason. I'll be putting up Sentinel coffer money to make this place presentable, and the hall can pay it back when it starts to make money."

"I don't know that we can."

Searn spun on Hanen with a stern look. "I saw what you did in Edi, Hanen. You had trouble with Thadar, true. But what you set up there was just the beginning. Understand that what you started there is a vision of the Black Sentinels' future. Until now the Sentinels have all operated independently. Those commanders on the council in Limae, whom I head? They're just Sentinels who have made bigger names for themselves. You, though? You're not making bigger names for your-selves; you're making a bigger name for all Black Sentinels. You're creating a bigger future for all of us."

Hanen looked down at the ground.

"Now," Searn said, "stop doubting, or at least keep it to yourself, and start doing. Can you do that?"

Hanen looked up and nodded. "Yes. I can do that."

"Rallia?" Searn looked at the other Clouw.

"We can do it," Rallia said.

"Good. Now let's discuss what this place needs to look like before the others arrive."

2

Blackiron Guildhall

Never forget Alvaria, that short-lived regal line.
Two brothers founded kingdom, but lost it all in time.
Liman Untellian, warrior strong and true.
Dothar the elder brother, with wisdom was he imbued.
They brought about a long peace, but like the flower wilts,
Their heirs fell down upon their own swords, buried to the hilts.
Listen now to Brase Turrian's tale, of Lomi's clan of woe.
As fate conspired to crush Unteels in Redot, ruling down below.

— FROM *BRASE TURRIAN, PRINCE OF WOE*,
BY ELLAVON GAVALIN, DÜRANI PLAYWRIGHT

Something floated on the edge of Hanen's vision as he awoke. It wore the black cloak of a Sentinel and stopped to stand several yards from him. By the dim light of predawn he thought perhaps it stood by the large table he had placed the night before. The cloaked figure moved away from the edge of his vision.

From the back end of the guildhall, Searn appeared with a lantern in his hand from behind the canvas he had hung to designate his own private area. As he made his way around the still-cooling hearth they had constructed from the old forge, Rallia shifted the door that leaned against the entrance and came to stand with him, warming her hands by the ruddy glow of the embers.

"Anyone active?" Searn asked.

"I just saw another Sentinel enter before me. I had been taking a walk overlooking the city, and the Sentinel came from the Abecinian Cathedral. Do we have anyone assigned to watch the Nifarans?"

"Not that I know of," Searn's voice said in the dark. "The Paladins made it clear we were not needed while the Nifarans were under their protection in the cloister of the Abecinians."

"Interesting," Rallia said.

"I'd like to go for a walk myself," Searn said. "Can you wake your brother?"

"I'm awake," Hanen grunted as he sat up on the cot.

"Cloak, money pouch. Clubs, no axes."

Hanen sat up. "What's going on?"

"Let's find some food. I'll explain on the way."

They stepped out in the pre-dawn light. While a few guards stood at their posts, they looked barely aware of their surroundings. The junk-yard that surrounded their hall was still a mess.

"If I didn't know any better, I'd think that the King agreed to let us use the old forge just to get free labor from us to clean this place up," Hanen said.

"That may be true," Searn said. "Probably not something to ask him when you meet him, though."

"Meet the king?" Rallia said, excitement in her voice.

"That's one the reasons we're leaving now. To make ourselves scarce for the morning, and putting together some deliveries for Blackiron while we're at it."

"Who are we avoiding?" Rallia asked.

"That Voktorra Captain—Abenard Navien."

"Why?" Hanen asked.

"Because he has a summons from the King for us."

Hanen stopped. "Why are we not at Blackiron then?"

"And did you just say *we*?" Rallia asked.

"Yes. We. I may have set up my own office in the back of the hall, but Blackiron is your office. It's best that way. We're avoiding the captain for two reasons. The first is I don't like him. He rankles me. The second is because I want him to sweat. He was given the message last night, and has chosen to wait until today to tell us, in order to keep us off our guard. He assumes if we find out almost too late, we'd appear before the King in a panic. But if we don't get the message, and we arrive even later, then it will fall on him."

"You're reversing the tables on him," Hanen said. "Why is he playing this game? What problem does he have with the Sentinels?"

"If I had to wager a guess, he feels threatened by the Black Sentinels. Perhaps he fears we're looking to replace the Voktorra in their role as royal guard—that we might wish to take away the old guard contract."

"I've heard similar stories," Rallia said. "Where tallow and wax candle guilds fight one another for their rights to sell?"

"Yes," Searn said.

"It didn't work out for either in Bortali, with the emergence of starblush," Hanen said.

"Then we had best not go to war with them," Searn said. "But a bit of subtle manipulation never hurt anyone," he said with a smirk.

They came to the plateau above the canal. The smoke from the smoker guild was being stoked into life, and the western wind took the gray pall out to sea. The fading stars continued to blink out just as a scent arose, first from the servants passing the three of them and then from the side street they approached. The rich, bready scents stopped Rallia first, and then Hanen and Searn.

"I want that," Rallia said.

The entire street was lined with shop after shop of bakers, and terminated in the facade of a guild, with stones carved to symbolize sheaves of wheat and the likeness of the goddess Nifara.

"Bread row," Searn said as they walked past darkened shops of those that opened up for business later.

Rallia led the way, deftly dodging servants running late with wares they needed for their masters. A gang of young men wearing tall brown hats with a single golden rope tied around the brim, marking them as journeymen from the rope-makers guild, made calls to passing serving girls, and jeered at another group of boys dressed in the red and white of the butcher's guild.

The smell of bread was overwhelming. Three young boys in the ochre of the baker trade stood out front of a few windows holding up loaves to sell to passersby, while one baker stood at the back of a wagon, and inside stacked the large, flat trenchers, dense and packed with various seeds.

A girl, perhaps twenty, stood speaking with the baker's son. The latter had a yellow pill box hat on his dark hair, and wore a simple brown tunic with a darker brown overcoat trimmed in yellow brocade. The customer was a pretty blonde girl who wore her hair down and free. She wore a light blue smock, and a similar brown overcoat to the baker's son, over which strips of blue brocade hung down the length of her thin frame. From under her smock and up her throat sat full fur lining, the color of her hair, propping up her chin. She turned to look as the baker's son indicated toward the three Sentinels in black. Both smiled. Hanen felt himself blush.

"Sticky buns?" Rallia asked, walking up to the young man selling the rolls.

He nodded and turned to the window behind him. His father placed down a fresh tray and gave him a smile with a thick, bushy mustache.

Rallia handed him a silver Baro, and he took it, smiling. Taking out a wax-lined paper sack, he placed rolls, one after the other, into the sack, but not before first slathering each with a brush covered in honey butter. He placed the twelfth one into the bag, and then took up a thirteenth and placed it in Rallia's hand. More carefully than before, he put a dollop of the honeyed butter on the top. As Rallia took a large bite of the roll, she muttered her approval. The baker's son gave the bag a rolled twist to seal the top, and then presented her the package as the rest of the one in her hand disappeared into her mouth.

Hanen, Searn, and the other girl watched the proceedings in silent appreciation.

"These are so good," Rallia said through a mouth full of sticky bun.

"I'm glad you like them," the young man said. "We used to just put honey on them. But I thought to mix it with butter. It doesn't take so long to spread it on top now."

"Smart idea," Rallia said. "I'm sure you've got lots of them."

The boy turned bright red.

"Are they as good as the ones on Kolaon Hill in Edi City?" Hanen asked.

"The bakers in Kolaon are good, but they produce so many at a time, each one doesn't have the care put into them like I can taste in these."

"Oh?" the other girl said. "Are you from Edi?"

"Most recently we came from Edi, yes," Rallia said. "But I'm from Bortali, along with my brother here."

"Brother?" the baker's son asked. "I wouldn't have guessed."

"Same father, different mothers."

"I guess that means this isn't him," the blonde girl said, indicating to Searn.

"Searn? No."

"Well, now I know his name but not yours."

"My apologies," Hanen said. "My name is Hanen Clouw. And this is Rallia."

"Alodda," the girl said, offering out her hand. Hanen took it in his and gave it a slight shake. The girl laughed a bubbly laugh.

"What's funny?" Hanen asked.

"I can tell you're new in town. But I like you, so let me give you a pointer. When a girl offers you her hand, turn your hand upward, and touch her palm with your fingers if you're feeling flirtatious. Take her fingertips and squeeze if you're just trying to be cordial, but taking it and shaking it as you did is reserved only for family or betrothed."

Hanen felt his heat rise.

"What if we just want to show a great deal of gratitude for amazing bread rolls?" Rallia asked, winking at the baker's son.

The young man laughed heartily. "I think it'll do just to know you loved it, Rallia. I'm Lilmar."

"We need to move along," Searn said.

Hanen nodded and turned to leave. Alodda walked up to Hanen and put a hand on his elbow. Even through the heavy scent of bread on the air Hanen could smell her perfume—both delicate and piercing, it reminded him of fresh sawdust and several flowers he couldn't name.

"I hope I didn't offend you," she said.

"Uh, no. I'm fine," Hanen said stoically. "I just didn't know."

"I was only jesting with you. My father is a tailor over in the Grotto. This brocade ribbon I'm wearing hangs on the mannequins out front of our shop. You should stop by. Perhaps we can make you some clothes for wearing around the city. You're a Black Sentinel, but most that I've seen only work for middle and lower classes here, because they don't wear fine enough clothes under their cloak. My family makes the finest clothes outside the upper district. Better than the upper district, in my opinion."

"I'll keep that in mind. Thank you."

"She's pretty," Searn said to Hanen as they walked away. Though it sounded more like a question.

"Yes, but a bit assuming," Hanen said.

"You haven't had a bun yet," Rallia said as she handed one to each of them and took another for herself.

"We'll need to send some Sentinels out for supplies later today," Searn said.

"Aurín has agreed to cook for everyone," Rallia said. "He started a list of things we'd need to have available for him."

"Such as?"

"Wheels of cheese, some dried meats. Things that are better invested in than purchased as needed."

"Money will go farther, and with less complaint, if you let him do the shopping. We'll give him a limit to his spending and see what he does with it. If he does well, then you can increase his budget."

"What should we assign Ophedia to do?" Hanen asked.

"She only just started with the Sentinels. Let her go out and find contracts and further herself."

"I think senior members may become jealous," Hanen said.

"Why is that?"

"This is a far change from what Sentinels sign up to do," Hanen replied. "We're bodyguards and escorts. Asking the other Sentinels to help us set up the office takes away from other duties."

"Unless," Rallia interjected, "we do as we did in Edi."

"What's that?"

"Identify Sentinels who aren't good at guard duty, but have a mind for other skills, and we give them something to do."

"This is exactly my point," Searn said. "I've proposed this to the leadership in Haven, and I am voted down each time."

"What's that?"

"Part of the growth of this organization is going to revolve around its specialists doing what they do best. Bounty hunting, administration. We can do it all internally and not need to hire out those jobs to poachers and scriveners."

They came to the canal street. It was called the canal, but no water was present, even though the roar of it could be felt under their feet as it coursed along the underground canyon toward the sea. The street laid flat, dropping a step every hundred feet, although a single ramp ran up the center for carts. The low sun flashed off the black scales of an ynfald skulking near an alleyway.

The creature was smaller than most of the ynfalds in the city, but bigger than the small ones found in Edi City that many ladies carried on their laps and doted upon. Large black scales overlapped along the entirety of its body, from the tip of its nose, to the end of its long, thick tail. A small tongue snapped out in anticipation as it sat eyeing a house-cör sitting in an upper window.

A woman walking a tall and elegant ynfald on a leash passed by. The two ynfalds rattled their scales at each other in acknowledgment but mostly ignored one another. Hanen put a hand out to stop Rallia, and Searn followed suit. The little black ynfald suddenly darted across the way, under the wheels of a cart, bearing no mind to it, and in its whispering silence the sleipnir pulling the cart didn't even notice.

It popped out the other side and slunk behind a large pot with a tree rising out of it, looking up to the window above. The disinterested cör swatted its tail back and forth, trimmed two inches back to remove the poisoned stinger it was born with, in attempt to make the thing less feral.

The ynfald suddenly leapt up onto the first window, its small claw-tipped paws finding purchase. Then it took another leap to a small overhang, and then took the final leap up onto the wooden jetty built out of the sandstone face of the house.

The cör panicked and disappeared into the room, as the ynfald scrambled up over the lip. As it tried to find purchase, it tripped the wooden prop holding the shutter open and came crashing down onto the armored back of the black creature. It began to yelp and cry out, and was met by the yowling of the cör within. Hanen unfastened his cloak and handed it to Rallia.

"What were you doing, Hanen?" Searn asked, but Hanen had already stepped up onto the planter, and reached out for the first windowsill.

"Just leave the thing," Searn said. "It got itself into that trouble, it can suffer the consequences."

Hanen pulled himself up, and then over to reach up and stand even with the window.

He placed a hand on its back. The scales all stood up on end, rattling together in stressed surprise.

"Quiet now," Hanen said. "Shhhh...."

The creature swung its head back to see what touched him, and smacked its nose on the leaded window pane.

"Ouch," Hanen said. "I bet that hurt. How about you let me take care of you?"

He could see the cör standing in the center of the room, back arched, and small quills standing up along its back.

"Best not to mess with manticörs and their kin."

Hanen leaned against the wooden frame, and placed an arm around the ynfald, and then nudged the window up with an elbow.

The ynfald scrambled backwards and fell out of Hanen's arm, almost pulling him down with it. It tumbled through the air, and came down nose first onto the stones. But rather than slamming, it curled up and rolled over in a spiraling tumble across the cobbles, then came up on all four feet.

Rallia was laughing uproariously at the whole sight. Hanen climbed down and eyed the ynfald, which sat trying to recollect its dignity. It looked over its shoulder, apparently embarrassed by the whole turn of events.

"Give me a roll," Hanen said, as he came up to Rallia.

Rallia sighed and handed him one of her precious sticky buns. Hanen tore it in two and tossed it to the ground in front of the creature, who winced as it hit the stones, and then turned and sniffed at it, tasting it with a flicking tongue. Then it opened its mouth to show small razor teeth as it took the whole thing in its mouth. Turning, it regarded Hanen, letting its heavy scaled tail fall left, and then right. Each time it hit the pavement, the rattle of the scales made a sound. Then it stood up and approached, sniffing toward the other half in Hanen's hand. Hanen knelt down.

"You want this?" Hanen said, holding it out. "No more chasing cörs. It'll only get you in more trouble."

The ynfald regarded it, but did not take it from him until he opened his palm. He gave the creature a pat on its head, stood, and walked away.

"You could have gotten in trouble with the authorities, climbing up that house face," Searn said.

Hanen shrugged. "The ynfald needed a hand. It would have been dropped in the ocean if it had been caught. I did no harm."

"Hanen," Rallia said.

"No need to worry, Rallia," Hanen said. "It's done, and nothing bad happened."

"No," Rallia said, jerking her thumb behind her. "You have a friend."

The ynfald now walked casually beside Hanen, as though it had always been there.

"Wow," Hanen said, "it snuck right up with nothing more than a whisper."

"Good name," Rallia said.

"What, Whisper?"

Rallia nodded.

"Are you going to answer to that?" Hanen asked the ynfald. "Whisper?"

The ynfald looked up indifferently, and continued to pad alongside him.

Hanen soon noticed he was not the only person with an ynfald walking alongside them. One in three people had one following along. If he stretched his fingers down, he could not touch Whisper's back, unless the creature lifted his head high, and even then Hanen's fingers only just brushed the top of his skull. The ynfalds of Mahndür were taller and longer than those of the south. As one ynfald passed another, they would shake, rattling their scales at one another in recognition. Whisper, usually so silent, rustled next to Hanen's leg at each passing.

As they arrived at the docks, the fishmongers were picking up the day's haul from locals, while teamsters unloaded casks of foreign ale.

"Best keep that little ynnie close," a sailor said as he mended a recently frayed net.

Hanen stopped and looked at the man. "Why is that?"

"Black ynnies bring luck, and take it with them when they go."

"Are you tying an Aben's Knot?" Rallia asked.

The sailor nodded. "Know your knots, do you?"

"Our father is a netmender in Bortali. He learned the knot from his grandfather."

"Bortali's where I learned it," the man said, stopping to puff on his pipe while he looked the two of them up and down. "You Marn's kin?" he asked.

"That we are!" Rallia said with a broadening smile.

"Can't say I saw him when I was last in Garrou port."

"He may have moved on since we left."

"He's a good man," the sailor said. "Could have used a black ynnie like that though, for all the bad luck he's always had."

"It is good to meet an acquaintance who thought well of our father," Rallia said. "Can we have your name?"

"Doab Belmueller."

"Good to meet you," Rallia said, taking the man's offered hands. "You wouldn't know where we can get a large enough fish to feed twenty men and women?"

"I brought one in myself this morning," the sailor said. "I was supposed to have been met by a man an hour ago, but he never came. Since you're here, you're welcome to it. As sons of Marn, who taught me the best knot in the trade, I'll let the fish go for a dukt."

He rose and pulled himself into his boat, and motioned for them to look.

The fish easily had thirty pounds of meat on it.

"That'll feed us three times over," Hanen said.

"I wouldn't let it sit that long," the fisherman said. "My advice? You take this up to the smokers guild. For a silver Baro they'll fillet it in half, and smoke one half for you. And the other, you take home and feast on. But you make sure that Nall is the man who smokes it. You won't regret it."

"Thank you Doab," Rallia said.

They turned and continued down the pier, requisitioning the delivery of a large cask of ale before starting the climb back to Blackiron, making only one other stop at a cheesemonger to pick up several wheels of cheese and to hire a cart to carry their fish, barrel, and wheels to their base.

Hanen thought of the tailor's daughter as they passed the cavernous opening to the Grotto Market, and looked down at his clothes. He shook his head, knowing he couldn't afford new clothes if he hadn't yet lined up work.

They came up to the castle complex and entered the Stone, passing by Voktorra running their routines. One of them turned and ran the other direction.

"That'll be one going to fetch their captain," Searn said under his breath.

They entered Blackiron and Ophedia approached with Aurín, who took command of the cart. He moved the goods off the back, and then rode back down with the driver to the smokehouses.

"That guard captain?" Ophedia said. "He's been looking for you. I think he's come by every hour."

Searn nodded. "I expected he might. Was he getting ruffled?"

"Yes. Very."

Searn chuckled.

"Who is this?" Ophedia said, crouching down next to the ynfald by Hanen's side.

"This is Whisper."

Ophedia reached out and gave the ynfald a scratch on the back of the skull, and the creature half collapsed toward her in acceptance.

The door behind them opened. Captain Abenard Navien came pushing in, gasping for breath.

"There you are, Sentinel," he said to Searn. "The King wishes to see you immediately."

"Perfect!" Searn said, flashing a smile. "The Clouws and I will be along shortly. If you'll give us a moment."

The captain looked around, and then stepped back outside.

"It looks like we're off to see the King. Be on your best behavior. And keep your mouths shut. I'll do the talking."

Rallia nodded. Hanen turned to Whisper. "Stay here with Ophedia."

The ynfald followed Ophedia as she walked away, and threw himself down on the ground by her feet, watching the Clouws leave with Searn.

3

Blue Room

Ynnie-faldy, lucky day.
Knowie not to make he stay?
Iffy go he takey away.
Baddie Lucky back again.

Hanen could tell the Voktorra Captain, Navien, was in a hurry. He waved off those subservient to him with a dismissive hand as he marched through the tunnel leading under the Voktorra Guildhall and into the courtyard directly outside the main castle keep. The plain gray building loomed over them as they walked toward the dark stained wood of the door. Navien walked across the grass toward another door, its iron-banded entrance held open and guarded by two more Voktorra. They saluted as he passed, the three Sentinels in tow.

They turned back and toward the main entrance hall, lit only by the interior torches. A servant in house colors stood from a small desk.

"Captain Navien," he said. "The King has been awaiting your presence all morning."

"We were delayed," Navien snapped. "Where will he see us?"

"Escort your wards to the Blue Room."

Navien gave a short salute and marched on. The hallways were as gray as the outside, down to the deep gray carpet on the floor.

"Rather bleak," Rallia said under her breath.

"It's a means of preparing you for surprise," Searn replied.

"What do you mean?" Hanen asked as they turned a corner. Two footman in black wool uniforms pulled open the wooden doors they stood outside of.

Hanen found himself holding his breath as he entered the room. That it was called the "Blue Room" only spoke of the accents of blue carpeting and ornamentation on the white marble fireplace. The dominant color, however, was the gold leafing that covered the pillars, candelabra, and accoutrements. The ceiling had been silvered and polished to a mirror.

There was no one within, so Hanen spun and admired his surroundings.

"This is more impressive than the Aritelo Receiving Room," Rallia said.

"Agreed," Hanen said.

"Quite the display, isn't it?" Searn said.

Hanen nodded.

"There are three others like it in other arms of the Stone, but this one is the most impressive."

"You are to remain silent as the King enters," Captain Navien said. He stood at attention and looked toward a door by the fireplace mantel across the room.

"Do we bow?" Rallia muttered to Searn.

"It can't hurt," the man replied.

The door opened, and a small man wearing blue and gold to match the room entered. He carried a tall staff topped with a silver capricör head, the symbol of the country. He took a single step to one side and knocked the staff on the marble that lined the outside of the room.

"His Royal Majesty, Velab Erdthal II, King of Mahndür and Nasun. Grandmaster of the Fulharian Guilds."

The King entered the room wearing a floor-length, white, linen tunic. Over one shoulder he wore a fur-lined mantle of blue velvet, which dragged over the floor behind him. He cradled a golden scepter, crowned with a much more elaborate capricör head. The diadem that sat on his head had a jewel-encrusted set of stylized horns curling down the side of his face. He had a trim black beard and piercing blue eyes. Upon closer look, he wasn't much older than Hanen's twenty-nine years.

He walked to the hearth and turned, striking a very intentional pose.

Rallia bent at the waist, and gave a low soldier's bow, her feet straight and together. Hanen and Searn did the same, although Searn did not bow more than his head.

"Rise," the King said. His voice was tight and controlled.

As Hanen looked up, he saw anger burning in the King's eyes.

"I sent word for you last night," the King said. "You were to appear over an hour ago."

Captain Navien stepped forward to speak up, but Searn interrupted him.

"King Erdthal," Searn said, "we only just received the message and came immediately. While we were readily available to take the messages last night at Blackiron Hall, if the messenger was not able to visit us until this morning, I was out in the city with my two colleagues."

The King shot a look at Navien and sighed. "And who are your two colleagues?"

"This is Hanen Clouw, and his sister, Rallia Clouw."

"Clouw," the King said. "I don't recognize that last name."

"We're originally from Bortali," Hanen said and then added, "Your majesty."

"Bortali. Still, that is not a surname I recollect. What is the purpose for their accompanying you?"

"Your majesty," Searn said, giving his head another nod. "While I am the Master and Commander of the Black Sentinels, given authority to do so by the council of commanders in Haven, the capital of Limae, the Clouws will be taking up the helm of the guildhall here in Mahn Fulhar."

"They are captains of your organization?"

"Yes they are," Searn lied. "I take it you summoned me here to discuss updates to our charter?"

"Do not presume to know why I summoned you here. Just because you were associated with my uncle Bakkdin, although I fail to understand why he never mentioned you in his communications before he died those years ago, does not give you permission to presume."

"Very well, your majesty."

"I do wish to discuss the charter. I've looked over the old charter, and I'm not sure that it will answer the questions we had for you at the feast."

"That is why I wished to discuss renegotiation with you."

"Say your peace, and then I'll say mine."

"The charter simply covered the kings's allowance for individual Sentinels to operate within the borders of Mahndür. It is not as extensive as the charter in Œron, nor the charter I recently negotiated in Macena. I should like to enter into negotiation with the Crown of Mahndür, to request full guild rights for the Black Sentinels within the cities of Mahndür, and permissions at the borders of Mahndür's neighbors."

"Just what do your foreign charters offer you that the current Mahndürian charter does not?"

"In Œron and Macena, we have permission to act as the hand of the law, most specifically in regards to brigandry and cutpurses."

"And just what are you offering in return for this increased authority?"

"As a full guild, the charter taxes paid to the crown would improve, as having guild status would improve our standing in the community."

"So what you're really asking for," the King said, "is my seal of approval."

Searn bowed his head cordially in agreement.

"And the fact that I granted you temporary use of the Blackiron smithy provides another level of authority, because your clientele will have to visit the highest authority in the land, this castle complex, in order to make their agreements with you."

"The improvements the Black Sentinels will be making to the Blackiron Guildhall will pay for themselves, I should think, improving a much disused portion of the grounds."

"I think that goes without saying, and behooves you to do so. That does not provide any assets to the benefit of your argument to me."

Hanen stepped forward, and waited until both men looked at him.

"What is it?" the King said.

Hanen's voice caught in his throat. He stalled for a moment by giving a curt bow. "Your majesty. May I speak?"

The King gave a casual flip of his hand.

"Your majesty," Hanen said, "I am a Black Sentinel, originally from Garrou in Bortali, with an office of operations in Edi City. I have traveled between both of those cities multiple times a year since before I was made a Sentinel. And there is one thing I've learned, at least regarding the border guards of Bortali, Düran, and Edi."

"And what would that be?" the King asked.

"That one of the only ways to cross a border is by paying first a tax to the city you've left from, in order to gain writ of passage, and then to pay additional bribes to the crossing guards."

"That is part of the business of running a border."

"Part of the issue I see with this, is that the guards often sent to work a border are those who would cause trouble if left stationed in a city. They care little for who crosses, merely that they line their pockets with their bribes."

"I fail to see the point you're making."

"My sister and I have crossed borders, as I said. But we've found success by pooling resources from the merchants we take payment from, and negotiating smaller bribes, although in a larger pool for these guards, and thus with considerably less hassle than if each merchant had needed to negotiate crossing on their own."

"Your point, boy?"

"None of that money ever reaches the crown. It allows those less-than-adequate guards to continue in their ways. I've known plenty of merchants who, after experiencing a poor treatment from a border crossing, refuse to do business with that country. I would make a proposal to add to the guild responsibilities in the charter that eliminate most of these issues."

"And what would that be?"

"The Black Sentinel Guild would collect from the merchants all tariffs and import taxes, along with an additional surcharge that could be called the King's Writ Charge. This earns them a writ of passage directly from the crown, co-signed by the Black Sentinel Guild."

"What good would that do?"

"Those bribes, usually paid to corrupt guards who throw the money away on gambling and prostitutes, would be paid directly to your personal coffers as neither a bribe, nor illegal."

"The border guards would not appreciate losing that income. The bribes keep them from committing acts of brigandry, if we're being honest."

"I understand," Searn added, "that each guild takes on a responsibility in the kingdom, to further its respectability. The butchers' guild is in charge of cleaning drains and maintaining sewers alongside the chandlers guild."

"And the Voktorra," the King said, "while solely guarding the castle complex, each must give a day guarding portions of the city."

"Yes, your Majesty."

"What are you offering?"

"Improvements to the border crossings," Searn said. "The Black Sentinels would invest a certain amount of capital to improve facilities at the crossings. By making the crossings more respectable, and if you deem it wise to station better men at those crossings, trade to and from Mahndür will improve."

"I see," the King said.

Servants carried several chairs in and placed them facing the fire. The King gave a wave to have one of them turned to face the Sentinels and Captain Navien, who still stood nearby. The King sat, though he gave no indication for them to join him.

"The authority you're proposing will take time to establish."

"That, I do not doubt, your majesty. It will take time to convince the guards at those crossings that we are acting under your authority."

"That also provides no real benefit to the city of Mahn Fulhar," the King said.

Rallia cleared her throat.

Searn shot her a look.

"Your majesty," Rallia said, giving a deep, respectful bow. "I may have a solution to that."

The King smiled. "Rallia, is it?"

"Yes, your Majesty."

"Go on."

"The Black Sentinels act as bodyguards and escorts on the road. Work can, at times, be unsteady. Bodyguard work more so in the colder months, and road escort work further still in the warmer months. But we have no ready form of income."

"That sounds to me," King Erdthal said, "as though you're advocating against your own people."

"On the contrary, your majesty," Rallia said. "I think there is a way for us to establish our legitimacy around Mahn Fulhar readily, and at the same time provide a stronger authority to the crown by granting a single request."

"To the point, Rallia Clouw."

"The Sentinels could also act as messengers."

"Messengers?"

"Rallia," Searn hissed.

Rallia gave Searn and Hanen an embarrassed look.

"If I may continue," Rallia said to the king.

"This dissension among you amuses me. I'd like to see you dig your way out of this one. Continue."

"The Black Sentinels are, depending on how you look at it, already messengers. We guard the assets of our wards. We escort merchants and their goods. Messages travel slowly—messages between normal people, that is. Envoys and couriers for the crown carry important writs between government officials, of course.

"But if we begin to take messages between people, both in city, and abroad, I expect people would pay. A badge of office to those Sentinels who are trustworthy would mark them as ones who can keep a secret. One who can deliver a message reliably. The return on these messages would be substantial, and the benefit to the crown, before you ask, is that we would be beholden to carrying official documents for the crown at no charge. If the only people who know these messages from the crown are important documents, they can be covertly moved as needed."

"That is an interesting proposal. Who would issue these badges for messengers?"

"The Black Sentinel Guild would," Searn said, stepping forward and placing a hand on Rallia's shoulder to show his support. "And a portion of the messenger fee would be paid to the crown, of course."

"Messages are cheap to move. Set what price you will on them, but a fourth is paid in the form of taxes and a fourth is paid along with the writ fee for border crossings."

"That is substantially more than is paid from merchant fees," Hanen muttered.

"That is what I ask," King Erdthal said.

"Then you agree?" Searn said.

"I am still perturbed that you did not come sooner," the King said, looking to the chairs and now food being set up behind him. "But it seems the message did not arrive with the urgency the beautiful Rallia here proposes your Black Sentinels would be acting with."

He gave a stern look at Captain Navien as he spoke.

"I will agree to all we discussed, on the condition that you'll be under the watchful eye of Captain Navien. You're to pay his fee as a guard to your guild, and he'll be reporting your actions directly to me."

"Your majesty," Navien began to protest.

"Be quiet Navien," the King said. "I've already made my decision."

The door opened behind them, and several Paladins entered, their hammers at attention.

"Now, Navien, I have guests, and I ask you escort these three back to their guildhall by way of the other side door."

Navien gave a curt bow and spun to walk to the aforementioned door. As they walked toward it, Hanen saw the Prima Pater and other ranking members of the Paladins of the Hammer appear, as well as the white mitre of the High Priest of Aben. Paladinial guards stood around them, obscuring Hanen's view.

As they left the room, they heard a voice announcing the guests, "His Most Holy Authority, Prima Pater of the Paladins of the Hammer, Dorian Mür."

The voices became muffled by closed doors as the herald announced the High Priest of Aben, as well as others of rank, before Hanen could no longer understand the words being said.

"It appears," Captain Navien said tersely over his shoulder as they walked, "that we'll be working closely with one another. Let me make you aware of one thing. When I act as guard, I observe no privacy. I will have an eye on you and your company at all times of the day. I will report anything I deem illegal or treasonous to His Majesty and any other proper authorities."

"As that is no different than what you are already doing," Searn said with a smile, "I don't see a problem with this."

"Before," he said, "I assigned guards to Blackiron smithy out of my own suspicions. It was, at that time, voluntary. Now it is an assignment, given by the king, and paid for from your own coffers. So now I have the incentive to keep an eye on you with a great deal of pleasure."

"And just what is your current rate of employment?" Searn asked.

"You'll be paying me a gold Royal a week."

Hanen stopped in his track and almost choked on his tongue. Searn gave him a stern look to silence himself.

They walked on in silence and came to Blackiron.

"I'll give you an hour before I start my first shift as your personal escort," Navien said.

Without another word, he turned and marched away.

Searn watched him leave before walking into the hall. A few of the

Sentinels were sitting around the hearth, nursing ales poured from a recently arrived barrel.

"Let's go and talk in my area," Searn said, walking with Hanen and Rallia to his back corner. He lit a candle and placed it on his table. "It would seem we have a guild," Searn said, flashing a smile.

"True," Hanen said, taking a seat opposite him.

"Rallia," Searn said, turning to look at the younger Clouw.

"I'm sorry I spoke without consulting you. It felt we needed another weight to tip the scales, and it was something I have been thinking about for a while."

"Not something you ever said to me," Hanen said.

"I'm not going to deny it's a good idea," Searn said, "but you've now volunteered all of our company to act as messengers. It's not something they're going to appreciate."

"Which is why I suggested only those deemed worthy will get a badge of office."

"That will add an entirely new facet to the organization," Searn said.

"It will allow us to recruit and vet younger men and women who perhaps won't make good guard material, but might prove valuable as runners and administrators."

"You mean treating more as apprentices," Hanen said.

"Like any other guild," Rallia added, "runners first, then you either earn your first club, or become a higher level messenger."

"And receiving the cloak?" Searn asked.

"Journeymanship. Gaining captaincy is effectively becoming a Master in the guild, and a true Black Sentinel."

"Speaking of which," Searn said as he turned and pulled up two bundles, and placed them on the table. "Each of these are for you."

Hanen reached out and took his, and handed the other one to Rallia. They were heavy, and awkward to unroll, but each revealed a new crossbow and a case for bolts.

"You're both captains now," Searn said.

"Why?" Hanen asked.

"You can't run a guild like this without being a Master, as Rallia put it. And this also allows you to control the prices of your caravans without needing someone like Thadar around to legitimize it."

He turned to Rallia. "If you're going to legitimize this messenger side of things, then you're to head it up as the first captain, and you'll need that badge of office designed and created. I'm assigning you to do that."

"I need Rallia's help to plan for the caravan."

"Hanen," Rallia said, "you have always been the brains behind that. I'll act as someone you can talk to, but you don't really need me. And I need this, something for me to do on my own."

"Very well," Hanen skulked.

"No more making big decisions without my approval, though," Searn said. "Or at least that you've both talked about together, so you're acting in tandem."

"Agreed," Hanen and Rallia said together.

4

Dark Stave Inn

Companions neared to hear him,
As he told the fated tale,
They drank, caroused, and urged him on,
    Heartily and hale,
    Quaffed heavily the ale.

—THE TRAVELER

When Hanen entered the Dark Stave Inn situated along the upper canal, just below the Overdist, as most Mahnfularians referred to the upper echelons of the city, half of those carousing at the tables were Black Sentinels. Several of the drovers who had delivered supplies to Blackiron were present, too, most sitting as near as they could to the table with Ophedia and a Mahndürian woman, Sälla Fyfe.

The two of them were both quaffing ale from tankards, the dark porter running down their chins and soaking the necklines of their white linen blouses. Ophedia lapsed into a fit of coughing and laughter as Sälla, a tall broad woman with a nearly white-blonde braid running down her back, continued to empty the tankard to the jeers and pounding fists of those around her.

At the sound of the pounding, Whisper, who had entered on Hanen's heels, pulled in as tight to Hanen as he could, nearly disappearing into the folds of his cloak. As Hanen stamped his boots free of wet, slushy snow, it revealed the ynfald again.

"Whisper!" Ophedia called, as she approached the barkeep and received two more tankards. The ynfald quickly forgot its fear and ran to join her. She turned back to the tables and put both of the tankards in front of Sälla and then sat across from the woman.

Rallia was already sitting across from Aurín and a Sentinel, Diben Läur, a friendly man from Limae who had spent a great deal of time in Mahndür, albeit mostly on the western coast. He had been a source of country customs, and was teaching the two of them a game on a small grid of lines like that of Edi-Fŏz. Though instead of colored beads, the men moved pieces more reminiscent of the Hrelgren game, Thallat. Most looked like standing sticks, and three pieces moving about with more ornamentation.

"Hanen," Rallia said, not looking up. She moved one of the large black pieces into a space surrounded by opposing white pieces, then looked at Diben. "They join my band now, right?"

"Correct," Diben said, and Rallia replaced the smaller white pieces with black ones of her own.

"Looks interesting," Hanen said.

"It is. It has elements of Edi-Fŏz, but it's unique, too." She looked at her teacher. "You said it's called Garrison?"

"Correct," Diben said.

"Have you seen Searn yet?" Hanen asked.

"He said he'd be here," Ophedia said. "He's probably off trying to find a way to sneak into the Crysalas convent, or something."

"What's that supposed to mean?" Hanen asked.

Ophedia shrugged.

"Hey Hanen," Ophedia said, pulling his shoulder around to face the others. "Tell that story you told on the road to Birin, the night before we fought the manticör."

"Which story?" Hanen asked.

"The Brazen Man."

"I'd rather not, right now. Searn wanted us to gather here, and I'd rather not keep him waiting when he arrives."

The Sentinels began to beat the tables, goading him on. Ophedia took the opportunity to get a tankard of dark ale for him and shoved it into his hand, while another fed the hearth to get it blazing. Rallia gave him a shove from behind toward the vacant storyteller's chair.

"This is a good time to establish rapport with them," Rallia muttered.

Hanen sighed, but couldn't help letting a smile play on his lips.

"Fine," he said, as he took his seat and sipped the dark liquid. It was a rich, hearty, dark beer, not the yellow beers of Düran and Edi.

"What's the storyteller's price?" the barkeep shouted over the cheer of everyone scooting chairs and benches nearer to listen.

"If you deem Hanen's story worthy," Rallia announced, standing next to her brother, "you each owe him an ale. Paid out when Hanen asks."

Everyone responded with the bang of their tankards on the tables.

Whisper rushed over and sat next to Hanen, who gave the ynfald a pat on the head.

Hanen pulled his cloak further across his shoulders and took another draw from the tankard. His silence was matched by everyone settling in. Sap crackled in the heat of the fire, signaling him to begin.

Hanen began in a hoarse whisper that drew everyone in. A few more turned, drawing in to listen, as though all shared in a dark secret.

"Hear now the tale of the Brazen Man, a man who sought to be a hero and became immortal.

"Hear now the tale of a coward, who sought to slay a dragon, and ceased to be a man.

"Hear now the tale of a hero, who, like all heroes, succumbed to their folly.

"It is said the tale took place before the Hrelgrens enslaved mankind. There was born a lowly blacksmith's son, who had no strength in his arm to lift a hammer, nor precision of mind to strike the iron while it was hot. The tale tells that he was simply known as VeSmith, or Son of Smith. For his name comes from a bygone era, from which only the 'Ve' in a Morriegan's name still holds clout.

"And yet, do not forget, that the man was no Morriegan, but from that ancient race of better men who lived after the Destruction.

"Even he, a lesser man, was better than most who live today

"—and so listen to his folly, and know you would just as easily fall prey.

"VeSmith was worthless, and cast from home, for none would take him as an apprentice. And so he traveled the world. He ate what he could find, and drank only what fell from the sky. And VeSmith found himself in the wilderness. It was then two people found him. One tall and thin, the other short and round. They both wore hooded robes, the first of red, the other of gray. The first bore a spear of purest silver, while the other wore two massive gauntlets made of obsidian. One of the gauntlets looked freshly carved from a single slab of black glass, while the other, perhaps at one time identical, was somehow larger, and seemed to pull the wearer down with its weight, giving him a permanent hunch.

"They invited him to join them around their fire, and the food they both prepared was truly inspired. The tall one knocked down fruit from a tree, and with his spear split it open, to reveal a sweet nectar, that none have ever tasted since. The shorter one gathered up grass and with his gauntlet beat it in to flour, and mixed it with water from a brook, and poured it out on a hot stone and made the world's first bread then, they say.

"Together they ate and drank, and as VeSmith became drowsy, he listened to the two speak of their friend and brother, who had left them, sundered in mind by a betrayer. He had gone mad and done the unthinkable, hunting down and killing the greatest of dragons, leaving only the dragon's mate alive. It was said the cloak of a dragon could not be pierced. And in his dreams, VeSmith knew he would become as great a hero as this fallen friend, and slay a dragon, for all peoples knew that dragons were mad, and killed with wanton slaughter.

"He arose before dawn. The tall one still slept. But the other tended the fire.

"'I see you rise early,' the short one said. 'That is good. You must rise early to begin the hunt.'

"To which VeSmith said, 'You hunt, good cook?'

"And the one said, 'I always hunt. But I also make gifts.'

"'What gift would you give me?' asked VeSmith.

"'I would give you what your heart most desires,' said the figure.

"In the dawning light, VeSmith saw that the cloak of gray was in fact a pelt. And the scales fell from his eyes, and he knew that the Great Gift Giver, Kashir, sat before him. They say that Kashir did not fall until much later. He did not become known as Kos-Yran until during the enslavement of men. But who can know? Even before his fall, Kashir's gifts were said to teach a lesson. It was only later that the gifts became spiteful curses. But again, who can know?

"The man asked for his gift: that of a strength to withstand all attacks. For what good does hunting a dragon do if you still wind up dead? He was told his gift was granted, and he left before the other arose. And thus, VeSmith walked to the east. For many months he walked, the summer sun beating down upon him.

"All at once, he was set upon by a great creature. It struck a blow with claws that would kill two men, but VeSmith felt nothing. He rose up and, with a rock, beat the beast to death. He continued on, and one by one larger creatures came, and each struck death upon VeSmith and he felt nothing. Each day he was able to walk farther, and farther, until after one long night of walking, he never slept again.

"The hot sun beat down upon him, and his skin turned to bronze, while the cold nights tempered the metal. He came to a mountain range and climbed to the top. A great escarpment stood there, looking out over the lands to the east. And knowing now the gift had been granted, he cast himself from the cliff and fell with a mighty clang of metal. He looked upon himself and saw that he was now made entirely of bronze. He rose and sought out the dragon, knowing now nothing could hurt him.

"It took many months and years. He did not know how long. But it is said he found the cave of the dragon. He bided his time, and watched her go to and fro. She was great to behold. Her wings held her aloft. Her numerous feet could skitter upon the ground. He envied her power. And thus, the man of bronze waited and watched for one hundred years to find the right time.

"As it was said before, he was a coward. For that reason, he never ventured close enough. Sometimes she would be gone for months, other times for days. He mapped the stars and sun, and found that she left for the greatest time on the longest day of the year. And thus, as the summer tide turned, she left.

"The Brazen Man entered the cave from which she hunted, and ventured deep within. And there he saw the thing for which the dragon lived—hundreds of eggs laid out for any to take.

"He lifted the first, and it weighed like a stone. He cast it against the wall, and the remains of the dragon inside spilled out. And VeSmith felt nothing.

"Again and again he did the same, and each dragon killed let out a shrill cry. For over a hundred years they had grown and awaited their birth, which never came. Knowing he could rid the world of dragons that very day, he set upon the destruction of the race.

"His mighty heroic feat completed, he left the cave and went to sit outside the place and await her return. The month of days came and went, and the dragon arrived. She paid no heed to the flash of bronze on the mountainside and entered her abode. A scream echoed forth from the cave like a hurricane. No scream such as that has ever been heard since the dragon first lost its mate.

"In her anguish, the mighty beast threw itself against the inside of the cave, mangling her own body. When the fury had settled, the Brazen Man slunk back into the cave, and there he saw her shattered remains. Her wings had been torn from her body, and she lay there breathing deeply in sorrow.

"He stole those wings and took them for himself, a trophy to take back to his people.

"The walk was just as long. He walked the day, and during the night worked to fashion for himself a cloak made from those wings. And thus the Brazen Man entered the place of his hometown, now in the black cloak of dragon hide, and skin made of bronze. And yet no one recognized him. For since he had been gone the hrelgrens had come, and the hrelgrens had left. Generation had come and generation had left.

"And thus the Brazen Man, a hero to all, but none remember, walks the earth, seeking to show off the gifts he was given and gifts that he took. For it was he who slayed all the dragons of Kallattai, and took the wings from their queen.

"But they also say the dragon did not die in her anguish. For she still had eggs to lay. But dragons no longer have wings, and only skitter upon the ground like insects. And all dragons fear man, for what one man wrought. One man wrought from bronze who has no name, for he was a coward."

The fire continued to crackle in the hearth. Then a *tap, tap, tap* began to sound, coming from the barkeep. Others joined in, until soon the entire room was roaring with cheers and the sound of tankards on tables. Hanen smiled.

"Looks like you'll be drinking free for a while," a voice said from behind him. Searn leaned against the wall.

"I hadn't seen you come in," Hanen said, looking around. He saw Captain Navien by the door, refusing an offer of ale from the barkeep, and eyeing everyone suspiciously.

"I came in right about the time you took that seat."

The Black Sentinels were filling up their own tankards with the barkeep again, and talking amongst themselves.

"You wanted to talk to everyone, didn't you?" Hanen asked.

"I did. But I can wait a minute or two."

Ophedia walked up and gave him his own tankard.

"All these ales you're passing out," Rallia said, "I hope you're keeping a penny for yourself."

"I was a tavern girl before," she said. "I know how to get an extra coin or two. Haven't paid for one of my own drinks tonight."

"Rallia," Searn said, "I hope you're ready for the deluge of questions you'll get when I mention your idea."

"I'm sure I'll figure out something to say," she responded.

"What did you call us all here for?" one of the Sentinels called from across the room.

"Not entertained enough?" Searn shouted back, to the laughter of several.

"We just know you're a busy man," Sälla said. "Probably need to get your peace said, and go back to the arms of whatever woman you fall into."

"What makes you think there's a woman?" Searn asked with a smile.

"What else would keep you from returning to Blackiron until just before dawn the past three nights?"

"Indeed, business does keep me away at odd hours," Searn said. "But there's no woman."

Searn took the seat that Hanen had vacated.

"I did call you all here, for a celebration of sorts, and it felt right to do it here rather than at Blackiron. No need to mix our business and our pleasure."

"Alright," someone said. "Let's hear it then."

"I just came from a final meeting with the King," Searn said.

A few whistled at that.

"If you haven't heard rumors yet, or pieced things together for yourself, the Black Sentinel Charter for Mahndür has been updated, and several beneficial addendums have been made that will make business much smoother and more readily available to you all. Namely, the Black Sentinels are recognized as a Guild in Mahn Fulhar, and Blackiron Guildhall is recognized as such."

"But what's the downside?" Aurín asked.

"Not too much of a downside," Searn said. "Only, to act in Mahndür, an additional guild fee will need to be paid in order to have authority as a Black Sentinel in the country."

"How is that going to help us?" another asked.

"Right now, besides a guard job here or there, it's difficult to get work. And that's because the guilds control everything. Once you're paid up at Blackiron, you're a guild member. That means better jobs. Guild jobs."

"And just what exactly does that mean?" Sälla asked.

"It means besides guard work, you'll be able to get work alongside others, assigned from Blackiron itself, by captains Hanen and Rallia Clouw."

"Like the caravan route you ran to Edi? Only here in Mahndür?" Sälla asked.

"Exactly," Searn said.

"The caravan pays well," Aurín confirmed. "Better than scrounging for work, day in, day out."

"The Black Sentinels are also going to be taking on a new task, unique to Mahndür for now. Those interested in picking up small coin, but ready coin, will need to interview with Rallia to be considered for exclusive membership to the Black Sentinel Runners. Rallia, would you care to elaborate?"

"It's fairly simple," Rallia said. "Those who can prove themselves trustworthy will start acting as couriers, delivering sealed messages, personal, official, or otherwise. This'll be important for caravans, as at least one runner will need to be in most caravans, to carry posted messages down the route."

"Add to that," Searn said, "we'll start letting young boys and girls interested in joining the Sentinels act as low grade runners, to prove they have the cunning minds and strong will to become more."

"This is all well and good," one said, "but why?"

"You mean why Mahndür," Searn responded.

"Yeah."

"Because for whatever reason, there are less Sentinels in Mahndür than in any other country. So this is the place to start the change from the ground up. You prove you've got what it takes, and then I can convince the other commanders in Limae to make this a normal thing across Ganthic. If you prove you're a leader, perhaps one day you'll join their company as a member of the leadership in Haven."

"I wouldn't mind that," Aurín said, raising his tankard.

The rest of them quickly joined in with their agreement.

"Navien is gone," Rallia muttered.

Hanen looked around. "For someone ordered to be suspicious of us, it's rather frequent he's not around."

The door opened, and a portly man entered. He wore a dyed gray wool robe, felted and thick. Across his shoulder, a mantle of pink, the color of fish flesh.

"Smokers guild," one Sentinel muttered towards Searn.

He was followed by two other men his age. A tall, thin man with a mantle of red over his shoulders. The third was a man with obvious fight in him, and a thick brow. He wore a brown leather apron and leather hat.

"The last one is Org Nellsun from the Blacksmiths Guild. I think the thin man is the Flax Guildmaster."

"We're looking for Searn," the blacksmith said.

"I am Searn VeTurres, Master and Commander of the Black Sentinels," Searn said, stepping forward.

"Quite the gathering here," the fat man said.

"We're just having a celebration," Searn said. "You're welcome to join us if you'd like. You didn't bring any attendants with you, so I assume you're here cordially."

"No need for an ale for me or my friends here," the fat man said. "We won't stay long. We understand you've been given a charter."

"I wouldn't say we've been granted a charter," Searn said. "We already had one of those. But it was updated specifically to grant Black Sentinels the title of Guild in Mahndür."

"The same Black Sentinels who founded their little band of brigand guards in a country founded by criminals," the tall, thin man said.

"It is true," Searn said. "Limae was once a haven for many who could call no country home. Hence the name of the capital, Haven. But that was a few centuries ago. Plenty of time to establish itself as a sovereign nation. Similar to the way the guilds of Mahndür, founded by men with no title, built their strength and influence by the sweat of their backs in the middle of one of the strongest monarchies in the continent."

"Monarchy Mahndür may be called, but the King rules at the express permission of the guilds. He does not approve new guilds. The guilds do."

"We've inquired to be heard by the guilds, but no answer has come."

"The guilds meet four times a year. You could have waited until then. If your claim is approved, then the guilds go to the King and request his agreement."

"And just when is the next guild meeting?"

"In two days," the fat man replied. "On the Solstice, once the sun sets."

"Very well," Searn said. "We'll come with our platitudes."

The fat man smiled, turned, and left the tavern. Someone without held a torch for him to light the way. By the light of the torches Hanen could count dozens of men with trade tools held in their hands, prepared to defend the three old envoys. The mob of men walked away into the night.

"Did you see?" Rallia asked.

"I saw," Hanen said.

"This presents an opportunity," Searn said to the two of them. "And one you'll be answering on your own."

"What do you mean?" Hanen asked.

"I'm leaving town on an errand the King asked me to take on," Searn said. "And I will not be back in time for the guild meeting. You two will be going on your own. Well, with anyone else you invite to join you."

"What are we going to say?" Hanen asked.

"That's up to you. Convince the guilds we're here to benefit them and their city, and through that their coffers and their country."

"For coin and country?" Rallia said, lifting her tankard.

Searn lifted his with a smile. "For coin and country."

5

Winter Road

Purity in Form, Purity in Mind, Purity in Choice. All three have their purpose and their beauty, but no greater purity can be found than in that of perseverance and patience. There need not be an Aspect taken, for all should strive to practice such things.

—*SAYINGS OF MATRIARCH DESWYN*

The carriage trundled out of Zebüdé, slipping left and right in the dry, powdery snow. From atop her six-legged sleipnir, Katiam Borreau kept a close eye on the back of the carriage, and constantly worried about the people within. The Matriarch Superioris had taken possession of that carriage, along with a second one. Meanwhile, the Paladins, under the leadership of the Matriarch's husband, had journeyed forth toward Mahn Fulhar to see that all was ready for her arrival, and that of the Monks of Nifara.

It had taken a day of debate to convince the Black Sentinels to consider their contract more or less completed, providing Katiam and Esenath the privacy they needed to tend to the ailing Archimandrite, who slept in the carriage with the Matriarch.

The carriage took another slip and came to a halt in a snowbank no deeper than Katiam's foot. The sleipnirs strained at their harnesses, but could not budge it. The line of Nifaran Monks stopped, scarves wrapped over their shaven heads, and several of the Paladames dismounted and fell to digging the wheel out, until the carriage budged back into motion.

"We should have harnessed Aurochs," Astrid Glass said with a frown as she remounted. As captain of the Matriarch's guard, she was the only Paladame to remain in her armor. She adjusted the plates, which sat awkwardly over the thicker padded clothing, and then made sure the winter cloak she wore over all prevented cold from reaching the metal.

"They are stronger," Katiam replied, "but infinitely more stubborn. In the cold they'd refuse to pull."

"I suppose," Astrid said, shivering as she urged her own sleipnir back into a trudging march.

"The Matriarch said you could put your armor away."

"If my discomfort becomes unbearable, I will."

"Alright," Katiam said, smiling. "Just remember that discomfort is not one of the Aspects of purity."

Astrid gave her a weak smile with no joy behind it.

The seven monks on foot began to sing a song, to set the pace and give them something to break up the white landscape and howling wind. The elderly Cräg Narn led their line. Katiam knew him by how diminutive he was compared to the others. That he was able to walk with the rest of them surprised Katiam, but, as ever, he cheerfully continued his vigilant pilgrimage. Kerei Lant, the acting Archimandrite, while Pell Maran suffered under the malady caused by the poisoned blade, sat in the carriage with him and the Matriarch Superioris. Katiam could hear her voice join with the others', albeit muffled by the cushioned carriage.

"I suppose we ought to take comfort," Katiam muttered.

"Why?" Astrid said from beneath her heavy woolen hood.

"The plain and simple life these monks lead, and they sing amidst this snowy landscape."

"The mountains out of Boroni were cold enough," Astrid said, "but this is almost too much."

Another sleipnir pulled up next to Katiam as Astrid urged hers on ahead.

Katiam glanced over and stifled a laugh at the overly-bundled Esenath Chloïse. Katiam could just make out her eyes and dark skin under the frosted wool covering her head and shoulders.

"What?" Esenath asked.

"Nothing," Katiam replied, and then sighed, watching Astrid ahead. "I miss the old Astrid."

"What do you mean?" Esenath asked.

"Before the vül attacked us on the road to Garrou, Astrid was the life of our order. The first to offer her meal to the weary, a song or verse to the dispirited, a broad smile from across the room."

"But then she lost her brother," Esenath said, "to that gold-consuming monster."

Katiam nodded.

"Grief is a long road that never truly ends," Esenath said.

"You speak from experience?"

The road straightened out and was visible for a time as the wind blew the surface clean, before obscuring it again under drifting snow.

"You said she offered comfort," Esenath said.

"Yes. To any and all."

"And what did she receive in return for it?"

"Adoration," Katiam said, "but she did not seem to seek it out."

"What comfort has she been offered now that she is dispirited?"

"I…" Katiam bit her lip.

"I'm not admonishing you, Katiam. I'm just asking. It seems that after all this time, perhaps we ought to provide her a way out. With simple smiles, and proffered hands."

"And if she does not want that?"

"She does not need to take the help, if she does not want it. But should we not be there when she does?"

"That is true," Katiam said.

"Have you been good, and not disturbed the Rotha?" Esenath changed the subject.

"I have done as you said," Katiam replied. The wooden box, now full of warm dirt dug up from the Ebrw grove, sat in the carriage as well, under the protection of the Matriarch Superioris. Esenath had taken the role of nursemaid to the little pod, ordering botanical care for it, now that it had opened.

"I poured the measured water into the funnel," Katiam said. "But nothing has happened since that day at the Green Bastion."

"Nor should you expect to see anything for some time." Esenath said.

Katiam sighed.

"Katiam, the development of a plant takes time. You must be patient. If you took charge of an orphan child, would you expect it to know how to read? Dance? Speak?"

"No."

"It is the middle of winter; the most we can do is provide the Rotha warmth to keep it alive until spring. Perhaps then we'll see something. Until then, take comfort in the fact that you've discovered how to awaken it."

"Accidentally."

"Yes, accidentally. But you did. Hundreds of women over the years have cared for that pod, and now it awakens. That is something to take pride in. That is something to concentrate on."

*　*　*

They took shelter in a barn that night. The farmer and his family took shelter with them there, offering their bed to the Matriarch and the ailing Archimandrite. The sky was cloudy and still, and the smell of capricör clung to the air along with the deep, earthy aroma of sleipnir. Katiam approached Sabine Upona, the Matriarch's assistant, as she spoke to the farmer.

"Give yourselves time to stop," the man said. "A calm like this usually means the Lupinfang will send the clouds away, and bring a crystal sky."

"That should mean a warm sun then, no?" Sabine asked.

"At times. But the nights will be colder than the Mad Gift Giver's heart."

"Thank you for the warning."

As they filed out onto the road, the clouds slowly broke up. Three miles down the road, and the hills that had blocked their view to the sea leveled out, and the gray-blue chop of the waves stretched to the horizon, light from a clear sky highlighting the white caps on each break. The breeze that played across Katiam's hair sent a sudden shiver down her spine, and she pulled the cloak around over her head. She was grateful the Matriarch allowed them to remove their armor and bundle it in the second open-topped wagon full of supplies, and, today, two of the monks, who were tired from a poor night's sleep.

The wind turned to gales by midday, the clouds disappeared from the sky, and the sun worked to remove the vestiges of the approaching winter by melting off the snow that had fallen over the previous days.

The sun began its descent toward the horizon before them, and Katiam watched Sister Upona move from sister to sister, the only one agitated and concerned with the coming evening.

She raised her voice as she rode alongside the carriage, speaking to the Matriarch within.

Katiam urged her mount forward as the carriage trundled to a stop.

"I understand your concern," the elderly voice of the Matriarch said, "but I see no shelter, and we are already so far behind the Paladins. We ought to continue on."

"Matriarch."

"Upona, I have already decided."

Sabine lowered her head and pulled at her reins.

A gust of cold air off the sea extinguished the sun on the western horizon like a candle snuffing out. The black sky above gaped wide as stars blinked themselves awake. Crystals of frost clung in the air, multiplying the number of the stars in the sky by the frosty light of the silver moon, Umay.

The wind was not strong, but what breeze there was caressed with fingers of ice. The light of a distant farm appeared, and then suddenly went out. A few moments later, a wind came howling off the sea, bringing more cold, and now the wet of freezing rain.

"What was that light?" Sabine said, with little hope in her voice.

"I saw it too," Katiam said.

"Are the monks still on foot?"

"No," Esenath said from nearby, "they're all hunkered in the wagon."

"I'll speak with the Matriarch," Katiam said.

"She's being stubborn," Sabine said.

"I'll see what I can do."

Sabine gave a nod to Astrid, who took her own sleipnir to the front of the line of riders and motioned for the carriage to stop.

Katiam dismounted and approached the carriage, giving a light rap on the door.

"Why have we stopped?" the Matriarch asked. "Night only just fell."

"Auntie," Katiam said, pulling open the door and pulling herself into the carriage.

Maeda Mür sat next to the snoring Pell Maran. Several blankets nearly smothered the man, who looked content.

"Why aren't we moving?" the Matriarch asked. She had her white headdress on her lap, and ran her fingers through her thin white curls.

"Why are you being so irritable?" Katiam asked.

The old woman across from her was not much shorter than Katiam, and she assumed that if she ever lived to be the same age, she'd shrink to be just as tall. Whether she'd ever reduce to such a lean frame and lose the thicker hips that pressed against the sleeping monk next to her remained to be seen.

"Don't be petulant, child. And close that door; it's letting in cold air."

"The cold air the rest of us have been riding in all day?"

"Don't speak to me like that," the old woman snapped.

"Auntie," Katiam said, "you have always asked me to speak so with you when we're alone."

Maeda glanced over at the old man across from her.

Katiam closed the door. "He's fully asleep. We're as alone as we've ever been since leaving the Green Grove."

"And he hasn't been much company, with all the sleeping he's doing," the old woman grumbled. "The sun was out today?"

"It was. It was beautiful. But cold."

"And I'm stuck in here."

"Is that what this is about?" Katiam asked. "You're lonely?"

"Of course I'm lonely!" Maeda said. "My husband leaves us to go on ahead and prepare for his ceremony—leaves me with this sleeping invalid, in this blasted waste, with nothing to see through leather covered windows."

"Has Kerei Lant come and sat with you?"

"Yes," the Matriarch said. "But only when Pell is awake. And even then, her conversations are as dry as bone. None of you have come to sit with me."

"Auntie," Katiam said sternly, "you know that we've not been granted permission to do so."

"What has that got to do with anything?"

"Astrid, Sabine, and myself are the only women who left from Pariantür with you. Our numbers have increased, but only at the expense of everyone else being reassigned along the way."

Maeda furrowed her brow. "Then why don't the three of you come and visit?"

"Astrid cannot. She's the head of the guard. And Sabine and I cannot just come sit with you, without generating some jealously."

"You're my physician, and Sabine is my personal assistant."

"Yes, and the rest of the women with us are semi-content to be in your presence, but you have not invited them to join you here, so they would not presume. You're the head of our order and our religion. That makes you as unapproachable as a queen."

Maeda leaned her head back and stared at the ceiling.

"Of course it's my fault."

"I'm not pointing blame at you," Katiam said apologetically.

"Oh, I know, Katiam. I'm just realizing it. I've been so petulant myself, I hadn't realized what gave me my irritation was on my own shoulders. Now, why have we stopped?"

"So I could speak to you. We need to find shelter; it's far too cold to be traveling after dark."

"We can't shelter here on the open road."

"No, but there was a fire a ways off. If we can get to that, perhaps it will provide shelter. And tomorrow, we'll make sure to stop before nightfall."

"As Sabine suggested." The Matriarch paused in thought. "It will take us that much longer to reach Mahn Fulhar."

"Yes. But without endangering ourselves unnecessarily."

"You're right. I should trust Sabine to lead us there. She'll want to see her own husband as much as I do mine."

The inn they arrived at had only one other patron. The innkeeper was more than accommodating, and made their cold journey worth the extra effort.

Overnight a heavy snow fell, leaving the landscape pristine and white, but altogether impassable for the carriages.

"We'll never make it to Mahn Fulhar before the Solstice," the Matriarch complained as Katiam brought bread and pottage from the inn's kitchen.

"The innkeeper said tomorrow the roads will be clear. The weather changes almost daily for the next month."

"Then tell everyone we'll leave as early as possible tomorrow."

"Yes, Auntie."

"And have you tended to the Rotha?"

"It is there under that blanket near the fire," Katiam said, pointing to the pile by the hearth.

"Amazing to think that it was brought to life by the Dweol petals."

"What does that mean, though?"

"If only I knew. You probably ought to bring it with you when we journey to Precipice in the spring."

"I was thinking that."

A knock came at the door, and Sabine Upona entered.

"We'll leave as early tomorrow as possible," Maeda informed her as she opened her mouth to speak.

"Very well, Matriarch Superioris." She stopped and stood at the edge of the carpet by the fire.

"I assume that those sisters who wish to sit with me have been compiled into a list?"

"Yes," Sabine said, "but that is not why I am here."

The elderly woman looked up from her thick pottage, and indicated for her to speak, her mouth full of food.

"There is a Pater Minoris Gladen, who arrived from the south, along with an entire unit of Paladins. He heard you were here and requested an audience."

"Gladen...." the Matriarch pondered.

"He is the ranking Paladin of the Aerie in Limae."

"Journeying north to see the Prima Pater, I don't doubt."

"He didn't seem to know that the Prima Pater was nearby."

"Then show him in, and stay as my attendant."

Upona bowed and left.

"I'm afraid you'll have to excuse me," Maeda said to Katiam.

Katiam rose and made her way down to the common room. Upona and the leading Paladin passed her and walked up the stairs. Gladen and the other Paladins wore black cloaks over their frames, protecting them from the cold. Those who remained in the common room made small talk with the sisters and monks. One Paladin, a Primus, spoke in the silent hand language through a translator to Esenath. He stood taller than the others, but his frame didn't match his height. Katiam then saw the modified boots he wore, giving him several extra inches.

Katiam approached Astrid, who sat by herself, tearing off pieces of bread.

"New people to talk with, and you're over here?" Katiam said, sitting across from her.

"I wasn't feeling talkative."

"Did the Paladins say where they're coming from or why?"

"They're riding up from further south in Varea, and are headed to Mahn Fulhar to meet with the King."

"But they came originally from the Aerie."

"They haven't said so, but I know they are. How did you know?"

"Their leader told Sister Upona, who just escorted him to meet with the Matriarch Superioris. How did you know?"

"I know the Primus over there. Slate."

"How do you know him?"

"He worked as my father's apprentice, and joined up with the Paladins at the same time as my brother."

"And he's already made Primus?"

"Slate was always ambitious. And a hard worker. Though my father trained him, he became a leather worker at Pariantür. A skilled one at that. When the Aerie requested a new master for their leather shop Slate volunteered. That was the last time I saw him. Five years ago, actually."

"Has he spoken to you yet?" Katiam asked.

"No. Nor do I want him to."

"Why is that?"

"For one, he'll ask about Killian. Secondly, because he fancied me back in the day, and I'd rather not go into that again."

"Aw," Katiam said, smiling.

"The Aspect of Honor paired with the Aspect of Compassion takes up too much of my attention."

Katiam nodded knowingly. Most thought the Aspect of Virginity the most common Aspect taken at Pariantür, seemingly the surest way to purity, through Vestal Virginity, but it was the Aspect of Honor, setting themselves aside as a Paladame guard, that so many more took on. Katiam had considered taking the Aspect of Virginity herself from time to time, but had not felt the need to set herself aside in that manner. Her own Aspects of Purity, from the Diet of St. Klare to the wooden mace at her side denoting pacifism, and even the bound sleeves of the Aspect of restoring dignity to the ailing, all performed their duty— something she was all too painfully aware of with or without another Aspect on her shoulders.

An hour later Upona and the Pater Minoris descended the stairs.

"Brothers," the Paladin announced loudly.

Half looked up sharply. Others looked over with eyes glazed by long days of travel on the road.

"Tomorrow morning, we're to leave before dawn. The sisters and our fellow dedicates from the Nifaran order all travel to the same destination as we do—Mahn Fulhar. That being said, I have agreed to assist the Matriarch Superioris's journey, and travel alongside her. Apparently, the Prima Pater himself is already in Mahn Fulhar preparing for a rather momentous meeting of the orders. It is only right that we travel to join them."

"Hear hear!" The Paladins shouted.

"Excelsior Loth," the Pater Minoris said to a Paladin nearby, "it appears that you'll need to travel to St. Nonn without me. We part at daybreak."

The Paladin he addressed dropped to his knee. "Yes, Pater Minoris."

"Now, I'm hungry. Let us eat and rest, for tomorrow, we begin the long road to Mahn Fulhar."

6

Rose Convent

Shelter my roses, and gather up a garden of them, that they may together unlock the secret knowledge hidden within their garden, and heal that which is scarred.

—FROM *NAELA'S EPIPHANY*

The Paladins of the Aerie were a great encouragement to the company as they journeyed along the frigid road. They seemed almost acclimated to the cold, and their knowledge of the road to Mahn Fulhar allowed them to travel longer hours to destinations the Paladames would have struggled to find.

When Etienne Oren arrived at the inn they were staying at to announce they were but a day away from Mahn Fulhar, the sisters cheered and fell to revelry, singing hymns and drinking to the health of Pater Minoris Gladen.

By dawn, Brother Oren had already left to report their arrival to the Prima Pater, and everything was made ready for their departure. The Paladins informed them it would be a warmer day, and so those with armor to don put on their formal regalia under their travel cloaks.

The monks of Nifara took the suggestion by Gladen to ride in the wagon, at least until the city was within view. The pace set by Gladen himself brought another level of cheer to the company, moving faster than they had since meeting up with the monks near Bremüm.

The rolling hills to the south of Mahn Fulhar covered their view to the city like waves blocking the view of a harbor in a storm, but the sun beat down and filled the air with the aroma of mud and a false spring. It was the Flame of Aben they saw first. Although the flame in the iron arrow itself was not visible from the distance, the arrow, pointing to the heavens, provided them something to ride towards.

The Matriarch, while she often complained of bumpy roads, called for her windows to be opened and the carriage encouraged to ride faster. And faster they did ride. At times, Katiam worried about the jostling of the elderly woman's frame, and that of the sleeping Archimandrite. But at times she caught glimpse of her great-aunt's face smiling in the sun, and she knew better than to protest.

Five Paladins rode out from the city to meet them and added to Gladen's numbers, including the Primus of the Mahn Fulhar Bastion, Primus Melit, who greeted Pater Minoris Gladen as a brother.

Everyone fell into formation, and they rode toward the city. The walls, manned by gray-clad guards, boomed open for them, and they began their stately march through. The southern section of the city was filled with sights of clean, well-populated streets, and the smell of smoked meats wafting through the air from vast smokehouses. The people of Mahn Fulhar stopped to watch their procession march past, some making signs of respect, others gawking in curiosity at the armored women and monks of Nifara, who were escorted by Paladins of the Hammer in black travel cloaks.

Their journey took them back and forth over a canal with the water of autumn dwindling along its course. They came to a set of wide stairs alongside an even longer ramp for carts, and made their way up to the sight they had anticipated for weeks.

Across the wide green lawn, next to the gray cathedral of Aben and the dark-stoned castle of Mahn Fulhar, stood the rose-vine covered white marble of the Crysalas convent. It climbed into the air like the shrubs growing along its lower walls, white, clean, and pure. Atop the tallest tower, a glass framed structure in the form of a rose glinted in the bright sunlight.

Pater Minoris Gladen called commands, and the Paladins pressed forward in a parade march, taking the long, wide road around the green toward the gate of the Crysalas complex.

The gates to the structure opened, and women in white poured out, silver-clad Paladames among them. They all started in a cheer that slowly resolved in a hymn of gladness as they watched the head of their religion come to them, and they greeted their sisters with open arms.

Over the roar of the song sung by over five hundred women, Gladen shouted that he would take the monks on to their own quiet rest at the Abecinian complex. Katiam glanced back across the green to see several dozen monks of Aben loitering outside their own complex, watching the proceedings in wonder.

As the Matriarch's carriage neared, the throng of women enveloped them, bringing their movements to a halt. Sabine dismounted and approached the carriage. She turned to the crowd, which fell utterly silent.

"Sisters of the Crysalas!" Upona said in a clear, clean voice. "I present to you the head of the Order of the Rose, Abbess of Pariantür, and the Matriarch Superioris of the Crysalas Integritas across the face of our world, Maeda Mür!"

The door flung open, and the Matriarch stood up out of the door. Astrid Glass stood below, ready to offer assistance if the Matriarch asked for it. The Matriarch wore her headdress, which looked like a rose bloom, and smiled the largest wrinkled smile her face could afford. The tight slits of her eyes cast looks across the crowd, who roared a cheer. The sun beat down on the white robes of the sisters, who parted as a group of six, red-clad Sisters Superiorii approached, led by one in a headdress more ornate than the Matriarch's.

To the gasp of those around her, the self-important woman reached up, took off her own headdress, and fell to her knees.

"Matriarch Superioris," the woman said, "I, the Abbess Superioris of Mahndür and the Crysalas Convent of Mahn Fulhar, Oditte Foi, welcome you with heart-filled warm embrace. Please, enter our garden of flowers, and find rest."

Katiam felt the weight of the crowd suddenly pull her forward and through the gates of the convent. White walls, sprinkled with pink marble adornments, rose high above. Flower petals littered the brick walkways. The vault-like doors that led into the building consumed them all and embraced them in various degrees of warmth by fires lit in hearths.

Before she knew what had happened, she was in a room with steam, her bundle of armor taken from her, and white linen robes given to her to wear when she had concluded her bath. Hot water poured in from some ancient cistern. The attendant excused herself, leaving Katiam to her own devices.

She snapped from her reverie and stood up out of the water after what felt like hours, the Rotha suddenly bursting into her mind.

Dressing in clean robes scented with some northern climate flower, she rushed out into the hall.

"Sister?" an attendant called beside her.

Katiam spun to see the young girl smiling at her.

"May I show you to your rooms?"

"I had a box in the carriage. It holds something very dear; I must retrieve it."

"We will send someone to the Abecinian complex for it. Please follow me."

Katiam wrung her hands as she followed the girl.

"It was such good news to hear that the Matriarch herself was coming to visit. We had to make haste to be ready."

"Did you not know?" Katiam said, her mind not on the conversation as she made small talk with the girl.

They walked under a wide arch into a small meeting room. The black and white tiles of the interior stretched across the room to the walls, adorned with plasterwork between the mirrors that lined the sides. The Matriarch sat up on a cushioned lounge, a fur-lined blanket pulled over her as Upona and Abbess Superioris Foi stood speaking with her.

"But why," the Matriarch asked, "did you not know before the message came from Precipice?"

"I do not know what to say to that," Abbess Foi replied.

"We sent the message over a year ago," Sabine replied.

The abbess looked at both of them with consternation across her face.

"Abbess Foi," Sabine placed a hand on the woman's arm, "we do not blame you for not knowing. But it is an issue and source of irritation that both the Matriarch and her husband, the Prima Pater, have been fretting over for many months now."

"I can show you to your own room," the girl next to Katiam said.

Katiam turned to consider the girl, and saw dark-skinned Esenath standing over her shoulder, working upon the Rotha's box on a table. She rushed across the room to stand across from the other woman.

"I've been worried!" Katiam said as Esenath looked up, a smile playing across her lips.

"I wondered where you might be," Esenath said.

The box they had selected for the Rotha, no longer than a forearm and half as deep and wide, popped open as Esenath levered the chisel in her hand. Some dirt scattered across the marble table, cold to the touch.

Esenath touched the dirt in the box and frowned.

"What's wrong?" Katiam asked.

"It's very cold. Nearly frozen."

"And what does that mean?"

"For some plants, that's good. In fact, some plants won't grow without having gone through a deep chill. But usually those plants haven't already sprouted."

She stirred the soil softly, took hold of the large clump of dirt in the middle, and lifted, clicking her tongue as the dirt broke free of the seed pod. Before it opened, it had fit comfortably in both hands. Five tendrils now grew from the split along its seam; the longest had grown to over six inches, and the others were half the length. The pod had split open entirely, hinged at the bottom with waxy plant material. At the center, where all five tendrils came together, a small, gourd-shaped mass no bigger than Katiam's thumb nestled with soil filling most of the inside of the shell.

But all five vines lay limp, and yellowed.

"Bring me the bucket of soil I have over there by the fire," Esenath said.

Katiam turned to the roaring hearth across the room. A wooden bucket, brimming with fresh dirt, lay warming.

As Katiam came back with it, another sister entered, carrying an ornate box. She placed it next to Esenath and bowed, before excusing herself.

"What is in that?" Katiam asked.

"First, we warm our little Rotha here. Then we'll use what is in that box. Is the soil in the bucket warm?"

Katiam put a hand into the dirt.

"It's hot."

"Good. Can you touch it without burning yourself?"

"Yes."

"Then I'm going to hold the Rotha at this end of the box. Please put double handfuls of the warm dirt in and mix, until you can get that half of the box a uniform temperature."

The damp cold of the soil in the Rotha's box was tempered by the shocking heat of the bucket's contents. Katiam worked back and forth, watching Esenath tenderly clean the Rotha in her hands, leaving the tendrils untouched.

"Will the Rotha stay in this box now that we're here?"

"I'm going to speak to the wood shop," Esenath said, "and see if we can't build a new container. Something a bit finer, don't you think?"

Katiam smiled.

"Now, how is the soil? Cool like a spring soil?"

"Yes. Not warm, but not cold."

"Good." She reached out and touched it with a free hand. "That is good earth. Make a space in it."

Katiam cleared a hole, and Esenath placed the Rotha there.

"I have a theory," Esenath said. "What we've done here may be enough, but could take time and require diligence on our part. We ought to practice diligence anyway. But I'd like to try something that may help our little Rotha here faster."

"What is that?"

"Please open the box," she said as she half buried the Rotha, leaving the longest vine exposed, as well as a portion of the shell.

Katiam reached over with dirt encrusted fingers and opened the ornate box. A blushing glow emanated from it as she flipped the lid.

Seven crystalline Dweol petals lay on satin cushioning. They pulsed with a glow deep within.

"How many?" Esenath asked.

"Seven."

Esenath nodded. She pulled back some of the soil, so she could see each tendril. "Bring one over."

Katiam took one up gingerly between two fingers and brought it over.

"On the longest vine, place the petal on its tip."

As she placed the crystal down, the vines it touched quivered feebly, and then fell still.

Esenath sighed, reaching to grab more soil and cover up the pod.

"Esenath," Katiam said hesitantly, "look."

The vine was slowly changing color, from the starved yellow, back to a fresh green. The tendril moved in small, weak gyrations, took hold of the crystal, and began retracting toward the center. The other four vines jolted as the first one did, then fell still themselves. Even as the crystal was pulled into the shell, it began to lose its glow.

"Bring the others!" Esenath hissed. "Quickly!"

Katiam pulled the small treasure box closer and handed each petal to Esenath, who placed them at the ends of the vines. In turn the tendrils blushed to a bright green of new growth, and, taking hold of the nearest crystals, pulled each of them into the shell. The four smaller arms pulled dirt in around the center, and then pulled the shell tightly around itself. Not closed, but protectively, like some sand creature retreating into its own home. Then, the vines fell still, albeit with the healthy green color within the waxy surface.

Esenath sighed and gave Katiam a triumphant smile.

"We won't need to warm the other half of the soil. We can just find a warm place to put this box. In the meantime, though, let's keep the extra soil warm by the hearth, just in case."

"What about these last two crystals?" Katiam asked.

"One a day. We'll give one a day to the Rotha, and just see if that's what it needs to continue to grow."

7

Feather Through Stone

Words cannot describe what we have no context for. Anka Six-Wings does not convey the truth of his nature. Hammer is the only word we have for what hangs upon the belt of Grissone, yet these words mean nothing. They are paradoxical in nature. That a hammer be used for protection does not stand to reason, yet our Order is the hammer that protects.

—PRIMA PATER SLEIN VRAGG, IMPERIAL YEAR 2136

Frost hung in the air, looking for additional places to paint the landscape with its frosty touch. The brown stones of the paladinial Bastion contrasted with the light gray of the Abecinian compound surrounding it when the full light of day arrived. But here, in the early morning gray, all shone the same, with hints of light upon the frost-covered surfaces.

Jined Brazstein, made Brother Adjutant by divine ordination, warmed the legs of the six-legged sleipnir with the saddle blanket before it could be let into the stall. He had thought such a chore beneath someone of the rank of Adjutant, but no humble task was below that of the Vow of Poverty, the Vow he had taken on top of his first Vow of Chastity.

Jined had many new tasks hoisted upon his shoulders over the past month's ride from Boroni, through the Belvh Pass, and across the dying autumnal fields and forests of Mahndür to their long journey's end, Mahn Fulhar.

The timing could not have been better, if he was honest with himself. The Prima Pater's entourage had arrived at the upper gates of Mahn Fulhar just as a light flurry blew in off the Lupinfang, dusting their walk with large, welcoming flakes. A battalion of Mahndürian soldiers, along with the gray-clad castle guards, filled the field before the castle, which was colloquially referred to as "the Stone".

Young King Erdthal sat atop a perfectly black sleipnir, alongside a temporary stage and pavilion, on which sat the High Priest of Aben, Klent Rigal, who appeared not much older than Jined. With his own entourage of high-tiered priests and rectors, the High Priest welcomed the Prima Pater and his company, and introduced the King as protector of the Church of Aben.

The ceremony and introductions continued as the light faded, and they were eventually given leave to escape into the Bastion to rest.

It had been one week since their arrival. Just before dawn, Etienne Oren, who was assigned to ride out the day prior, had returned with the news they had been waiting for—the Crysalas Integritas would be arriving by midday, accompanied by a platoon of Paladins who had come across them on their own journey from the south.

Where most Paladins were credited with their time served on various duties, Jined understood his new Vow meant continually humbling himself. No compensation would be given for his work, and thus additional work was often taken on by those of the Vow of Poverty to warrant justification of needs—in Jined's case, the planning of the Solstice Council with his now mentor, Pater Segundus Nichal Guess, of the same Vow.

And so, Jined rushed off to relieve the Bastion stable keepers, and see to Etienne's mount.

"The provisioners wondered why you weren't there for the meal," a snide voice said from an entryway. Jined didn't turn around as he continued to brush the sleipnir's coat. He heard the clatter of a wooden bowl placed down on a bench.

"I suppose," the other Paladin said as he approached, "they just can't understand why someone would need to show off their selfish, false humility by taking on a second full Vow voluntarily."

"I'm sure you were quick to explain just how self-righteousness is best displayed, Dane Marric," Jined said. "You are the most experienced man I know in that particular skill."

Dane gave Jined a sneer, one fist resting on his hip, the other holding the signature hammer just under the head while the twenty-two linked chain connected the butt of the haft to his belt.

Like Jined, Dane wore full paladinial armor. Over the heavy knee-high boots and split leather skirt he wore bands across his torso, and a heavy breastplate and tower gorget that nearly obscured his jawline. Mail ran down his shoulders, under the shoulder pauldrons and onto his heavy leather gauntlets. The back of his wrists were lined with riveted plates on the leather of his glove. Across the front of the gorget, green cordons marked his rank of Brother Excelsior, while the bead on the end of a tassel marked him for his Vow of Chastity. That bead was identical to one of the two beads on Jined's own white cordon tassels. The loose jowls under Dane's chin oddly juxtaposed the sharp features of his face. It shook like a bird's wattle as he moved his head back and forth.

Even in his full armor, he stood nearly a head shorter than Jined. Most men did. The rigidity of his eyes and nose felt forced and intentional compared to Jined's own stocky nature. The breaks in Jined's nose, and the heavy brow many had jested was placed there by the gods to keep rain out of his eyes, both furrowed.

"You're in no place to openly insult me," Dane scoffed, cocking an eyebrow. "As a Brother Adjutant, you ought to show dignity for our order, and rise above such things."

"For one," Jined said, "dignity does not exude humility. And secondly, it is not your place to admonish a brother of higher rank."

"So you do, indeed, think yourself better than I? Because you're the son of nobility? Brahz was nothing to look at. How such a small village came to have a jarl at its head, I shall never know."

"I will not deign to answer that insult, if only because I forfeited all rights to any titles I may have once held when I took on the second Vow."

Dane opened his mouth for another attack.

"Brother Marric," Jined said, spinning to look at the Paladin. "As you are of little help standing there, I would ask why you remain, and what you intend to accomplish by doing so?"

"Brother Adjutant," Dane said with a feigned look of shock, "I only intended to keep you in conversation long enough to ensure that your porridge, left over by that cold wall, had reached an appropriate temperature before you ate it. I understand those of the Vow of Poverty do not eat food that is hot."

Jined gritted his teeth. "There are those who do so," Jined said. "I am not one of those."

"My mistake," Dane said, giving a salute to hide the smile growing on his lips. He turned and marched back into the bastion.

Jined led the sleipnir across the stable toward its own stall, where its oats and fresh hay awaited.

"It was a cold night to be out riding," Jined said.

"But probably no colder than the porridge brother Marric brought you," a voice from behind said.

A smile grew broad across Jined's chiseled jaw, and his hard, heavy brows softened as he turned. The Paladin stood a head shorter than Jined, and while no light struck his armor, a soft glow seemed to emanate from him. On his belt hung no hammer, but instead the hint of a hammer that was not there. Where Jined wore armor over leather, the figure before him was the armor that gave him his figure.

Jined dropped to one knee. "Grissone. My god."

"Please rise," Grissone said. "I'd like to walk with you, and long platitudes can be saved for prayer given to me from the quiet of your cell. I would simply like to walk."

Jined rose and followed the softly glowing figure out of the stable and into the yard, where the color of the stones was showing through the melting frost.

"My mother told me of the day she created frost. She felt it a stunning balance of the beauty of her flowers. It gave her the freedom to paint in so many hues, no matter the season."

Jined shuffled alongside Grissone, his head and shoulders hunched in involuntary obeisance.

"You ought to stand taller," Grissone said. "The neckache you'll get from walking like that will not be agreeable later on tonight."

"I..." Jined said, "I fear standing taller than you."

Grissone stopped and turned to consider Jined next to him.

"As the creator of man, do you think I would have made a mistake? Allowing you to grow so broad and tall?"

"I was not questioning you," Jined said, "I..."

"Jined," Grissone said, touching his shoulder softly. "I was jesting with you."

"Is this your actual size?" Jined asked.

"This?" Grissone said. "No. In my full glory, I am... it is hard to describe the actual size of a god. It is not measured in space. I am smaller than the others, however. Since part of my size is accounted for in Anka."

"Your twin-soul?" Jined asked.

"Yes," Grissone said. "When we are together, he sits upon my shoulders, and together we come to full height. Still, we're not nearly as tall as Kea'Rinoul once stood, or as powerfully built as Rionne was."

"But why limit yourself to a shorter stature when you walk among men?"

"It provides me a different perspective, I suppose."

They walked through a gateway into a back orchard garden. Priests of Aben tended the place, spreading old hay around the bases of the trees.

"Can they see you?" Jined asked. He straightened his back every few paces when he realized what he was doing.

"Yes," Grissone said, "although they will likely not recall me in a few moments. I am just another Paladin to them. Or perhaps they consider me a priest. They see what they wish to see."

"Were you in the stable before you spoke?"

"You mean to ask me whether Dane could see me?"

Jined nodded.

"Yes. You were busy and didn't see me, but I was there, and he glanced my way once. He thought me a stablehand."

Jined chuckled.

"What is funny?"

"Dane Marric, a self-righteous Paladin, gave his god a glance, and didn't know he looked into the divine face of his god."

"Jined," Grissone said sternly, "do not be one to cast shame upon Dane. You do not know his heart. You do not know the lengths of internal mortification he goes to to make himself presentable to the world."

"I am sorry," Jined said, taking a deep breath. "Forgive me."

"Of course," Grissone said. "Now, do not think I am not at work to save him. But I expect his will be a long road, and not one you can adjust by cunning repartee with him when he attacks you. You did something he wished he had thought of himself."

"It was by your suggestion that I did it," Jined said.

"I put you on the path, it is true. But you took the step and took that Vow."

Grissone walked over to a stone wall.

"Now," Grissone said, "while I did wish to walk with you, I also came to you for a reason, and we're going to be late if we don't go now."

"Where are we going?"

"To watch an event unfold."

"At this stone wall?"

"No. In the castle, the Stone."

"We ought to turn back and go the way we came, then."

"We ought to not question how your divine god will get you there," Grissone chuckled.

"What do you mean?" Jined asked.

Grissone took up the empty hammer from his belt and touched it to Jined's chest. Jined's form filled the space of the hammer, but he still stood there next to his god. The sun peeked over the garden wall and struck his armor, but left no reflection, instead running through him.

"I'm not here?"

"You are," Grissone said, watching with amusement as Jined lifted a hand to consider it. "I've just removed... threads. You're mostly still here, but no one can see you. That is to say, if someone looked directly at you, they won't see you. Though we might appear in the peripheral of some. Dorian for one, is likely to note you, though he won't be able to say for certain."

The wind struck them like the beats of large wings, and suddenly Jined and Grissone were up and over the wall. They moved like a feather. Jined grasped at Grissone, who took the man's hand in his, and they lit across the sky toward the castle. Its bleak gray stone threatened to dash them to pieces as they flew directly toward it, but when Jined's head should have struck the stone with enough force to fell an auroch, he instead fell through the rock, and plummeted down through a library, and another antechamber, before coming to rest on carpeted flagstone.

Three Black Sentinels walked, escorted by one of the castle guards, away from a room.

"We've missed introductions," Grissone said, "but you will know most, anyway." He walked toward the door the four figures had exited from and pulled Jined through the wood.

The room within was decorated with an ostentatious amount of gold leafing and blue accoutrements. King Erdthal was taking his seat between High Priest Rigal and Prima Pater Dorian Mür.

Only the three seats had been provided, forcing the two Pater Segundii, Nichal Guess and Gallahan Pír, to stand behind the Prima Pater. The aquiline accents of the Prima Pater's armor, the modified armor of St. Hamul himself, seemed to reflect some of Grissone's own glory. This contrasted with the gray robes and the mitre of the High Priest of Aben, and the duller uniform of the King.

"Are you doing that?" Jined asked.

"I'm reminding the other two of the authority Dorian has, and that Nichal and Gallahan deserve respect, too. Since they sit to inherit Dorian's authority, along with the other Pater Segundii still at Pariantür when he is gone."

"You don't think your father will be upset that you've made Dorian appear greater than his own High Priest?"

"No," Grissone said, "I'm not particularly worried."

"I didn't know you could be so..."

"Facetious?"

"Well... yes."

The three men in the chairs sat in silence for a moment, awaiting the valet to pour cups of wine for them. The man finished his service, and once the men held the goblets in their hands, he bowed and left.

"I thank you both for coming to see me," King Erdthal said. "It fills my heart with both a pride and humility, if one can have such a thing occur, to know I have such holiness in my city."

"One need only look upon the beauty of Mahn Fulhar," High Priest Rigal said, "to know Mahn Fulhar does not need multiple heads of churches within its walls to be blessed."

"An interesting turn of phrase," Dorian said, "as I received word, not but a few minutes ago, before I came here, that the Matriarch Superioris of the Crysalas Integritas is to arrive at the city today. She is expected at her own temple by midday."

"Ah, I'm very interested in meeting the head of our sister religion. But perhaps not so eager to meet her as you are, Prima Pater."

"I have missed my wife," Dorian agreed. "We shall have our time to see one another later. I imagine she'll need rest, and the demands of her church will keep her quite busy for a time. She asked to take on the task of escorting the ailing Archimandrite to the city while I rode on ahead to see to the planning of the Solstice Council."

"Yes," King Erdthal said, leaning forward in his chair, "the reason we're meeting."

"King Erdthal," Rigal said, "I am most eager to hear what you wish to speak about, in regards to this momentous occasion. And what allowances the city shall provide for it."

"I need to know what needs you have, and then I shall make all allowances."

"Four churches and their heads," Dorian began, "as recognized by most of the known world, will be gathered as the sun sets on the upcoming Winter Solstice. But it is also to be a private gathering."

"I have no doubt of that," the king said.

"It is to take place in the Abecinian Cathedral, and only members of the holy orders are to be in attendance, to discuss matters."

"Surely the god-ordained King of Mahn Fulhar will be allowed, if only as my guest," Rigal said.

Dorian shook his head. "If we allow you to join us, then all of the other nations will assume you are favored by all four churches. That we're already meeting here in your capital will be talk enough."

The King sat back in his seat.

"The King's authority as monarch would perhaps be questioned if he was not," Rigal said.

"As protector of the realm," Dorian said, "I was considering asking you to stand guard with your military might, on the green outside the complex. It would establish authority, provide us secrecy, and show yourself a servant of the churches."

"A very wise idea," High Priest Rigal conceded. "A proper helping of humility and might."

The king gave a faint smile as he nodded his acquiescence.

"I've learned what I needed to know," Grissone said to Jined.

"What is that?" Jined replied as they turned.

"The High Priest of Aben is in the King's pocket—his sycophant."

"And how does this help?"

"There is nothing I will do about it. He's not my priest. But now you know, and you can watch him. I do not trust him."

They turned to walk away as the main door to the blue and gold hall opened and a servant entered.

"What is it?" the king snapped.

"Pater Minoris Jakis Gladen has arrived with news."

"Gladen?" Dorian muttered to the two men behind him. "From The Aerie?"

"Very well," the king said, rising from his seat.

The servant turned back around and left the room.

The man who strode in wore a flashing smile, but moved like a storm cloud. Jakis Gladen fit his paladinial armor perfectly and wore across the frame of his gorget and shoulder pads a black cloak to keep the winter winds at bay. His chiseled chin and jawline were harsher than Jined's.

Behind him several Paladins followed, including the Pater's Primus, who, oddly enough, wore blocked boots to provide him several extra inches.

"Pater Gladen," the king said, cutting a regal stance. The Paladin gave a curt bow to the king, and then turned to the Prima Pater.

"Prima Pater. Pater Segundii," he gave a salute to each in turn.

"This is an odd surprise," Dorian said. "I did not expect to see you until after our time in Mahn Fulhar concluded. Our itinerary indicated we'd travel through Limae to Birin on our return trip."

"I did not know I would see you in Mahn Fulhar myself, Prima Pater," Gladen said. "Not until I came across the Matriarch Superioris and the ailing Archimandrite as I rode north toward bastions I was inspecting."

"You did not expect us?" Dorian said, looking over his shoulder to Pater Segundus Pír.

"Another missive gone astray?" Pír asked.

"Indeed," Gladen said. "I knew that you had planned a trip to the continent, but we had not heard that you would be traveling across the Northern Scapes. Given the turmoil in Hraldor and Temblin, I could have thought a southern route more likely."

"Temblin is always at war," Dorian snapped. "I want to know why our meticulously planned mission across these domains has been unknown to any save the Paladins of St. Hamul."

"Regardless of whether we knew of your arrival or not," the High

Priest of Aben said, "we are all here now, and if what Pater Gladen says is true, and the Matriarch Superioris has safely been delivered, then we can hold the ceremony on the Solstice the night after next without hesitation."

"Indeed," Dorian said, sitting back in his chair with a sigh. "Nichal, will you please go and inform Adjutant Brazstein of our additional paladinial guests that have arrived? And have him add them to his seating plans for the ceremony?"

Nichal saluted and quickly rushed out the door.

"We ought to get you back to the stables," Grissone said, turning again. "Nichal might beat us there."

"That," Jined said, "and my porridge has probably gone colder."

8

New Alvarians

Faith, it is said, was Grissone's first love. She never had form, nor name, yet he awaits her arrival by practice of her virtue. And thus we emulate his patience, waiting for that which has not, but will one day, come.

—*THE IKHALLE STONE*, LINE 37

An hour spent with his god seemed to fill a void he had always known was there, but had never acknowledged. Jined wandered the Bastion with the empty porridge bowl in his hand, recollecting the events of the morning as a distant memory brought visibly to present.

"Brazstein," Pater Segundus Nichal Guess said, finding him as he gave his bowl to a cellarer in the kitchen.

He was almost as tall as Jined, with thick eyebrow lashes and a head of coarse black bristles that fought to remain unshaven. The weight of the world always seemed to rest on his shoulders. Now that Jined bore the same Vow, he was starting to understand why.

"We have guests who have just arrived. Pater Minoris Gladen of the Aerie brought the Crysalas in, having met them on the road. Can you see that five more places are set for dinner tonight? In the Prima

Pater's private chapel, I think. We'll use it to finalize planning for the ceremony."

"Yes, Pater Segundus."

Jined stopped by his cell, one he shared with Etienne, who also bore the Vow of Poverty. Despite their difference in rank, unlike other Brother Adjutants of other Vows, Jined would always share a cell, since he could call no cell his own. The younger Paladin lay quietly in his bed, attempting to get some rest from his late-night ride. Jined grabbed his satchel, which contained his notes for the ceremony.

He closed the door behind him as he left, putting the satchel across his body. He felt the last vestiges of the elation he had worn since meeting with Grissone slough off his frame as responsibility once more took hold.

Dane approached from down the hall and opened his mouth to speak.

"Brother Excelsior," Jined said with a voice of authority that spoke of business rather than common talk. Dane straightened his back, ready to take an order, even if his eyes shone a hint of haughtiness. "Please see half a dozen seats brought to the Prima Pater's chapel. We're to add guests to his dinner tonight. And then I'd like you to go and check with the Abecinian church and ensure that they have prepared the number of candles we requested to be ready for the ceremony."

Dane saluted and left without another word.

Jined turned the corner and almost collided with Loïc and Cävian, the twin brothers who had both taken the Vow of Silence, giving up their familial name. The two of them chatted idly with each other in the hand language spoken by those of their Vow.

"What are the two of you up to right now?" Jined asked.

We're idle, Loïc signaled with a smirk on his face.

"Then can I ask the two of you a favor?"

Both nodded.

"There will be additional guests at dinner with the Prima Pater to-night. Please see that the kitchen has what they need. If they don't have the supplies, will you offer to go and purchase the goods for them?"

I will go, Cävian signed. *Brother has other duties later on.*

Jined moved about the Bastion making notes to himself, asking others to help him prepare things for the dinner, and doing what needed doing when no assistance could be found. It disappointed him to feel the effects of having walked through walls with his god quickly dissipating. But, as he wrapped his mind around the new responsibilities, he knew that changing from a simple guard to an organizer would do just that.

An hour before dinner, Jined sat himself down on a bench in an alcove for a moment to himself and closed his eyes.

"It's important to take time for yourself," a voice said. Jined opened his eyes to see the figure of Pater Jakis Gladen standing over him. He still wore the black travel blanket over his shoulders. "Especially for those with the Vow of Poverty on our shoulders."

"You are of the Vow of Poverty?"

Gladen laughed as he reached up and pushed back the black cloak to show the bead of poverty hanging on his gold cordons. "I've been so busy all day long I hadn't realized I still had this on. May I?" he asked, indicating his desire to sit next to Jined.

"Of course," Jined said.

Gladen sat next to him with a sigh and then untied the cloak, folding it on his lap.

"Pater Minoris Jakis Gladen," the Paladin introduced himself.

"Brother Adjutant Jined Brazstein."

"The Paladin with two Vows," the Pater replied.

"So you've heard that?"

"Who hasn't? A very talkative Paladin, Excelsior Marric, was it? He told me all about you."

"Ah," Jined said.

"Quite the adventure you've been on. Found a lost book. Took on a second Vow. Fought a giant savern-man?"

"He was cursed by Kos-Yran, and had control over wyloths, saverns, and furies."

"Sounds like Grissone has favored you," Gladen said. "That is good; a mote of his power, sitting on your shoulders. What a great and wonderful burden to have in your possession."

"I've disavowed all possessions," Jined said.

"All worldly possessions," Gladen said. "But we cannot turn away the gifts of our god. We should hold onto them; use them for the good of all, when it is time."

"We can't contain Grissone."

"No," Gladen said, "we can't contain a god. But when a god uses their power through us, there are, some might say, vestiges of that power that remain, like a thin coat on a white fence."

Gladen rose and stretched.

"That may not be true," he added, "but I like to think that it is. It helps me get through the day when the burdens stack up; as though I can draw from that power invested in me. Now, from here, how do I get to the Prima Pater's chapel? I'd like to be there before the bells strike to call for dinner. I'm starving after all that travel."

"I will walk with you," Jined said.

As they turned the two corners to reach the chapel, Loïc was carrying a bread basket from the kitchen and placing pieces of the rich, dark bread on each platter.

"One thing I'll give Mahndür," Pater Gladen said, "their use of flax in their bread is to be admired." He negligently reached out and fixed a piece of bread that sat half off the plate.

You did not have to go so far as all this, Jined signed to Loïc, *if you had other duties.*

I did not, Loïc said. *And you know the philosophy I follow.*

To perform each request.

Loïc nodded and left.

"You speak the Silent language?" Gladen asked.

"I have been learning it as we traveled. Loïc and Cävian are good teachers and have proven to be good friends."

Other members of the Prima Pater's entourage, as well as those from the local Bastion ranked Brother Adjutant or higher, began filtering in just as the bells for dinner began to toll. A few Brother Paladins and

Brother Excelsiors served food in front of them all as they waited on the Prima Pater and his two Segundii. They all rose as the little elderly man entered. He nearly hopped in, spry as ever, and came to stand at the head of the table.

"Welcome, all," he said. "And we welcome Pater Gladen from the Aerie, who happened to be traveling north and came to visit our table. Welcome."

Everyone gave greetings to Gladen and his second, the tall but quiet Primus Slate, who had come to take his seat next to him.

Everyone tore open the bread on their plate and put portions of smoked fish upon it. Into their bowls they put thick short noodles from a common server, and tore off portions of sauce-covered anda, a water bird often kept on farms in the surrounding countryside. The aroma of tart berries cooked to sweetness and the nuttiness of the sticky noodles rose to match the brotherly cheer in the room.

"Pater Gladen," the Prima Pater addressed the Paladin sitting next to Jined, "tell us of the Aerie citadel. What happens in its holdings, that you find yourself on the road as winter sets in?"

"Prima Pater," Gladen said, "I am often found traveling up and down the length of our assigned domain. More so these past six months."

"Why is that?"

"There are rumors of insurgents causing trouble in Varea and Redot. News of them started to filter in while I was here visiting King Erdthal this past spring. He asked that I look into the situation, and so I spent all of the summer in those countries looking for the trouble."

"Insurgents? To what aim?"

"Restoring Alvaria," Gladen said in all seriousness.

"Alvaria? A country that existed for no longer than forty years, centuries ago?" the Prima Pater smiled.

"More a banner to unite under," Gladen said, "than actually looking at history."

"What makes you say that?" Pater Segundus Pír asked.

"Alvaria encompassed Varea, Redot, southern Mahndür, and Limae.

That being the case, rumors in Limae should also abound. As those rumors have yet to spring up, I can assume it is more banner than true vision."

"You mentioned King Erdthal asked you to go and seek these Alvarians," Pater Segundus Guess said, "in countries separate to his own."

"Yes. We Paladins can cross borders and ensure that potential causes for strife do not come to that point."

"And what did the Council of Elders in Redot have to say? Or the Lord Regent in Varea?"

"They did not protest," Gladen said.

"Did you discover anything?" the Prima Pater had stopped eating and had both hands on the table.

"Am I to be admonished? For doing what falls under my responsibilities as a Pater Minoris of a Fortress-Citadel?" Gladen glared at the leadership.

Dorian Mür forced a smile and closed his eyes. The smile warmed to a genuine one.

"I am sorry, Pater Minoris Gladen," he said. "Please allow me to explain my frustration. You see, we chose to take this trek across what Pariantür has considered the relatively quiet Northern Scapes, to ensure that reports to the positive were without error. And what do we find?

"The countries of Bortali and Boroni are threatening war. Messages sent through St. Hamul to Düran, Limae, and even Mahndür have gone amiss. And so, to find out that more potential strife exists between Mahndür, Redot, and Varea, not to mention the usual problems found in the southeastern countries of Temblin and Hraldor, you can see why I am eager to quickly identify the trouble and prepare a plan to combat these issues. I am not attacking you; I am aiming to calm the muddy waters."

"I understand, Prima Pater," Gladen said, albeit through clenched teeth.

"What were your findings?" Nichal Guess asked.

"Of?" Gladen replied.

"The insurgents."

"I found some evidence of their presence. But I have not yet been able to uncover their leadership, or even what their goals are."

"What do you suspect?" Dorian asked.

"I believe the New Alvarians are seeking support from either the Redotian Elders, or the Regent of Varea. If they have the support of one of the countries, they can mobilize to absorb the others. Finally they can turn that combined might on Mahndür."

"Why turn against Mahndür?"

"The southern portion of Mahndür, once part of Old Alvaria, has qualms with a crown so far north. Having a government more centralized to their own needs would fit their demands."

"Which are?"

"The southern Mahndürians are required to grow the country's flax, but are restricted from pasturing capricör. So they must import their wool from directly across the border, or are charged excessive fees by those who bring wool from the pastures north of Mahn Fulhar. Yet the guilds of Mahn Fulhar demand flax seed and linen as an essential good, so the tax on the flax product is minimal."

"That seems odd," Pater Segundus Pír said. "Wool is much more important to warmth. Shouldn't it be taxed as an essential good?"

"As a livestock product, it has a separate tax levied on it."

"I have a suggestion," Primus Dikun Polun, the entourage purser, said. "You may not like it, but the Black Sentinels may be in a position to help us out."

"As bodyguards?" Dorian asked, looking at the tight voiced man.

"No, Prima Pater," Polun replied. "Perhaps you recall that the Black Sentinels who joined us were coming north only as escorts to the Nifarans, but they've come to Mahn Fulhar to set up a caravan route from here to either Aunté, or Nor-Vio in Ormach, as their destination."

"And how will that help the situation?"

"Rebellion may be avoided if we simply alleviate the issue with relief."

"And how do you suggest we do that?"

"By requesting they requisition wool from Ormach."

"I see three problems with this suggestion," Pater Gladen said, "if I may?"

Polun nodded.

"First, relief with wool given from Ormach will only temporarily solve the issue, as it will continue to be a constant need. Secondly, this will cause strife between King Erdthal, whose subjects will no longer be reliant on him or his protection, further causing strife with Ormach. Lastly, one should not trust the Black Sentinels if money does not exchange hands."

"You have first-hand experience with the Sentinels, I take it?" Dorian asked.

"Their entire organization is headquartered in Haven, as close to the Citadel as the Bastion here is to the Church of Aben, and they do nothing if it won't make them money."

"As one can expect from one not of a holy order."

"And yet," Gladen said, "they wish to be shown the respect of an equal, often appealing to the Citadel as servants to the people. They have a very well-educated view on what the Grissoni church is required to do."

"Perhaps we could appeal to their leadership with benefits better than money?"

"The commanders who run the Black Sentinels would need to be entirely in agreement for something like that to work, and they rarely agree."

"We won't need to speak to their council," Dorian said. "We'll just speak to their Master and Commander."

"Last I heard," Gladen said, "their Master and Commander was off in the east. Macena, or Temblin."

"Searn VeTurres is here in Mahn Fulhar. He came to the city with us."

"VeTurres is here?" Gladen said.

"Yes. Anything we should know?"

"Yes. He's the shrewdest man I've ever known, and strangely enough, we've never met. But decisions made by him are law among the Sentinels, and they always benefit them in the end, even when they seemed a sacrifice."

"Let's move on to better subjects," Dorian said. "We've talked of enough strife for one dinner, I think. We all have things to consider, regardless."

"Is all ready for the ceremony, Brazstein?" Pater Segundus Pír asked.

"I have final planning to go over with Brother Upona," Jined said, "but I have no issues that I see in the plan."

"I should like to be in attendance at the ceremony," Gladen said to the Prima Pater.

"I would like that," Dorian responded, "if Brother Brazstein is able to accommodate you and the brothers who traveled with you."

"There is room," Jined said. "The Nifarans take up only the one pew behind the Black Bench."

"I forgot that the Abecinian Cathedral here has a Black Bench."

"Made from a qavylli mahogany, no less," Upona, the Prima Pater's seneschal, spoke up. "I've not seen its equal in craft."

"I often forget I promoted you to my assistant from the wood shop," Dorian said. "I hope you find time to practice your craft while we're here."

"What time I have to spare," Upona said, "is spent with my wife."

"Jurgon Upona's wife is a Paladame of the Crysalas Honoris," Jined muttered to Gladen, "and personal assistant to the Matriarch Superioris. The selection was made to keep gossip between only the two couples. Upona is the most tight-lipped man I know, and his wife is equally private."

Gallahan Pír's own assistant, Primus Aeger, was signing to the Pater Segundus.

"Primus Aeger says that he has always found the tradition of the Black Seat an odd one," Pír said, "and one his own studies have never uncovered the true history behind."

"Not so much a tradition," Dorian said, "as a requirement from the church of Wyv-Thüm."

"Surely the church of the Judge of the Dead is not real," Pater Gladen said. "The Judge sits upon his throne, and has the souls of the dead delivered to him by Nifara. What need would he have of a priesthood?"

"They do exist," Dorian said. "There is not much more I am at liberty to say. They are a secret Mystery, but many of the old legends are based in facts."

"Such as the secret gates into Noccitan?" Upona asked.

"I heard a tale when I was a boy," Nichal said, "of people stumbling upon one of the gates into Noccitan, and entering, but not dying. The act of finding such a place obligates them to become a priest of the Judge."

"Most chapels," Pater Gladen said, "such as the one in the Aerie, have only the single stool made of black wood. Why is the one here so large and elaborate?"

"Because Mahn Fulhar was a city long before Mahndür was a country," Pater Segundus Pír said. "And those who live and die within its walls require burial here, within these walls. The catacombs below the cathedral are extensive, as I understand it. For every body buried there, the three coins paid to Wyv-Thüm, one for each of his eyes, are collected for the maintenance of the Black Bench."

"And only those of Wyv-Thüm's priesthood may sit there," Dorian said with finality. He rose from his seat.

"If you'll excuse me now," Dorian said. "I have an appointment to visit my wife. Jurgon?"

His seneschal followed him out the door into his office to prepare himself for the walk across the green to the temple of Crysania.

"It's a wonder there is not a tunnel between the two churches," Nichal said.

"There is rumored to have once been one," Gladen said. "But as the priests and monks of Aben are required to remain celibate, it would only benefit those Integritas who are wed to Paladins, and this Bastion is a small one."

"It is an odd turn of doctrine," Polun said, "that the priests of the father of the gods cannot marry priestesses of the mother of the gods."

"I imagine it was not so much a matter of doctrine," Gallahan Pír said, "but a matter of necessity once the Paladames came to seek refuge at Pariantür those centuries ago."

9

Interlude

The forge heat had reached its climax. The smith took his hand off the bellows and pulled on the chain nearby. A gong resounded, and the door opened. Two men entered, a strong box between them. The smith could tell from their vacant expressions that they had little say in their actions. He envied them their mindless ways, yet the knowledge he held was more precious still. They placed the box onto a table as he approached. He lifted the door on the top of the finely carved wooden ark and put his hand into the cavity.

Feeling around, he pulled out a clump of the metal. This one already had the right weight. He held it up and turned it over in the forgelight. The veins and cavities of the twisted skyfall metal were tight. This one bore a wide scratch upon its surface that no natural thing, save the metal itself, could make. Indeed, only when an extreme searing heat brought it to temperature could it be manipulated. But this scratch upon its surface, as if from the claw of some great beast, had been caused upon its surface while cool.

He pondered that for a time, and then gave a wave of his hand. The two men turned and left with the heavy fortune between them.

He turned back to the forge and opened the door. Taking up long tongs, he pinched the skyfall and set it into the furnace.

While he waited, he cleaned around the special anvil. A spherical cavity placed there was brushed free of motes of dust. The hammers were hung within reach.

He turned to the forge after an hour and clicked the tongs a few times before opening the door. Within, the metal glowed white hot. Grasping it, he lifted. He had never bothered to confirm it, but he felt that when heated it was, beyond all logic, heavier. He took a few steps back and placed it onto the anvil, the top of which was made of the same stuff.

To test the purity, he took up his largest hammer and struck one of the mangled protrusions. The hot metal gave no sign of change. Then, placing his hammer aside, he picked up the hammer made of the same stuff and struck. The metal gave like putty. He smiled to himself and began to work it into shape, forcing the metal and the mangled portion of the surface into a general round shape.

He could see that, even with the inner glow continuing to emanate from its surface, the pits and veins would never go, even after it was made into the desired shape. That had always been the case. It was as though at one point the metal had been a single thin sheet, and then, by the hand of some elder being, crumpled into its final form; even the metal refused to touch itself.

When the metal had cooled too much, it began to cause a thrum he could feel in his hands. If he continued to allow it to do so, his ears would start to bleed again. He turned to the forge, and put it back in to reheat.

When it came out, he put it down in the half sphere and gave it probing taps. He had made enough of these before, so bringing it to the uniform shape he wanted was easy. Still, he would not be proud of it. It could not be shined; it would be dull. Not like the polished finish of the Plate that sat in the vault. Who had crafted it? What had it been quenched in that made it look as it did?

The metal began to thrum—he could feel it with every strike. It mesmerized him. Though he could not hear it, he could feel it. He continued to beat it into shape, wiping the sweat forming on his brow and touching the moisture at his temple. His wrist came back with fresh red blood from his ear. He sighed, turned, and put the metal back into the furnace. He had worked it too long. He closed the forge door and could feel the banging on the door to the room.

He opened it to see one of the Paladins standing there, holding his head and shouting something at him. It was the taskmaster, one of the servants of the commander. He shrugged and indicated for the man to follow him in. He pointed to a stool, and the man sat.

While the taskmaster watched him intently, he began filling the quenching trough. He had tried so many liquids—water, various oils—and all produced the same effect. The man sitting on the stool impatiently shouted orders at him. He paid him no heed. The taskmaster knew he had gone deaf from work with the thrumming metal long ago, so why did he bother?

He took up the tongs and opened the forge. The man across the trough waited for him to bring the sphere of metal over.

It was the shape the smith desired. He smiled confidently.

He walked across the room, tongs in both hands, hot metal extended. He prepared to drop the sphere of metal, its surface a twisted minutiae in veins and folds. He looked at the Paladin, his look smug, rage-filled, and shouting.

He had never quenched it in blood. It might answer the tinge of red seen in the shining surface of the Dread Plate.

He finished the work and washed the sphere clean, smiling broadly. This sphere, unlike the others, shined brightly, though he would still describe it as a black metal. The veins were as red as the dawn. Oddly enough, the scratch could still be seen. No amount of hammering had seemed to remove it. It was his finest work.

He took up his skyfall metal hammer and tapped it lightly. Even in the recesses of his skull, he thought he could hear the sound. Before it began to give him a headache, he touched it with the hammer to absorb some of the vibration, which slowed, then stopped. He could tell that this accursed sphere would be used to destroy something far greater than itself. It had been made for that.

* * *

Primus Melit sat down across from the scribe. The scribe gave an indication for him to wait as he finished writing a line on the page.

Aeger looked up at the man across from him.

How can I help you, Primus, he signed.

"Eight hundred years ago," Melit said, "a wiseman brought a truth to Pariantür. It enlightened many."

You speak of one many consider a heretic.

"Yet his teachings persist."

Among some, yes.

"Among the knowing."

Aeger rose and locked the door.

He went to the sideboard, poured two goblets of fortified mead, and gave one to Melit.

I don't know that we've ever met, Aeger signed. *What name have you adopted?*

"My master was the scholar, Goblet."

Aeger laughed voicelessly. *His brother was called Cup—the name I've adopted.*

"Fitting," Melit laughed. "The students of two brothers, separated. Cup and Goblet."

I wonder at why you have sought me out.

"I received a message today, meant for one called Cup. I've been trying to figure out which of your company bore the title. And now, we meet."

The message?

"Dusk sent it along. He says someone in your company has something for me, but he does not say who it is. Do you know who it is?"

I might, Aeger signed. *But if they have not yet sent it, then there is a good reason. And I must say, while you show loyalty to Dusk, I also see in you a hint of loyalty to Vanguard. I do not yet know if I can trust you.*

"I admire caution. Who is your loyalty to?"

Fidelity holds the title of Canon at Pariantür. To him I owe my allegiance.

"And is Fidelity here? Does he stand here with your chain in his hand?"

Aeger shook his head and took a sip of the drink before him.

"Then you only hold loyalty to one who stands over you."

Do not we all?

Melit pulled the note from his robe and handed it to Aeger, who lifted the seal, already broken, and read the words within.

Dusk means to betray Vanguard.

"And asks that we bring him, and his life's work to Waglÿsaor," Melit said. "If we can do that, and consolidate the Motean power there, he believes we can establish something great."

Until I journeyed through Bortali, I thought that Haven would have been a better place. I might have even thrown in my lot with Vanguard. The lawless nation would have been ripe for harvest.

"And now?"

The desperation of the Northern Scapes is a fruit in season. I think Dusk is right; a new religion would take there like a wildfire. Moteans would flock to it.

"And what of Piedala?"

I think we can convince them. If not, they and the Citadel could be sacrificed to ensure Motean strength.

"So, shall we speed the failure of Vanguard here?" Melit said, rising as he finished the cup of mead.

Aeger nodded.

Melit let himself out.

Aeger took out a small ledger. Next to the name of Melit he wrote the word "Goblet" and then made a note.

~Goblet shifts loyalties like the waves of the sea.

He finished the mead next to him and sat back in his seat, considering how to send a message safely back to the sect at Pariantür, and warn them of the changes coming to the secret order.

PART 2

10

Friends and Allies

As purse drew near to empty,
His work he took back up,
He plied his trade for any,
    And took the coin for sup,
        Regathering his luck.

—THE TRAVELER

Whisper trotted alongside Hanen as he walked past the massive guildhall. It stood overlooking the city, across the Upper Estates from the Crysalas temple. Nearly everyone who walked the well-kept streets bore signs of guild membership, and none seemed to notice the looming presence of the massive timber-beamed hall that crowned the hill. Several Voktorra stood atop the marble steps leading up to the doors, confirming what Navien had shared. The guilds controlled the city, and their enforcers were the Voktorra.

"How are we going to present our value to the Guild Masters," Hanen spoke to the ynfald next to him, who sat upon the stone walkway. "And how can we be sure the guilds won't just take our suggestion and do it themselves?"

"A well-presented plan often convinces those hearing of it that the presenter is the best solution to the problem," a reedy voice said from behind him.

Hanen turned to see the tall, slender figure of the qavyl spice merchant Ymbrys Veronia standing there. Qavylli stood a head taller than most humans, with their soft, flesh-covered, knobby horns rising a few inches still above that. Two tendrils fell from his upper lips like a lake fish's over the flashing smile across his triangular face. Two long ears went out horizontally from his head. He wore thick robes of a red material over his frame, furs lined his long throat, and he still held the leather-bound staff, from which hung various pockets and bags. His flat tail was hidden under the robes that nearly touched the ground.

"What are you doing in Mahn Fulhar?" Hanen asked. "I thought you were going to remain in Birin for a time."

"For a time. And then I traveled north to Garrou. I caught the last ship from Garrou to Mahn Fulhar before the winter storms made it impossible."

"I hope you're not too cold, here in the north."

"The qavylli do not mind cold. Our capital is in the highest of mountain valleys, after all."

The qavyl bent over to pet the ynfald, who readily accepted the attention.

"It is so very fitting that you have an ynfald like this," Ymbrys said.

"Why is that?"

"Ynfalds were created by the Arbiter, and acted as guards in the first city, before his fall. A black ynfald, as black as your Sentinel cloak, is apropos."

Hanen shifted the weight of the crossbow that hung under his cloak.

"Many things have changed in the short time since we've spoken. A captain now, I see?"

"Yes," Hanen said. "Rallia and I were both given the rank by Searn after a meeting with the king."

"You've met King Erdthal, then?" Ymbrys said. "I had the pleasure of meeting his father many decades ago, when he journeyed to the qavyl continent of Hannica. A shrewd boy, though not as cunning as his brother."

"What took you to Garrou?"

"I had never seen the Glowing City, and I thought to find my quarry there. It was not to be. Rumor has it they've come here, to Mahn Fulhar, and here I find you."

"You seek Paladins, then?"

"The Prima Pater of the Grissoni church?" Ymbrys replied. "No. Although I find it interesting you were here along with the leadership of the Paladins. How did that come to be?"

"Searn spoke with the heads of the Nifaran Templum, and convinced them to allow us to escort them here."

"And now you stand conspicuously talking to yourself as you stare at the guildhall."

"I have been charged with making a presentation before the Guildmasters, for the guilds of Mahn Fulhar to accept the Black Sentinels as equal."

"I see the comparisons to be made," Ymbrys said. "Your organization is already run like a guild. Why do you need approval of the guild masters? Have the Sentinels no charter with the King?"

"We did, but Searn requested the charter be updated and the Sentinels recognized by him as a guild, so we could negotiate with other guilds."

"I see now. And these guilds require that they recognize a new guild, and not just the word of the King."

"Exactly," Hanen said, pulling his cloak tighter. "I have to return to our hall at the castle."

"It was a pleasure running into you again," Ymbrys said. "Until we meet again."

"Likewise," Hanen said, and he turned to walk in the opposite direction.

When Hanen came down to the bridge crossing the city canyon, he thought better than to continue up to Blackiron, instead turning toward the Grotto Market.

Rallia had agreed to meet him there before going to the guildhall at nightfall, if they didn't run into each other before then, and so he decided a bit more time to himself would help.

Half of the cavern sat open to the sky above, and those market stalls with no shelter had tents erected over them. At the back of the grotto, the stream trickled out of an inset marble fountain, and down into the pool that people gathered water from. Set into the same wall was the Grotto's own guildhall.

Along the walls, façades of the houses of higher-status merchants had been painted in colors that juxtaposed their neighbors. Above each shop, some windows were obviously fake, to provide a look of perceived wealth. On another level above the homes ran a columned walkway, through which a fair number of well-dressed members of the aristocracy observed those they considered below them.

Hanen stopped and watched one young woman with an elderly chaperone behind her paying little attention. The girl gave Hanen a small wave of her hand. He waved back as she continued to make odd gestures. He was certain she flirted in some way unknown to him. She turned her shoulder to him before turning back. He looked around to see if someone had seen him making a fool of himself, and saw a man-servant making similar return gestures as he held up odd trinkets from the merchant cart he stood next to.

He blushed in embarrassment as his suspicions were confirmed. The manservant, now laden with purchases, walked to the Voktorra-guarded staircase that rose up to the level of the girl, so she could approve the finds.

Hanen shook his head and walked away through the barely-straight rows of merchant tents. While the tent tops were temporary, it was apparent by the fixtures within that they were mostly permanent shops, presented as tents to give the feel of an open-air market in a southern climate.

He came to the back and turned to the right to find a small, quiet section inhabited almost entirely by Hrelgren merchants. The green-skinned, soft-beaked figures spoke with one another and gave little attention to him as he walked by. Usually Hrelgrens were so quick to hawk their wares, it was odd to see them so far from their own people without the desire to sell.

He soon noticed that their own stalls had few wares, save for some small trinkets. He stopped and looked at one young hrelgren, no more than their own coming-of-age of twelve.

The hrelgren eyed Hanen and stood up, looking him in the eye.

"Azho. Sint-hati-oi-zidil-moni-palitan," Hanen greeted him.

The Hrelgren's face, and those nearby, lit up in wide smiles.

"Ashini! Eti-bo-sha'shina-zidil-palitan," the hrelgren said back. The others nearby were now saying *ashini* and *azho* over one another.

"You don't seem to have many wares," Hanen said.

"Alas," the hrelgren said, "I was sent here by my father, who himself said he came here as a young hrel."

"If you've no wares, then have you sold them all?"

"I wish that were the case, my friend. We all came here together a month ago, with goods we were told would sell well in Mahn Fulhar. But a week after we arrived, our goods, Tach'eynese ceramics, were stolen. From Boun they stole a pot of Eybor pepper seeds. From my friend Delit, a satchel full of finely dried meat. If we return home so soon after we arrived, our families may ostracize us."

"Surely they can't fault you for being taken advantage of," Hanen said.

"Indeed they can," the Hrelgren said. "Blessed people as we are, touched by our god, returning with the knowledge that we were stolen from will be a sign of our cursing."

"So what do you wait for?"

"For enough silver to pay for our return trip home. And we can admit that the we squandered the money earned from the profits."

"That makes no sense to me."

"It is not meant to." The hrelgren came out from his booth and held out his hand. "I am Zhag *rm* Tellis, of the Tach'eyn Isles."

"Hanen Clouw."

"You're a Black Sentinel."

"I am. My sister and I arrange a caravan for merchants to travel from here to Ormach."

"Tell me when you expect to leave."

"In the spring, as soon as the roads will allow and not spoil goods."

The hrelgren leaned in and whispered up to the taller Hanen. "I will speak to my friends. We may look to join you."

Hanen said his farewells.

As he came around the curve, he looked up into the windows of the permanent shops. One shop was nothing more than a home with a desk in the window for selling coal tickets. Another displayed dried fruits in rows of clear Alnír-crafted glass jars.

As he passed an ointner, a customer came out wearing a cloud of recently purchased perfume that even Hanen could tell was cheap. Whisper began to sneeze uncontrollably while Hanen found a catch in his throat and began to cough.

He almost ran into a woman as she stepped out of her own shop to situate a mannequin, wrapped in blue brocade ribbon over the shoulders.

She turned and startled as she saw him approach. "Hello, Hanen. I thought perhaps we'd never meet again."

Hanen smiled. "I apologize. I'm terrible with names, but I never forget a face. You were at the baker's stall last week?"

She nodded. "It's Alodda. And who is this?" she said, her voice going up in register as she knelt down next to the ynfald. The smaller black-scaled creature slunk low and approached, his thin tongue whipping out to taste the air around her. She chuckled as she reached into her pocket and pulled out a small piece of dried venison.

"This is Whisper. I saved him from some trouble right after you and I met."

"Black ynfalds are good luck," she said, offering the piece of meat to the ynfald and scratching the back of his head.

"Perhaps meeting you is what brought him good luck," Hanen said. "If I hadn't met you, I wouldn't have been in the right place to help this little guy out."

"Would you like to come in?" She indicated toward her store, painted in white with blue highlights, and stepped up into it.

Inside there were several mannequins dressed in fine outfits. A young girl who looked to be Alodda's much younger sister was pinning a woman's outfit while the customer tried on a gown in a mirror. A middle-aged woman stepped out from the back and approached Alodda to consult her.

"The ynnie won't cause any trouble, I don't doubt." A voice shot out from behind Hanen, and he spun to see a very old man sitting in a window seat, hand-stitching brocade into a vest.

"Father," Alodda said, walking over. "The ynfald is fine."

"That's what I was saying," the old man shouted. He was obviously hard of hearing.

"Your father?" Hanen asked.

"Yes. My mother, Eimeé, is his second wife. She was a shop girl here who helped with sales and tailoring. My father is Abgenas Dülar. His hand-stitched brocade has been worn by kings and generals since the Protectorate Wars."

"That's a very long time."

"Yes," she said with a smirk. "My father is a very old man. I'm learning from him, though I doubt I'll ever be as good as he is."

"May I see some of your work?"

She smiled again and led him over to the opposing wall. She pulled out a deep blue sash, embroidered with a fine lighter blue detail. Hanen took it from her offering hands and held it up.

"This is fine work," he said. "You used an Aben's Knot for the mesh background."

"Aben's Knot?" she asked, taking back the piece and holding it up to look closer. He pointed at the lattice work that covered the entire piece.

"You mean Abgenas's knot. My father invented that knot."

"Well," Hanen said. "I learned that knot from my father, a net mender. And plenty of fishermen use it to make nets now. It can't only be sixty years old."

She marched across the room to stand by her father.

"This is Hanen, father. He told me your knot is used by fishermen who make nets, but they call it Aben's Knot."

"No. I never taught it to any fisherman. I can't think of a soul I've ever taught it to outside my family. Coincidence, perhaps? Give the boy a bit of thread. Let's watch him tie it."

Alodda ran into the back and came out with a bit of string. "Go ahead, show my father."

Hanen took it and deftly tied it into a series of knots that made a small mesh.

The old man took it, looking confused. Then he looked up, light dawning in his eyes.

"I remember! I taught it to that Paladin, back during the war. He could never do it my way. He always did the third pass backwards. Nethendel! That was his name. Nethendel Unteel. Maybe he passed on that knowledge?"

Alodda turned back. "There you go," she said. "Perhaps your father learned it from someone who learned it from the Paladin Unteel."

Hanen still had the blue bolt in his hand. He handed it back.

"Is there anything you'd be interested in while you're here?"

"Not that I can think of," Hanen replied. "Though you did suggest I might need some new clothes last time we met."

"I remember."

"I could use a new outfit for spring. But I'd want you to do the embroidery work, rather than your father."

She lit up when he said that. "Let me and my sister take your measurements while we discuss what I'll make for you."

Whisper trotted alongside Hanen with his head a little higher, with the black ribbon tied loosely around his neck. As the day wore down to a close, there were less people, and more of them had attentive ynfalds walking alongside them.

The people of Mahndür took obvious pride in their pedigreed ynfalds. All of them stood with backs and heads twice the size of Whisper, indicating he was some wandering mongrel from another land, or perhaps from the farming countryside. Some of the taller ynfalds walked with long gaits, built for speed to match a sleipnir. Others were powerfully built for taking down heavier prey. A few of the ladies carried tiny gray ynfalds, as seen in some of the patrician members of society of Edi City, reminding Hanen that cultures had nuances and styles of garb, but most remained the same the world over.

"What were you doing on the streets of Mahn Fulhar?" Hanen said to the little creature.

"Probably waiting for you," Rallia said as she walked up with a small pouch of dried fruit. She offered one to Whisper and then the bag to Hanen.

"Where have you been?" Hanen asked.

"Running messages all over town," she said, smiling. "There were two flippant young girls who thought the idea novel, and sent me back and forth to each other three times. I wouldn't have been surprised if it was just for sport with the messages empty. But they paid what I asked for and I got my exercise in."

"How much did you make?"

"If I had been running the messages to the same part of town, say from the castle to one of the estates, I would have asked for a copper Lora. Because one lived on an estate and the other was out in the North Holdings, I asked for a Baro each time I ran."

"Are you serious?" Hanen said. "A day's labor-wage for a message?"

"I imagine as this catches on, the rate will go down. Sälla and I are the only ones running messages right now. And the agreement is, we let them pay us, but never in anything but a single coin. If someone offers a single copper Nit, and that's not enough, we will ask for more. Thus far everyone has paid in either Loras or Baros."

"You know that once the others hear what you're making, they'll all want to do it."

"Which is why we'll be controlling who gets to. Young boys and girls who want to become runners for us will only be allowed to ask for single copper Nits for their services, until they earn their rank."

"Shall we head back toward the Guildhall?"

Rallia nodded and stuffed several more fruits in her mouth.

Together they left the Grotto and crossed over to ascend toward the north hill. Rallia asked Hanen to follow her down a narrow street that belonged to the woodcarvers guild and had a lesser known, well-cared-for set of stairs that climbed up and out a tower looking toward the rest of the city. As they came out of the door, they startled a flock of black gryphs, which took off into the sky, cawing their frustration at the two Clouws.

"Where are we?" Hanen said. The sun was fading behind clouds in the west, preparing to start the long dusky hours.

"You can just see the tradehouses over there, overlooking the harbor below, so we're not far from the cooper guild and after that the guildhall."

"How do you already know your way around here so well?" Hanen asked.

"I'm up so early, and it's been too cold to practice. So I've been exploring."

Rallia took a turn down another alley and came out into an empty street lined with empty shops.

"What's here?"

"I understand that farmers and merchants from the south come up here in the summer and set up shop, and then go home before winter."

"And those boys walking toward us in green and blue?"

A group of ten boys and young men were approaching. They had wide metal bowl-like hats on their heads, and held leather straps with metal balls fastened to the ends.

"Whitesmith guild," Rallia said, "from the looks of it."

For a moment it seemed as though the whitesmiths were just walk-ing past, but they soon shuffled to walk down the middle of the road, intent on walking right up to the two of them. Whisper's scales began to rustle next to Hanen, and the susserus grew louder as the ten men stopped twenty feet from them. One of them held a hand out for them to stop.

"You the Clouws?" he asked.

"That depends," Hanen replied.

"On what?"

"If you're looking for trouble or not."

"We're looking to talk to you, as we understand you're looking to present some information to the Guildmasters tonight."

"And if we are?"

"Then don't."

Rallia took a single step forward. "If we came to you with all of our Sentinels at hand, and told you you needed to stop making tin pots, and leave town and become potters, would you?"

"Of course not. We are a guild; our livelihood can't be taken away from us."

"Then what about our business threatens your way of life?"

"You went to the King when you should have shown respect to the Guildmasters first."

"Who goes to craftsmen, no matter his rank, when he can go to the King? That's how every country on the face of Kallattai works."

"Mahn Fulhar is not most countries. This is how things are done."

"So, you lot drew the short stick on who had to go rough us up and make sure we didn't arrive?"

"No short stick," a boy no older than fifteen said. "We volunteered."

"Ten is too many," Hanen muttered, "And I'm not that great a fighter."

"We have our crossbows," Rallia responded.

"Unloaded ones."

"Then you threaten to shoot if they approach you, and I'll just have to see how I fare. I've been running all day, so I'm limber."

Hanen turned back to them. "So, we agree to leave, and you just let us go?"

"If you agree to leave," the leader said, "then we follow you the whole way back to your hall, and make sure you stay there."

"We could walk away," Hanen offered to Rallia, "and hope we find more Sentinels."

"That's a good idea."

"We'll go," Hanen said.

The whitesmiths began to laugh and provided each other a few slurs regarding the two of them.

They took the causeway over to the upper district, and walked past the Dark Stave Inn, where Ophedia, Aurín, and several others were drinking.

Hanen suddenly broke from Rallia and ran inside.

"Arms!" he shouted.

Chairs fell over backwards as the Black Sentinels reached for their clubs and axes and poured out, just as the whitesmiths realized what was happening.

The numbers were almost matched—eight Sentinels against their ten.

"What's wrong, Hanen?" Ophedia asked.

"These men thought to escort us back to Blackiron, to ensure we didn't go to meet with the Guildmasters."

"Those old codgers who asked Searn and the two of you to come?"

"Yes," Rallia said.

"Break bones," Hanen said, "if you must, but don't kill any of them. I'll give a Baro for everyone that is down on the ground and moaning."

"What are you talking about?" the lead whitesmith said.

"You're not in the position of power now. I've told my Sentinels to break bones. Arms preferably, so you can't practice your trade for a while. Seems fair, to what you were threatening us with. Now, if you want to step away from this fight, I'll buy you all drinks. If you want a fight, that's what you're going to get. Understand?"

To make his point clear, he pulled back his cloak and revealed the crossbow.

"Ha! Not even loaded!"

"But I can load it before one of you gets through my Sentinels, and then I put it between your eyes. Understand?"

Ophedia lunged forward, her long, heavy, club-topped stave swinging wildly around. Everyone fell silent as she rushed forward and brought the heavy implement around and into the upper arm of one of the tin-smiths.

The loud crack of the arm breaking, and the yowl of the whitesmith falling to the ground, forced Ophedia back as the whitesmiths surged forward with their leather thongs swinging wildly.

One of the tin balls struck the side of a Sentinel's head, bringing him down, but the sling quickly became useless in the skirmish. Rallia spun her heavy-ended quarter staff around and hit two men in quick succession, while Aurín, his axes still in their leather sheaths, still broke skin on the back of the hand of the leader.

Hanen watched in awe and horror as the Sentinels went to work. One whitesmith broke through to him, but Whisper suddenly rushed forward and nipped at the man's legs, sending him back.

It was over in a moment, the ten blue and green clad artisans now black and blue and moaning in the street.

"I don't doubt," Aurín said, walking up to Hanen, "that the Voktorra were notified of this ahead of time. And our friend, Captain Navien, will be here soon. You and Rallia ought to go to your meeting. I'll stay and take the fall for this fight. Try not to be detained."

"What will you tell them?"

"I'll think of something."

"I'll go with you," Ophedia said as she approached. Her lip was cut, and her hair hung around her face, but she looked unharmed.

"Clean yourself up, first," Rallia said, "and grab your cloak."

11

Guildhall

Thief don't knock, hunter traps, burglar is a knave.
Follow rules, and bow to crown, we all end up in grave.

— FROM *THE THIEF'S BRIDE*

C aptain Abenard Navien stood at the entry door to the Guildhall.
"What are you doing here?" he said, a startled look on his face.

"I suppose that question answers the question I had for you,"
Hanen said.

"And what would that be?"

"You were commanded by the King to trail us. You knew we were due
to appear here tonight, and yet you were nowhere to be found, and now
you question why we're here. You're either terrible at your job, behind
the attempt to have us beaten, or else you're disloyal to the King."

Navien's face turned red with anger.

"Honestly," Rallia said, "I wouldn't be surprised if it was all three."

Hanen put a hand on Rallia's shoulder as the shorter Clouw balled
her fists.

"Before you say anything," Hanen said to Captain Navien, "know
this. It takes a lot to make my sister angry. She remained calm when

a vül assaulted us, and when a fellow Sentinel threatened me with extortion."

"And when that Manticör attacked us," Ophedia added from over her shoulders.

"And that too," Hanen said. "Most importantly, you should know, Rallia is the best fighter I've ever seen. And I've watched Bortali Ringers go for rounds and rounds."

"What is your point, Clouw?" Navien asked through clenched teeth.

"Let us through to make our presentation. You lost the battle today. Don't lose the war at the end of my sister's fists."

Navien took a step back and pursed his lips.

Rallia and Ophedia walked past, Whisper shooting along beside them before they could be told no ynfalds were allowed. Hanen stopped. "Captain Navien, before you say, 'This isn't over,' please understand we're not here to usurp the Voktorra. We want to make a living. If you'd come to terms with that, perhaps we could come to an agreement. Until then, stay out of our way."

The long hall into the entrance was wide, and groups of different men and scatterings of women, all dressed in garb denoting their guild, grew quiet as they passed. The light from two open fire pits in the hall ahead shone off a gilded ceiling, and on higher benches sat a group of men in nondescript gray robes, although in front of each of them hung banners marking their guilds. Others sat on plain benches, their own banners hanging from poles, and those around each banner wore similar colors.

"Remind you of that arobola match we escorted that Dürani merchant to in Morriego?" Rallia asked.

"Arobola originated in Macena," Ophedia said.

"Regardless, you'd think this was a sporting event."

The portly guildmaster from the smokers guild, as well as the other two from the flax guild and the blacksmiths guild, sat among those on the higher benches. All save one empty stand, with green and blue on the banner.

"I think we may have beaten the Guildmaster of the whitesmiths," Hanen muttered.

"I think it was me," Rallia said.

The man in the center of the bench wore the same gray robes, although he wore a wrap around his head with golden threads, denoting a sort of crown. In front of him hung the black and white of the stone cutters guild.

"I see you've arrived," the bearded stonecutter announced.

"We apologize for the later-than-expected arrival," Hanen said, giving a bow.

"Where is your grand master? Master and Commander Searn Ve-Turres?"

"He regrets that he could not be in attendance. He had more important things to attend to. However, as the co-heads of the branch guild, my name being Hanen Clouw, and this, my sister, Rallia Clouw, we speak for the Black Sentinel guild, as recognized by King Erdthal."

"While you've arrived later than expected, things are not lost. After all, this is one of the quarterly meetings of the guilds. We are currently listening to grievances. We will proceed to dining, before all come back to assemble and make decisions as guilds of the city, uniting together in cause."

A gray flag with a black square hung in front of the rightmost Guildmaster. Hanen glanced to see Captain Navien come to stand behind the man who sat there. The man held a staff, acting as officiator, and bore the stern look of a Voktorra himself.

"Have you any grievances against any of the guilds, be they present or not?" the High Grand Master asked.

"We have none," Hanen said.

The Guildmaster of the Voktorra stood and struck a stone with the heavy staff.

"Grievances are concluded," he announced. "Food will be served in the great hall."

The Guildmasters stood together and left by way of the door behind them.

"Do we follow everyone?" Rallia asked as she watched everyone file toward a long ramping hall down toward the lower level.

Hanen shrugged, then glanced down to see the ynfald at his side, and sighed. "I had meant for him to stay with Aurín."

"The men over there in green have hunting ynfalds with them, and I saw a matronly lady carrying her house cör in her arms."

"I recall something I learned in Macena," Ophedia said. "When Searn met me, I was a member of the Bounty Hunter's Guild, and in arrears with the guild for lost bounties. That's beside the point. Macena was founded by Morriegans, and a few Ikhalans, all seeking to escape their oppressive situations. When they founded the nation, they looked at other countries to decide which model they would use. And they chose the guild law of Mahn Fulhar as their basis for trade."

"And?" Hanen asked.

"Being invited to a guild meeting specifically by a Guildmaster does not mean you've been invited as a guest. It is an invitation to the fraternity. If you do not show, they never extend another invitation. If you do show, you have shown them the honor of meeting their requirements."

"So," Rallia said, "are you saying that just by being here, we've succeeded? We have a guild?"

Ophedia nodded. "As long as we do nothing to get us expelled from guild meetings."

"Like assaulting a guildmaster," Hanen muttered.

"He attacked us," Rallia said.

"And I threw the first punch," Ophedia said. "I should leave—go and make sure that Aurín has the guildmaster detained."

"I don't know if that's a good idea," Hanen said. "Nor if we should send you back to have him released. The trouble we could get in with the Voktorra for detaining the whitesmiths could have worse consequences."

"Well then," Ophedia said, "we're here, and there is free food. We might as well enjoy ourselves until they give us a swift kick out."

She marched off, throwing back her cloak over her shoulders. Rallia joined her, their staves tapping on the flagstones as they followed the hundreds of others making their way to the banquet hall.

"Shall we?" Hanen said to Whisper.

The ynfald's tail flopped over once with a clatter of scales on the tile.

"Clouw," a sharp voice said from behind him.

Hanen internally groaned as he turned around. Captain Navien approached with the gray-robed guildmaster.

"Hanen Clouw," the Voktorra said, "I have been asked to introduce you to the guildmaster Silab Rork of the Voktorra."

The man's perfectly-kept blonde beard had been well waxed, and gave him the appearance of an oil painting.

"I have heard much of the Black Sentinels," Rork said. "Of course, we've seen individuals from your organization around the city, but never in the full force your Master and Commander seems to enjoy flaunting."

"It is not perhaps my own preference, but as Master and Commander of the continent-spanning organization, it is in his right, I suppose," Hanen said.

"You came to the city along with several other important individuals," Rork said. "Prima Pater of the Paladins of the Hammer, a handful of influential Nifarans, and Captain Navien reports you've been to see the King, and batted no eye at that event. Were you not nervous to be in the presence of such grandeur?"

"To tell you the truth," Hanen said, "there is little that will surprise me. And keeping a straight face in the presence of royalty or holiness is part of the job."

"And what credentials have you and your sister?"

"A successful caravan organized from Edi City to Garrou, traveled three times yearly over five years. Once we established ourselves, we organized additional groups, three in all, almost constantly moving up and down the continent, for three-quarters of the year."

"And you intend to do the same here?" Rork said.

"That is my intention."

"And your sister? What credentials does she have?"

"She saved the lives of three of the most important men in Edi City in a single night. Lord Tergon Aritelo personally made Rallia a standing offer to be his own bodyguard."

"Tergon Aritelo?"

"Head of House Aritelo."

"Yes," Rork said, impressed. "I know who he is. House Aritelo is not only one of the richest exporters of Edian Silk, but Tergon is a military man. He led an attack against Castenard in the Trade Wars twenty years ago, and nearly broke Castenard's back, financially and literally. My father was there to see it. If your sister received special commendation from him, and that could be confirmed..."

He turned to Navien and gave the man a nod before they both marched off toward the lower level.

Hanen sighed a relief and turned to go the same direction, but took a longer time walking down the ramp.

The beam rafters along the white, plastered ceiling hung low, but not so low Hanen could touch them. The black and white marble tiles reminded Hanen of a gala at an Edian estate.

Rallia and Ophedia stood across the room speaking to the large guildmaster of the smoker's guild. Food sat on tables along the side, and many people inched their way along it, taking bites as they went. In the far corner, a small group of musicians played on horns and woodwinds to an up-tempo kept by a single drummer.

"You might imagine for such a dour group of people when up above in the council hall, that the party would be just as quiet," a man next to him said. Hanen turned to see the tall, thin guildmaster of the flax guild.

"I have found that no matter what country I am in, if you give people free food, their tongues will wag, and their enmity with one another mostly forgotten."

"That is very true, Hanen Clouw," the older man said. "I am Zenn Abar."

"That is a Zhigavan name, isn't it?" Hanen asked.

"Indeed. You've known Zhigavans then?"

"As we were raised in Garrou, there were a few Zhigavans in town, when the border was not contested. And I've escorted a few in our caravan. How is it you came to be in Mahn Fulhar?"

"My grandfather came here after the Protectorate Wars, and we became flax farmers."

"The business is good?"

"It grows better here than in Zhigava."

"It seems wool does better," Hanen said.

"Only because you've arrived in the winter. In the summer, our southern Mahndürian linens will come out. You'll see."

Hanen smelled the cedar and porumarian oil on her before he saw her move through the crowd. Her blonde hair was pulled into two braids down the back of her head, and she wore her blue embroidered ribbon tied around her neck, with a flat, demure, blue-felted dress, with only the sleeves decorated, increasing extensively the further down toward the wrist. The dress brushed the floor, keeping her feet from view.

"Alodda," he said, walking up behind her.

"Hanen," she said, turning with a smile and offering her hand. He reached out, took only the tips of her fingers, and gave them a squeeze, adding the flourish of an Edian bow.

She touched her chest with the other hand, and her legs gave in in a slight curtsy as color came to her cheeks.

"I've never seen a bow like that. I'm not sure what to make of it."

"It is a bow from Edi City. It tells the potential conversation partner that if they are willing to seek them out, then they should enjoy their company."

Hanen had seen it done a number of times by those he guarded. He dropped her hand, turned, and walked away, his ears burning. To have a friendly face to speak with would be good. To provide a means for her to escape when she wished, and come and seek him out, put the burden of choice on her.

Hanen and Whisper ducked between people talking and came to the tables. An ynfald stuck its head out from under the table and rattled its scales at Whisper, who cowered in surprise and flicked his tongue in apology to the other animal.

Hanen ignored the creature and began filling a plate with food for himself. He tossed a scrap of meat to Whisper who swallowed it whole, and thought better of it when the second piece came at him from Hanen's hand.

"It took me a moment," Alodda said, pushing through the crowd to reach him. "Your walking off like that almost embarrassed me. But then Nera, a friend of mine, repeated what you had said. I thought that was noble."

"I apologize if I embarrassed you. I thought teaching you a bit of culture I've been exposed to was only fair for your own lesson from when we first met."

"I expect you've just started a new tradition in Mahn Fulhar."

"And I'm sure the other guilds will be just as mad at us for that, too."

"As long as you intend to reform the Sentinels from what they're often known as here in Mahn Fulhar."

Hanen turned and looked at her. He held out his plate so she could take pieces for herself. "What do you mean? How do people think of the Sentinels?"

"Extorting bullies, to be honest. A poor man's Voktorra."

"Ouch," Hanen said.

"I'm only saying what I've heard. But I've heard it all my life."

"There are Sentinels with that attitude. I was on the receiving end of one of them in Edi."

"What did you do?"

"He was shot with a crossbow bolt for brigandry."

"Oh my."

"What do the Voktorra do? Besides look sharp, and stand guard?"

"I think that's it," she said. "Do Sentinels do something more than that?"

"We act as escorts for merchants. Carry messages. Act as guards, yes, but shoulder-to-shoulder with our clients. Not stand at entrances as house guards."

"So there is room for both of you, perhaps."

"Yes," Hanen said, "I think perhaps there is. Thank you."

"For?"

"Reminding me of what I need to say."

After more than an hour, the music stopped, and people began to move back up the ramp to stand as a throng around the walls of the meeting hall.

A few older members tried to bring up grievances, but were turned down. One of them tried again, rewording his grievance in the form of a decision that needed to be made. Once more, the council turned him out to wait until the next quarterly meeting. Rallia and Ophedia came to stand with Hanen again, and he could see Alodda standing with her family and other merchants from the Grotto Market.

A figure came out from the Guildmaster's door and took his seat at the council. It was one of the whitesmiths who had come to see Hanen away. He had a bandage tied around his head. Captain Navien, standing behind the master of the Voktorra, took an order from his commander, and turned to make his way toward Hanen. Guildmaster Rork stood from his own chair, and moved over to kneel next to the whitesmith, and they whispered to one another, before the whitesmith nodded, and Rork took his seat again.

"You are next to speak," Navien said, as he approached. "And you are not to speak unless spoken to."

"Is that true?" Hanen asked Ophedia.

"I'm not an expert at guild law. I only remembered that one thing."

Hanen turned back. Guildmaster Rork stood and tapped his staff.

"The council will hear from Hanen and Rallia Clouw."

Hanen pushed through the crowd, excusing himself as he went. Rallia followed close behind. They came to stand in the small gap left by the crowd in the center of the room.

"Hail, Hanen Clouw. Hail, Rallia Clouw, of the Black Sentinels. You have come to request admittance into the record of Mahn Fulhar Guilds, this day, Wovyr the 20th, of Imperial Year 2155."

"Honorable Members of the Granddmasters' Council. The Black

Sentinels seek ratification of the Charter granted by King Erdthal as a legitimate guild in the country of Mahndür and city of Mahn Fulhar."

"And where will your guildhall be located?"

"We have been granted lease of the old forge within the walls of the Stone, known as Blackiron, in order to afford a private place of business, and privacy for deals brokered with our clients."

"And what services will the Black Sentinels provide that benefit the city and guilds of Mahn Fulhar?"

"The Black Sentinels provide personal protection to those that hire individual members, not to be confused with house-guard duties provided by the esteemed Voktorra guild. Those Black Sentinels bearing a badge of a Black Sentinel Runner are also approved by the Black Sentinel charter to carry messages safely, both within Mahn Fulhar and abroad."

"And this rumor of caravans?"

"Trade caravans, from Mahn Fulhar to Nor-Vio and Aunté, and on to Ormach, by land, will deliver goods to towns not on normal sea ports, nor be endangered by sea storms, and under the stronger might of tested and trained Black Sentinels, acquired and paid for by the Guild."

"And why cannot the Guildhall arrange these caravans?"

"You would not, because separate guilds would be required to provide the manpower and guards, to guard goods that are not theirs, and make arrangements afresh each and every trip. Our experience, and use of locals' knowledge, allows us to move caravans along efficiently, without problem."

"Is there anyone who wishes to lodge a grievance why the Black Sentinels should not be allowed to become a paying member of the greater Guild of Mahn Fulhar?"

Many turned their eyes to look at the whitesmith, who simply stared ahead and said nothing.

"Why is he not speaking?" Rallia asked.

"I told the head of the Voktorra that Lord Tergon Aritelo owed you his life. He knows of Aritelo, and it impressed him."

"Very well," the Grandmaster said. "Then the Black Sentinel Guild has been approved. Inter-guild business can be conducted with the Black Sentinels with no prior permission needed by the council. Adjourned."

12

Solstice

Each shall select their own Vow, for it shall act as an usher to a greater faith in Grissone. But weigh and balance each, for each Vow comes with its own demands. Its own sacrifices. Choose not the sacrifice that you can best handle. Select one with the greatest sacrifice to you. For then you shall be forged into a new man. A better servant of Grissone.

—*PALADIN NOVITIATE PRIMER*, **PAGE 87.**

Jined opened his eyes as the light of morning came in through the window. He sat up and put his feet on the cold stone ground. He prayed under his breath, "Give me strength to face this day," and thought he felt a warmth in his heart begin to flare.

After going through his morning routine, he arrived at the cathedral entrance, looking at his ledger while distractedly looking at the beautiful edifice that reached to the sky.

Built in an almost pyramidal shape, so that from all angles one could see the iron arrowhead that topped it, gouts of flame burned from within.

The massive reinforced wooden doors sat open as gray-clad priests and monks of Aben moved in and out, delivering candles and taking old tapestries out for a final beating. Citizens of the city gawked as they passed by, and a handful took the side door to the commoners' chapel for sacraments to be administered to them.

Jined noted the missing adornments in the urns outside the doors, and then took a step through the lintel. Most of the Abecinians used the side aisles, setting new candles into their candelabras. One of the higher ranked priests gave orders to a troupe of monks scrubbing the altar, above which hung the iron lantern of Aben. Behind it, a carved display of interwoven symbols of an arrow, a chalice, a path, and behind it all a great creature of the deep, could be made out from all the way down the nave where Jined stood. He touched the mosaic-tiled basin, in which the form of a Deep One swam. Then he proceeded down the nave, his hammer held at attention and his eyes averted from the unlit lantern.

The thick Mahndürian glass mounted inside windows kept the wide, open space warmer than it ought to be with the winter chill settling in outside. A few older priests held lanterns for the workers, supplementing the light coming in through the frosted glass of the clerestory.

The Paladins of the Hammer would sit on the right, and the Paladames of the Rose directly behind them and before the rest of the Crysalas Integritas.

On the left, the throng of Abecinian priests and monks would sit by rank. It was the arms of the choir that Jined had come to check. To the left of the altar, the Black Bench sat freshly oiled, directly behind which a pew for the Nifarans sat with blue decor being put in place. Across from these, the leadership from Pariantür would sit beside the central dais, where the leaders of the four churches would preside. The Prima Pater had requested seats for all three leaders of the Nifarans at the table, and a black chair symbolically left empty for the leader of Wyv-Thüm.

All looked ready, and according to the last bell that pealed, they still had hours for the ceremony to begin.

Grissone's standard bearer, Valér Queton, had come in at some point after Jined, and was situating the holy standard of Grissone into a pole-post at the head of the aisle, where the Paladins would sit. Usually quiet, he spoke to another Paladin. The old man gave a nod and turned to leave the figure, who looked at Jined, and then to the ceiling, which was painted in a mural from one end to the other, showing the story of the creation of Kallattai.

"My god," Jined said, approaching the short Grissone as he admired the work.

"When the artist who painted that mural died," Grissone said, "he was taken directly to Lomïn. Wyv didn't even bother making a judgment."

"Is that so?" Jined asked. "I had heard he was quite a sinner in his day."

"Rhotar Ülen was indeed," Grissone said. "But you murdered a man before you became a Paladin, so I'm sure you understand that people can change."

"You were speaking to Brother Queton," Jined said.

"Do you think you're the only person I speak to?"

"I would never presume."

"It's alright, Jined," Grissone said, putting a hand on his shoulder, "jealousy is a normal feeling."

Jined looked into Grissone's eyes in embarrassment. Grissone had a broad grin on his face.

"I speak to many people. Most don't speak back. Valér is a very devout Paladin. He may subscribe to the Vow of Pacifism, but has the heart of a Vow of Prayer. He and I are often in conversation. And unlike many others, he sees me."

"And does he know it is you?"

"He suspects it is so. But he has never admitted it openly. I prefer it that way."

"Are you here to join in the ceremony?"

"I am afraid not. I have things to attend to. But my father asked I come and ensure that everything is in order."

"The father of the gods himself?"

"It is his cathedral."

"And can he not see what happens here?"

"Of course. But there are things set in place to occur during this ceremony that the gods have vested interest in. His gray watchers, after all, are on the move, along with the servants of Wyv."

"Wyv?"

"We all have our agents and interests in the mortal realm. It takes much of our effort to provide the balance against the darkness the Black Coterie continually brings to bear."

"And this council, it is important?"

"It is historic. And it is the threshold of a new era. And I can feel the Deceiver nearby."

"If the Deceiver is to be here, should you not stay?"

"It is not my fate to stay his hand. I can only strengthen those who must suffer under and strive against his attacks."

"But you cannot stay?"

"We gods have plenty of responsibilities. As much as I'd like to be here, I cannot. It is enough for us to know we each have witnesses here to see that all is done well. Speaking of witnesses...."

Jined followed Grissone's eyes to the door where Dane entered and approached with three hrelgrens and a qavyl following him. When Jined looked back to Grissone, his god was gone.

"Pater Segundus Nichal," Dane began, stepping aside to allow the other figures to come and stand alongside him, "requested that I scour the city for any hrelgrens who might act as representatives of their own god, Kasne. As a result, I found these three merchants willing to come and take part in the ceremony."

"We welcome you," Jined said, giving a bow. "And we are honored that ones touched by the god Kasne *et* Terral should come to at least sit in observance of this ceremony that occurs tonight."

"Thank you for your invitation," one of the hrelgrens said. He smiled with his soft beak, flashing the bar of white teeth across his green face. He touched a knuckle to the silver banded hat that covered his hairless head. "Paladin Marric explained that he sought us out to ensure that each member of the White Pantheon would be represented. I am Zhag *rm* Tellis, a humble merchant. It is rather unfortunate that it should be us that stand before you this day, though, being the only Hrelgrens in the city."

"Why unfortunate?" Jined asked.

"My companions and I, along with several others, came to this city to seek prosperity, but instead found only grief after being robbed of our possessions."

"And yet you remain here," Jined said.

"Perhaps it is testimony that they ought to have remained, to be here for such a time as this," the qavyl said.

Jined turned to look at the qavyl. "And may I inquire your name?"

"I will gladly give it," the qavyl said. He stood taller than Jined, but likely weighed half as much. His long flat tail had been mostly obscured by the layers of silks he wore. "My name is Ymbrys Veronia. I am a scholar and a merchant, and I just so happened to be speaking with these merchants when your fellow Paladin approached. Having heard his reasoning for asking three of the hrelgrens to come to you, I made the point that I was the only qavyl currently in this city, which seems both odd, and fortuitous. And thus, I have come to show representation for Lae'Zeq, god of the qavylli."

Jined gave a nod to the qavyl and turned back to the hrelgrens.

"You have selected a number from your group to represent Kasne *et* Terral then."

"We three, being his holy number."

"Very well," Jined said. "I see no issues. As a race chosen and blessed by the Prince of the Forest, you are welcome to the ceremony when it begins."

"My companion," Zhag said, "Ethri *nu* Rhizog has agreed to return to Kandargurn after the ceremony and report what has happened to the priests of the One Enthroned on Kallattai."

"Thank you," Jined replied. "And you, Ymbrys Veronia?"

"Lae'Zeq would be most certainly honored to have me here to act as representative. I don't presume that you will give me a seat at the table with the leadership of the other churches, a seat in the room, to observe, will be enough."

"The same can be said for us," Zhag *rm* Tellis said.

"I think we're in agreement, then," Jined said. "Brother Dane, could you see that our four guests are occupied until the ceremony?"

Dane gave a salute, albeit with a hint of sarcasm as he looked Jined up and down, his eye falling on the white cordon across Jined's chest. He turned and led the four out of the cathedral and toward the paladinial Bastion.

Jined kept himself busy preparing and denoting a bench for the hrelgrens and the single qavyl near enough to the front to be afforded honor, and thought on what Grissone had said, including his indication that the four of them ought also to be in attendance. It was only right that representatives from all seven members of the White Pantheon be there.

* * *

Thousands had gathered on the green outside of the cathedral complex to watch the beginning of the ceremony.

Jined stood at the door of the cathedral alongside Nichal Guess and Valér Queton, who carried his hammer in one hand and the sigil of ceremony in the other. It reminded Jined of the Prima Pater's own sigil, with two wings instead of hammer heads.

The three of them watched as the throng of Abecinian priests continued to filter into the vast cathedral in a slow, solemn procession. They had started there, then proceeded down to the pier, where they had each taken a cup of sea water and carried it back to empty into the basin outside of the doors, singing a chant to Aben as they did so.

Following after them came the white-robed priests with gray mantles over their shoulders. Then came the archrectors, and their leaders, the council of bishops, who walked in formation around the High Priest, Klent Rigal. While Jined had made sure his private carriage was ready, the head of the Abecinian church had surprised Jined and chosen to walk the entire procession.

The gates to the Stone boomed opened, and the assembly of the castle guard guild, the Voktorra, marched with King Erdthal upon his black sleipnir. Rather than march directly to the cathedral, they took the long walk in the opposite direction, stopping before the entrance of the Crysalas complex where singing issued forth. They continued their march, and a choir of white-clad members of the Crysalas Integritas came out singing a repeating chorus.

Behind the first choir marched the armored Paladames of the Rose, mostly those who had journeyed from Pariantür with the Prima Pater's entourage, but they were joined by others from the city's secret vault to join in the ceremony. Behind all of these walked the Matriarch Superioris herself. On one arm, her great niece and physician Katiam Borreau provided her stability. On the other walked her assistant, Sabine Upona.

As the Voktorra and King came around to the cathedral, they left the procession, and pushed into the crowd in a move that, to Jined, felt far too authoritarian. But it was what King Erdthal had asked to do in his service to the ceremony, and the Prima Pater had agreed to it.

The Crysalas coming after the Voktorra were stalled in their arriving, as the Matriarch stopped to bless babies held out to her by the people. When she did finally arrive, High Priest Rigal stepped out from the bishops and took her arm, and the two of them walked to the door arm-in-arm, and turned to face the crowd.

The parade march of the Paladins came next. Jined's fellow guards appeared as the six-beated clop of their steel-shod sleipnir echoed off the walls of the Stone. Jined had suggested they have Valér Queton at their head, but the Prima Pater had turned it down on behalf of the other churches having no standard.

Behind the guards marched the rest of the paladinial entourage, along with the Paladins of the local bastion, and those who had arrived in Mahn Fulhar with Pater Gladen. Behind those came a cart, pulled by a pair of matching black sleipnir. Atop it stood the Prima Pater, along with the Nifaran Monks and their ailing Archimandrite, Pell Maran.

The monks had insisted on walking, but the Prima Pater prevailed on them, to ensure that the Archimandrite would be rested enough to take part in the proceedings.

As they came around to the front of the cathedral, the Prima Pater hopped down from the carriage, and turned to help the Archimandrite and the rest of the Nifarans down.

The Paladins and monks solemnly entered the cathedral, leaving the Prima Pater and the three heads of the Nifaran order alongside the Matriarch Superioris and the High Priest of Aben.

From the back of the cart, the Prima Pater reached into a cage with a heavily gloved hand and withdrew a trained ælerne—a four-winged eagle. He lifted his hand, and, with the other, raised his sigil. The ælerne beat all four wings and took off to circle the green. A flock of white four-winged dwovs were released from the Crysalas complex and swarmed, darting and hovering, their white bodies moving above the heads of the crowd with a zip and warble. As the ælerne continued to circle, a small ruckus rose as a flock of black gryphs, which kept roosts in the castle, and who the Voktorra had insisted would not make trouble, took to the air. They took off after the dwovs, and the ælerne took off after the black birds in defense of the white ones, driving them off after some effort.

The Prima Pater turned his attention away from the sky and toward the crowd. Jined could see a look of irritation on his face, which quickly faded.

First, the High Priest stepped forward to address the crowd.

"Today marks a momentous day. Four heads of church convene to discuss the future. And here we stand on the continent of Ganthic, named for the gods whom we represent—Grissone, Aben, Nifara, Thüm, and Crysania. Humanity shall be stronger after this day, knowing once more that we are united. The path of humanity is led by the guidance of our high king in Lomïn, from whom all kings derive their earthly power. Aben, Full of Grace, see us now gathered, and breathe your will into us."

"Purity and health to one and all," the Matriarch Superioris said. "The Mother of All, the wife of Aben, wishes well upon you. Let us therefore continue our fast this entire day, for after this day the light grows stronger, and the White Pantheon unites."

"Justice come to you, and let a contrite heart be your only desire." Kerei Lant looked nervous, despite her usual confidence. "Nifara gladly takes each soul to their final stand before the judge. Let us then make her job easier, by being fair to one another and finding it in our hearts to help those who are helpless."

The Prima Pater spoke last. "Grissone was humanity's first god, for it was by his hand that we were created. Let us then remember him in our faith. For he is never one to turn away those who seek him. Let us now convene, the Guides of the Path, the Roses of Purity, the Scales of Justice, and the Pariantür, to discuss what is to come."

They turned and walked one after the other into the cathedral.

Jined, Nichal, and Valér entered behind, pulling the doors closed as they went. Each leader moved to their respective people and began to pray with their followers, as monks of Aben began lighting the great torch-ensconced lanterns. The prayers ended as the monks turned to the final torch next to the black pew. The monk holding the candle that would light it fell back as the torch lit on its own with a flame that had no color.

The heads of church had come to stand on the platform by the altar. They turned to consider the eerie flame, and Jined thought he saw the Prima Pater nod, having perhaps expected this to happen.

Everyone murmured as they watched the invisible flame burn. Far to the left of the altar, the black doorway that led to the catacombs beneath the cathedral opened. From the gaping maw into the earth, figures clad in even blacker robes shuffled up and out. They each carried unlit candles, and with no more ceremony they simply slid into the black pew and took their seats. The place grew silent as all eyes fell on them.

One of them stood. He was taller even than Jined, but thin and reedy. He stepped forward and walked up to stand next to the other four. When he spoke, he spoke with a voice that seemed rarely used. None could see his face beneath his hood.

"Thus know that Wyv-Thüm, brother of Aben, and Judge of Souls, has sent his representatives. I am Kadok Galistine, Pontifex of the Sect of Thüm, Keeper of the Dead, and ally. My legates join us now to represent our holdings in the mortal realm."

13

Pantheon's Council

Record their deeds. Take note their sins. Tally their weight. Present to him.

—UNKNOWN ORIGIN

"We welcome this most unexpected visit," High Priest Klent Rigal said, his voice wavering.

Dorian Mür stepped down from the platform and approached Kadok. "I have enjoyed our past conversations via letter, Kadok. To finally meet you is my pleasure." They both clasped hands.

The Matriarch Superioris gave a reverent nod of her head, and Kerei Lant, as acting Archimandrite, gave a deep bow.

"I can only assume your appearance holds a great deal of meaning," Dorian said.

"It does," the Pontifex said, "but I have no doubt that in due time we shall each present our agendas."

"There is little need for me to introduce myself," Dorian said, "but let me introduce to you the other heads of religion at this assembly.

"First, I present Maeda Mür, Matriarch Superioris of the Crysalas Integritas and High Matron of the Crysalas Honoris branch—the Paladames of the Rose."

"Greetings, Keeper of the Dweol," Kadok said.

The Matriarch gave another slight curtsy.

"Our brother in gray," Dorian said, "is Klent Rigal, High Priest of the Abecinian Church, Abbot of the Monks of the Lamp, and Confessor of the Monarchy of Mahndür."

"I give my humble welcome to the priesthood of our father god's brother."

The High Priest of Aben gave a reverent bow and then took his seat, looking everywhere but back at the black-clad figure.

"Of the servants of Nifara, we have the acting Archimandrite, Kerei Lant, and her two councilors, Pell Maran, and Cräg Narn."

The three monks stood and give their bows.

"Is not Pell Maran the Archimandrite still?" Kadok asked.

"I am poor in health," the former Archimandrite said, "and thus, I have selected to give Kerei my seat, and I shall act as her councilor."

"It shall be an honor to speak with the three of you, regardless. Our churches' goals so oft align, I do not doubt the ancient Cräg Narn shall agree."

The quiet and very old Cräg gave a smile and a nod, but said nothing.

"It is a great honor to us that we meet," Kerei Lant said. "And while I am new to the position of leader of our order, I shall endeavor to see the relationship between us strengthened."

"This may be truly needed," Kadok said, bowing back, "these times are trying, and will require our vigilance.

"I see too that you have also invited representatives of the gods of the forest and of wisdom," he said, looking out over the congregation, his eyes falling on the three hrelgrens and the single qavyl. The latter rose and gave a reverent bow, to which Galistine took a step back, and then composed himself, and gave an even lower bow himself. The three hrelgrens also rose and acknowledged the Pontifex in their own way.

"Please, Pontifex Galistine," the Prima Pater said, "will you join our circle?"

He indicated toward the table, and to the black chair already set between Kerei Lant and Dorian. The tall figure almost seemed to float up the steps to the table, where he took his seat.

The council sat in a semi-circle, facing the congregation. The three sight-bound leaders of Nifara, the Pontifex of Wyv-Thüm, the Prima Pater, the Matriarch, and, on the other end, the host of the meeting, the High Priest of Aben.

"While it was at our request this meeting occur, and we certainly thank all in attendance for coming," Dorian said, "let us give the floor to our host Klent Rigal, High Priest of Aben."

"I thank you for arranging this, Prima Pater," the High Priest said, standing. "I need not elaborate on what we all know. The church of Aben, divided as it is in all its factions, from the secluded cloisters of the Morrig Church to the fewer and far between Luzoran Hermits, is united in our worship of one god, Aben, High King in Lömin. The monks and the priests of the Abecinian Church welcome you."

He gave a long pause, waiting for an applause that never came.

"When our good friend, Dorian Mür, asked us to address this collected crowd of brotherhood, I was not certain where I might begin. To speak of the status of the affairs of one religion to another might require us to speak to small points of contention that, in the grand scheme of things, matter little. For what man or woman among us can say they are truly at peace? Daily we strive along our path toward the Ever-Day, to put bread in our mouths and seek the good of all around us.

"And thus I determined to present what good our church is doing in this world, from the far north in Nasun to the foundling nation of Macena, where our church grows daily.

"Our priests, ever on the path, act as guiding light, surrogate to the Gray Watchers who are present yet invisible. We offer a chalice of goodwill and a unity against strife, as I have commanded our brothers of the cloth to strive for."

Jined caught movement and turned to see Loïc and Cävian speaking to one another with hands in their laps.

He doesn't say much, does he? Cävian asked.

No, Loïc replied, *but he does use a lot of words to get there.*

Jined chuckled silently.

"Indeed, even the Church of the Common Cup, as rife with violence as they have been in the past, have remained peaceful, reporting no acts of violence to me in their regular communiqué. The Monks of Nifara walk peacefully, where once they were endangered, and the Paladins of the Hammer no longer need go out of their way to reach their own people. It is safe to say, that if the High Missioner of the Common Cup reports that these brothers and sisters of the faith travel safely where his sect holds sway, then even too the Hidden Sects of the Crysalas are safe."

The Matriarch Superioris stood. "Despite what the High Missioner may have reported, the Crysalas Integritas have been subject to some persecution in the past ten years, both in Œron and beyond. We serve the helpless in communities that would be endangered if they were found out by their oppressors. And while we have been able to retain our anonymity in Œron, they continue to attempt to flush us out. The downtrodden women we protect, as well as their children, continue to flock to us, but those who seek to harm them have continued to seek them out. It is a constant struggle."

"If that is so, we shall adopt a more proactive approach to stopping this," said the High Priest of Aben. "I shall send an envoy to Aunté as soon as the spring thaw begins."

"It would be important to note," Kerei Lant added as she rose from her chair, "that the reports you have received are only from the High Missioner's pen, not from the churches he reports are left unharmed.

"It is true, the violence against the monks of Nifara has diminished as of late, but we still face persecution in some places. In the Oruche Marches we are not safe, and certainly not protected by the authorities from Œron, who control the area. While in Œron proper, we are treated as foreigners under the watchful eye of the Missioner's Doyens. We are not permissioned to provide any judgment that would supersede the altogether stringent laws of Œron, despite our millennia-long authority to do so, given by the pantheon itself."

"I am astonished to learn such things," the High Priest said. "And to have this come to light at such a time as this fills me with great anxiety. I shall endeavor to see that the accusations brought to bear are given their due diligence. That a sister church should be endangered within a realm that is predominantly Abecinian grieves me. Indeed, even the smallest of grievances against you brings me more sadness than I can say."

He sat, his hand going to his forehead with a cloth.

"High Priest Rigal," Dorian said, standing, "do not despair. It is for this reason we meet. To discuss such things with no need for miles and months between us. We aim to bring all errors and grievances to one another, and promise to act diligently to ensure all is brought to light. Have you anything left to say?"

The High Priest waved a dismissive hand, embarrassment written across his face.

"Perhaps you'd like to continue on with your report, Kerei?" Dorian said to the monk.

"Thank you, Prima Pater," she replied. "As you are all generally aware of our pilgrimage from Birin, escorted by the company of Black Sentinels, set upon by brigands, and attacked by a creature cursed by the Mad Gift Giver, this road of trials is nothing compared to what our order faces regularly the world over. For it is our calling to face the road and its dangers to bring justice to those who need it.

"Of those in attendance, perhaps we are most situated to speak of what is happening in the south. Sidierata and Edi continue their mercantile strife with one another. Generally speaking, their economic warfare has little effect on the poor and downtrodden, and indeed, their justice system is one of the more commendable ones.

"However, because of this, it would be hard to rely on either of them in a time of need, as they will not risk marching to stop a conflict in, say, Temblin, if it might expose their flank to their enemies. This of course brings me to Temblin. They have continued to bark threats of war, and it is the Nifaran Council's belief that Temblin and Hraldor will come to blows in the near future."

"And what of the Fortress of Piedala?" the High Priest of Aben asked. "Do they not act as go-between with those nations?"

"Our reports from Temblin," the Prima Pater said, "elaborate on the growing issue. Hraldor is a constant ally of the Empire and is quick to adopt treaties proposed by Piedala, but their patience wears thin. Hraldor was, you recall, officially founded after the Protectorate Wars, carving out a portion of Kar-Aghar as an act of charity from the Empire during the treaties."

"Yet Temblin continues to hold enmity against the Hrelgrens and the people of Hraldor for past grievances," the High Priest spoke with a passion Jined had not seen in his usually-composed face.

"Indeed," the Prima Pater said. "The Tambii were very adamant during the treaties that they be given their own portion of Kar-Aghar, Minor Hrelgreens. To give them a portion of the country would have meant to give them Eruhk, one of the only two major cities in that peninsula. Instead, all agreed to grant survivors of the Protectorate Wars who wished to settle in a new land the very small northern spike of Minor Hrelgreens, and the Hrelgrens were quick to agree, so long as they retained Eruhk."

"If I may," Kerei Lant said.

"Of course," the Prima Pater smiled, "we digressed. Please, continue."

"Thank you," she smiled. "While I brought up the strife of Temblin, they have one thing that should be admired. In their passion, they are quick to right injustices to their people. It is an easily understood thing that men and women can oft overlook the treatment of the downtrodden, but in no other nation do the people react so quickly when their sins are pointed out and admitted.

"Our fellow monk, Seriah Yaledít, recently visited the country and found that a large number of orphans had been mistreated and sequestered away by a corrupt official. When Nefer Yaledít brought this grievance to the local authorities, they immediately responded in kind, by giving us a rather extensive charter for an orphanage. Large enough for the children already without family or home, and then for more.

Fortunately, it seems that this was guided by the hand of our goddess, because it will be needed should war come to those southern lands."

"Orphanages of the Nifarans are well known both near and far," the High Priest chimed in.

"And as of late, we have founded more and more of them," Kerei said.

"Commendable," the High Priest replied.

"But why is this so?" Kerei Lant chided.

"What do you mean?"

"Why must these orphanages come to be?" Kerei said, turning her head toward the sound of the High Priest. "Why do orphans continue to grow in number, and where are the extended families of these children? Why must it fall to the Nifarans—blind, surrogate parents—to care for them? Why must the Vaults of the Crysalas fill to brimming with the downtrodden and beaten? Why must the Paladins ride to negotiate peace with those in conflict with one another? Why can we not come to peace?"

"The Deceiver and his fallen brothers stalk about, drawing people from the paths of righteousness," the High Priest said softly.

"We cannot blame the Deceiver for the sins of man," Kerei raised her voice. "We are each to blame, and none can stand before the Judge and lay their sins before his throne and claim them as grievances of Achanerüt!"

Kerei stopped, the soft hand of Pell Maran weakly touching her arm.

"That is all I have to report," she said sullenly, sitting down and crossing her arms.

"These," the Prima Pater said, standing, "are all good questions, and ones we ought to all raise. You are right, Archimandrite Lant. Why must these grievances continue? The numbers of our various orders are filled with those who have neither mother nor father. Perhaps that is why our orders are ones who often found and support such charters. But it is good to ask why it comes to that.

"That strife continues in Temblin, that the Œronzi continue to secretly persecute those of other faiths, that the Northern Nations of

Boroni and Bortali sit on the verge of a Great War, all seems staged for a series of wars that could be the demise of the world as we know it. What we can do to stop such recklessness, I do not know. I am old. My wife, she is aging. It falls to the next generation to do what we were not strong enough to initiate. Archimandrite Lant, High Priest Rigal, it will fall to you, and the Pater Segundii who follow after my passing, to answer these questions."

He sighed, looking out across the congregation. "It falls to each of you. I have done what I could. I have placed my best negotiators in Bortali and Boroni. Some of our wisest diplomats sit in office at Piedala. Indeed, even the Aerie in Limae proactively seeks to stop further conflict between Varea and Redot, who have grievance with Mahndür itself. But we must hold true, or else we'll falter. And we'll have a conflict to rival and exceed the loss of the generation who fought alongside me in the Protectorate Wars."

The Matriarch Superioris stood slowly, patting the top of the Prima Pater's head.

"Do not despair," she said looking around at those at the table.

"Do not despair," she repeated, looking up at the throng of priests and holy warriors.

"Do not give up your hope, fleeting as it may seem. For I have looked into the Future Tapestry, and I see great things. Terrible things. Good things. And all is not lost. Things may change. Change happens. Even if the elderly, such as myself, do not oft welcome it, change will come. It is how we react to this change that defines us.

"The Crysalas Integritas continue to grow. Indeed, ever since the Protectorate Wars, the pains of the pogroms of centuries past seemingly healed, we have thrived. Ours is a secret growth, in every major city in the continent. And in those places where we are public—the college in Nemen, the Convent here in Mahndür, and now a hospital being founded by our order in Waglÿsaor—all of these places bring a new a public face to the world. We are strong in our suffering, and should hope that this is a sign of what is to come."

"Did you not say that persecution continues, though?" Kerei asked.

"Yes. Of course it does," the Matriarch said. "To see our women continue to find success in one nation can cause bitterness in those who have little of their own, and they foment grumbling, and act to destroy what they cannot have. But is this not always the case? Do not children break the toys of those who are happy, to make others as miserable as themselves? How much more corrupt and able of destruction are those who come to maturity? Do we outgrow the petulance of childhood? No. We only grow in our ability to cause suffering in others.

"Take your example of Temblin. Why do they hate Hrelgrens and Hraldor so? They claim it is the grievances of the Hrelgrens before they were called such, enslaving humanity over two millennia ago. It was those same Hrelgrens, centuries later, having been brought under the guidance of the god Kasne *et* Terral, who came to the southern nations of men and offered as consolation an unrivaled sum of money to purchase the peninsula we now call Minor Hrelgreens.

"The Tambii people were glad to take the money and go, sojourning to what we now call Ikhala. Some even to Bronue Jinre. And centuries later, when some of those Tambii returned, driven off by vül to the north, they began railing for the land to be returned to them. They were those who had failed, and sought to take from those who were successful. Even today, they seek to take from those who have peace. The Œronzi persecute the Nifarans, the Crysalas, even the Parianti, because we rejoice in our community. Because they are under the lash of a church that, in my opinion, subjugates their people to the common purpose."

"What do you propose we do then?" the High Priest asked.

"Continue on," the old lady said, "and do not give up hope. We need not give in to those who brandish flame and wrath, but give what we have to those who have not, and seek solace among us. For it is in those who do not act as petulant children where our future lies—where the right future lies."

She sat down and placed her hands into her lap. Jined watched the Prima Pater's own hand reach over and join hers. They both smiled.

The black robed Pontifex stood.

"I know that our appearance may be a surprise to many. Indeed, it was not even our wish to make an appearance. Our public existence will cause a stir across all of Ganthic, and perhaps the world, bringing myth and legend to fact. But I have come for good reason; doom comes to rest upon us all."

The entire congregation began to murmur once more. The leaders each raised hands to silence them.

"First, let me explain the purpose of our sect. We are the keepers of the greatest of secrets, for we record the fate of every soul who dies. We know of each judgment made by the Judge Wyv-Thüm, and we have seen a growing list of deaths that claim to come by ways unknown. This has not happened since Achanerüt first appeared and sent those hundred souls to the gates of Lömin those millennia ago—those first deaths that marked the demise of peace and prosperity.

"These deaths are not small ones, either. High Priest Rigal, your right-hand man, a priest of standing, one Dolle Vahn, died only last week. He is one of these victims. Prima Pater, a Primus died but two days ago. You have not even heard of his passing, but it was close to here. He too, was a victim."

"What is this?" the High Priest said in rage. "Murder? I was under the impression that Dolle died in his sleep?"

"Hear me out. We do not understand how they die. In the last several years it has been with alarming regularity. Something dire approaches, and yet we know nothing of what it is. They remain a mystery and become more and more enshrouded in darkness."

Dorian stood and leaned against the table. "This... is not how I expected this meeting to play out."

"Please understand, we would not be here if this were not so serious. But our auguries cannot determine the cause, and so we reveal this to each of you, to do with as you please."

"I have a request to make of you, Kadok," Dorian said.

"I will grant any request from you, Dorian Mür."

"You must lower your hood, so that we know you speak the truth."

The tall man nodded and dropped his hood. His visage was formless, gray, and imperceptible.

"You are not the mortal Kadok, are you?" Dorian asked.

"I was Kadok," the being said, "who was a servant of Wyv-Thüm. But I too was murdered, not two weeks ago, and do not recall how. As servant to the Judge, I was made a Gray Watcher, as others before me."

"And you believe that you were murdered in this unknown way?"

"That is all that can account for my lack of knowledge. How I could have been murdered thusly, unless he who took my life could pass beyond the threshold that no mortal can return from? I cannot know. But even Wyv himself does not know or understand how this came to be, for his far-seeing eyes cannot pierce the veil of this mystery."

"This is darker news than simple wars of men," the Prima Pater said.

"My time in this realm draws to an end," Kadok said. "I must return with my brothers here, to the service of he who claims us."

He turned to face the three leaders of the Nifaran order.

"Passed from life into true death, my mantle also passes to another. The new Pontifex, when selected in the coming months, shall send a message through the Nine to you, for it is time our orders worked together."

Cräg Narn was quickest to stand and give a deep bow.

"The Nine shall await your news," he said.

The black-clad figures stood together, pushing back their hoods to reveal similarly gray and ephemeral forms. Then, as though a breeze came upon them, the robes collapsed to the ground, formless.

"This ends the public meeting," Dorian announced abruptly.

He turned to the congregation. "Everyone is to return to their complexes and places of rest. The heads of church will remain here under my guard for us to continue discussing what has just happened."

A slow and rising panic washed over everyone. The Paladins took the perimeter and began to lead everyone out of the cathedral. Once the place was empty, the Paladins came to stand before the four who had remained seated.

"Nichal, Gallahan, you will stay," the Prima Pater said. "The rest of you will leave and will await our return."

Jined turned to follow the others.

"Jined," the Prima Pater had risen and walked quickly toward him. "The Bastion of St. Nonn, on the road toward Alnír, it's a day or two ride from here. Did they send any representatives to this meeting?"

"We sent a message, but never heard back."

"You will ride there tonight. Take whomever you wish. I suspect you'll find a Primus there is dead. Discover what you can."

"Prima Pater, who were they?"

"The Watchers? Few know. However, Kadok Galistine was a real person; I've had contact with him before. If he was allowed to return back from the dead to speak this to us, I believe it. Wyv does not allow many to leave his domain except by his will or by darker means. I do not suspect the latter. I saw enough of that in my youth during the Protectorate Wars to know what it looks like."

Jined turned and approached Cävian and Loïc, signing, *you will both join me. We ride immediately to St. Nonn.*

14

Coldness

A stone's throw away, coldness beckons ye caper with him.

—FROM THE *CÖR'S FINAL MEAL*

As Seriah Yaledít, a Nifaran monk, walked the streets of Mahn Fulhar, she was shown respect, and given wide enough berth to move freely down the street. In Birin, the monks so proliferated the place that everyone took them for granted, and it became a fight at times to move through tight crowds. Here she didn't feel crushed and could move freely with the help of her staff.

"Holy Nefer!"

She turned toward the voice and began the practiced shuffle of her wooden sandals clacking on the cobblestone. She did not move quickly. It encouraged those calling out to instead go to the Nefer to make their request.

She heard and felt a sizable man approach her. He smelled of produce, though not in a bad way.

"Holy Nefer," he said again.

"Greetings in the name of our Holy Virgin of Justice," she said. "Nifara be with you."

"Ha! Yes. Though I hope not too soon."

Nifara made many people uncomfortable, being the goddess both of justice and the ushering of the souls of the dead to their judgment.

"Nefer," the man said, "I am a humble grocer. I should like to speak with you."

"It is my service to listen."

"Very well. I have this trouble I hope you might settle. You see, my son fancies a girl."

"I do not settle disputes of marriage," she said.

"Of course, I understand. But if you'll hear me out."

Seriah smiled, gritting her teeth.

"He fancies this girl whose father is a blacksmith. A good one at that. But he will not agree to marry her into my family. The trouble is, he is indebted to me for a bill of sale from last winter. I've offered to clear the debt in return, but he will not agree."

"And your son does not wish to be a blacksmith?"

The grocer was silent for some time. He finally spoke. "I hadn't thought of that. He could go and apprentice to Barl. Writing off the debt could be his apprentice fee. Holy Nefer, thank you! Thank you! Please, let me fill your satchel. I have some fruit you'll find delightful! And it won't go bad for a time!"

It was a common occurrence. Many times she solved problems without solving anything. Sometimes it only required listening, and the troubles took care of themselves.

"Holy Nefer!"

She made it perhaps twenty more steps. Two figures approached. Both women.

"Nefer, Nefer!" the second one said. "Our daughters both work for a master dyer, but they are not being given their fair pay."

Seriah smiled. "Please tell me the facts and we shall go together and meet with this dyer."

They soon discovered the girls had stolen bolts of cloth from their master and he had found them out. He had not sought to embarrass them, so in his kindness he had kept them employed, garnishing their wages instead.

They had not shared this with their mothers. Instead, it fell to Seriah to give a judgment on the girls at the request of their parents. All but the two now-disgraced girls were happy when she left. The girls were now forced to work extra hours over winter to make up for the coins they had not been bringing home to their families.

As she came out into the street, people approached her in a mob. The press of bodies pushing her up against a wall quickly grew out of control, their demands filling the air. She held up her staff to silence them.

"Is there a Judgment Tree in this city?" she shouted.

"There is," a booming voice said.

"Take me there, and we shall sit the day in judgment."

A figure approached her and offered his arm. It was clad in chain and plate. The smell of oiled leather gave her comfort. A Paladin.

"Sister Nefer," he said, "I was only just walking by. Let me escort you to the Judgment Tree, and I shall see to it that you can cast your judgment in due order."

"Thank you, brother. I feel I recognize your voice. I am Seriah Yaledít."

"Yes, I know. We traveled for a few days together earlier this year."

"Of course! Pater Noss! I rode with you on the Amstonhotten road. Why didn't you say so?"

"I did not wish to embarrass you if you did not realize it."

"Do not be silly. I am always happy to walk with someone I know and can trust."

"It is good to once more walk with you then," Noss said.

"Tell me," Seriah asked, "how many people follow us?"

"There are probably fifty of them."

She sighed. "Very well. Today will be a long day."

"The things we do for our beliefs," he said.

They walked along for a time in silence. People behind them muttered and whispered harsh arguments with each other.

"Do you know where this Judgment Tree is?" Seriah asked.

"No," Pater Noss laughed, "but no one has corrected us, so I assume we're going in the right direction."

Seriah laughed along with him.

"Nefer, may I ask you some questions as we walk?"

"Of course."

"I have asked many Nefers the same question. You see, I am a scholar of the gods' interactions with mortals."

"I'm sure it's an interesting subject."

"Yes, I find it so."

"Very well, what is your question?"

"Have you any awareness that Nifara performs miracles? Or miracles through the Nefers?"

"No. It is a question often asked of us, and the answer is we do not know of any. I cannot imagine the amount of energy the gods must exert to perform miracles, whether through the blessings of Kasne upon the Hrelgrens, or miracles of Grissone, performed through you."

"I'm sure none of us can fathom it."

"But I am sure she expends her energy elsewhere. She has, after all, taken up the role of her once betrothed. Kos-Yran was the god of order. The god of justice. It was his responsibility as the Walker-Between-Worlds to guide souls on to their rest. And yet..."

"And yet Nifara was forced to take up the role of her fallen love. The miracle she must perform with each delivery of a soul to Noccitan."

"As you say."

"We have arrived," Pater Noss said.

"Please, guide me to the tree."

"It is a tree that has grown out of the cobblestones, and it seems it was once burnt by a fire. But a second tree grew out of the remains."

"Fitting. Thank you, Pater Noss."

"I'll take my leave of you now. I still have a ways to go on my journey."

"May Grissone be with you," Seriah said.

"Thank you, Nefer. May Nifara protect you."

She was provided a stool, and she sat with her back against the Judgment Tree and heard the cries for justice through the remainder of the day and well into evening. All had left the street, and Seriah sat alone. She often did after a day like this, sitting in the silence of a town or field where farmers came to her.

She never felt scared or threatened in her time as a Nefer. After all, regardless of criminality, no man wished to offend Nifara. Steal from another man, take something from a child—but to harm a Nefer would surely be heard of immediately by Nifara, and nothing on Kallattai would save you from eternal imprisonment in Noccitan.

Yet the air this night had a deep chill that set into her bones. Only one other time had she felt like this, sitting with travelers around a fire, the embers all that were left, and the howls of beasts in the woods drew nearer. The fires were fed, and the fear had subsided. Yet here it only felt colder. There was no approach of a figure. No breath of some back-alley thief or murderer. Just a presence.

"Have... have you come for judgment?" she asked hesitantly, probing into the darkness.

There was nothing there.

"Nifara grants me the power to judge and discern. Come and reveal yourself."

"Now why the cold air?" a voice said from behind her. The chill that had set around her snapped, and warmth flooded back into the street, but the shivers in her spine did not. This voice, gravelly, and old, was not the source of the fear. Instead, the voice seemed to capture and consume the fear, tucking it away. "Shoo, cold. This kind monk is just enjoying the cool sea air."

His voice was not perhaps gravelly, the more she heard it. Instead it was silky, full, like it spoke with a mouth filled with wool. "Perhaps I can sit with you?" the stranger offered.

"If you'd like," Seriah said.

The person threw themselves down with a slump next to the tree.

"It is a fine night. The turning of the seasons. I like winter."

"Why is that, fair stranger?"

"Hah! I am not fair. Nothing good to look at here. Life has been hard enough to see to that."

"Very well, stranger. Why do you like winter?"

"Because death provides perspective, and the life that comes after is sweeter. Perhaps bittersweet, but sweeter."

"I always preferred the autumn as a little girl, because it meant the work was done, and harvest had begun. Winter is not to me a death; it is rest."

"They each, I suppose, have their purpose. Have you ever spoken with Nifara?"

"Spoken with? No. I should hope the only time I ever see her is when I leave this world."

"That'll be some time from today, I don't doubt. But I ask you this: if you ever should see her, please tell her that I wish my love had not shunned me. Things might have turned out differently if she hadn't. The things I have seen and done might not have come to be if I had not been shunned at the very beginning."

"I do not know that I will be allowed to do so. I have never heard of Nefers passing along messages to the afterlife. That is not what we are here for."

"All the same, I should like it if you would do so."

"Perhaps I might have your name then?"

"She will know when you tell her so."

He pulled himself up with a heavy groan. "Come along, brother."

He walked away, and then she felt the remnants of the chill pass by her to follow the stranger, fading away until she was left in the street alone.

15

Those Who Remain

Of St. Klare, so much can be said of someone who said so little. After all, it is said she was chosen by Crysania, and never spoke a word, even before she took her Vows. She never learned to read nor write, and so we have no records of teachings, for she had none. Her ascetic diet is attributed to her, or at least those that followed her ways, serving the poor, and avoiding impact on those around her. But there is a legend that she did speak, and only once. She stood in chains before the king of Ancient Zhig. And her words melted the tyrant's heart and set about in motion the end of the pogroms of the north.

— *THE HISTORY OF THE CRYSALAS*

The crystalline ringing of the convent bells pulsed and called. Katiam found herself drawing closer to consciousness and fighting back against the urge, hoping for a few minutes' extra sleep. And yet, after so many months on the road, the sound was a welcome one, harkening to her life at Pariantür.

She sat up smiling and looked across the other beds, each with a simple bedside table. The crystal goblets rang in unison with the great bell, pulsing out a call for the morning to begin. Katiam had poured out the contents into the Rotha's soil next to her before turning over to sleep, and her goblet rang empty and true.

A group of women in red robes entered the room and began to sing a sharp song to wake those who still had not roused. Several of the younger sisters groggily rose and begrudgingly reset their beds. She remembered being that age, growing used to the short night's sleep of those only recently joined.

It only took a few moments before those with an easier time waking began speaking about the recent night's events. The appearance of the black-robed Wyvian Watchers, the strife between the High Priest of Aben and the others, and the Prima Pater ordering everyone back to their own complexes.

The Abbess Superioris did not seem happy returning to her convent while the Matriarch Superioris continued to speak with the other heads of church. She had been quick to leave the others to corral the sisters when they arrived back.

Katiam gasped and leapt toward the door, and Sister Sabine Upona stepped up and into her way. "Sister Borreau?"

"I didn't see the Matriarch to bed last night. She'll be needing her medicine."

"I saw to it when I returned with her. She was very understanding last night, especially after staying up so late."

"How late were you out?"

"If she slept, she's only had a few short hours. She probably ought not to be disturbed."

"What are you doing awake, then?" Katiam asked.

Sabine smiled under the dark circles around her eyes.

"I haven't been to bed yet; the Abbess and I have been speaking since I returned."

"Until dawn? About what?"

"The order, the Matriarch, the... Unfortunately, it's really not my place to say. Especially here. And I'm tired."

"I understand. If you'll excuse me, I still need to make sure the Matriarch has everything she needs."

"Of course," Upona said. "I may join you to see that she's resting before I find somewhere to sleep myself."

"You could use the spare bed in her room. It was provided for me, in case I needed to stay nearby her in times of need."

Maeda appeared not to have moved since Upona had tucked her in. While Katiam puttered about preparing medicines for later, Upona took to the spare bed. By the time Katiam turned to leave, the Matriarch's assistant was fast asleep.

As Katiam left the room, a figure in red approached. "May I speak with her?"

Katiam turned, smiling apologetically, and looked into the face of the aging Abbess Superioris.

"Abbess Foi," Katiam said, "I'm afraid she still sleeps."

The Abbess sighed.

"I understand that the same ought to go for you."

The old woman shook her head. "I am used to that. I have nights I don't sleep much, and staying up to see the dawn through seems to be all that will help with that."

"The Matriarch Superioris used to suffer the same way. My predecessor prescribed a tonic for her that seemed to help. I could prepare the same for you, if you'd like."

The woman next to her smiled. "Thank you," she said, "but there are times I cherish the extra work I'm able to do in those still hours."

Katiam gave a small bow and excused herself.

She walked the long back hallway to the grand stairs that circled inside the glass-enclosed tower overlooking the extensive rose garden orchard that stretched out behind the complex. Beyond the far walls she could see other estates, and, to the south, the hill of South Mahn Fulhar.

She passed by the formal level, devoid of most women except in times of propriety and ceremony, and came to the lowest, where water flowed from a spring and the kitchen prepared the meals. The smell of the food being brought back after the meal wafted past her. She picked up her pace, hoping she'd reach the dining hall in time to find at least one scrap of food.

The din of cleaning came to her first, and the sinking dread that she'd have to ask for food from the less-than-pleasant head provisioner washed over her.

She rounded the corner. Most had already left the dining hall, and those who had taken up the duty of cleaning moved between pillars that held up the building above.

Katiam turned into the kitchen as her stomach groaned in hungry protest.

"Katiam?"

She turned to see Astrid Glass sitting at a table. "I saw you leave the dormitory with Sabine, so I saved you some food."

Katiam smiled and took the seat opposite her.

"Thank you, Astrid," she said. "I owe you."

"Nonsense," Astrid said. "You've been busy enough caring for the Matriarch Superioris and helping Esenath; it was the least I could do. I have nothing else to do, anyway."

"What do you mean?" Katiam asked, tearing up the bread and shoving it into her mouth.

"You probably noticed, there are no Paladames here," Astrid said. "Well, at least none in armor." She motioned to the white robes she wore. As Katiam thought back, the only time she had seen Astrid in armor was at the solstice ceremony.

"The Abbess explained that to the Matriarch," Katiam said. "Those who act as guards in the single Vault hidden in the city don't even wear armor, or it would be too easy for someone to uncover it as they travel to and from the Convent."

"I understand that," Astrid said, "and so I can't wear mine. But I don't have any guard duty, either. The others from the convent want the honor of standing guard near the Matriarch."

"Have you spoken to Sabine?"

Astrid nodded. "She knows. She's just too occupied with things to find anything for me to do."

"It looks like you're in a position I wish I had been in at Thementhu college."

"What's that?"

"You have freedom."

Astrid gave her a look.

"What I mean is you can do whatever you want. Go explore the convent. The city. Anything, really."

"I can't," Astrid said. "I need something to occupy me. Something to think about, or rather not think about. Or else..."

"Or else what?" Katiam said, and then she remembered. "Oh."

Astrid stood abruptly and left without another word.

Her brother, Killian Glass, had died due to her own rash actions when the vül had attacked them in the mountains between Nemen and Bortali. It had changed Astrid from the lively girl she had once been, into the morose and professional guard she had remained ever since.

The dry bread in Katiam's mouth turned to ash to match the sinking feeling and gnawing hunger in her gut.

She rose, gave her platter to a passing sister collecting dishes, and returned to the dormitory, which sat empty. Katiam approached her bed, only to have her heart join her sinking stomach when the dirt-filled planter was nowhere to be seen. Another sister moved among the beds, tidying those that weren't up to her inspection.

"Did you see a box here beside this bed?" she asked.

"You know we encourage personal items not be left in the common dormitory." The woman finished straightening a bed and then looked up to Katiam as she joined her. "Ah, you're a member of the Matriarch Superioris's party; perhaps you didn't know. We may be sisters here, but we're still human. Someone probably took your box. I can ask around, see if anyone has seen it."

"It was a box full of dirt," Katiam said. "Who would have done so?"

"Oh!" The woman exclaimed. "I saw one of your party take that planter as everyone was leaving this morning."

"One of ours?" Katiam replied.

"Yes, the dark-skinned Sidieratan," the sister replied.

"Thank you!" Katiam said, turning to leave.

Now she moved through the convent with purpose. With the cold winter enfolding everything in its grip, the convent kept only the one south-facing hothouse warm, to keep certain southern herbs in season for the kitchen.

Katiam laughed to herself to think anyone would wish harm or possession of the Rotha pod. She walked past the clattering kitchen preparing for the next big meal, and pushed open the big wooden doors that led out to the eastern courtyard.

Several women led sleipnirs in a circle by leads, to work the animals' muscles, while another group worked away in the smithy nearby, preparing to shoe another six-legged creature.

The framed glass of the hot room next to the smithy appeared as Katiam circled, and she could see two figures within. She pushed open the door and quickly closed it behind her as the heat and humidity washed over her.

"You ought to have brought a cloak," a woman before her said. "Leaving here to cross that cold courtyard is going to be difficult after you've been here a few minutes."

"I'm looking for Esenath," Katiam said.

The woman trimmed off another herb and placed it in the basket next to her. She shrugged and indicated with her chin toward the south window. Katiam recognized the brown-clad woman from behind, if only from the back of her shaved head.

"What are you doing?" Katiam asked as politely as she could muster. Her voice quavered as she saw, with relief, the dirt filled box in front of the other woman. "I thought someone had taken the Rotha."

"Why fear that?" Esenath replied. "None really know what it is, save you or I."

"It...it was foolish, I know."

"You're growing fond of it," Esenath said, smiling. "To tell you the truth, so have I."

"What are you doing?" Katiam asked again.

"I thought it might do to bring it somewhere it could get full sun."

"The dormitory has those big windows."

"North-facing," Esenath said, "and very drafty."

"It is warm here," Katiam admitted.

"Yes. And the Rotha already appears improved."

"What?" Katiam said, pulling in closer.

The tips of the five tendrils peeked out from the dirt.

"It's growing!" Katiam said.

"I told you it would."

Katiam reached out with a tentative finger to feel the soil, and then placed her entire palm upon the surface. The sunlight coming through the glass kept it warm. Esenath had already moistened the dirt.

"Have you offered it a Dweol petal yet?"

"No," Esenath said, smiling. She motioned to the wooden box nearby.

Katiam flipped open the box and took out one of the rose-colored crystals. The vibration of the crystal pulsed ever so slightly in her hand. This increased as she drew it nearer to the top of the planter. The five tendrils began to quiver, matching the feeling running through Katiam's fingers.

The tendrils reached up another quarter inch. She placed it next to the central green tip. The dirt under the crystal moved slightly, and took the crystal down below the surface. The tendrils fell still.

"Satisfying, isn't it?" Esenath asked.

"Yes," Katiam said. "I'm starting to see why you cherish your time among the greenhouse plants."

"Just as you find purpose in the administration of medicine, I'm sure."

"It's not the same," Katiam said.

"Nothing is the same," Esenath said, "yet all is the same."

"What do you mean?"

"It means I can hear the frustration in your voice. Perhaps even dissatisfaction. And I would point out that all responsibilities have their ups and downs. I'm sure there are aspects you cherish, and others you could do without. And I would also point out that the same is true for tending a garden. Why am I so very stringent on what we do to replicate each moment spent with the Rotha, now that it has sprouted?"

"Experience?"

"Because I fear it could all be for naught. I have had prized bulbs eaten by vermin. Or a single morning's missed watering kill an herb I had cultivated for a year. Have you not experienced the same?"

"I suppose that is true," Katiam said. "A change of diet, and an elderly patient edges near death."

"We all face the trials of frustration along with the triumphs. Don't lose sight of the fact that both lead to the same thing."

Katiam looked at the woman next to her.

"Satisfaction."

As Katiam reentered the convent, she walked with a renewed purpose toward the Matriarch Superioris's study. Within, the old lady sat in front of the blazing fire, a book across her lap, and her head bowed.

Katiam smiled and walked over to the apothecary cabinet. She went about her business, preparing a goblet of foul-tasting tonics, and then proceeded to cut it with wine and rosewater.

She approached the snoozing old lady and knelt down beside her to wait.

"I was merely praying to Crysania," the old woman said.

"Yes, Auntie," Katiam said.

"Ah, Katiam," she said, looking over fondly at her great niece. "Come to give me my just earnings?"

"Come to see you live another day," Katiam said, taking the book off the woman's lap and placing the goblet in her hands.

Maeda Mür lifted it to her lips, wincing at the smell, and then grimacing at the taste.

"Drink up. The faster you take it down, the sooner you'll be done."

"No need to chide me with the pleasantries a child can see through."

"And no need for you to fight me on it," Katiam said.

"Stoke the fire, dear," the Matriarch said.

"It's blazing," Katiam said, "and I'd rather see you finish your medicine."

"I'm not going to spill it out on this fine carpet," the old woman said sternly. "It was one time, two years ago."

"But the carpet was handwoven qavylli."

"An ugly rug which I always hated."

"Gifted to you by the oracle in the Sanae Massif."

"I promised never to do it again."

"Very well," Katiam said. "Now finish your medicine and I'll feed your fire."

She rose and walked toward the hearth.

"And if you spill any of that on your gown," Katiam said over her shoulder, "I'll make the next one without any of the rosewater you love."

She chuckled to herself as the Matriarch grumbled, and then did as she was told.

Sister Upona entered and took a chair to sit with the Matriarch.

"Sabine," the woman said, making a face as she took another sip from her goblet.

"Matriarch Superioris."

"What is wrong now?"

"Wrong?"

"You've not sat down in three days, and now you are pulling up a chair next to me. What is wrong?"

"Nothing," Sabine said. "I'm just...tired."

"And?"

"And the Abbess Superioris is conducting a mass, so you and I can finally speak without interruption."

The Matriarch's assistant turned to speak to Katiam.

"You may finish with that fire, and leave us," she said.

Katiam stood and turned to look at the two women.

The look on Sabine's face turned to dread.

"Katiam!" she said. "I am so sorry, I thought you were a convent attendant."

Katiam smiled. "I understand, Sabine. I can leave."

"No!" Sabine said, standing and walking across the room. "I'm sorry, I did not mean to be terse. I'm sorry I interrupted your time with your aunt. Let me get you a chair. Perhaps we can all three sit."

She rushed to grab another chair as Katiam took the Matriarch's empty goblet.

"Perhaps some of the wine from the decanter?" the Matriarch asked.

Katiam bowed her head and poured a cup for Sabine, refilled the Matriarch's own, and then poured a crystal glass of rosewater for herself.

She came and sat with the two women, offering the other glasses to them.

They sat for a long while in silence, sipping gently.

"It's been too long since we've done this," Maeda said finally.

"The ship from Obeceñas to Poray, I think," Sabine said.

"The ship creaked, the sailors swore," the Matriarch corrected. "We have not sat in silence, we three, since we left Pariantür."

They fell to another round of quiet. Katiam closed her eyes and let the roar of the fire fill her ears.

"Did you have something to say, Sabine?" Maeda finally asked.

"I had hoped to speak on the events of last night, without others around."

"I can leave," Katiam offered again.

"I mean without those who we do not know nor trust," Sabine said.

"I should like to speak on the events of last night as well," the Matriarch said, "but I'd rather not repeat myself fifty times. Perhaps we could arrange a meeting of all of our attendants from the journey."

"Besides Katiam and myself," Sabine said, "I believe Sister Glass is the only remaining attendant from Pariantür."

"This is true," the Matriarch said.

"Shall we call for her?" Sabine offered.

"No. I'd like the others. Perhaps everyone who has joined since then, up until we crossed into Mahndür?"

"I will see to it. An hour then?"

"Eager, are we?" the Matriarch asked.

Sabine smiled awkwardly.

"Speaking of Sister Glass," Katiam said. The other two gave her a look. "She is feeling purposeless."

"What do you mean, child?"

"She came as a guard, but is not being allowed to do her duty."

"The Paladames assigned here have desired the honor to guard the Matriarch," Sabine said.

"And I should think the respite to be a good one for Astrid," the Matriarch added.

"It might have been," Katiam said, "but I fear the rest only dredged up memories she has fought to keep down."

"Ah," the Matriarch said, glancing over at Sabine. "We had feared this may happen, did we not?"

"She'll have to face the loss of her brother eventually," Sabine said.

"Yes," Katiam said, "but her mother and father serve at Pariantür. I imagine she'd like to do it with them on her own terms."

"Very well," the Matriarch said. "I'm sure between Sabine and the Abbess, we can find some menial duties to occupy Astrid."

"Why don't we ask sister Glass to gather everyone, and arrange a private location to meet?" Sabine said.

"Very good, Sabine. Katiam, will you please go and ask Astrid to do so?"

The Matriarch looked over at her assistant.

"I can see my attendant here would very much like to speak with me alone, despite her protestations to the contrary."

Sabine grimaced and gave Katiam an imploring look.

Katiam rose, took the empty glasses from her companions, and returned them to the sideboard before excusing herself. She turned her attention to finding Astrid and the upcoming meeting with her fellow road companions.

*   *   *

It was an odd feeling, seeing the collection of women. They had not had a moment to meet since arriving in Mahn Fulhar, and Katiam felt outnumbered as she considered how few of those who had left Pariantür were still with them. So many had left their company, from Captain

Sigri Smith, now establishing the hospital in Waglÿsaor, to the silent sister Narah Juevan and her constant companion Lutea Calimbrise—both of whom stayed on at the convent near Garrou. The Matriarch Superioris, Sabine Upona, Astrid Glass, and Katiam herself were all that remained of the eleven Crysalas Honoris who left Pariantür.

That was not to say that those who had joined them were not welcome. She considered Esenath a friend, and a few of the others had brought welcome skills on the road, from Jaspine's cooking to the vocal talents of Pash Deluma.

The Matriarch Superioris had taken a seat at the head of the summer room, warmed only slightly by the sun streaming in through the southern windows and the hearth at the north end. Astrid walked around the group, counting the heads of the twenty women. She nodded to herself and made a motion to Sabine.

"Thank you all for coming," Sabine said. "The Matriarch thought it fair to gather those of us from the road together, to provide a forum for each of you to raise any questions you may have since the ceremony. I know I have a few of my own."

"Did you know about the church of the Judge?" Esenath asked, not waiting for the awkward silence that proceeds groups waiting for someone to speak up.

"That they would make an appearance?" the Matriarch responded. "Or that they existed?"

"Either," Esenath replied.

"They are certainly not mere rumor. But just as you did not say the Judge's name, due no doubt to superstitions you hold, few speak of the followers of Wyv-Thüm, and fewer still give thought that he would have dedicates to his will."

"What is their purpose? And why did they appear?" Another asked.

"I think they confirmed most of that," the Matriarch said. "Their role is to worship Wyv and record the dead. Those who appeared have passed away in life, but it is said that there are portals into Noccitan, where, should the living pass through, never to return, they remain as mortal followers. They add to the number of followers, observers to the testimonies of those Nifara brings before the Judge's Throne."

"Gray Watchers, then," Sabine said in a tone denoting her own curiosity.

"If you'd prefer to call them that. The Gray Watchers of Aben were formed from the souls of the fallen race of Aben's creations, the Serabim, who were destroyed in the wars leading up to the Destruction. Wyv-Thüm followed his brother's practice and turned fervent servants to the same sort of specter—observers who can pass between realms. I'd imagine only at the behest of Wyv and his purposes, though; it is something only gods can do, after all."

"And now I wish only to return to Pariantür, to see if any of our own texts speak on such things," Sabine said.

"There is little," the Matriarch said, "and those who I have known to become obsessed with such things are often called away by the Judge, by death or by worship. I'd prefer you on this side of mortality, Sabine."

Her attendant blushed.

Katiam glanced over to Astrid, who was usually lost to her own thoughts, and saw her chewing on her lips. A wave of worry washed over Katiam. Then the other girl turned to the front as she inhaled deeply through her nose.

"Matriarch Superioris?"

"Yes, Astrid?"

"I need not remind you, nor anyone here, of my role as a Paladame, and thus my responsibilities include guardianship of those given to my care. But just as importantly, I am taught to be suspicious, and to keep observant eyes open for those in danger, as well as watching for those who would cause danger."

"Understood, Sister Glass. That being said, what have you observed that you wish to share?"

"I fear the opinion I wish to share may only be my own, but still, my gut tells me I ought to share."

"Often our mother goddess shares such insights. What is it?"

Astrid gave a quick glance around the room, and back to the Matri-arch's kind smile.

"It is regarding the High Priest of Aben," Astrid said.

"Go on, Astrid."

"His denial that there are problems in Œron. It spoke to me not of ignorance, but of something else."

"You suspect he knows of such things, and is perhaps dishonest on the subject," the Matriarch stated.

"Well, yes."

"You are not the first to bring this up to me," the Matriarch said, "and given it comes from different circles, I believe that perhaps we ought to consider this more thoroughly."

She looked about the room, where others fidgeted in discomfort.

"Let me first state that there are other possibilities. After all, men, perhaps more so than we women, are good at ignoring problems that do not stare them in the eye. Better to deny the existence of the problem, in order to ensure focus on the present situation. And then it may also be he denied it to save his own pride.

"The Church of Aben is not so unified as he might wish it; they have four distinct branches. And while all give lip service to the High Priest of Aben, we know that the Church of the Common Chalice in Œron has their own high priest, and members of their country's re-ligion that would never outright admit their own prophet is second to one from the north. So it may be that Klent Rigal is covering over that wound to ensure a show of solidarity before three other religions— well, four, considering the Watchers of Wyv—who all show singularly unified sects."

"But as you have said to me in the past," Sabine piped up. "If the same question is raised by multiple people from various circles, it bene-fits us to further investigate."

"As you say, Sabine."

"Could the High Priest be hiding something?" Esenath asked.

"Let us not jump to any conclusions," the Matriarch said, raising a hand. "I am going to speak further with Abbess Superioris Foi. She has a longer lasting relationship with the young High Priest. I will value her testimony on the subject, and will see to it that a proper investigation is made. On that subject, though, I would ask the rest of you to refrain from further gossip, lest it lead to slanderous tongues. Please let those better suited to the task do so."

"Matriarch Superioris," Sabine said, "if I may…"

"Of course, Sister Upona."

"Regarding the urgency the Pontifex spoke of, does this move up our plans for visiting the shrine at Precipice?"

"It may. However, that remains to be seen. Dorian dispatched three Paladins at the conclusion of the public ceremony to investigate the dead Primus the Watcher referenced. I have reason to believe that what they uncover will be something that affects us all. This was confirmed by the Abbess Superioris, who tells me of a sister in residence here with the gift of Oracular vision. The girl awoke in the middle of the night and bid us pray for the safety of the three of them."

"And did she say anything else?" someone asked.

"It was, unfortunately, a fleeting dream. She only knew that they headed toward danger. I've already informed the Prima Pater."

"Should we prepare for something?" Astrid asked.

"What would you have us prepare for?" the Matriarch asked. "The return of three battle-hardened Paladins a week from now?"

"I did not mean to insinuate they would be incapable," Astrid blushed.

"Of course, sister," the Matriarch smiled. "I did not think you had. If the Prima Pater believes they are in greater danger than they can handle, he'll dispatch help for them. Just as at Pariantür, just as cities we have holdings in, we have our own troubles and responsibilities."

"Matriarch Superioris," Sister Upona said, "do you recall the orders you gave the Vaults of Boroni and Bortali?"

The Matriarch gave her a quizzical look.

"You asked them each to prepare plans of escape for their cities, should a siege threaten the women and children of the city."

"I recall the request, yes."

"You have yet to ask Mahn Fulhar to do so."

"Do you share in Astrid's fears, Sabine?"

Sabine smiled. "No. But we find ourselves in a unique situation. Astrid is one of the better ledger keepers in the Paladames. Perhaps Astrid could take on the task, to prepare a plan and archive the plan for future use."

"Ah," the Matriarch sighed. "In regards to the conversation you and I had earlier. Of course."

She turned to Astrid. "Would you take this task on?"

"Yes, Matriarch Superioris."

"You'll need to visit the vaults, as well."

Astrid gave a curt bow. Katiam thought she caught a smile playing on her lips.

"Now," the Matriarch said, looking around the room, "are there any other questions?"

16

St. Nonn

May your prayers be four, to rise like the four-wings of the ælerne.
Swiftness to the defense of the helpless,
Protection from those who cast doubt,
Solace in truth to speak words required,
Might to weather the trepidations of evil.

**— THE ONLY RECORDED WORDS OF THE FIRST PRIMA PATER,
KELLIN SIARN**

The night was cold and dark. The snow wasn't deep, but wind threw it across their vision and made it hard to keep track of where the sleipnir's hooves hit hard dirt. They planned to ride all night and through the next day.

Jined felt weariness settling upon him. His eyes involuntarily began to blink.

"Grissone, grant me wakefulness."

A shock of energy seemed to flow through him, and a string of verses came to mind:

"Grissone-Anka lift us up.
Our faith lies in you.
Give us your wings.

We shall fly.

We shall fly.

We shall fly."

Over and over, he repeated the psalm. The snow stung harder and the wind slapped them across their faces. The sun began to rise above the snow, and they came upon a farming village. The first smoke was beginning to rise from chimneys.

"Let us find out how far we've traveled," Jined said.

They approached the first farmhouse. Jined walked up to the door and knocked. Hesitantly, a farmer peeked out. Seeing the three Paladins standing there, he threw the door open.

"Paladins! Please, come in."

Jined and the twins knocked the snow off their boots at the door as they entered. It was a large farmhouse, with twelve family members within helping prepare for the morning meal.

"Will you join us for the breaking of the fast?" the farmer asked.

"We would be honored."

Jined was given the seat at the head of the table. The twins sat at the other end. The mother and grandmother brought around bowls of gruel with chunks of sausage in them and placed them before each person. Little ones shared bowls. Before they ate, though, the father turned to Jined.

"Brother Paladin, will you pray?"

Jined nodded. He took his bowl in his hands and lifted it as everyone copied him.

"Grissone, I pray a blessing over this household, and upon our mission. Let those who share in this meal be drawn to do what is good—to those we love and also to strangers."

Soon the older children, finished with their food, began clearing the bowls for the little ones.

Several children clamored to sit up on the Paladins' laps, which they obliged. They asked a hundred little questions, which the twins could not answer, and looked to Jined for assistance.

"They have taken a Vow of Silence," he said.

All of the children went quiet at this.

"They can't speak?" a little girl asked.

"We Paladins take Vows, to draw us closer to Grissone, the god of Faith. Brother Loïc and Brother Cävian have taken the Vow of Silence; they choose not to speak."

"And why do they look so much alike?"

"They are twins," Jined said. The little girl was confused, and someone told her they'd explain it later.

"What about you?" an older girl asked.

"I have taken the Vow of Chastity. And of Poverty."

One little girl with bright red hair threw herself over Jined's leg. She was no older than three.

"Tell us a story," she begged. "I need a story."

"Uh... I don't know many."

"Leave the man alone," their mother said, attempting to pull the little girl away.

"It is no trouble," Jined said. "Let me think of one to tell."

He glanced at Loïc and then Cävian, who merely shrugged and smiled wryly at his discomfort.

"Do you know the story of St. Ikhail?"

The children fell silent, shaking their heads.

That's an easy one to tell, Loïc signed

Quiet, brother, Cävian responded. *I don't see you telling a tale.*

Loïc shrugged.

"Ikhail was a blacksmith. He never amounted to much, charged only with making shoes for sleipnirs and nails for carpenters. Yet it is said that his hammer never faltered, and rang evenly all the days he worked.

"One day a man came to his smithy and sat down to watch him ply his trade.

"'What shall I craft for you, stranger?' Ikhail asked the man.

"'I have a hammer with no head. I would have you craft that hammer.'

"'With what?'

"'Why, with your arm.'

"At this Ikhail laughed. 'I mean what would you have this hammer head crafted from?'

"'Whatever can be found.'

"Ikhail laughed again and walked to a pile of unused shards of metal. He took it up and walked forward, placing the piece within the stone forge, and let the metal heat. Taking it out, he began to beat the rose-red iron.

"'How many faces will this hammer have?' he asked.

"'I ask that it has two; one for striking, and one for defending.'

"'This will be a weapon of war, then? Against whom?'

"'Prepare the hammer, and I will show you.'

"He worked long into the night, reheating and striking the metal until the head was complete. He quenched it in a barrel of water and took it to the man, placing it in his hands.

"'This is a finely crafted hammer, but I need one made of faith.'

"Ikhail looked at the man once more. 'I have no faith with which to build a hammer for striking, nor for defending. How can you propose this?'

"'If you would seek to make such a hammer, then you would become more than a simple horse-shoe farrier.'

"Ikhail turned back to his forge. When he turned back around the man was gone, the hammer he had built was left behind with a finely hued haft of the strongest wood he had ever seen. And thus he took it up, banded the haft, and used it as his smithing hammer. For five years he stayed, and all said that his smithy could make anything, for his new hammer was the finest crafted hammer in the realm.

"One day the anvil stopped ringing. The people came to the smithy to find it empty. Ikhail was gone. The forge still glowed, but Ikhail and his hammer had disappeared.

"One day, word came to the people near his smithy. He had found the means to forge a hammer made of faith, but it could not be made by one man. It took no convincing. Every man, woman, and child in that village heeded his call. It is said that they were the metal from which he forged his hammer of faith. For no town on Kallattai completely left their homes behind as the people of that now-forgotten village did."

"What happened next?" one of the children asked.

"Ikhail found a hammer made of faith, and he smote the T'Akai who invaded."

One of the children gasped. "Did you know Ikhail, grandpapa Mechit?" she asked.

The old man smiled. "I did not. But I've seen T'Akai during the Protectorate Wars. And I've seen the hammer Ikhail built with faith—Pariantür."

Jined stood and bowed to the old man. "Your service to the Hammer is admirable. Perhaps you can continue the story I started; we must away to St. Nonn."

"Be careful then. Things have been silent of late," the old man said.

"How far is it to the bastion?"

"St. Nonn's? Ten leagues, perhaps."

Loïc gave a look of surprise. *That's almost forty leagues we traveled last night. Did you pray something in that snow storm?*

Jined just nodded before turning back to the farmers. "Thank you again, for your hospitality."

*   *   *

They saw the Bastion while they were still a league off, atop a bluff a half mile from the main road. Outside, a single Paladin stood guard. They slowed their mounts to a trot for the last mile.

"There are supposed to be only two Paladins at this bastion. A Brother Adjutant and a Brother Excelsior. And yet, one stands guard. But over what?"

The Paladin watched them approach. He wore a black cape of mourning on his back.

"Grissone protects!" Jined called, a smile on his face.

The Paladin walked over to the door and stood in front of it.

"Where do you hail from?" the guard asked.

"We just rode down from Mahn Fulhar, where we attended the meeting of the churches."

"Which meeting is that?"

"Brother Excelsior, you and your fellow brother were summoned to appear. We sent word well over a week ago and didn't hear back. Now I've come to see how you fare."

The door opened from the inside, and three Paladins came out. They too wore black capes.

"Brother Adjutant," the center one said. He wore the cordons of a Primus. "Please, let us show you hospitality. Brother Hichel here is often overly cautious."

Jined dismounted and said under his breath, "To another paladin?"

They entered the bastion. It was a single room, with a stairwell into the cellar near the back. Ten Paladins pored over a table and maps.

"You are the Primus here?" Jined asked the one who had come to their aid outside.

"Yes, I am Primus Loth. I was just made Primus after last week's incident."

"Incident?" Jined asked.

"Yes. Primus Giller died."

"Did he? My Primus had not heard that."

"Why would he? Giller was leading us up from Grisden. He died mysteriously after we arrived."

"Ah. That seems to explain why there are so many of you here. Are there not only two Paladins stationed at this bastion?"

"Yes. We have reassigned them to Alnír. They left a week ago."

"I see. My fellow brothers here, Loïc and Cävian, and I, will need to prepare a report of the Primus's death."

"We are still preparing our paperwork. We were sent out from St. Justyn's to take a census."

"St. Justyns? In Redot? But this Bastion is subject to the Precipice Fortress, and by that, beholden to the Aerie."

The Primus took a quick step back as another Paladin from Jined's blindside swung his hammer at his head. Jined spun and leaned forward.

The hammer glanced along his shoulder and dropped to strike the flagstone instead. Jined shot out with a backhanded blow, the plates of his leather gauntlet slashing across the paladin's face. Loth had stepped away, putting distance between himself and Jined.

"Attack the faithless," Loth ordered. "They seek to stop our good mission."

"Faithless?" Jined asked, looking at the twins. They both shrugged, their hammers now in their hands.

The guard, Hichel, came at Cävian with his hammer raised high. Cävian struck out with the hammerhaft, doubling the man over, and then brought a knee up into his face.

Jined and Loïc leapt forward as four Paladins came at them. Jined swung wide with a blow meant to force them back, while Loïc quickly struck overhanded onto the skull of another. It glanced the side of his face and struck his gorget, crumpling the metal into his cheek. He fell immediately. Two of them rushed to tackle Jined, while the fourth began swinging wildly at Loïc.

"Grissone!" Jined shouted. "Give me strength."

Jined shoved up on the two Paladins that now held him back. They both flew off of him as though they had been kicked by a sleipnir.

Cävian stood by the door and began motioning a prayer with his hands repeatedly.

Swift as the bird, terrible as an aelerne....

Swift as the bird, terrible as an aelerne....

Loïc began striking back at the other Paladin with swings far too fast to follow. The enemy was hit multiple times before he fell to his knees, begging for mercy.

Four Paladins still stood, the Primus among them.

"What in the name of all that is holy are you about?!" Jined shouted.

He swung his hammer against the wall next to him. The stone leapt from its place and fell outside. The four looked upon him in astonishment. Shaking himself from his stupor, Primus Loth began shouting orders.

"This is what we've prepared ourselves for. Be of the New Faith, brothers. Find your greatness."

The four took up their hammers, which Jined could now see were not chained to them, but leaning against the table they had been looking at.

Loïc turned to Jined. *Where are their chains?*

"Let's ask our questions afterwards."

The three Paladins rushed forward, striking with heavy swings that, if left unblocked, would crush armor. Jined leapt back and Loïc stepped in and struck a Paladin on the back, but the man countered with a thrust of his haft, striking Loïc between the eyes and laying him out.

"Cävian!" Jined shouted. "Focus. Get in here!"

Then under his breath, Jined said, "Grissone, protect me."

He struck out quickly with his hammer across the breastplate of a Paladin. The man fell, holding the crushed metal, gasping, and struggling to breathe. Cävian stepped up and put a boot against him, knocking him back. He was unable to defend himself as he gasped for breath.

Then, stepping forward, Jined and Cävian both swung from either direction at the next Paladin. Both hammers hit home—Jined's on the paladin's shoulder, and Cävian's on his knee. He fell, howling.

The third Paladin came out of nowhere, making a heavy strike down upon Jined's head. A blinding flash of light exploded where he hit Jined, blowing the enemy back against the nearest wall. Jined blinked his vision clear.

Only the Primus remained. Jined kicked over the table rather than go around it. Loth now stood under the statue of the Anka, which Jined only now saw was messily painted black.

"What is this heresy?" he asked.

He could see fear building in Loth's eyes. Loth dropped his own hammer and fell to his knees. Jined grabbed him by the throat and lifted him to stand. "What have you done?" he asked, forcing the man's head around to look at the statue.

"We are changing things. The hammer was just weighing us down. We will make things better by being active."

"Cävian, find some rope in the cellar. We'll be marching these heretics back to Mahn Fulhar."

Cävian rose from kneeling over Loïc who was just starting to wake.

A few minutes later, Cävian came back upstairs. He had in tow another Paladin who had been stripped down to his robe and covered in bruises both old and new.

He was tied up and locked in a cellar room, Cävian signed.

Jined found him some water. "What is your name, brother?"

"Silas Merun. Thank you for the water."

"Rest, brother. You can tell us your story after you have your strength."

"Thank you."

They chained the heretical Paladins to a pillar together, then proceeded to look through the bastion. They gathered up the maps and papers they had with them and put them in a leather satchel. By nightfall they had searched over the entire place. They found outside five graves, recently made. Loïc made dinner for the four of them. The heretics were given nothing.

Silas was ready to speak after they had eaten.

"The time in the cellar was long, confusing. I don't even know what day this is," Silas said.

"Yesterday was winter solstice."

"Then it has only been a week."

"What happened? Please start from the beginning."

"Excelsior Rann and I answered a knock at the door and found Excelsior Loth and his nine Paladins. They were traveling the road and begged us to provide a place to stay. Of course we obliged. But once in and fed, they began bolstering the place, locking the doors from the inside, and telling us they were being pursued by an enemy.

"Another knock came at the door, and I heard the voice of Primus Giller, who had arrived from Precipice many times, so I knew his voice well. They would not let him and his Paladins in. The Paladins outside did not press their advantage, but stayed without. That night we heard a wail in the middle of the night. Paladins came and rushed to the door and began banging on it to let them in, stating that Primus Giller had been murdered by some specter.

"Loth and his Paladins finally relented and opened the door. They struck down the Paladins as they entered. I tried to flee with Brother Rann, but they cut down Rann, too. I was a coward, and they captured me, and they have been torturing me ever since. They keep mentioning the New Faith, and they say that we need only faith in ourselves to join them."

"Brother Merun, you have been very brave in sharing your story," Jined said. "We come from Mahn Fulhar, in the company of the Prima Pater. Would you like to meet the Prima Pater?"

"With all my heart."

"Then you will help us take these Paladins to him in chains, and I ask of you only this: do not act out in vengeance against them. Justice will be had."

17

Interlude

The Paladin placed the package down on the table. Searn reached across and took it up in his hands, clutching it to him. The sailors who sat nearby paid them no heed as they edged themselves deeper into their cups of grog while singing a shanty together.

"Thank you for returning this. I had hoped to meet you in Haven when I passed through."

"After I went through Birin and sent the Bulwark off, I traveled up into the southern pass of Boroni. There was so much talk about the Prima Pater and his Entourage that I followed their trail down into Mahndür. I almost joined up with you the day after your company joined theirs, but felt it might cause trouble, so I held back to try and keep a day or so behind you. But with the attack by that creature, and then the Paladames slowly escorting the Archimandrite, I restlessly took my time to finally reach you here."

"Very shrewd of you," Searn said. "When I passed through Haven, the Bulwark had not yet arrived. I suspect they took the pass to the south of Birin, to ascend to the Limae plain. So I suppose that makes sense."

"Do you suspect that Vanguard converted them to the cause?"

"If he didn't, then he destroyed them," a voice said from the next booth. The figure of another Paladin appeared over the lip. He came around to stand before them.

"Bell," the Paladin said. "Shroud."

"Cup," Searn said.

"May I sit?" Aeger asked.

Searn scooted over, and the Primus sat down with them.

"Is that your Shade, returned to you?"

"How did you know?"

"I spoke to Dusk while we were in Waglÿsaor. He was very interested in discovering how you do that. And I also noticed your Shade was missing when we spoke on the journey north."

"Why are you here?" Bell asked.

"I happened to be running errands for Pater Segundus Pír when I saw you walking with that Nefer, and recognized you. I thought you ought to know that I had done so and that if you're spotted in your full regalia it's going to cause a stir among the brothers, especially since Vanguard has played his hand and is here now, too. So many Pater Minorii here who shouldn't be. You'd think something was going on."

"Vanguard is here?" Bell asked.

"Yes. With his second, Slate. And also, I believe I recognized a very emotionless Pater Koel from the Bulwark marching with him as well."

"Pater Koel," Bell said, "is never muted. He is a passionate man."

"I suspect Vanguard had something to do with that."

"Regarding your visit with Dusk," Searn said, "has he deduced how the Living Shade is made?"

"No. Nor would I tell him that I was the one who taught you how to do it, unless he offered me something dear in return."

"You taught it to Shroud?" Bell asked.

"Yes, Pellian. I discovered it myself. I was at a low point in my life, and the discovery of it, and my subsequent survival through the ordeal, gave me a new lease on life."

"I have what I need, so I am going to leave now," Searn said. "Bell, take what Cup has said into consideration. You ought to hide your armor somewhere while you're around."

Searn stood, taking the package with him.

A few minutes after he left, another Paladin entered the small tavern. Cup sighed.

"What?"

"Slate."

The thin Paladin marched to the table and put both hands on the table.

"Who was that Black Sentinel?" he asked.

Bell cocked an eyebrow. "I don't know that we've met, but it seems Primus Aeger here knows who you are. Your name, Primus?"

"I saw the two of you talking. Aeger is under the Vow of Silence, so if he's talking, it means you're a member of the brotherhood."

"Confident accusation," Bell said, "as you are, yourself, a member of that vow as well. And you'll still treat me with the respect of my rank as Pater Minoris. But you will call me Bell."

Slate took a seat. "I'm known as Slate."

"That's also his name," Aeger said. "He arrived with Vanguard."

"Who was the Sentinel? And how does he know about us?"

"That is none of your business," Bell said, "but my own."

"How did you convince Pater Koel to join your cause?" Aeger asked Slate.

"He was persuaded. We have some means by which to convert more to the cause now."

"It was said the Plate had powers like that in the Protectorate Wars," Bell said. "You've unlocked it, haven't you?"

Slate smiled smugly, but said nothing. He turned to Aeger.

"Vanguard has left me here in the city, to keep a watch out for his flock of followers. And he also asked me to find a moment to speak to you privately, away from the prying eyes of the others."

"And just what message did he have for me?"

"To stay out of his way when he acts. You're in his territory, so you'll play the part you're required to."

"I am here under the authority of Fidelity. And while he's no longer here, you should know that we're now all under an even higher authority in the brotherhood. Shroud is among us. And he has at his disposal a tool ever more powerful than that bundle of armor you've taken so long to unlock."

"Shroud is a myth," Slate said.

"He is very much real," Bell said, "and you'd be wise to stay out of his way."

"Vanguard, and by proxy I, will do what pleases us. It is time for the Moteans to act. If you do not support us, then you are against us. Consider that."

Slate rose and left without another word.

"Well," Bell said, "he's a fool. And he's going to get us all in big trouble."

"Yes," Aeger said, thinking to himself.

"I will warn Shroud, when I am able."

"But do not do anything brash," Aeger said. "We act better in secret. And having seen what Shroud's new tool can do, I don't wish to anger him."

PART 3

18

Badge of Pride

Nine times she knocked. And upon the final knock the ynfald died.
—LAST LINE OF THE CHILDREN'S TALE *THE CÖR'S FINAL MEAL*

The door to Blackiron flew open and Rallia marched in and across the room as though Nifara had come to take her soul. Hanen looked up from the table where maps were strewn across the face as well as a piece of rolled hrelgren reedpulp marked with notations. She stopped across from Hanen, snow still on her bare head and shoulders, and dropped a wrapped package on the table.

"What's wrong?" Hanen asked.

"They finished it early," she said.

Hanen looked his sister in the eye. "What is it?"

"The Runners badge," she said.

"You came in here like the Voktorra were about to torch the building."

"I'm sorry," Rallia said, forcing a smile. "I marched up here so fast I've hardly any breath left. And I'm excited."

"Have you looked at it yet?"

"I thought you'd want to see it, too."

Hanen waved towards the package. "Well? Open it!"

Rallia pulled her knife from her belt and snapped the ribbon. The silk opened, and out fell a purse of velvet.

"Nice looking parcel," Hanen said. "Who did you have make it?"

"I was referred to a man in the mid-district who does minting work for the guilds."

"How did you get someone to do minting work before our meeting with the guilds? Is he not guild?"

"No. The crown requires minters belong to non-guild, so their loyalty is to the crown."

Rallia lifted the pouch and gave it a shake. A single coin-sized piece of gold fell heavily into her hand.

She leaned over the table while considering the piece.

It was slightly oblong, but certainly looked like a coin. Upon the face, an abstract shape of the Sentinel's peaked hood encompassed a sealed scroll. She turned it over to reveal the steel pin installed into it. "This way it can be worn on the outside of the cloak. Did you know up here no one has ever heard the term Coin Cloak?"

"I think it's a good thing. Is that what you're implying with the coin?"

"Yes," Rallia said. "I figured that if this idea starts circulating to other countries, maybe they'll start thinking that this is where the term originated, as though the Black Sentinels thought of it themselves."

"To make the derogatory term lose its bite."

"Exactly."

"So, the coin. Who wears it?"

"Effectively this gold coin medallion is the equivalent of a fully ranked messenger, approved to carry royal messages."

"So you'll have other coins, too."

"Of course," Rallia said. She poured out the rest of the contents of the pouch, revealing three more gold coins and a paper wrap that upon opening revealed a single silver one. "The silver one, he sent as a test. You'll note the hood is down on this one. This is for those with Sentinel status, meaning they have earned their cloak, and can carry messages."

"What will you do for young boys and girls who are just starting off?"

"I'm having a rod made. A special club of sorts. It'll have a compartment for hiding messages in it, and it'll be the rod of office we all carry."

"You've thought this through."

"I've been thinking it through since that Hrelgren in Deld gave me that message to deliver."

"Why have you never said anything about it?"

"I wanted to make sure I had everything ironed out first."

"I could have helped."

"Hanen, you have all the good ideas, and they always seem to come out ready to go, as you think them out."

"First off," Hanen said, "all the good ideas aren't mine. It was your idea to put the office in Edi on Aritelo Hill, on the street set back away from the larger markets, to provide a better privacy for the clients."

He shuffled the papers on his desk, cleaning some of the space and pulling up a bottle sitting underneath, along with two mugs.

"Secondly, I make up the ideas on the spot and fix them as we go. None of them are fleshed out as I speak."

He poured out the glasses, and handed one to his sister.

"To the Sentinel Runners. Is that what we're calling it?"

"Yes," Rallia said, lifting her cup. "Sentinel Runners. I'll have the rank of Courier. And thirdly?"

"Thirdly?" Hanen parroted.

"List of three. You said two things."

"Thirdly," Hanen said. "To the Sentinel Runners. Rallia's idea. The best idea a Clouw has had."

Rallia smiled, and touched her cup to Hanen's.

"What are we celebrating?" Searn said, appearing from behind the curtain of his area.

"The Sentinel Runners," Hanen said. "When did you return?"

"Middle of the night," Searn said, walking up and picking up the coin, considering it. "Coin Cloak," he said. "Funny. And who have you already approved to wear one?"

"Myself and Sälla," Rallia said.

"And will all captains get one?"

"I'm not sure. I wanted to ask you. This silver one will be made for those who have proven themselves, but aren't ranked for royal missives. And the first message rod is almost done."

"Rods?" Searn asked.

"Equivalent to the first club."

"So, three ranks. Entry, Trusted, and Courier. I approve. I think that a Captain needs to have at least a silver Trusted badge"

"If you think so, then I agree," Rallia said.

"How did the meetings with the guilds go?"

Hanen told him what happened that night.

"And did the whitesmiths say anything afterwords? Has there been any retaliation?"

"None," Hanen said. "But I haven't given it any thought."

"You'll need to. They may have been under orders from another, but the fact is, you beat them soundly, and probably embarrassed them."

"What would you suggest?"

"Send them a gift, probably."

The door opened and a man walked in. His head was shaven, and he stood tall, despite the cold outside, with the bearing of nobility. The brown traveler clothes he wore spoke otherwise, but Hanen could tell there was more to him than met the eye.

The man opened his mouth to talk, but Searn interrupted him.

"Greetings Pellian," Searn said. He turned back to the Clouws. "I have to go meet with this client." He looked around and affirmed no one else was in the hall.

"Could you perhaps find something else to do?"

Hanen rose as Rallia put the coins back in the pouch.

"I'll take one of these gold ones for myself," Searn said.

Rallia nodded and handed him one.

Searn turned and escorted the man to the back of the hall.

"There is a problem with Slate," the man muttered.

"In a moment, Pellian," Searn said.

The man turned and watch Hanen go. Hanen stopped and gave a

little whistle, which brought the still-sleeping Whisper up and out from under the table. They left the hall and closed the door behind them.

"He had the bearing of a Paladin," Rallia said.

"What makes you say that? Because I was thinking the same thing."

"He held his chin up, as though he was trying to keep it from catching on a gorget that wasn't there."

Captain Navien walked toward them from the stable yard.

"I understand your commander has returned," Navien said.

"He is meeting with a client," Hanen said. "He's not to be disturbed."

"I have an important message from His Majesty, to be delivered to him upon his return."

"I can take it to him," Rallia said.

"It is to come from me," Navien said.

"Captain Navien," Rallia said, "I am an official Courier of the Black Sentinel Runners." She pointed to the gold coin now hanging from her cloak. "It means I am authorized to carry royal missives. I'll even deliver this one to Searn free of charge."

"That may be true," Navien said. "Frankly, I don't trust you."

Rallia scowled. "And I don't appreciate the attitude you've had towards us since we've arrived." Rallia stepped up to Navien. "You've all but admitted that you were behind the whitesmiths attacking us. And I'll remind you that the Black Sentinels have done everything by the book, and earned every authority required to operate. Fortunately for you, I'm much more in my right mind than I was the night of the Guildhall meeting. But don't try to match toe-to-toe with me. We both hold the rank of captain. And neither of us wants to start a war."

"I don't care for your rank, nor your charter. I care that the King gave me the authority to keep an eye on you. And if I want to go into that building and speak to Searn, regardless of if he is busy, then I will."

He pushed past Rallia to head towards Blackiron.

Rallia's hand shot out and grabbed Navien's wrist, stopping him in place.

"Give me a reason to start a war with the Sentinels," Navien said through gritted teeth, looking down at the hand on his wrist.

"What do you have against Sentinels?" Rallia asked, meeting the other man's dark gaze with her own.

"Let go of my wrist, or are you going to continue to use threats, as all your kind do?"

Rallia removed her hand, and Navien stomped away.

"Let him go," Hanen said. "And let Searn deal with him. He's right. We don't need a war."

Rallia spun and marched in the opposite direction. It took a jog to catch up as she marched past the Voktorra guard at the gate, ignoring their comments and platitudes.

"Rallia," Hanen called. His younger sister didn't stop.

"Rallia, please slow down," Hanen said.

"Now I'm mad," Rallia said. "I need to walk it off. Once I've cooled off, I'll find you."

"Where?"

"I don't know. Where are you going to?"

"The Grotto, I guess."

"Then I'll find you there."

Hanen shook his head and turned to follow the upper canal streets, meandering his way down to the Grotto Market.

Zhag *rm* Tellis and the other hrelgrens gave him a wave as he circled past their booths. He saw a couple of Black Sentinels here and there speaking with merchants, but he paid them little heed as he continued toward his destination. He cut through the last bit of market stalls, past the smell of a boiling cauldron frying root veg, and a woman working dried flowers and herbs in a mortar and pestle.

He stopped across the narrow street from the tailor and looked up into the window. Three customers, young women in fine dresses, stood in the shop speaking with Alodda's mother and little sister. In the other window, Abgenas sat cross legged, his eye more on the piece he embroidered than the street below him.

Hanen felt a nudge on his thigh and turned to see Whisper looking up at him imploringly.

He kneeled down and scratched the scaled back of the ynfald's skull.

Whisper gave his tail a flop and clatter on the paving stones.

"I don't even know why I came down here," he said.

Whisper nudged his chest, almost knocking him off his crouched feet.

Hanen stood, turned towards the shop, and walked across the space, raising his hand to open the door. It swung open. Cedar and porumarian oil washed over him as Alodda nearly bowled into him in a rush to leave on some errand.

"Oh! Hanen!" She shouted. Her countenance went from surprise, to recognition, and finally the look blushed into sullen irritation.

"What are you doing here?" It was not a kindly asked question.

"I was just stopping by to say hello," he said, stepping back off the stoop, to give her the space to join him there. She remained standing in the door.

"I don't have time to speak today," she said. She turned back into the shop. "I'm going to Batrik Dyers, father."

Hanen heard murmured response as she closed the door behind herself.

"May I join you?" Hanen asked. "If you'll allow the company."

"I am not in the mood to speak," Alodda said. Her cheeks were flushed red, despite the chilly day. "I've got several errands to run."

She gave a look of surprise and glanced down to see the wet nose of Whisper nuzzling at the pocket sewn to the outside of her blue dress. She smiled, and knelt down, pulling out a sweet meat for the creature.

"But time to stop and pet Whisper," Hanen said.

She spun her head and gave him a glowering look. She stood abruptly and marched off in a huff toward the back of the grotto and the stairs leading to the smokers' district.

"Did I say something wrong?" he called to her.

She stopped at the bottom of the stairs.

"It wasn't but a few days ago at the guildhall we last spoke. Did I say something then to upset you?"

She turned, her face flat. "Do you know why the guilds questioned you, before offering you a position among them?"

Startled by the turn, Hanen frowned. "They resented the King offering us a charter for our guild without consulting them."

She shook her head and took a tentative step toward him.

"When you and your company arrived in Mahn Fulhar there were only a small handful of Sentinels here, and most of them only arrived recently, and would likely move along soon. Did you ever wonder why that was?"

"I mean, we asked them. And they said most Sentinels here in the north stay on the move from town to town. I didn't think much of it, since my sister and I move from town to town, too."

"So you're just like the others," she sighed. "That's what I feared."

"What is that supposed to mean?"

"You Sentinels move from town to town as the coin dries up. You avoid sticking to one place, as it'll draw attention to what you are really doing. But the Guildmasters were right. They were catching on to what those who live in fear of you have never been brave enough to speak up against. And now, with the power of the charter behind you, it'll only get worse."

"Alodda. I don't understand what you're talking about."

"A few of the minor guilds caught on last year—the glovers and the bucklemakers. They pooled their money and bought off the most influential Sentinel and convinced him to leave. Those friends I have who were under the thumb of a few Sentinels finally got the spine they needed to stand up to those who were bullying them. And now, that bully king..." She looked around to see who might be listening, stepped forward, and glared up at Hanen.

She lowered her voice to a whispering hiss. "Now that bully King has invited the whole tangle of viperous Sentinels back to town with a Guild Charter to back them up."

"I still don't understand what you're talking about," Hanen protested. "What have I done?"

"Veli Mütse and her husband Goev?" Alodda's eyes were brimming with hot, angry tears. "They had finally made enough money to convince the last Black Sentinel to arrive in their part of town to leave. He wasn't gone for more than a month, and now he's back, with your Blackiron Guild to provide him with a higher rate. Goev will have to go back to work for his father. At least then he'll have the protection of numbers. But he'll never own his own shop again. Not if that black-cloaked shunt has his way."

"Alodda!" Hanen put his hands on her shoulders, surprised to hear the coarse language from her. "I don't understand what you're talking about."

She glowered up at him.

"And I can't fix what you won't explain."

"I had hoped you were different. That you were bringing something new to Mahn Fulhar. But it's worse than before."

"Worse than before? What do you mean? We came to provide protection. Safety."

"Protection at what cost? Our dignity? Our hard-earned gold?"

"Well," Hanen said, stepping back, "certainly not your dignity. But you would have to pay us."

She turned, scoffing, and stormed off up the stairs.

"Alodda!" He called after her, watching her go.

"Was that the girl from the bakery?" Rallia asked, walking up with a pair of partially dried apples. She tossed a half-eaten one to Whisper, and gave the other to Hanen before pulling another out of her satchel.

"Alodda Dülar," Hanen said.

"She's pretty," Rallia replied. "How'd you scare her off?"

"It seems like the Sentinels did something bad to the town before we arrived. First I've heard of anything like that."

"Sure," Rallia said through the bite of apple. "Sälla Fyfe was talking to Ophedia a few days ago. I guess back in the day the Sentinels were known for running a racket on the merchants and shaking them down for loose coin."

Hanen sighed. "I don't think it was 'back in the day.' I think it was more recent than that. And the legitimization of Blackiron may have been a blaring invite for those rotten elements to return."

"What are we going to do about it?"

"I don't know," Hanen said. "But if we don't act fast we'll have a whole gang of Thadars running around Mahn Fulhar."

"Of course, fixing it will also put you back in good graces with that girl."

Hanen gave Rallia a faint smile.

"Let's go up to the Dark Stave and see if anyone is playing Garrison. If Aurín is around, then I bet we could scrounge up a game of Edi-Fŏz."

"Yeah," Hanen said.

"It'll take your mind off the girl. Or the stink of the tavern will at least wipe away the scent she left in the air."

Hanen took a bite of the apple and noticed the cedar and porumarian oils that lingered on his hand where he had touched her shoulder.

19

Justice

Down the axe,
> Drop the blade,
>> Hangman's noose,
>>> Judgment made.

She makes her case,
> He speaks his word,
>> Lomïn or Noccitan,
>>> Judgment heard.

—THREE EYED KING

It seemed almost daily that new men and women came to join the Sentinels. Rallia often greeted them and introduced them to Searn, who took Rallia's impressions into consideration. Rallia had three young boys and two young women who she deemed fit enough to be runners and had them taking messages from one end of the city to the other.

Over the three weeks since the meeting with the Guild Masters, Hanen's paranoia that friends and companions were extorting the merchants of Mahn Fulhar grew. To him, each new recruit looked like trouble, and Sentinels who already held cloak and clubs, and had journeyed to Mahn Fulhar to see what the Blackiron Guildhall was all about, reeked of deeper corruption. Searn's ease around all the Sentinels only told Hanen that he had to build a case before he could say anything.

That a month had nearly gone since the solstice doubled down his own pressure to have the caravan route planned and ready to accept merchants for southbound passage.

Aurín Mateau had taken an interest in Hanen's work, and sought out a handful of merchants interested in being on the list. Hanen suspected that Aurín was hoping to make Captain and be in charge of one of the caravans. His knowledge of his homeland, Œron, had been useful, too.

Although the Sentinels were finding a great deal of work, the cut they were paying Blackiron for the jobs Searn was finding for some of them wasn't much, and since most of that went to paying for the expenses accrued by Aurín's cooking and the barrels of ale that needed constant refilling, Hanen couldn't wait to see the caravans off bringing in real coin.

"You haven't made a mark in over an hour," Rallia said. She sat on a stool with a leather strop, sharpening her set of razors. "What are you thinking about? That girl?"

"The caravan."

"And?"

"Just the caravan," Hanen said. "It occurred to me that we can raise our rates compared to what we charged in Edi."

"Why is that?"

"We made some money," Hanen said, "over our usual day rates, but we were never fully profitable, since there were costs you and I didn't really understand until later. I had planned to raise those rates when we made Captain, to compensate for those costs. Now we can."

"We should be able to take in some extra income with messages I carry, as well."

"I factored that in, too."

"What else is on your mind?"

"I expect I should have everything finalized in a week."

"That's good. A week sooner than you anticipated."

"Yes."

"And then we can concentrate on what's really bothering you."

"And what's that?"

"What the girl said to you. About Sentinels extorting merchants."

The sinking pit in Hanen's stomach deepened. It had hung over him like a dark specter, and he had found out little since his argument with Alodda. He hadn't really returned to the Grotto in the eight days that had passed. When he did find time to walk the city, Sentinels he passed often dropped what they were doing to ingratiate themselves to him, if only to position themselves to take part in the spring caravans.

"I haven't forgotten," Hanen said sullenly.

"I'm not saying you have. I can see that burden sitting on your shoulders. It's weighing you down."

"And it doesn't bother you?" Hanen said.

"It does," Rallia said. "But, like you, the work I've been doing has kept me from doing anything about it either."

Hanen turned back to his figures. He made a few notations, and then looked back over at his sister.

"Are we naive in thinking it's perhaps only a few outliers who do so?"

"I think it's because it's not something we have come up against. Save from with Thadar, we were ignorant, not naive."

"But it's a problem even in Edi?"

"In Edi? I highly doubt the problem is rampant. The merchants and their house guards had too much power for it to be a problem. I can think of a couple times a Sentinel ended up in the stocks. They often left town after that to look for opportunities elsewhere."

Whisper looked up from his warm place by the hearth as the door to the hall opened. Milu Gentry and Stanis Bok, two young Sentinels who had come to the city a day or two before the meeting at the Guildhall, entered.

They had been a force to be reckoned with, taking on more jobs between the two of them, and quickly earning their second club from Searn, who felt their charm and ambition would be a good face for recruiting more members to the guild.

Each threw themselves down into a chair and grew silent. They usually chattered idly, but their sullen looks at the ceiling told Hanen they had something they intended to say.

They resorted to sighing after a time. Hanen looked up to see Stanis break the sudden eye contact with him.

"What do you want, Milu?" Hanen asked.

Stanis stood and walked over to the wall to stretch out his legs. He was the larger of the two, and often goaded Milu into doing the greater share of the work for him. He looked back at Milu, who gaped at Hanen, and gave the smaller man a look.

"We're looking for a contract," Milu said, hesitatingly. "We heard you had one down in the Grotto Market."

"I did have a contract for that area. Why are you asking about the Grotto again?" This was the third time they had asked for a job in that area specifically.

"Well," Stanis said, coming over to stand next to Milu. "It's the only place that stays warm in these winter months."

"Aren't you from here originally?"

"Yeah, so?"

"Then you should be used to the cold."

Milu ribbed Stanis, who turned with a fist, and stopped himself.

"Just tell him," Milu said.

Stanis chewed his lip and then said. "There's a girl. She hawks smoked fish."

"Why should that matter?" Hanen said. "You know that gets in the way of all contracts. Besides, I already gave the job to Rallia."

"It's just a low-level guard job," Milu said, his irritation starting to rise.

"And you're a low-level Sentinel," Hanen said. "If you don't find your own jobs and set up the contracts yourself, if you come and ask me for jobs that have come to my table, then you'll take the jobs I assign you."

"I'll let them have the job," Rallia said. "I took it because no one else wanted it."

"See?!" Stanis said. "She didn't even want it."

Hanen glared at Rallia, who shrugged back at him. Hanen shook his head, handed them the contract, and waved them off.

He turned back to his figures, seething inside. Rallia came over next to him.

"I didn't appreciate that," Hanen said.

"I could tell. I…"

"Rallia, you completely undermined me."

"Excuse me?"

"I was planning on establishing some authority over them, and now they both know I'll buckle if you're nearby to save them. You've made me out to be the bad guy, and you get to be the hero."

"Hanen."

"No, don't start. You spend all your time making friends with the others, shaving their ugly mugs, fraternizing, and here I am planning this big operation. What am I getting out of this? Certainly not their friendship. And certainly not their respect if you step in to save the day every time."

"Can you give me a chance to speak now?" Rallia said calmly.

"Fine. Say your peace." He turned back to the figures.

Rallia gave him a gentle slap on the back of his head. Hanen spun and took a wild swing. Rallia deftly stepped back and took a quarter-staff up off the wall. Hanen put his hands down.

"I'm not going to fight you, Rallia. It's not something I'll win."

"Fine. Put your figures down and look me in the eye while I say what I have to say."

She tossed Hanen a pole and they knocked them against each other.

"First, you're getting flabby. You're not taking on any contracts for yourself. You need to. It's the only way you're going to get fit and get in the good graces of the others. Secondly, you want to be leadership, so be leadership. You could have not given them that contract. You could have told them 'no' and I would have gone and done the job."

"And thirdly?"

"Thirdly?"

"Yes. You always have a third thing when you make a list."

"True. When does the contract for those two start?"

"Did you look at it when I first asked you to do it? It's this afternoon, why?"

"Then how about you and I go and establish a little authority and see they get to the job on time? Perhaps it'll give you a chance to see that girl of yours."

"She doesn't want to see me, though."

"Maybe she's cooled off since then."

Hanen took a swing, and Rallia lowered her guard and took the strike on her upper arm, wincing.

"That make you feel better?" Rallia asked.

"You lowered your guard, so the shot was cheap."

"But still, felt good, right? We're even now?"

Hanen gave a weak nod. Rallia smiled in response.

"We're even."

They walked down into the city and found lunch at an inn near the Grotto, then entered and looked at a few of the stalls.

Whisper moved from stall to stall, seeking out merchants he knew would give him scraps, and stealing a bite or two from those who didn't. Rallia gave Hanen a nudge, and Hanen looked up to see Stanis and Milu walking down the next aisle.

Hanen was grateful Rallia had suggested they not wear their own cloaks. Milu looked Hanen in the eye and didn't register it was him.

Stanis Bok walked down the row like a king. He wore both clubs on his belt, his cloak held open to show them off. Next to him, Milu had his hood up and held a single club in his hand, the ugly end in his left palm.

"They look like us when we first started out," Hanen said.

"We weren't so arrogant," Rallia said.

Both of the younger Sentinels took a piece of fruit off a cart and began walking away until the merchant called after them. Turning, Milu flipped a single penny at the man and made a rude gesture.

They turned and cut through several tents to walk toward the permanent shops across the Grotto from Alodda's, stepping up into a cabinet shop. They came out a few minutes later and stepped into the shop next to it. They came out of each with looks of self-satisfaction, looking each way before continuing on. The reedy boy outside the patisserie saw them coming and leapt up into the shop. Stanis ribbed Milu, and they both laughed as they watched the boy disappear, before goading each other to follow.

They walked into the sweets shop and disappeared. A few moments later they came out laughing, cake in their hands, eating the sweets with disgusting aplomb.

Hanen surged forward, but Rallia held him back for a few minutes before motioning they both go. Hanen turned to Whisper as Rallia reached for the door.

"Stay out here, boy," Hanen said to the ynfald. Whisper made himself comfortable, his scales rattling on the paving stones.

Inside a woman leaned against the wall behind the counter weeping. Her husband, covered in flour, comforted her. He looked up and saw the two standing there.

"We are closed. I am sorry." He spoke in a thick Œronzi accent.

"We did not mean to intrude," Hanen said, turning to leave.

Rallia stopped him.

"Is something wrong?" Rallia asked.

The man looked up. "If you ask, then you know. You saw. It's those shunting Black Cloaks. They come in every day."

"Sir, I've never known a Coin Cloak to be disrespectful."

"Then you must have family with them. Because ever since the Guildhall gave them their power, they've come back into town and been nothing but trouble."

"What kind of trouble?" Hanen asked.

"Are you not from here?"

"No. We're from Bortali."

"Those two boys in particular have been in here demanding protection pay from us every day. I heard of other places where merchants are feeling the strain from those ruffians, too. I don't know if I can tell them 'no' again. They are costing me money from the destruction they've done to us. My wife is distraught, my sons hide from them, and the Voktorra guild does nothing."

"We are sorry to hear that," Hanen said, "and we're sorry to have intruded."

They came back onto the street and saw Milu and Stanis stepping out of another shop down the lane.

"I'm going to take it out of them in pounds of flesh," Hanen seethed.

"Don't do anything drastic," Rallia said.

"What do you mean, 'don't do anything drastic'? They are ruining our good name. How many merchants have they roughed up? What are they costing us in coin? I'll make them bleed every penny back. Slowly. And surely."

The two young Sentinels moved from place to place, causing trouble. They were approached by a group of three Voktorra guard, whom the boys paid a handful of coin to, and they were left alone.

"Then it's the Voktorra, too," Rallia said. "We could speak to Captain Navien, and work together to staunch this."

"No. We take care of this alone. Inside of the Black Sentinels only, I mean."

The two young Sentinels arrived at the location of the contract Hanen had given them, and entered the glassblower, going about their business, as though nothing had happened.

"Will you continue to watch them?" Hanen said. "I need to go find Searn and tell him what happened."

Rallia agreed and settled herself in as Hanen walked away.

Searn sat at his own desk, a ledger in his hands. He saw Hanen and waved him in. Whisper curled up outside the door. He had quickly learned he wasn't welcome in Searn's area.

"Have a seat, Hanen."

"Thank you."

"Have we begun to gain some merchants for the first trip south in spring?"

"We have. Though it's been slowing down over the past week. I think I understand why now."

"Oh?"

"Rallia and I just followed those two newer Sentinels, Milu Gentry and Stanis Bok. They begged for a contract in the Grotto for the third time in the past week. Something didn't match up, so we followed them."

"And what did you uncover?"

"They're extorting the locals."

"That's not how we do things."

"No, it's not. It makes me wonder if others are doing the same."

"I can see how you've come to that conclusion. It has not been unheard of in the Sentinels before. Just look at what Captain Saliss did to you."

"Believe me, it's all I can think about. What can we do?"

"If the local law had brought it up, we'd usually turn them over."

"We watched them bribe a set of Voktorra, so I doubt we'll hear anything from them."

"Which means Captain Navien probably already knows, and is letting it proceed, if only to sully our name."

"What can we do, then?"

"Since we have discovered it ourselves, it allows us to deal with it in our own way."

"Which is?"

"Ostracize them, and we'll chop off a hand for stealing jobs from us."

"That seems reasonable," Hanen responded cooly.

"Quick to agree." Searn smiled. "You're angry."

"Of course I'm angry. It undermines our authority. It ruins our name."

"Good. Then see that it's done."

Hanen froze as he stood.

"What's the trouble?" Searn asked.

"You want me to do it?"

"Well, yes. You're leadership. You need to establish your authority. I'll call a meeting tonight, and you'll be exacting the punishment. It will send a message that if anyone else is doing the same, they stop. I have several other things I'm doing right now, or we could talk more about it. Thank you ahead of time for taking care of it."

Hanen stood and excused himself. Whisper followed him as he walked out of Blackiron and into the streets of the High Quarter. He walked away from the central greens and down the street of shops reserved for the gentry servants. It was devoid of the sound of industry, only the clink and rattle of goods being sold.

They came to a back street and Whisper turned down the dead-end row and disappeared into the shop at the end. Hanen sighed and followed the creature to see what trouble he was getting himself into.

As he passed the window, he saw a tall figure talking with the confectionary baker behind the counter. Hanen stepped around the corner and into the door. Both figures were looking at the ynfald, who sat in the middle of the floor staring at them.

"I was wondering where you went off to," the merchant said.

The other figure turned around. He was wearing a long cloak to keep warm, which kept his tail hidden, but there was no mistaking it was Ymbrys Veronia. His broad smile was visible through the scarves and his hood over his head. As always, he had the leather bound staff in his hand.

"Perhaps you're following me, or is it the other way around?" Ymbrys asked.

Hanen smiled. He walked up to Whisper and patted the ynfald's head. "Is he yours?" the merchant asked. "He's been coming here almost every morning for a few weeks now."

"Yes. I'm sorry if he's been causing trouble."

"No trouble. I always pay my debts to a luck-bringer. That boy loves his sugar. Now, master Veronia, you were saying about that sour powder of yours...."

"Ah, yes. I'd be willing to part with it. It's not a cheap spice, though."

"It comes from where exactly?"

"It's an acid harvested from the myramith. They are an arthropod that forms a major staple in our culture. Like the small myrms that live here. Though I've seen a few that grew as large as that ynfald there."

The merchant reached behind himself and pulled out two broken pieces of gingerbread. He tossed a piece to Whisper, who snatched it out of midair. He handed another piece to Hanen, who took his time with it. It was good.

"Perhaps I won't say exactly where the sour stuff comes from," the merchant said, "but it'll be a delight to watch the faces of those who try it. How much you want again?"

"I'll sell you a whole bag for a gold royal."

The merchant scoffed, though Hanen could tell it was a forced sound.

"That's unreasonable."

"It is what I'm asking."

"You'd need to give me something else for that kind of money."

"It's all I have left to sell this trip."

"Ah. So I'm your last stop. No one else wanted it, huh?"

"Precisely the opposite. In fact, the Silver Fish bought two of these bags."

"I doubt that. Gerrol doesn't do business with outsiders."

"Gerrol, I heard, has been up in bed for the better part of a month now. His son bought the bags."

"Very well. I know you aren't lying, then. I'll give you a Royal, but you have to buy a loaf of gingerbread, and ten candied meats."

"How much?"

"One dukt."

Ymbrys pulled out a silver dukt and placed it on the counter. The man took it and handed back a gold Royal, along with a large loaf of gingerbread and a small bag. He took the sack of powder, which fit in one hand, and turned to Hanen. "What can I do for you?"

"Actually, he's with me," Ymbrys said. "Shall we?"

Hanen nodded silently and followed Ymbrys out onto the street. Whisper followed closely behind.

"I hope he didn't take you for too much," Hanen said. "A dukt for a loaf of sweet bread and a handful of sugared meat? I wouldn't pay a tenth of that."

"Oh, I didn't mind. The Silver Fish bought the two bags for three Royals. I made out just fine in the end. How does business fare for the Black Sentinels in Mahn Fulhar?"

"I was going to ask you the same."

"I have little left to attend to; my goods are all sold. Now I'll see about buying some local northern herbs to sell in the south. Varea, I think, is next. The number of your Sentinels I've seen around the city is staggering. You seem well adjusted."

"What does that mean?"

"I mean to say, you look comfortable. As though the new authority suits you. When do you plan to head south again?"

"When spring breaks," Hanen replied.

"Perhaps I'll consider finishing off winter here and join you."

They walked a short way in silence. Whisper nudged Ymbrys for one of the sweets, which the qavyl obliged to give him.

"Do you enjoy traveling alone?" Hanen asked.

"I never travel alone."

"Oh. I'm sorry. I just assumed."

"I always have myself to keep me company." Ymbrys didn't laugh, but he had a glint in his eye. "Why do you ask, young Clouw?"

"I am becoming tired of people. I'm tired of being demanded of and not being appreciated."

"Demands? What demands?"

"Others are constantly asking for favors, and then finding themselves disappointed when I don't meet their needs. Have you ever been in a position of authority?"

The qavyl chuckled.

"I have indeed been in authority. It's why I often travel with only myself for company. I have my own agendas, which are better served by me. Those I consider close—even family—are far away now. It's best if I leave them out of my plans; they'd only meddle."

"That was why I came walking myself. I have something rather awful I've been tasked to do. I'm not sure if I'm ready."

"You humans often struggle with that, don't you? You are more ready than you think."

"Thank you. I needed to hear that."

"What is this task? If I may be so bold."

"Two of our number have been caught extorting. The penalty is the loss of a hand. I'm to deliver the justice."

"That is not justice. That is punishment."

"What do you mean?"

"Punishment is simply an immediate payment for a crime. Justice takes a long time to pay back. My own family suffered from the same problem a long time ago. We are still digging ourselves out of the debt we owe those our wayward members have hurt."

They came to stand by the aqueduct. Water flowed lazily down toward its waterfall into the grotto further along.

"You see, my family was forced to accept one into our circle. We all knew it was wrong, but we were curious as to his nature, and allowed him into our lives. Instead he sowed seeds that ripped my family in half. I was the eldest son. When my father did not act, I should have. But I was hesitant. My closest companion stood up to that willful creature, and attempted to exact punishment, but lost his own life in return. We're still picking up the pieces of that fateful day, when punishment wasn't enough. You'll have a long enough road ahead of you rebuilding your good names."

"And that is why we need to take care of the problem quickly, so that it doesn't grow."

"It seems your mind is made up, then," the qavyl said, crouching down to offer another sweet meat to the ynfald, muttering some platitude to the creature in his own tongue. As he stood, Ymbrys looked around. "This is where I leave you. When I need to travel south, I will seek you out."

Hanen gave the qavyl a respectful bow, and began the walk back to Blackiron, where he'd have to face what he had hoped to avoid.

20

Responsibilities

Tip, tip, tip,
> the tinker's tap.
Clank, clang,
> blacksmith's trade
Jin, Jin, Jin,
> monk's office.
Scratch, scratch
> clerk's coin made.
Nip, nip, nip,
> seamstress's thread
Clip, clip-clop
> paladin's ride,
Silence from Deceiver's Web.
> You cannot hide.

—AN OLD CHILDREN'S RHYME FROM MAHNDÜR

As Hanen entered Blackiron, he found himself staring at the backs of every Sentinel in Mahn Fulhar. Searn was speaking.

"There he is!" Searn said, beckoning Hanen to come to the front. Rallia stood nearby, her arms crossed as she glanced sideways at Milu and Stanis, who stood together, unaware that they were in any kind of trouble.

"The Paladins and Paladames left seven days ago," Searn said to Hanen as he came to stand next to him. "We're not entirely sure where they were off to, but they seemed ready to travel. I only just learned of this an hour ago."

"The monks, too?"

"We wouldn't be here if they were. We've got a contract to fulfill, after all. I may pay them a visit soon, to discuss the terms."

"Any other business I missed?"

"Not particularly, unless you have something you'd like to share with the group?"

The Sentinels had stopped paying attention and started chatting with their neighbors.

"I do, actually," Hanen said, more loudly than he had intended. "We have something rather important to discuss."

"You decided who goes on the first caravan?" one Sentinel asked.

"Er, no," Hanen said. "It's two full months away before we even leave. There's no rush to determine who is going with the first one."

"Well, if some of us are waiting for the second caravan," Stanis Bok said, "maybe we'd like to go elsewhere until then."

Hanen glared at the boy, and then held up a hand to silence everyone.

"That is not what I'm here to discuss. Now, the King himself allowed us to establish this office. We've been good to you, sharing jobs that we are not obliged to share. It has been beneficial to you, and to the Blackiron guildhall.

"That being said, we agreed to follow the local laws—what one of us does affects the good name of the others. People trust us with their lives. Those who go up against us are made to fear us and our professionalism. But the fact remains that there are those who have decided to take some matters further and take money from good, law-abiding people. This could and will sully the good name of the Black Sentinels. It is not something we can allow to continue."

He glanced around the room, and moved his eyes quickly over

Milu and Stanis, who were nodding solemnly. Hanen rolled his eyes internally.

"Fortunately, this came to my attention before the Voktorra found out, or we'd be dealing with turning over one of ours over to their authority. Instead we have the duty to deal with the problem ourselves. And so, it's fallen to me to deal with the culprits and take a hand from each one, removing them from our services. Rallia? Could you please bring them forward?"

Everyone looked for Rallia, including Milu and Stanis, who turned to see she was standing directly behind them. Before they could duck and run, Rallia grabbed their collars and shoved them to the ground in front of Hanen. They fell on their hands and knees and tried to stand and scramble away. Two other Sentinels stepped up and offered to hold the boys down.

"Rallia, please report what you saw," Searn asked.

"Hanen and I watched these two boys go into over five different businesses and rough up the merchants, demanding protection pay. We verified with the merchants that this occurred."

"Is this true?" Searn asked the two boys who were now shivering with fright.

"We weren't doing anything untoward," Milu said.

"It was just a bit of fun," Stanis said over the other.

"And what exactly is a bit of fun?"

"We wanted them to know how important the Sentinels could be."

"By roughing them up?" Searn asked sternly.

"We..." Milu said, and began choking up.

"We're sorry!" Stanis said and began sobbing wildly.

"What you did was theft, and makes you no better than a corrupt official demanding excessive taxes and keeping most for themselves. You'll be paying the Sentinels back for the loss of our good name, in gold and in the loss of your right hands."

They both started hollering. A Sentinel, Kalle Bann, threw a swift fist across Stanis' jaw. Milu shut his own mouth in response and began whimpering.

"This is not a simple warning," Hanen added. "You weren't just pushing someone around, getting caught with your first offense. You're Sentinels, with enough rank to be above all this.

"And this is a problem," Hanen looked back around the crowd. Kalle, standing over Stanis, gave a frown and nod to him as their eyes met. "A problem, I've come to learn, of many Sentinels in Mahn Fulhar. Across all Mahndür, I'd wager.

"And so," Hanen said. "The two of you will serve as a lesson. Exploiting people, extortion, vandalizing possessions, all of these put together amount to so much more than simple bullying."

Hanen's voice was shaking now with nervousness. Searn stepped up next to him. "And it is not something we will tolerate among the Sentinels."

Searn offered his own axe, a large double-bladed battle axe that he had brought with him from Haven in Limae. Hanen took it and held it in both hands, gripping it tightly.

Searn gave a nod to Kalle for Stanis to be brought forward. Aurín brought a block of wood over, with the help of the Limaean Diben Läur.

Stanis was forced down to his knees, and Searn came forward and tore the cloak off Stanis' back.

"If any of you wonder what authority we have to exact this punishment here and now," Searn said, "you are welcome to read the charter, which, by agreeing to take jobs from Blackiron and paying your dues, you declare you understand. Brigandry is crime, and extortion is brigandry."

He looked back at Hanen and gave a solemn nod.

"Stanis Bok," Hanen said, "you are guilty of misconduct, extortion, bullying, and theft from the Black Sentinels, both here in Mahn Fulhar, and beyond. Do you have any last words before we take your hand?"

Stanis sadly shook his head.

Hanen nodded and gritted his teeth. He glanced over at Rallia who looked on with a sense of horror in her eyes. The proceedings had obviously come as a surprise to her. Rallia slowly shook her head and looked away.

Hanen lifted the axe. Kalle Bann sat on the ground, pulling on the exposed arm of the boy not much younger than Rallia had been when they had both started as Sentinels. Hanen took a deep breath and dropped the axe. The hand came clean off. Stanis passed out.

Roaring filled Hanen's ears, and his vision began to tunnel. He could not hear himself speak, but he recalled repeating what he had said, this time to Milu. Milu's own hand fell to the ground just as easily. Hanen set the axe head on the ground and let go of the handle. He heard it clatter in deafening brilliance.

The voices of everyone began to clamor. He walked out of Blackiron and into the quickly falling night. He became weak at the knees and steadied himself on a barrel. The tunnel vision cleared, and the world came back into clarity before he suddenly, and violently, vomited across the ground.

Several Voktorra lounging nearby laughed at him. Someone put a hand on his shoulder.

"Hanen?" Rallia said. "What was that all about?"

"Not now, Rallia."

"No. We need to talk about this."

"I said not now, Rallia."

He stood and walked off into the night. Whisper followed to keep him company, though he seemed to give Hanen a wider berth than usual.

The night had been a clear and very cold one. Hanen walked the streets until morning, and didn't return until well after the gray of dawn had fully bleached the clouds that rolled in before daybreak.

When he came back to Blackiron, Rallia was outside practicing her morning drills with her staff. She stopped as Hanen approached, and looked at her older brother.

"I've been waiting for you to return all night," Rallia said.

"You didn't need to."

"I did. I thought of following you, but you obviously needed time to yourself. Shall we go find some food?"

Hanen nodded.

He followed Rallia, who knew of a bakery that opened early. The wife of the baker kept a clean kitchen in the back and made other morning foodstuffs. They each got bacon and eggs cooked into the center of rolls of bread. There was a cör in the upper window that Whisper ignored once the mistress of the bakery tossed him a scrap of meat skin.

They walked along the cold streets in silence until they had finished their food.

"I did what was necessary. What was asked of me," Hanen said.

"I understand," Rallia said.

"Do you?" Hanen asked, stopping in his tracks. "You are always so agreeable, and amiable about everything. Do you have any thoughts of your own? Don't you have an opinion on the matter?"

"I've always trusted you to make the right decision," Rallia said. "There is no need to get upset with me."

"But I don't even know if they are the right decisions when I make them."

"That's what growing up is all about, Hanen. I think you got our father's wisdom when it comes to these matters."

Hanen shook his head. "Our father had the worst luck in the world. I think the only good quality that man had was patience. And that's what you ended up with."

Rallia ignored the comment, as she often did when people complimented her. And more importantly, she let the insult Hanen gave to their father roll off her back. "Searn has asked me to take a job, so I'll be leaving today."

"What job?"

"I'm supposed to go check something out in the west. He asked me to do it to test my qualities, he said. And I've a message to deliver, so that will be part of it. That's why I waited for you to return; I didn't want to leave with words unspoken. You'd think I was leaving angry. Last night—that was awful to watch."

"It...it was. But it was necessary."

"I suppose," Rallia said. "The city would have hung them for theft."

"Where are you traveling to?" Hanen asked.

"Due west. I guess there is a farmstead kept by an old retired Sentinel."

"Alright. I'll keep an ear out for news from there, in case something happens."

"I'll be back in a couple of weeks. In the meantime, I thought you ought to keep an eye on Kalle Bann."

"Kalle? Why?"

"Did you see how quick he was to help you out last night?"

"Someone had to."

"But after you left, the kegs were tapped, and he was very audible of his support of what you did."

"Again, I don't see the issue."

"I mentioned before you needed to spend more time getting to know the other Sentinels. Kalle is one of the rowdiest Sentinels I know. Quick to goad a fight. First to tell some ribald story. Self-righteousness is not a character trait of his. I think he was covering for himself."

"I'll look into it."

"You probably ought to look at the other locals, too—Diben Läur and Sälla Fyfe."

"And everyone else for that matter," Hanen muttered.

"But also," Rallia said, "be careful."

"I will," Hanen said.

When they arrived at Blackiron, Rallia double-checked her gear and left without another word.

Hanen went looking for Searn. Not finding him in his small, haphazard office, he took a look at some of the books Searn had sitting on his shelf. Surprisingly, he found a paladinial book of prayer. He leafed it open and saw Searn had made notations on the pages. It was marked as being owned by a Paladin named Roderig.

"Well done last night," Searn said from the doorway.

"I apologize," Hanen said, putting the book back in its place. "I came looking for you, and your books piqued my interest."

"Ah," Searn said, taking a seat behind the table. He motioned for Hanen to sit.

"Where is Rallia off to?" Hanen asked.

"I've got an important assignment for her, and she's the only one I trust who is capable of doing it. As the highest ranked Black Sentinel Runner, she's the best suited for the job, too."

"You probably ought to have consulted me," Hanen said.

"Why? I'm in charge. The two of you, siblings though you may be, are of equal status. I figured you'd tell each other anyway."

"But what's the assignment?"

"It's really not your concern."

"I think it is," Hanen said.

"Insubordination? It's not like you," Searn said, grinning smugly.

"Honestly, Searn, I'm tired of you asking me to continually distance myself from others by taking on authoritarian tasks, and then keeping me in the dark like I'm some sort of lackey."

"Showing your spine, finally? Sometimes you remind me of myself."

Searn poured a glass of wine for each of them and handed one to Hanen.

"I had something stolen from me several years ago. Almost everything I have done, every decision I've made, has been to gain the object back. Rallia is being sent to scout out its last location."

"What is the item?"

"Well, you may not think much of me if I just tell you without background. So let me go into a bit more detail. You see, as a young man I was a Paladin of the Hammer."

"Wait, what?"

"Yes. I joined the Paladins of the Hammer when I was young. I took the Vow of Silence. That book over there? Mine. My name was Roderig. I was given to scholarly pursuits, and I became quickly disenchanted with the Paladins. I felt that they were misleading humanity at the will of the gods."

"I didn't think you believed in the gods."

"I never said they didn't exist. I have said they are petty and abuse humanity at their own whim. Again, it's at their whim. I left the Paladins."

"Wait," Hanen said, "you can't just leave the Paladins. No one can."

"It took some doing," Searn said. "They think me dead. Anyway, I left with an interesting book I found in the depths of their library. I don't know how it got there, but it did. The cover was made of bone, and its text read of a way to throw off the shackles of divinity. Why the gods never sought to destroy it, I do not know, but with it I was able to begin a great undertaking. I discovered a way to keep the gods from controlling me."

"And the book, you stole it?"

"Yes, along with the object I began crafting. I became a Sentinel in Varea and began working on a project."

"And what was that?"

"It's called a boneshroud. Mostly, it's crafted from the bones of animals, blood from livestock, that sort of thing. But it was stolen from me, as I said, right before I met the two of you. It was why I was traveling in Temblin—to pursue the thief. I believe that thief has been continuing to craft this boneshroud, but he's begun using human blood and bone."

Hanen shivered. "That's awful. And you've sent Rallia to go looking for it?"

"No. She's simply going to see if the person I believe has taken it is where I think he is."

"Who took it?"

"A Paladin. Or, I should say, several Paladins. There is a group within the Paladins called the Order of the Feather, or Moteans, or something like that. I believe they have an even more sinister plan to unveil."

"Wait just a moment. This shroud. It sounds... wrong to me. Using bones? Blood? That doesn't sound right, regardless of whether it's made with animal or human. That sounds like some mythical dark sacrifice."

"There is more to it than that," Searn said, "but that's the summary. There is too much to it to go into greater detail."

"But why make this thing? What does it do that is worth your having faked your own death to craft it?"

"The gods can get into your mind and take control of it. Someone wearing the boneshroud would be unaffected by them."

"I get the sinking feeling you've sent Rallia on a mission more dangerous than she realizes. I need to go after her and help her."

"No. I need you here."

"Searn, my sister is walking into a death trap."

"I said no. And that's final. I suspect there are other Sentinels committing crimes equal to, or greater than those two boys. If we don't stay on top of it we'll risk the whole organization collapsing."

Hanen stood there, speechless.

"Please begin your investigation of the other Sentinels immediately."

"It will make me their enemy."

"It will make you their leader."

Hanen left, unable to comprehend what he had just learned. He went to his maps and figures and stared at them the rest of the day in order to look busy while he considered the facts as Searn had presented them.

As the day came closer to close, Ophedia del Ishé sauntered into Blackiron. Whisper padded over to greet her and received a scratch on the back of his skull. Once she finished, she came and stood opposite Hanen

"Do you have any ready work I could have?" she asked.

"Hrm?" he said, coming out of his thoughts. "Oh. Yes. What kind of work do you want?"

"It doesn't matter, really. I'm not looking to join Rallia's Runners."

"I've got a few single days as guards of clients who are considering joining the caravan in the spring. As long as you behave yourself, those will be both good for you, and for me."

"When are they?"

Hanen handed her both contracts. "One is tomorrow and the other starts a few days later."

She took them and turned to leave.

"Ophedia," Hanen asked. "How long had you been with Searn when we met you?"

"Four months? Why?"

"He tells me he's been searching for something that was stolen from him."

She spun and looked at Hanen with a look of confusion and suspicion.

"Stolen?" she asked.

"Yes. He mentioned it was stolen years ago. Did he ever go off investigating something?"

She relaxed. "Well, he was always off at strange hours doing this or that."

"So he was investigating? Seeking?"

"I suppose that makes sense. It wasn't my place to ask. I've never questioned him, because he's always been good to me."

"What do you mean by that?"

"Well, he's a handsome enough man and he's had his dalliances, but he never pressed his advantage on me. I appreciate that in someone. Enough of you let your wandering eye fall on me..." She returned to lean on the table, looking up from under her dark, red-tinged black hair. It was not accidental that her blouse was too loose, and too easy to see down. Hanen looked up at what he would consider the most inopportune moment, blushed, and looked away.

"I...Ophedia. Uh, could you..."

"What?" she asked. "All the other men in Blackiron have their eye on me. Don't you?"

"I'm not sure what to say," Hanen said. "I'm not saying that you're not easy to look at, but that just doesn't feel appropriate. I mean, you're not much older than a kid."

"But you admit I'm older than a kid."

She blew her hair out of her face, stood up, and, while she didn't think he was glancing her way, she readjusted herself and tied up the string at the top of her blouse. "I supposed you've been a gentleman. You always have."

Under her breath she said, "Not that you needed to be; others certainly haven't hesitated."

"What is that supposed to mean? Wait, have you been hurt?"

She laughed in her rich contralto voice. "No, I haven't been hurt. I've sent a few of the men around here limping off, though. I can take care of myself. I'm not some sweet, innocent, foolish barmaid anymore."

"We all grow up. Some faster than others."

He turned to look back down at his work, hoping to brush past the embarrassment of her advance.

"Ophedia," Hanen said, his ears burning hot. "I hope I've not just offended you."

"Offended me?" Ophedia laughed. "No, I'm not offended. A little put off, but..." she looked at him with dark, piercing eyes, realization dawning in them. "There's someone else, isn't there?"

"Uh...no," Hanen offered weakly.

"Alright," she said. "Now you and I are even. I feel better knowing there is another. What's her name?"

Hanen stood up and walked over to fill a tankard with ale. Aurín Mateau entered and approached the hearth to stoke the fires and prepare to cook for those who came looking for a meal.

"Hanen," Aurín said in acknowledgement.

"Aurín," Hanen returned.

"Ophedia," Hanen said, looking back at the girl's arched eyebrows. "Could you come over here?"

She walked over, stood behind Aurín, and looked Hanen in the eyes, confusion on her face, then, giving a knowing look, indicated toward Aurín. Hanen shot a look back, and shook his head, and mouthed the word "no."

She shrugged and looked away, her disinterest growing.

"I need some help from the two of you," Hanen said. "Aurín, you have everyone's bellies under your control, and Ophedia, you are familiar with nearly all of the men in the Sentinels."

"Well, I'm chatty with all of them," Ophedia offered. "It's the men, mostly, who get familiar with me."

Aurín shot Ophedia a glance, and then back at Hanen, then back to his cauldron.

"Regardless," Hanen said. "I need your eyes and ears."

"You're talking about last night's incident," Aurín said.

"That was something else," Ophedia said. "And very unexpected."

"Yes," Aurín said, "it got others talking."

"What about?"

"The Black Sentinels," Ophedia said, "Searn. You and Rallia. They think things are changing too fast."

"But what about me and Rallia?"

"They don't understand why the two of you are being moved so quickly into leadership. Some of them have been at this for years." She paused. "I tell you this because it's what I'm hearing. Some of them don't realize I was apprenticed to Searn. So they don't know I'm not just some dumb girl with curves."

"And that's why I need your help. They may not like that I've been made Captain, but I have. And Searn wants me to root out those who are of the same mindset as Milu and Stanis."

"I don't want to be singled out," Aurín said. "You don't name me as part of your investigation. They'd all stop eating my food and giving me coin for it."

"I understand," Hanen said. "Ophedia, will you help?"

"If that's what Searn is asking for, then I'll help. Everything has changed for the better since I joined up with Searn. And since you and Rallia entered the picture, it seems like I've been in all the right, and all the weirdest, places. I don't believe in fate, but I'm not going to insult it if it buys me a free dinner."

"Where do you want us to start?" Aurín asked.

"At first, just listen. See what you can pick up. I'd especially keep an eye out on those who are from here, or recently returned to town. Keep a log of where they say they like to visit. In three days' time we meet at the Ship Tack Inn, where we first stayed when we arrived. I'll buy you both dinner."

"Fair enough," Ophedia said. "Now, I'm off to gossip, and see if I can't figure out who it is you fancy."

She marched out of Blackiron, whistling to herself.

"What was that about?" Aurín asked.

"She made an advance on me," Hanen said.

"She's had her eye on you, since Edi."

"Really?"

"I wager you turned her down, though?"

Hanen nodded.

"Because you have your eye on that girl in the Grotto."

"Did Rallia tell you that?"

Aurín shook his head. "You're not the only Sentinel in the city, Hanen. I saw you down there visiting the girl a ways back. She's attractive. I don't blame you." He turned back to his cooking. "I've got to give this stew a bit of concentration now, if you don't mind."

Hanen excused himself and pulled on his cloak. Whisper gave Aurín's cooking a look of longing before joining Hanen and following him out the door and into the frosty air.

21

Cleaning the Wound

The guard stood 'pon the tollway,
To keep him from his road.
Path's champion asked for payment,
    He paid the dire toll,
        And onward did he stroll.

—THE TRAVELER

Hanen begrudged that he had no clothes other than his black shirt and leggings. The cast-off brown cloak he had on his shoulders provided some warmth, but he missed the Sentinel Cloak and its ability to block the movement of air, especially as he walked on the streets of the sky-exposed North Hill. The smell of tanning leathers certainly didn't improve the situation, and he hoped the Mütse Buckleshop was further along, and not near the stench of the tannery and its fetid out-pourings that ran into the street and down the backside of the hill towards the sea.

The frost-covered brass hanger up ahead told him he was arriving, and that the tannery would still be noticeable from the shop.

He stepped under the lintel of the shop and looked down the long room. Ten work stations, occupied by workers of various ages, tinkered away at brass fittings in front of them. A counter at the front was occupied by a woman a few years younger than Hanen. She wore a leather vest with buckles holding it tight across her middle. Her hair was up in braids. She looked tired, and gave a wane smile to Hanen as he approached.

"Good day, sir," she said.

"Hello," Hanen said. "I'm looking to speak to a Goev?"

She popped an eyebrow, then frowned. "What do you want with Goev?"

"Only to speak to him."

"My h...he's not here."

"I can come back another time," Hanen said.

"It may be some time before he's back here. He broke his arm."

"I'm very sorry to hear that."

An older man with broad arms walked up, wiping his hands down with a cloth.

"Who is this, Velli?" the man said through a thick beard.

"He's looking to speak with Goev."

"Planning on taking another cut of flesh from my boy, huh Sentinel?"

The man was in front of the counter now. Several others stopped what they were doing, and stood.

"Excuse me?" Hanen said.

"You're that Sentinel from the Guildhall," the master said. "You don't have the cloak on, but I recognize you in those black clothes. And that black ynnie was following you around then, too."

Hanen glanced back. Whisper had followed him again.

"You were supposed to stay with Aurín," Hanen chided. The ynfald gave his tail a few clattering flops on the ground.

Hanen looked back. Four men stood behind their master.

"I'll ask again," the man said. "What else do you want with my son?"

"Master Mütse," Hanen said, holding up one hand, and, with the other, opening his cloak to show he was unarmed. "If you recognize me, then you know what rank I hold in the Black Sentinels, and what position of authority I sit in at our guildhall. It has only recently come to light that there are members of my group bullying city folk, and I am personally looking into this, in order to rectify the situation."

The man crossed his arms and leaned back on one heel.

"I am here to find out just what happened, and who it was that thought it alright to demand protection pay."

"He did more than that!" The woman behind the counter screeched. Hanen and Master Mütse looked over at the hot tears streaming down her face.

"Velli," the man said, "let's let the man talk. Perhaps he can help."

"What help can you give? How can you pay back what was stolen?"

"Two nights ago," Hanen said, "I exacted punishment from two of my Sentinels. They're missing their right hands now. I plan to do the same to whoever it was that harmed your husband."

"I will tell you exactly what we told the Voktorra that came sniffing around for the same reason. My son has been pushed around by this Sentinel before. The man left as Goev's coin dried up in early autumn, but came back after your guild charter was established. Goev had no choice but to return to work for me. The Sentinel found Goev out and confronted him at a tavern a couple nights ago. Perhaps that very night you say you punished the other Sentinels?"

"That ruffian shunt," Velli interrupted, "got my husband drunker than ever, and then took him out back and beat him. Broke his good arm. Nearly crushed his eye. The doctors expect he won't see from that eye again."

"Who was it?"

"Kalle Bann," the girl spat.

Hanen nodded.

"How did you know to come and look for Goev?" the man asked.

"A mutual friend of Velli's told me."

"You're the Sentinel?" Velli said, coming around the counter. "The one that's been hanging around Alodda?"

Hanen looked at Velli, surprised that she had drawn that conclusion. He nodded.

"If you're looking to do the same to Alodda and her father's shop as that Kalle Bann did to my husband, then by Wyv-Thüm, I'll see that every woman on this street visits you in your sleep with a leather strap, and I'll personally pull the bag over your head before we toss you into the smoke house to dry into a lump of meat."

The master put a hand on Velli's shoulder, and pulled her back.

"The wives of Tanner Street are a very loyal gaggle," he chuckled. The smile disappeared from his face. "But very serious when they make threats by the name of the Judge."

"I understand," Hanen said, "and I can assure you, I mean no harm to Alodda or anyone else. I want to see justice done."

"Then see Kalle Bann made to fear," the woman said.

"May I ask why the threats you leveled at me weren't leveled at Kalle?"

"Believe me," the master said, "the threats were made, but that Voktorra came by yesterday. He heard her accusation and threat of vengeance, and asked she refrain for a time."

"What was the name of the Voktorra, if I may?"

"He was a charming man," Velli said. "A well-kept beard, gray uniform. I don't recall his name."

"He's the right-hand man of the Voktorra Master," Master Mütse said. "A Captain."

"Navien," Hanen said.

"Yes," they both said, nodding.

Hanen offered a hand to Master Mütse.

"Thank you for you information. Will you please draft up the costs and expenditures Sentinel Bann has accrued? Both in theft, and in medical bills for Goev? Our guild owes you and your family a weregild."

Master Mütse nodded. "Watch yourself, Sentinel. And don't let that man get the upper hand."

"I'll try not to," Hanen said. He looked to Velli. "I'm going to see your husband's injuries to his person and pride answered."

"Thank you," Velli said, bowing her head.

* * *

Night fell, and Hanen took food at Blackiron, hoping that Kalle might return amidst the crowd of other Sentinels, so he would have numbers to back him up when he made his accusation. He never came. The next morning the only other Sentinel sleeping off a hangover in the hall was Sälla Fyfe.

She poured herself an ale and sat sullenly in a chair, and took sips, wincing at the pain in her skull.

"May I sit with you?" Hanen asked, approaching with his own tankard.

She looked up with squinting eyes, and gave a nod.

"Late night, huh?" he asked.

She gave him a frown.

"I didn't see Kalle Bann last night, though."

"Haven't seen him since that night you took those boys' hands," she responded.

"No," Hanen agreed, "I haven't either. Do you know where he usually roosts?"

She laughed, then winced. "Funny you should say roosts. He is definitely a silvered cockatrice."

"Why do you say that?"

"He is a lot of bluster," Sälla said, leaning forward, "but he's also got a mean cockspur if you get him in a corner."

"Good to know," Hanen said, sitting back and pondering.

"You thinking of backing him into a corner?"

"I might have to."

"Good. He's nothing but trouble."

"How so?"

"You took the hands of those boys. But you know where they learned it from?"

"I'm going to guess it's the silvered cockatrice."

She pointed at Hanen and then to her temple, wincing at the touch.

"Do you know where I can find him?"

"Nowhere you'd want to go," she said.

"Bad part of town, then?"

"His brother owns an inn down on Dockside. It doesn't even have a name. But you can find it if you look around."

Hanen stood up.

"Are you going down there right now?"

"As hungover as you are," Hanen said, "I'm hoping that Kalle will have been sucking down his brother's cheap sailor grog. I have to hope he's at least as hungover as you."

"I'd love to come and watch, but my friend here—" she raised her tankard, "—tells me that might be bad for my health."

Hanen stood, pulled his cloak over his shoulders, put both axes in his belt, took up his crossbow and the case of ten bolts, and walked to the door. He gave a quick whistle and Whisper leapt up from his place before the fire and padded to his side.

"Everyone says you bring luck," he said, looking down into the eyes of the creature. "I hope that's true. Because I'll need it today."

Hanen had spent his childhood following his father to dockside inns and crate-strewn streets to look for work as a net mender, or to deliver finished goods. Half the time they made him watch as sailors gave his father a quick beating and half the money they had promised him for his labor.

The inn owned by Kalle Bann's brother was seedier than any tavern in Garrou. The squat building had been whitewashed at some point, but it had faded, and the filth that encrusted it matched the smell that emanated from the door, left open in the night. The way the door hung, it had likely not closed for years. The smell of stale beer and urine would have made Hanen gag if those same childhood memories hadn't toughened him to it.

As he stepped into the dark space, he heard the mutter of a drunk, passed out on a table. No one stood behind the bar, and the fire in the small hearth had reduced to cooling embers.

He thought he saw a total of three figures sleeping off their evening reverie. He put the crossbow down on the ground, and put a boot in the stirrup, pulled back, and then placed a bolt in the saddle.

"Kalle," Hanen said. "Kalle Bann?"

He heard a quick succession of sounds as someone quickly stood up off the ground.

"Who is it?" the man said. "I can only see your figure," Kalle said. "Another Coin Cloak?"

"Kalle," Hanen said, preparing to give the speech he had rehearsed. "It's Hanen Clouw. I'd like to talk to you."

"I wondered if you might," Kalle said. "Someone squeaked, huh?"

"What do you mean?" Hanen said.

"Heh..." the man chuckled. "Crossbow and an ynfald," he said. "You think that'll be enough, huh?"

"Let's talk," Hanen said. "We can step outside and talk like reasonable men."

"I don't reason to someone holding a crossbow bolt aimed at my heart."

Whisper began shivering his scales at Hanen's side.

"And my brother in particular doesn't like it either."

The drunk next to Hanen suddenly stood up and tackled Hanen from the side. The bolt shot off and into the rafters as Hanen and the man fell to the ground together.

Hanen looked up at the man on top of him, the spitting image of Kalle, but with a face covered in nasty scars.

The first fist fell and Hanen moved his head to the side, and it hit the stone.

"Son of a bitch!" the man swore. Then his cry of pain was met by another, higher pitched one.

The man threw himself off Hanen.

"Get the mongrel off me!" The man cried. Kalle was laughing as he came across the room and took hold of Whisper, throwing him toward the hearth. Then he turned to Hanen, who was scrambling backward across the floor.

"Thought you'd just come down here while I was drunk and make your threats? Never thought to ask how well I hold my liquor, did you?"

He took hold of Hanen's cloak and pulled him up onto his feet.

"Nocc," the man said, "you're no fighter."

Fear welled up in Hanen's throat as Kalle pulled a nasty dagger out of his belt. "Your sister isn't even in town. I can put a few nice-looking scars on your face, and have you off the end of the pier in an hour, and no one will miss you."

"He'll welcome the embrace of the water and the Judge after we're done with him," the tavern keep said. "I have a new rope knot I've been wanted to try on someone's knees. It's supposed to separate the joints when you tighten it down."

"That'd be fun," Kalle said. "Then we can go and see who it was who squealed. You been talking to those buckle makers? Or maybe that girl you fancy in the Grotto."

Rallia often spoke of times when she was training to fight, when someone struck her on the knuckles, and a pain shot through her hand, and buried itself deep into her heart like a dagger of ice. Any hesitation she felt seethed out through that quickly numbing bruise on her fingers, and was replaced by a warm anger, pulsing through her blood that fed the need to break the offender's will.

Hanen watched with interest as his hand shot out and hit Kalle's chin. The man stepped back in surprise, and Hanen matched his stride, his other hand slapping his exposed throat.

Kalle swung out with his knife just as his heel caught a fallen chair, and he tumbled backward.

"You little shunt," Kalle's brother said.

He jumped over the fallen Kalle, drawing a knife from his belt as he did so. Hanen had his own axe out and screamed in rage, raising it to block the wrist of the knife coming down over him. He charged into the man and lifted with his shoulders. The man fell over and onto the ground, and Whisper was suddenly in the man's face. Hanen struggled to his feet and ran into two drunks who were not fully roused. They swore as they tried to rise to their feet, whether to join the fight, or to get out of the way, Hanen didn't know. He rushed the table and pulled up on it, removing the stability of the two drunks. They tumbled to the ground in a heap.

Someone hit Hanen from behind, and he spun, a move he had seen Rallia perform several times. Kalle had his knife up again and rage filled his eyes.

"I'm gonna cut you!" he screamed.

Hanen took steps backwards, his own vision resolving back to clarity, just as he lost his own footing. His hand grasped for something to hold onto and got the collar of Kalle's shirt in his grip. They both fell to the ground. A stabbing pain tore through Hanen's arm, and Kalle's hot, stinking breath made him wretch as the man grimaced with malice.

Kalle turned the knife in his grip, and had himself in a straddled position over Hanen.

His brother stumbled over, taking hold of Hanen's arms, pulling them above his head.

"Now," Kalle said. "Let's see what kind of squealing we can get out of you before I go and do the same to the blonde girl in the Grotto."

Hanen roared in frustration, as the knife came down by his throat, and the malice turned to a dark grin.

"What the Nocc?" the barkeep holding his arms shouted. Kalle's face contorted, and a small spatter of blood hit Hanen's face from the bolt that came through the man's throat.

The other man scrambled to his feet before two more bolts hit him in the chest. Kalle fell over, clutching at his throat and gagging. Hanen looked up past the dying man to see the three figures in the door.

"Rallia?" he croaked. "Searn?"

"Not Rallia," the voice said.

Captain Abenard Navien approached and held out a hand to help him up.

"For a man who makes a living as a guard, you're very unaware of your surroundings," Abenard said. "I was staking this tavern out when you sauntered up and walked in to accost the criminals that usually frequent places like this."

"Why didn't you come in sooner?"

"I wanted to make sure my fellow Voktorra here were ready. And, I don't mind you getting roughed up a bit, first."

"Thanks," Hanen said flatly. "How did you know to come here?"

"I have been keeping an eye on Kalle since I heard the report from the buckle makers. Looks like you did too?"

"I've been investigating members of our guild who have been acting outside the law. I had hoped to take care of it quietly."

"Without we Voktorra here getting in the way."

Hanen nodded.

"Well, I'll be taking credit for this one. And it'll give me an edge when it comes to making demands of you and Searn. But you're alive, so I think you'll allow that."

"It's not like I have much choice."

"No, you don't. I still want to see your guild disbanded. But I respect you for taking matters into your own hands and trying to rectify the situation."

"I'll make a deal with you," Hanen said.

"What's that?"

"Report what you want. I'll even agree with whatever you say transpired here. But I have to ask you a favor."

"I saved your life today. Why should I do you a favor?"

Hanen ignored the remark. "Do you know the Dülar tailor in the Grotto?"

"Of course."

"Will you go and tell them what transpired? What really happened? You can say you saved my skin, but tell them I came here to stop the Sentinel harassing the Mütses?"

Navien laughed. "You like the girl."

Hanen grimaced. "She puts the blame of these few Sentinels on me. And I'd like her to know I did something about it."

"I'll think about it."

"I'll owe you one."

* * *

The light of the Ship Tack Inn burned bright as the sun set behind the city. Hanen could see Ophedia and Aurín sitting at the table by the window. He crossed the street and dropped his hood as he pushed the door in. The man behind the bar gave him a wave and a smile of recognition, and turned to pour him a beer. Hanen took the tankard from the man, walked across the room, and sidled into the seat next to Ophedia.

"Where have you been?" Aurín asked.

"Down in the city, why?"

"The other Sentinels," Aurín whispered, "they're getting hungry for more work. They've been grumbling that you haven't been providing enough for them."

"This is Edi all over again," Hanen said.

Aurín shrugged.

Hanen took a deep breath. "I suspect some of that may quickly die out, if we wait."

"Why is that?"

"This morning I set off early and found Kalle Bann."

"What did you do?" Ophedia asked, turning to consider him.

Hanen told them what happened and described how he helped the Voktorra remove the bodies, dumping them off the pier the same way Kalle had intended to do to him.

"Honestly," Ophedia said, raising her own mug, "I didn't think you had it in you."

"What?" Hanen asked.

"The ability to confront Kalle."

"I can't stand true injustice. I couldn't stomach him doing what he was doing."

"To the enemies of Hanen Clouw," Aurín said. "May they know better than to cross him, and may they flee before his wrath."

"Hear, hear," Ophedia called, pouring the remainder of her drink down her throat.

22

Trials and Shadows

His touch is but a feather upon our soul. Yet the weight of his mote is an anchor, from which we draw stability. And the seeds of power.

—PATER MINORIS IKAH SHON,
KNOWN TO HIS FOLLOWERS AS PATER PINION

"Go and notify the Prima Pater of our arrival," Jined called to the Paladin standing outside the bastion. Priests gawked as the three of them led the long line of captives, shivering in their brown robes, past their cathedral.

The Paladin standing guard had not moved.

"Inform the Prima Pater," Jined started again. The Paladin instead marched toward them.

"What are you doing?" Dane growled.

"I have returned with these prisoners in tow from a long, cold road. If you're not going to do as I asked and let the Prima Pater and Pater Segundus Guess know of our arrival, at least open up the stables."

Dane turned and rushed toward the door and opened it, ushering them in, while watching the Abecinians closely.

"These aren't prisoners," Dane said, "these are fellow Paladins."

"You're observant," Jined replied. He took hold of the chain of three men attached to Loïc's sleipnir and attached it to the end of the chain of men behind his own mount.

"You can't bring Paladins to our own Bastion in chains in broad daylight. The Monks of Aben are going to speak of this. The people of the city!"

The twins guided their own sleipnirs to stalls and began unsaddling them.

"Go and announce our arrival," Jined repeated.

"Tell me why you've brought these members of our order here in chains," Dane said, crossing his arms.

"That is none of your business," Jined said calmly.

"By Grissone, it is my business," Dane said. "If you've brought Paladins here in chains, as guard on duty, it is my job to protect the bastion. Perhaps these men are innocent, and *you've* been turned from the faith, to rain evil upon us all."

Jined laughed. "Dane Marric, your haughty disdain for me blinds you. You saw the miracle performed when I took on a second Vow. Even if you don't believe it divinely ordained, wouldn't you think that I had drawn more than my fair share of attention from our god by taking on a second Vow? Don't you think he would not only keep a closer eye on me, and bring wrath down on me if I've somehow turned against him?"

"Perhaps he only waited to let someone truly faithful perform the act of judgment."

"Dane Marric," Jined said, standing tall and rigid, "what we do with these prisoners, and why we escort them in chains, is not your concern. End this paltry squabbling, and do as I command, as Brother Adjutant, your superior, and march to Pater Segundus Guess and inform him of our arrival. We are to conduct a Pillory in the back garden, immediately. If you do not comply to this order, I'll see you tried under the same crimes as these men here: Murder, heresy, and the same sin you were found guilty of before—blasphemy."

Dane's eyes grew in horror, and he turned to leave at a sprint.

Jined turned to see Brother Merun still sitting atop his own Sleipnir.

"He doesn't seem to like you."

"Nor I him," Jined said, "but if Grissone wants us to continue to work alongside one another, who am I to question his will?"

Once the twins and Merun had seen to their animals, they led the way through the complex, Jined holding the chain—the other three taking up the rear behind their prisoners. They walked through the wide central hall of the Bastion, the Paladins there watching them pass with morbid curiosity, to the garden against the outer walls.

The local flock of black gryphs sat perched upon a large oak tree standing in the center and crowed at them as they took flight. Jined instructed the men attached to one another by the chain in his hand to drop to their knees. They shivered in the cold and seethed in anger toward their oppressor. Jined handed the end of the chain to Brother Merun, the twins standing alongside him, and then turned to the side door into the offices of the Bastion leadership. As the door opened, Dane was reaching to come out into the garden. Jined held a hand up for him to stop. Dane sneered, and then, peaking over Jined's shoulder, saw the prisoners there.

"That is far enough," Jined said.

"I shall go there, if I please."

"The Pillory shall be conducted by the leaders of our order, and only those present at the incident at St. Nonn."

"I am a guardian of the order."

"And you have performed perfunctorily, by delivering my order. Your service is done, and you are dismissed."

Dane opened his mouth to speak.

"Thank you very much, Brother Marric," Pater Segundus Pír said. "Please go and assist Brother Aeger in the library."

Dane gave a nod to the Pater Segundus and turned to storm off.

Nichal came out of the office and closed it behind him.

"Brother Upona prepares the Prima Pater," he said. "What happened, Jined?"

"In short, St. Nonn was under the command of a unit of heretics. They killed the Primus in command there, imprisoned his acolyte, and then tried to kill the twins and me."

"Very well," Gallahan said. "Let us be about our business."

He pushed past Jined, a tome under his arm. Nichal motioned for Jined to help him take up a table from the hall, and together they carried it out to place under the tree. Nichal gave a signal for the twins to bring seats.

Gallahan Pír took a seat at a table under the rustling boughs of the tree, the winter's leaves clinging for their lives and awaiting their spring fall. Nichal paced back and forth under the tree, the acorns littering the ground crunching underfoot as he observed each of the men before him. Jined, the twins, and Brother Silas Merun stood guard behind the heretics on the ground.

"Please have them state their names for the record," Gallahan said to Nichal as he opened up the heavy book and took the top off an inkwell next to him.

Nichal marched up to the first man. Like the others, he wore only his brown robes. Their armor had been removed and left at St. Nonn.

"Ryvene Dosque," the man muttered through a clenched jaw, held firm by the bandage Cävian had applied. The long, angry red scratch down his face, which Jined's gauntlet plates had left swollen on one side, left him with a drawl.

"Noted," Gallahan said, finding the name in his tome. In a second ledger he began writing with a charcoal rod. "Ryvene Dosque, Vow of Pacifism, stationed at Zaanlemm in Redot."

"Vahza," the second man stated with the prideful arrogance he had given his captors during the trip to Mahn Fulhar. "Of Grissen."

"Vow of Silence," Gallahan said, cocking his eyebrow, as he found the paladin's name in his roster.

Jined caught both Loïc and Cävian tensing out of the corner of his eye.

"Charges of Vow-breaking to be brought against them as well," Gallahan muttered to himself.

"If the short report Jined gave me is true," Nichal said, "that will be true of each of these men. If they all attacked Jined and his companions, the Pacifists fought, and the Silent spoke."

"The Vows were a construct to further..." one of the heretics began to orate, when the man next to him gave him an elbow.

Jined glanced over to see Primus Loth giving the man who spoke a glare to remain silent.

"And this is?" Nichal said, coming to stand before the two of them.

"Tzomis Goere," the man said, looking up into Nichal's eyes with a burning hatred.

"Goere?" Nichal looked down at the man in astonishment. "But you..."

"Were lost at sea on a mission to Aunté," Goere replied. "I'm sure that is what the reports would have said. I was freed from the Chalician prison."

"Then why didn't you return to Pariantür?" Nichal asked.

"Why return? You didn't free me."

Nichal clenched his jaw and turned. "Tzomis Goere of Pariantür."

They continued to have their names stated, eventually leaving only their leader, Loth.

"I am Primus Eralt Loth," he said. "Of The Aerie."

"I'm sure your commanding leader will have something to say about this," Nichal stated.

"Pater Minoris Gladen left last night or this morning," Gallahan said off-handedly.

Nichal turned and looked at Gallahan, who gave a shrug.

The door to the garden opened, and the Prima Pater Dorian Mür entered. He wore his full regalia, the stylized metal pinions rising from his shoulders, and his scepter cradled in his arms. The ornate filigree and symbology across the face of the armor glinted in the sun hanging in the pale blue sky.

He circled behind the tree and took a seat next to Gallahan. Jurgon Upona trailed behind him and stood behind his chair.

"Nichal, please come and join us," he said. "Gallahan, please state their names."

The elderly Pater Segundus read through the list as the Prima Pater eyed the men before them.

"If we're to conduct a pillory, it will be difficult without their hammers. May I ask why they are not armored, nor armed with the symbol of our faith?"

"If I may," Jined said, "these men no longer had their hammers chained to their belts when they attacked us. I deemed it symbolic to remove their armor and leave their hammers behind, having forsaken the faith."

The Prima Pater nodded. "Brother Brazstein. Could you elaborate the events at St. Nonn?"

"Yes, Prima Pater," Jined said. "As you no doubt recall, at the dismissal of the congregation after the ceremony on the Solstice, I left immediately with brothers Loïc and Cävian to ride to St. Nonn. Wings of Faith carried us there swiftly, to arrive by midday the following afternoon. The first sign of trouble was the Paladin standing guard outside the Bastion door."

"Which usually has only two Paladins stationed there?" the Prima Pater asked.

"Correct," Jined responded. "That the man, Loth, who kneels before you, felt it then important to intercept us at the door, and feed us a story of their arrival and dismissal of the two men who should have been stationed at the Bastion, was the first sign that something was afoot."

"And then?"

"And then they attacked us. It was sudden, and we had little time to react. Loïc, while recovered now, took the most damage of the three of us—a strike between the eyes. But Grissone protected us."

"No doubt. You made quick work of these eight men."

"Ten, Prima Pater. Two did not survive."

"I'm sorry to hear that it came to that," Dorian said.

"We had little time to distinguish whether we ought to," Jined said.

"You're not on trial, Brother Brazstein. We'll convene an inquest into that later to assure you followed proper protocol. For now, I'd like to determine what happened, why, and what we ought to do about it. Now, I understand that they took captive the Paladins actually stationed at St. Nonn?"

"Yes, Prima Pater. The only survivor of that incident was Brother Silas Merun." He gestured toward the fourth Paladin standing with them.

"Brother Merun," Dorian said, smiling to the younger Paladin. "Perhaps you'd like to tell your story?"

Silas stepped forward and retold what he had told Jined and the twins. When he finished, Dorian thanked him and stood, leaning over the table toward the men on the ground.

"These are rather dire charges brought against the eight of you," Dorian said. "Murder of a Paladin, and a Primus, no less. A treason against the Grissoni church. I haven't heard of this sort of thing for over fifty years. It has been fifty years, hasn't it, Gallahan?"

"Yes, Prima Pater."

"This is, of course, only our initial hearing. We'll be conducting formal inquests over the course of the next several days, and you'll each be afforded the opportunity to mount your own defense. But first, I have a nagging suspicion that I'd like to confirm. Nichal, take the robe off of their leader, Loth."

Nichal stepped forward and tore the front of Loth's robe open, exposing his chest to the cold. Across his chest a large tattoo of a feather was inscribed, next to an old, coin-sized burn.

"It is as I expected."

Loth spit toward the Prima Pater.

"I don't need to see any more—a Motean heretic."

"I am no heretic. I follow the truth now."

"You left the faith, yet continued to wear the armor of a Paladin, I don't doubt preaching and teaching your poorly-constructed theology to others, leading them astray to further your fallen religion. That is the definition of heresy. You say you follow the truth, but I say you follow deceit."

"Deceit?" Loth sneered. "We cast off the will of the gods—petty, spiteful beings. I've seen the destruction they create."

"The gods aren't petty. People are petty. We ascribe that to the gods when we cannot understand their greater plans. They only desire to improve us, and to save us from those who have fallen."

"That's where you're wrong!" he shouted, standing. The twins took hold of his arms and Nichal waved for them to escort him away. "You have the most to lose, along with your power. We will rise! And you will fall!"

His screams were heard as he was dragged further and further away. The others turned back to the Prima Pater.

"I suspect each of you has a similar tattoo. It is not a new thing. I'm sure you've been told this is a new idea—the concept of this hidden circle of Paladins who know the real truth. It is not new. Gallahan?"

The old scribe stood and pulled his robe off his shoulder. A brand had been burned over a now nearly indecipherable tattoo.

"Yes, even our Pater Segundus was once a member of your little sect. But he came to me long ago and admitted his guilt, and look how far he has come since then. Thus, I will offer each of you the same. Penance. But it will not come easily. The road of sin and heresy is a dark road, and it is hard to come back from.

"I suppose you wonder what will happen if you refuse my offer. It seems to me you're all murderers. You killed a Primus, whom I suspect was attempting to root out your sect. I will hand you over to the authorities of the crown. You will be executed as murderers, not as Paladins. For now, you'll be in the Bastion cells, under lock and key."

They went quietly, with little protest, as Loïc and Cävian, with the help of Brother Merun, took them in pairs.

The Prima Pater motioned for Jined to step forward to speak with him and the other leaders privately.

"What do you know of the Moteans?" the Prima Pater asked.

"I've never heard of them," Jined said.

"Good. Then let me explain. No one knows exactly when they started. Could be they go back to just after the foundation of the Paladins; perhaps they started more recently. We know they last reared their head after the Protectorate Wars. It is from Gallahan Pír that we've derived most of our knowledge; he was deep into the cult before he saw the truth and came to me. We were able to stifle it. Perhaps we acted too fast, and they simply ran away and hid. I suppose we'll find out soon enough."

"What is it, though, Prima Pater?"

"The Motean philosophy consists of several separate concepts. One line of reasoning says the gods perhaps don't exist. Another line believes in the gods, but that they don't care about mortals, or are simply liars. Regardless, they seek deeper secrets as to why the Paladins perform miracles. Or why the Paladames can foretell the future. I call it a divine gift, prayed for. They call it magic. Tell me, Jined. What do you think?"

"I don't need to think. I know."

"Know what?"

"That the gods exist."

"And why is that?"

"Grissone has visited me several times now. I spoke with him the night before the ceremony. He told me the Gray Watchers would be coming."

Dorian's face split into a large smile. He sat back and folded his hands.

"Did he now?"

Jined looked the Prima Pater in the eyes. "Yes, and you know it. You saw my cordons miraculously change colors. Grissone warned me that something big was coming."

"Intriguing."

"What is the Moteans' purpose though, Prima Pater?"

"Their purpose? It has always been to keep secrets. Even though they simply become the tools of the Deceiver, Achanerüt. It seems that now he has decided to turn his tools into ones of destruction. Let's have a look at that map you brought back."

Nichal grabbed the roll that contained the map and opened it up across the table. It was a large map of the continent of Ganthic. Birin in Düran was blotched out with black ink. A large black circle was made around the Aerie Citadel in Limae. St. Hamul had the same, as did St. Justyn in Redot. Several small "x"'s were marked across the map.

"It seems they have marked two citadels for targets, as well as fortresses in the center. Either the Bulwark in Birin is compromised, or it has been taken out of the picture."

"Prima Pater," Nichal said, "it looks like a war map."

"It would seem that way. Though you'll also note there are no marks in Bortali or Boroni. So for now we're going to assume these two different circumstances are isolated events."

The Prima Pater continued to pore over the map. "What do you think, Gallahan?"

"Prima Pater, this was something the Moteans always talked about—the perfect time to move. To further the agenda and reshape Ganthic. I always thought it was about enlightening people to their supposed truth about the gods—this is about power and dominion."

"I fear the worst as well, Gallahan. I fear we're gazing into the heart of the problems we've faced on this road from St. Hamul. And I fear the problem is gazing back."

23

Darkness

By blood in steel, the fallen find again,
The life and mem'rie lost by those they hate.
Sink now into this too-real face upon
the book of my soul.
                    And unto undeath.

— FROM *THE SPIRIT KING OF ŒRON*,
BY ELLAM GAVALIN, DÜRANI PLAYWRIGHT

The Prima Pater set aside his schedule for the remainder of the day to speak with every Paladin in Mahn Fulhar, questioning their histories and their backgrounds to determine what they knew of the Motean Faith. Jined suspected it was also to determine if they were secretly involved. Suspicions and murmurs filled the halls, dwindling to silence over the course of the day and evening.

The following morning, Jined was summoned to appear before the Prima Pater and his Segundii. When he arrived, Nichal and Gallahan sat along the sides of the Prima Pater's desk, while the Prima Pater stood leaning against the table. He turned as Jined entered, and straightened up.

"Brother Brazstein, please come over here."

Jined stood at attention.

"No need to be tense," the Prima Pater said, "I'm not particularly worried that this inquest will reveal anything about you we didn't already know. The Grissone-granted miracle performed on you when you took that second Vow, and those I've heard about in further questioning surrounding the incident at St. Nonn, confirms to me that you're blessed by our god."

"Prima Pater," Jined said, giving a curt bow of his head.

"For formality's sake, I'd like to have it stated for the record that we'll be interviewing Jined Brazstein," he said, turning back to Pater Segundus Pír.

He circled the desk and came to stand before the much taller Jined.

"Jined, I am going to admit a few things that may come as a surprise to you, but then, they may not. Firstly, let me say, I do not know why I brought you on this trip.

"Don't misunderstand me. You have a great track record at Pariantür. You're an efficient guard. You've more than proven yourself as a fighter while on patrol against T'Akai incursions near Pariantür. But you came to us as a penitent. That mark alone tends to keep one from being promoted as quickly as you were. In fact, now that I think of it, I think you're the only penitent who came on this journey. Actually, Gallahan did serve a time of penance after he admitted he was a Motean, but that's beside the point."

"If I may speak frankly?" Jined asked.

The Prima Pater nodded consent.

"It is something I've questioned in silence. I do not rightly understand why you invited me along myself."

"Very well. One might say, 'perhaps Grissone told him to.' But the fact is, I don't actually remember inviting you. Nichal states he did not add you. At some point you were added to our roster, and we simply never got around to taking you off. You know that has to be a very odd thing. Jurgon Upona—very attentive to details—never once mentioned a problem with your being on the list, so let's just say that it's odd, and a quandary that you're here."

"Very well," Jined conceded.

"As it turns out, you state you were visited by Grissone. Once more, a quandary. Due to my Vow, and seventy-five years of practice at it, I am in what you might call a constant conversation of prayer.

"Usually it is with the Anka, and sometimes Grissone. Let's not get into a theological discussion about how they are the same. They are, and they aren't. The Anka is farsighted, to things that have happened, but are not yet known. Yet I had no idea Grissone spoke with you. I'm a bit jealous, to be honest. I suspect he has spoken secrets to you that are perhaps for your ears only. But, I also feel an urge to ask if there is anything he might have told you that perhaps needs to be shared."

A sinking feeling hit Jined in his chest.

"Prima Pater, there is something. And, for the life of me, I cannot explain why I have not been able to share it."

The Prima Pater turned and looked him full in the face.

"Explain."

"Prima Pater, Brother Hammer, er, Grissone, spoke initially to me in nothing but verses. The first several times I met him, before I knew who he was, this was so. But the first time we met, at St. Hamul, he spoke a verse I did not know. But I feel unable to share it."

The weight that bore down on Jined was nearly physical. It moved from his chest to his shoulder, trying to pull him away from the Prima Pater, like a parent keeping a child from entering a road. As Jined pulled back against that touch, a chilly feeling of shame washed over him.

"When I was met with the chance to share it with someone it was meant for, I was waylaid by the minor Vow of Service," Jined said with a shuddering voice. "And even when Grissone revealed himself to me, he reminded me once more that I needed still to share this secret, but that it was perhaps too late. It seems to slip my mind at the slightest breeze. I cannot explain why."

The chill ran up and down his spine in pulses, screaming in his mind that he needed to flee this place, and keep the secret to himself.

"You are held back, I suspect."

"What do you mean?"

"Something dark keeps you from speaking. Chosen you may be by Grissone, but you are still mortal. You are compelled by another."

Jined felt himself break out in cold sweats. Fear and doubt filled his mind. He turned and began to walk away from the Prima Pater, and could hear the old man calling from behind, but his vision clouded, and each step took an eternity. He reached up to his face, hoping to pinch himself awake.

It was now an audible voice, screaming at him through the watery depths of the dream, drowning out the voice of the Prima Pater behind him.

"It was not Grissone who had been visiting you all this time," the voice raged. *"It was me."*

"Who are you!" Jined shouted. "What have I done to draw the attention of a dark god?"

Nichal was on his feet now. Jurgon rushed in from the antechamber, and Loïc came in the door from the hall, his hammer at the ready.

Jined's mind spun to think of each dark god. Kos-Yran was said to enthrall people. Even Rionne, the Destroyer, might do so. Perhaps even Achanerüt himself.

"Jined," a voice said, breaking through the living nightmare. "Look me in the eye. Now pray to Grissone for deliverance."

Jined could not focus. His mind was reeling, and he could barely hear the Prima Pater. From the corner of his eye, he thought he could see a figure standing there, its hand upon his shoulder. Its breath was icy and full of acid. Another figure came and put his hand on the other shoulder, shoving him down to his knees.

The Prima Pater's hands took his face between them, and drew his gaze to his own.

"Jined, look at me and hear my voice. Call on Grissone, and he will hear."

"If you do that," the icy voice said, *"then all you have done will be taken away. The mote of power you have been given will mean nothing."*

"Mote?" Jined muttered.

"Grissone," he whispered, "take back what strength you have given me, if it will ease this nightmare."

The figure next to him seethed in anger. Silent anger.

"Grissone," he said in a louder, more determined voice. "Come to my aid."

There was flash of light, and another figure stood there. He took the empty hammer from his belt and swung it at the shadowy figure, shattering it into a thousand pieces. Jined collapsed forward, his face on the cold stone.

The single shard of the shadow that had stood there wriggled towards Jined and leapt into the satchel at Jined's side.

The leather buckled and heaved, something within trying to escape.

"Open it," he heard the Prima Pater say.

Nichal crouched down next to Jined.

From the satchel a package tied in red silk ribbon fell onto the stone, and jerked and bucked of its own accord. The red silk burst into flame and burnt away, revealing a small handbook of black leather, a feather embossed upon it. The Prima Pater picked up the booklet which tried to tear itself free from his hands. Opening it, inky letters began fading in the light, as though they fled from his touch. He dropped it to the ground and pulled his winged-shaped scepter out and struck it, cleaving it in two.

"What in the name of all that is holy was that, Brazstein?!"

"I...don't know. I..." It came back to him. "I was given it at the Citadel of St. Hamul to deliver to someone. But now...I can't remember who."

"And you never opened it? You put it in your satchel to deliver it here?"

"Honestly, yes. How could I forget?"

"It is a shadebook," Gallahan Pír said from across the room.

"It is darkness, and evil," the Prima Pater added. "If what you say is true, Jined, then I expect, perhaps, it was given to you as a means of controlling you. I was able to guess that something like this was being done to you from our interviews with those who were deeper into the

Motean cult. We must ascertain who it was for. And more importantly, who gave it to you."

"This is happening too fast. Was that...thing...the Grissone that visited me? Has this all been a lie?"

"Jined," the Prima Pater said, touching the big man's face and drawing his gaze once more to him, "before you forget, now that you are no longer beholden to that thing, what message did Grissone tell you to convey? The one you were held back from saying?"

"She sees now a rose whose petals wilt." Jined said, though he felt the words were not his own. "She sees now a vine that has been cut. Prepare then a hedge of thorns. And be vigilant as a dwov watches over her nest."

As the verse came to an end, Jined's vision began to darken once more. He felt Nichal, and then the arms of others, lift him up and carry him in his delirious daze, and place him on the bed of his cell. The poison that had assaulted his mind slowly leeched away his sanity, like the sickness he had experienced as a child, and he wondered if he would ever rise again, and if Grissone had ever truly blessed him, or if he was now damned by that evil book given to him those months ago.

24

Holy Presence

Heresies start small, as slivers of doubt, as ideas half-formed and not finished. It takes one negligent comment by a sage, taken and dwelt upon by a lesser mind, to grow into a festering falsehood. Compare each new thought against the scriptures, and then, even then, find a means of drawing deeper into Grissone and weigh his own words in the silence of your heart against them. You will know through your faith and through your doubt whither the word comes from. Pay no heed to Deceit.

— ST. EMENTHUM JURAN, VOW OF PRAYER

Consciousness came and went. At one point Etienne fed him. Other times the twins took turns sitting with him, knelt in prayer. Yet another time the Prima Pater visited, resplendent in his armor. But he saw other figures visit. The gray, featureless visage of the priests of Wyv-Thüm stood over him. Perhaps to observe. Perhaps to prepare to escort him to the next life.

He was taken up toward the form of an ælerne eagle made of living embers, and plunged into the burning depths. It was not hot, and Jined watched his soul begin to glow in the furnace. Taken from the eternal flames, his soul was placed upon an anvil. The cool of the metal threatened to quench those flames. A hammer devoid of form but full of power struck him. He flinched at the sound as it struck time and again, in rhythmic resonance.

Doubled over, he was placed into the flame once more, and drawn back out to repeat the process.

Then, it was done. Brother Hammer stood next to him, replacing his empty hammer on his belt. He took Jined by his hand and helped him to his feet. "Now you have been reforged," he said, as the metal of Jined's soul cooled.

Jined took a deep breath, a relief washing over him. The pain he had not realized had followed him since St. Hamul was gone. The cracks in his soul were restored.

"What happened?" he asked, looking at the god next to him.

"You and I must take a journey," Grissone said.

"Where you go, I will follow."

"You cannot follow, but I can carry you there."

Jined felt himself being pressed into the void where Grissone's hammer did not hang from his belt. He swung there, aware that he was the hammer. His Pariantür. And Grissone began to walk.

"You will not be able to speak, but I will know your thoughts. And I will answer them as I can. First, we must find my sister."

He was able to look in any direction without turning his head. He was aware still of the furnace above, the Anka, circling overhead.

"You were oppressed by an unknown thing," Grissone said. "I have never encountered such a secret. Nor do I know why I did not know of it. We will seek out now what happened. But we must be counseled by the others. Thus, you may listen, but do not look fully onto members of my family. No mortal can look on us and live. How then can you look at me, you ask? You cannot. I have lessened myself. The Anka stays away, or else the two of us would blind you."

But am I dead? Am I damned?

"Damned? Of course not. You are chosen."

Then it has been you I spoke to all these times? Not that specter?

"I do not know what it has said to you, but when you and I walked, it has been me who spoke."

They walked through the Nothing. A blue streak, like a dancing ribbon, flitted and flew this way and that, gathering up something like a bird building a nest. Grissone moved toward her, and her form grew brighter and brighter. Jined the Hammer looked away. A blue glow blended with the dampened orange glow of Grissone.

"My brother," she said. There were two voices speaking. One in an ancient tongue he could almost understand. The other came a moment after, repeating the words in a language he could understand.

"Sister mine. You have been busy."

"I am always busy. And I have many errands to attend to."

"Then let us be quick. You must take me to the Throne."

"Little Brother's? Or our Father's?"

"Let us visit Little Brother first."

"I have much to attend to. Everything feels imbalanced."

"What we are about is more important."

A blue light enveloped them, and they moved swiftly across Nothing toward a forest that sat growing in the mist. The verdant paradise breathed. As they rushed toward it, pricks of light seemed to stretch out as candles as far as the eye could see. They came to stand behind a fern and waited. A figure, all in green, with horns, and a sword that glowed brighter than Jined-Hammer could look upon, reached out into Nothing. A pin-prick of light bloomed into two lights, and left.

"Welcome brother, welcome sister," he said. "I see you have found your Hammer."

"Yes," Grissone said, "and I see your influence grows."

"But a tentative hold it is," he said. "You have not visited in a while. Either of you."

"I pray you are not lonely, little Kasne," the blue light spoke.

"No. The work I do here pleases me."

"I am afraid we must be quick," Grissone said.

"I agree. I have many more to touch today," Kasne said.

"Have you ever seen a black figure hovering over the shoulder of a follower?"

"I have not. But when have I left my throne?"

"Very well. I have encountered just this. A figure, unseen by me, influencing and hampering my own. I must know the reason for this."

"Describe it," Kasne said.

"Like a Gray Watcher. Only it does not serve our Father, nor the Judge. It dressed in blackness, and was able to keep one of my own from speaking words. And it was bound to a book."

"Bound to a book? This is not the magic of Dream then."

"No. It is something new to me. Something darker."

"You must consult Father. And, if he is to be found, our eldest brother. We need his wisdom. And he knows the power of books."

The blue surrounded them again. They quickly left the Nothing and Jined could feel that they were going in a direction unknown to him. It was not across, nor up and down, but in a different direction.

"Now you will now see what most have not. Thus, I am going to put fetters on your eyes. For if you see the Kingdom of my Father, you will not wish anything but to stay in Lomïn."

The light burst forth on the horizon, like the sun. And a land appeared. Jined felt his eyes change and see things as they were, yet, only a portion of their true form. The place was arable, and figures worked the fields. They were gray in form, but rather than a gray that seemed drained of the life it once held, it was as though their true form was released from confines, and more solid than ephemeral. Some stopped to wave their greetings as they passed overhead.

They came to a mountain and began to climb. People lived upon the sides, and soon Jined realized it was not a mountain, but a city. Atop it sat a second city, and the walls had no gates. They came and lighted on the entrance to the temple that stood itself a mile high.

"It would have taken me a month to get here," Grissone said. "Thank you, sister."

"Let us go and speak with Father and Mother."

The single throne room stretched back for miles to a bright horizon of light. Grissone and his sister stopped beside a pillar.

"I will leave you here," Grissone said, "and you will listen but not see."

The Hammer-that-was-Jined was leaned against a pillar, and he saw only the backsides of the two figures walking into a passing cloud and disappear.

"Father," he heard Grissone say.

"My son," a voice boomed. It was far off, and yet all around.

"Mother," the blue one said.

"My beloved daughter," a rich voice of beauty and age said.

"Have you seen what has occurred?" Grissone asked.

"Something new," the Father said. "Or at least something renewed has begun."

"A being, like a Gray Watcher, yet enshrouded in inky black, set down oppression on one of my followers by contact with a book full of darkness. It is nothing like that of Dream, so can it be called magic?"

"My Paladames say that Wyv sent word," the Mother said. "There are deaths unaccounted for. They have been kept from our memory. Only the Judge and his Watchers know of them."

"I have not seen a death as such," the blue one said. "And I have seen every death."

"Something confuses us," Grissone said. "Something stirs."

"His web is growing stronger," the Mother said. "But what of the others?"

"Rionne still sits upon his throne," Grissone said. "And Kea'Rinoul refuses still to leave the Desert of Mourning. I know not of Kos-Yran. He moves with such stealth, yet his stink is smelled everywhere."

"Let us all consider these things," the Father said. "You have already spoken with Kasnetaoral. I hope we are able to reach out to Lae'Zeq; his silence continues to perturb me. But in his wisdom, he chose this new lot in life. I will allow it to continue."

A hand took hold of Jined, and once more they moved back toward the world, back through the threshold, and he was in his own room once more. Grissone was there, and seemed to fill the whole room with his being. The Hammer on his belt hung empty.

"You have your voice again," Grissone said. "You will remember this moment you shared with me as a fleeting dream, but you were witness. You are now cleansed and reforged. I have seen to it that you shall never again be afflicted by any outside source. If you can ascertain anything about these beings, I will know."

Grissone reached out and touched him between the eyes. "My eye is here now. I will see what you see. Be my eyes. Continue to seek deeper faith. There is more to learn, and I have more to demand of you."

Grissone was gone. It felt as though the air had left him. After a long moment Jined gasped for breath. The room was empty except for himself. He walked to the door and opened it. Loïc stood guard outside.

You are awake, he signed. *The Pater Segundii wish to see you when you are ready.*

I am ready, Jined replied.

They came to the Prima Pater's study. They could hear Nichal speaking with a voice that Jined couldn't quite place.

"Your service is commendable," Gallahan Pír said. "The Prima Pater is very impressed by how you've run the bastion."

"Then I should like to repeat my request, Pater Segundus. I should like Pariantür's permission to improve it into a fortress."

"As I said," Nichal replied, "we shall bring it up to discuss with the council when we return to Pariantür. Until then, you'll have to exert patience."

"Now, I should like to discuss the prisoners."

"We shall decide what to do with them later. For now, they remain."

"There is a larger Bastion in the north, the Gray Crag. It could be turned into a penitence jail. Better there than sullying the name of our Bastion here."

"Primus Melit," Gallahan said. "It is best that they remain here under our watchful eye until the Prima Pater returns and decides what to do with them."

"Melit?" Jined muttered, putting his hand on the door. Loïc put his hand on Jined's arm to make him pause. Jined shrugged his hand away and pushed his way in.

"Brother Brazstein," Nichal said, looking up with some surprise. "If you'd please wait, we are having a discussion with Primus Melit here."

Jined ignored the Pater Segundus, whose face turned to astonishment.

"Primus Melit," Jined said. "I ought to have recognized you by name when we first arrived."

"Brazstein," Nichal said. His voice was turning from irritation to anger. "We're conducting a private meeting with the Primus here."

"I understand. Though I think what I have to say and do is pertinent."

Though he did not fully understand why he did it, Jined lifted a palm out toward the Primus and prayed a silent prayer in his heart. He opened his eyes and stepped forward with his palm held out.

"You will, of course, forgive me for what I am about to do."

His hand wandered forward and he laid it upon the Paladin's shoulder. Melit hissed and jumped back, grabbing his shoulder as though swatting a biting fly.

"How dare you! What is the meaning of this?!"

"Adjutant Brazstein, stand down!" the Pater Segundus shouted.

Melit was spinning around trying to tear off his robe. His gorget clattered to the ground, and he pulled his robe up over his head, now shouting in panic. He tripped and fell to his knees. The skin on his shoulder was bubbling and steaming, the ink of the feather tattoo across his shoulder blade turning into a burning brand.

"Well," Gallahan said from the desk, "I suppose that does justify a bit of interruption."

"Pater Segundii, I am very sorry for this," Jined said to the two of them. "I recalled who it was I was supposed to deliver that heretical object to."

"I think that's apparent now."

Melit continued to breathe heavily. The bubbling on his skin slowed. The ink was gone. All that was left was a scar in the shape of a hammer.

"This...is why we have our New Faith," Melit said, panting. "You are evil in your ways. Claiming the power of a god who does not exist to enshroud your enslavement. You mark us the heretics when you are the heretics, standing in the way of humanity."

Melit's anger seemed to fill him with strength. He stood now and faced the three Paladins. Loïc had his hammer in his hand, holding it behind him. Jined held a hand up to signal pause. Nichal stood by the desk Gallahan sat at. The latter leaned forward, staring amusedly at Melit, who was now only in his undergarments.

"You wish to seek us out? You wish to burn us out as witches or practitioners of dark arts? There is nothing dark about our message, only freedom. Freedom that man can do whatever he sets his mind to. We will set man free from the shackles of your false divinity. We will unite them."

"Are you quite finished?" Gallahan asked. "You are wrong, you know. We shall not conduct a witch hunt. We only wish to seek a way to discourse with you. I only wish to help you see the errors of your ways."

"Grissone is very real," Nichal added. "He is as real as you or I, or more so."

"Your Grissone is false. Grissone is only an invention made by your desire to shackle rather than protect humanity. He is nothing but your own falsehood created to enslave people under your power. We have been freed."

"Freed by what? By whom?"

"Freed by ourselves."

Melit took out a long metal pin. He lifted it up and closed his eyes.

"Jined, stop him."

Jined made a move but it was not soon enough, as Melit thrust the long pin of metal into his own heart. He gasped and fell once more to his knees. His mouth continued to gape, and his eyes went blank. Black blood seeped from his heart. Smoke began to billow from his open mouth. It formed into a being standing before them like an empty black robe.

"Grissone grant every protection," Jined heard Gallahan say as his own ears began to dim and his vision tunneled. He felt Loïc come to stand shoulder to shoulder next to him.

"What are you?!" Jined shouted.

"*Transcendent*," the figure hissed from its own presence, and from the mouth of Melit on the ground.

Jined leapt forward and swung with his hammer, hitting the thing across the middle. It simply split like a waft of smoke, then congealed together again. Jined let his hammer drop and he grabbed at the thing with his hands. Surprisingly, it worked. He tore the cloak open to reveal nothing there. It began bucking, as it tried to escape his grasp.

"Let this thing not escape. Let my hands be its shackle," he felt himself say. The cloak dissolved, then coalesced again in his hands, unable to leave.

Melit's body collapsed to the ground, dead.

Jined held the struggling shade. To him it was as real as a person. But he could see it was ephemeral. Nichal came over to stand next to it.

"It seems to be the ghost of Melit."

"But Nifara takes every soul."

"Not if she's not allowed to, it would seem."

"Why would anyone wish to be a wandering ghost, as in the tales of old?"

"Because this shade knows what it will face if sent to stand before the Judge," Gallahan said. "Shade, look me in the eye."

The thing looked away.

"You know you spoke falsely," Gallahan offered kindly. "You will face the Judge one day. Your falsehoods, misleading the weak-minded, will be punished."

"Pater Segundus," Jined said, "do you suppose a shade like this is what was bound to me? A man made into a ghost of some sort?"

"I expect that is so."

"But how do you bind it then to a book by words?"

The Pater Segundus pulled the metal piece from Melit's chest.

Dripping with gore, he held it up to the light of the nearby fireplace. It had a quill for a tip.

"By writing with this," he said.

He walked over to the fire. The shade began to thrash about wildly, trying to escape to stop the Pater Segundus from what he was about to do. He threw it into the flames. The shade went into convulsions, then exploded like a column of smoke being hit by a sudden gust of wind.

"I think that answers that question," Nichal said. "Now, what do we do with this knowledge?"

"We have to tell the Prima Pater," Jined said.

"He left," Gallahan said.

"Left?"

"After you passed out," Nichal said, "he immediately traveled to the Crysalas Convent. It was empty. The women had, the morning you arrived, locked the place for a day of fasting. We thought nothing of it. But then your prophecy came, and Dorian went to deliver it to them personally. They had gone. All of them. It took the rest of the day to determine they had gone south, to the Oracle. Dorian mounted his sleipnir and left to pursue them."

"And how many days ago was that?" Jined asked.

"Two."

"Then unless they were led swiftly on the wings of the Anka," Jined said, "we may not be too late. We can go after them."

"If Melit here is a sign," Gallahan said to Nichal, "then the Prima Pater may be in danger from other Moteans."

"I don't like this discovery that we are infiltrated and surrounded."

"Nor do I, Nichal," Gallahan said, "but it appears we have no time to decide our course. We must instead tread swiftly on the path."

25

Interlude

Rallia opened the door to the tavern and stepped out into the street of the small town of Verír. The talkative smuggler had not seen the man she sought for Searn in over a fortnight, although she suspected he lied. The old man was still asleep on the bench he drank at from the night before. He'd be there when she returned.

The wind was calm, and the sun had not yet risen, though the early light began to sweep the stars free from the sky.

She walked down to the pier and then took a right, walking the long length of stone until she reached the end. A few old men had their poles in the water. They'd catch enough to feed their families before the rest awoke, and perhaps a few extra to sell at market. She passed by three old men murmuring with one another, and came to a large rocky outcropping. She scrambled up and over to the small cove beyond. It was heading towards low tide, so she would have all the time she needed.

She took off her outer tunic, lay her cloak over a rock, and found a patch of sand she liked. Then she took up her staff and began running through the basic motions she had learned from the Edian guard captain, hired to teach her proper spear etiquette. It was simple, formal. She moved her staff in sharp movements that looked professional. She had impressed plenty of people she had guarded with the movements, even if they were just for show.

She planted her toes in the sand and began to drill through the moves she had learned from the qavylli artisan in Düran. The strange creature had taught her more in one week than she had learned in three years about footing and balance. She had given the qavyl her attention as the two-hundred-year-old creature regaled her of his travels as an artisan and a legionnaire in the qavylli republic. Rallia's staff swung in wide arcs to keep the enemy at bay, and then closed in as she advanced a few quick paces so her staff could counter close quarters.

She came to a rest and dropped to her knee.

"That is not a human form of combat," a voice said.

Rallia spun and saw a very old man in a gray robe of an Abecinian priest sitting on the rock next to her cloak.

"Qavylli," Rallia replied, wiping the sweat from her face and then leaving it as a smudge on her trousers.

The old man had one of the longest beards Rallia had ever seen, almost tucked into his belt. He cast a silhouette that made his features hard to distinguish as the sun began to bleach the sky behind him.

"I expected as much. Strange to see a woman practice it."

"That is true, holy father."

"You rise earlier than most."

"I always have."

"Yes, I understand that is so."

Rallia came to stand next to the old priest. She pulled out a water skin and offered it first to the old man.

"Thank you for the offering, freely given."

"It is a small thing to offer."

"It is the simplest, and most genuine gift a man can give another— clean water. It was Aben's first domain, water. His people lived there."

"The Gray Watchers?" Rallia asked. "I thought they came from Lomïn."

"No. They came from the depths. Lomïn was Aben's own garden. Now it is a kingdom of the dead."

"My name is Rallia Clouw."

"Yes, I know."

"And how do you know that?"

"Word came to me from a small chapel in Düran. And I followed your movements from there through Mahn Fulhar."

"Father Diono?"

"Yes."

"How does he fare?"

"He has passed on to Lomïn."

Rallia sighed.

"He tends the kitchens in Aben's garden now."

"Yes, I expect he would."

"I understand you traveled with a qavyl, with a tall staff?"

"Ymbrys Veronia? I did."

"Have you seen him recently?"

"No, but he has a way of showing up in strange places. Why?"

"Because I have been seeking him. Will you pass a message along to him?"

"I can try. But who shall I say is seeking him?"

"Tell the War Breaker that Aben speaks: The Father wishes to converse. The Sister fears something moves. The Mother is half blinded. The Brother has a wound."

"That is quite the message," Rallia said. "I did not know the priests of Aben spoke in riddles like that."

"The priests do not; they are straight speaking. Those of Lomïn are not."

"You are a Watcher then?" Rallia asked.

The old man said nothing.

"There is more to this world than meets the eye, isn't there?"

"No truer words have been spoken."

The old man turned to leave.

"Please wait," Rallia pleaded.

The old man stopped, but did not turn.

"There are many tales of Watchers—gods, mortals, messages and wisdoms imparted, but no one ever seems to simply stop and speak with the Messenger."

The old man turned, and smiled.

"Have you ever been offered a meal and a conversation?"

"No. Never."

"Will you sit and eat with me? I have many questions."

"I'm sure you do."

The old man came back and stepped down onto the sand.

"Will you wait?" Rallia asked.

"I will wait."

Rallia rushed up over the rocks towards the old men who were fishing. One had a line anchored into a tide pool.

"How long until the tide turns?" Rallia asked.

"A few hours still."

"Do you have a fish there on your weigh line? Big enough to feed two?"

"I do. Who asks?"

"A customer."

Rallia gave the man three silver, double what she might pay for a fish at the market, which the man greedily took. She grabbed the fish and ran back to the beach, hoping the Watcher still waited, and sighed with relief when she saw he was still there. Rallia worked silently, glancing over her shoulder every once in a while to check that the old man was still there as she gathered up driftwood and made a fire, cooking the fish over it.

Finally the fish was done, and Rallia offered the Watcher the fish. The old man took a bite or too, nodding his approval.

"Another fine offering. You are a good woman, Rallia Clouw."

"Only a girl."

"You said you have questions?"

"The same questions anyone else has. What is Lomïn like? What is Aben like? If I have killed, can I hope to journey there?"

"You have a heart of precious metal. If you continue to ask such questions, and do not turn left or right from your path, I do not doubt you shall reach the Kingdom. The best way to know Aben is to meet him. And to meet him is a blessing."

"They say the world began with a single word spoken."

"Begin."

"And it was spoken by Aben and Wyv, together."

"Yes. They spoke it as a reflection of the word that spoke them into being."

"By the Existence? Where has he gone?"

"So few ask after the Existence. But the Existence is not gone. The Existence is always here."

Rallia sat back on the sand. "Have I kept you too long?"

"No, I have enjoyed this. It has been too long since I have tasted fish."

"Ever since you were mortal? As a Watcher when you lived in the sea?"

"I never answered you when you asked if I was a Watcher."

Rall looked up, startled.

"The Watchers attend me."

Rallia saw then ten tall figures standing up on the rocks, they wore gray robes, and she could not see faces inside the cowls. They held in their hands tridents, and some with short bows.

"You are not a Watcher?" Rallia asked. She tried to rise, and fell to one knee.

"I am not. Thank you, Rallia Clouw, for the meal."

Rallia found she could not speak. She opened her mouth, and no words came.

"You have another question?"

Rallia gasped for breath. "What can I say?"

"You need not say anything. You have treated me fairly. Take the knowledge of that with you."

"Why have you visited me?" Rallia asked.

"As I said. Seek out the qavyl. That will lead you in the right direction."

Rallia nodded. "Thank you."

The beach was empty.

She kicked sand over the ashes of the fire and took up the stick that the fish had been skewered on—the one from which Aben had eaten. She tucked it in her cloak and walked back to town, a smile that had not been there before stretched across her face.

PART 4

26

Fated Path

So much is unknown of the Dweol. The World Rose is a mystery that hails back to before the Destruction, long before any one woman called Crysania her goddess.

—SAYINGS OF MATRIARCH DESWYN

"Matriarch Superioris," Pater Minoris Jakis Gladen said, "the Prima Pater has asked that you seek refuge at the Massif."

The Paladin had blown in with five other Paladins just after the evening meal. They all had black cloaks over their frames, ready to travel themselves.

"Please start at the beginning," the Matriarch said. She took her seat by the fire, and Katiam handed her her goblet of evening medicine.

"As you likely recall," Gladen said, "after the ceremony, Brother Brazstein was sent by the Prima Pater to St. Nonn. We received message that he is returning with news that the Bastion is a single cell in a network of apostate Paladins. He uncovered a map with notes containing a plot to kill Prima Pater Mür and yourself. If you have means to escape the city, go to the Massif with haste. The Prima Pater feels you'll best be safe there."

"I should think weathering the storm here, or in a Crysalas Vault, the safest immediate place for refuge," the old lady said. "Abbess Foi? What do you think?"

"I only just completed reviewing the report your captain, Sister Glass, prepared. If we need to move, she has identified a safe means of leaving the city in times of war or panic."

"And is this, Pater Gladen, a time of war?"

"Given the scope of what the map indicates," Gladen said, "I believe so."

"I should like to confirm this with my husband first," she said.

"He has already ridden out."

"Aeger?" the Matriarch called.

One of the Paladins accompanying Gladen stepped forward. It was Gallahan Pír's personal assistant.

"Is what Gladen says true?"

Aeger nodded sternly.

"And where is Gallahan? Did he not ride with Dorian as his squire to war, as he did in the Protectorate Wars?"

Aeger made several signs.

"Administrator. Yes, I don't doubt. Then I charge you to act as courier to my husband. I'll draft a letter for you to take to him while Abbess Foi makes arrangements for those who will accompany me."

"The entire Convent," Gladen said.

"Excuse me?" the Matriarch said, arching a brow.

"The Prima Pater made it clear that the news Brother Brazstein brought was a danger to the entire order. He fears pogrom."

Abbess Foi gasped.

"What Paladin in their right mind would not only turn traitor, but threaten such things?" the Matriarch asked. "One in three Paladins has a Paladame as a mother, cousin, or aunt."

"Apparently, it may pertain to what the Pontifex of Wyv said. It may be related to the reports you gave. Perhaps these traitors ally themselves with the Church of the Common Chalice in Œron."

"This is very sudden," the Matriarch said, "but we were planning on taking the convent on a pilgrimage to the Oracle. It might as well be now."

Gladen smiled. "Very well. If you have your means out of the city, I shall prepare my own sleipnir and meet your company outside of the city."

"You're to escort us, then?" the Matriarch asked.

"And see you safely to your destination."

"I think I can safely say we shall meet you by the western gate before dawn."

"Very well," he said, dismissing himself.

The Matriarch turned to Abbess Foi. "Please move quickly."

"It is very hard to believe this story he tells," Foi said.

"Hard," the Matriarch said, "but not impossible. And Aeger confirmed it. If my husband rides without so much as a notice, he must think the need urgent, or easy to suppress. Since he asks that not only myself but the entire convent go, under cover of dark, then he must believe the danger great. And so, let us go. We'll travel with haste to the foothills, and then begin our pilgrimage, and await good news from the Hammer."

The plan Astrid had prepared worked, although it had to be stretched to compensate for two hundred of them. Finding Sleipnirs for all of them was almost impossible, but the winter storm the night before had stabled many within the city, and the Convent's coffers had enough to pay for their use. A couple of hours before dawn, and they were saddled and riding through the calm night, the prayers of Pater Minoris Gladen and his platoon of Paladins sped them along their way. Katiam felt the wind whipping across her face as they traveled through until morning with no trace of tiredness bearing down on their shoulders, at speeds no mortal was meant to travel.

By dawn they slowed to a canter. The six-legged sleipnirs seemed to be no more tired than if they had traveled for a single hour, and yet a weariness settled over every Paladin, Paladame, and mount as they resumed a normal speed.

Stopping at an inn, Katiam could not think straight through the weariness, but she made her way to the room offered the Matriarch and her closest attendants. She swore the innkeeper told them they were only a short ride outside of Alnír, a city known to be more than a full week's ride from Mahn Fulhar.

When she awoke, the sun was setting once more, and she knew the night would be the same as the one before. After several hours' ride, the mountains of the Mahndür Massif grew quickly to consume the stars upon the horizon. They came to a mountain pass and began to ascend, no longer pushed to miraculous speeds through prayer.

At dawn they came to the Fated Path. The pass narrowed to a tall, gray canyon. A paladinial Bastion stood there, looking like it had been built between the two walls, which had closed in to crush the Bastion in between.

They came to the door and knocked. It took some time for the two Paladins to wake and meet them at the door. All helped unsaddle the sleipnirs, setting many of them free in the large paddock, now bursting with hundreds of the animals. Katiam followed the others into the chapel, where everyone found places to lie or lean for several hours of uncomfortable respite.

The Bastion's stores were nearly emptied, and all shared cheese and dried meats as Abbess Superioris Foi walked the congregation through what would unfold over the next three days' journey up the Fated Path.

The summit would be taken with rigorous orthodoxy that the Grissoni church and Crysalas Integritas had long ago agreed to follow.

At midday, a bell pealed—one for each pilgrim in the company. The bell pealed continuously, and then it continued to echo for what seemed like hours as they each left on foot, up the first stage of the Fated Path known as the Burden. The erratically-built steps of the path climbed up the canyon. Some rose only a few inches, others took three steps at a time. Yet none were allowed to offer help to another; each must climb alone. At times the Paladins forgot and offered their help to the sisters, who stoically refused. Katiam could tell the climb was the hardest thing Maeda Mür had ever done in her life, given her age, but still the elderly lady pressed on.

The sun set in the west behind them, though it disappeared behind the walls of the canyon long before the dark crept in. A couple of the Paladins, as well as Katiam and few other Paladames, intentionally took up the rear as the Matriarch Superioris moved ever slower. The temperature continued to drop, and light gave way to utter darkness. The cold clouds overhead made it even darker. Only the stark white stone stairs were visible, though even they were difficult to make out in the pitch black. No torches would be lit. The silence grew as others pressed on ahead to the first shelter, leaving the handful who took up the rear behind the elderly lady alone in the night.

A light began to glow up ahead, and they all let out a grateful sigh as the first rest came into view. The Matriarch Superioris saw it too, and seemed to gain a skip in her step as she completed the first stage. Like the stables below, this was built across the entire canyon. Within was a temple to Crysania, made of white marble. Rose-colored glass stood backlit by torches in unseen passages available only to the custodians of the place. There was no one to greet them; simply a place to stop. Their beds had been made and food was prepared, but the entry into this place was the first part of the next leg which was known as the Silence.

Katiam followed the Matriarch Superioris, and in silence went about her nightly ritual of checking on her health and ensuring she felt fine. She was asleep before Katiam had finished her ministrations. Katiam took off her own armor and checked the moisture of the soil in the bag hanging from her hip. One of the green tendrils of the Rotha peeked out. She poured enough rose water into the leather satchel to keep the dirt moist, but not so much as would dampen the brown leather. Then, hanging it from the post of the Matriarch's bed frame, Katiam laid out on the floor and fell promptly asleep.

Dawn came too early, but the Matriarch Superioris rose without complaint as they prepared to leave. The canyon walls were white marble, the same stone the temple was made of. It was a gradual path, with few steps and an easy walk. Even the wind, which at times swept through the canyon, did not utter a whistle. And no one dared to break the silence.

Katiam walked with the Matriarch Superioris taking her arm. Maeda Mür smiled to herself, and Katiam did not worry so much for her great aunt's health. It was an easy walk, though it took the entirety of the day. Katiam was prompted by Abbess Superioris Foi's instructions, contemplating her walk as a Paladame of Pariantür. She had visited the Oracle in the Crysan Massif near Pariantür plenty of times. It had a different set of prompted stages to the summit. This time, though, was different, because it was new.

She felt the wonder of Crysania's intentional purity. Not purity for the natural sake of being, as many women are told they are by remaining virginal, but instead the purity of choice. To intentionally deny an action that might sully such a purity was one thing. But this, the action of choosing silence for silence's sake was an intentional purity. The purity of pushing through the pain of a climb, as the Burden was, was intentional.

They arrived at the final stop before entering the Brilliance. Attendants at the last way-stop wore veils, which Katiam envied for the day's next route. They were given a place to stay and told that they would be prepared to leave as dawn began. And thus, everyone chattered on for a short time before finding a place to rest.

She was roused by the chiming of a crystal gong that pierced everyone's ears. It continued to ring, and Katiam found her head hurting. It subsided, but as everyone prepared to leave the last stop, they all found they had become temporarily deafened. The doors opened and dawn light flooded across the now very shallow canyon. The wind swept hard, clearing away freshly fallen snow, revealing a sparkling landscape that was filled with so much beauty.

From what she could gather from a couple of other sisters who had visited before, this had been an amazing natural defense against pogroms before the foundation of the Paladames. It had kept those persecuting the Crysalas Integritas from ever coming and destroying this most sacred of places.

Far ahead she could see the summit temple. It stood in the full sun that had not yet risen to view. At times the trail steepened, blocking the view to the top, while at other times the grade rounded into long stretches that wore on their legs. All this made it impossible to determine how far they had to go.

Suddenly the sun rose into view, shooting across the crystal fields before them, and the light struck them with full force. Katiam thought she saw others double over as though struck with a hammer. She braced herself as the white light washed over her. Suddenly everything faded in a bleaching whiteness. Closing her eyes could not hide the light, for colors flashed behind her eyelids in great showers. The light in their eyes, and the reverberating ringing of the crystal gong, left her stumbling forward, deaf and blind.

She found an arm at one point. It was huge, and belonged to Pater Minoris Jakis Gladen, she surmised, but his low voice was too muffled to be understood, and she could only vaguely make him out next to her as they walked together.

The sun broke over its zenith and moved down their backs. It provided warmth, but they continued to fumble around well into evening until the sun went down. She expected to see better, yet it became noticeably worse. Now they walked in utter blackness.

Soon they heard feet rushing toward them as people took hold of their arms and guided them up to a wall, where a large door opened for them, and they were led into a paladinial fortress built to encompass the Temple of Crysania.

Their guides walked them down a long curving walkway, and the air grew cooler as they descended into the earth. A sudden warmth washed over her, and she could only just barely register the voice of the Matriarch being led into the same room.

The muffled voice of her attendant reached her through the tinny ringing in her ears.

"What regimen does the Matriarch Superioris follow? So we can see to her needs."

"This is the Matriarch's room?" She blinked the spots from her eyes, only just able to make out the forms in the room.

"It is. Does she require a certain portion of food? Does she eat much or little?"

"If you prepare a normal portion, she will take it. But she also has a medicinal schedule she must keep to."

Katiam gave them a list of medicines, and the women promised to provide it and also replenish some of Katiam's stores of several items the Convent at Mahn Fulhar did not have.

Katiam was shown to her room, where she placed the satchel containing the Rotha on a writing desk against the wall. She felt around, sniffed at the basin of rosewater, and splashed some of the contents into the dirt in the satchel to remoisten it before throwing herself onto the bed and falling into a deep sleep.

*   *   *

"The city stables report they came and requested all the sleipnirs they could muster, in the middle of the night."

"But why, Nichal?" Dorian asked.

"They do not know. But the Matriarch Superioris herself paid them from her own coffers."

"And were they accompanied by anyone?"

"They were on their own when a few cloaked women came to them with the request."

"The Voktorra at the eastern gate report that they led their beasts out his gate before dawn," the Herald Amal Yollis said. "And met with ten figures, which carried themselves as Paladins."

"And which way did they ride?"

"South."

"If I had to wager," Gallahan Pír said, "they are making their way to the Oracle."

"The words again," Dorian said as he paced the room.

"She sees now a rose whose petals wilt," Gallahan read from the book in front of him. "She sees now a vine that has been cut. Prepare then a hedge of thorns. And be vigilant as a dwov watches over her nest."

"And it is no known verse."

"I've spoken to several priests at the Abecinian complex who know the holy texts, those specializing in Crysalas texts, and they know no verse like this. And it does not match up with the normal rules of prophecy either."

"Which rules?" Nichal asked.

"All Oracular prophecies," Gallahan said, "verify themselves by sharing a known past. Something occurring at the same time as the prophecy, although not often in the same location, and then something from the future."

"But this does not," Dorian said.

"No," Gallahan said, "the entire piece is vague, but reeks of worry; like a mother who feels in her heart something goes wrong with her child."

"Six months!" Dorian said, banging his hand down on the table. "The shade placed in Jined's pocket kept that secret from us for six months."

"How many other shadebooks are there?" Nichal asked.

"Who can know?" Gallahan said.

"They ought all to be found and burnt."

Dorian turned and looked at the Pater Segundus. "If discovered, perhaps. But we'll not conduct a witch hunt."

"Why not?"

"We are the protectors of mankind, not the enemies of ourselves."

"You've seen the map," Nichal said. "We're at war. And we didn't even know it. I'm not convinced the Northern Scapes were not intended to act as a trap for us."

"Nor am I," Dorian said, "but let us find the Crysalas and determine whether the first major act of war has begun."

Nichal stood. "I'll send riders south."

"It is almost night. Jined still lies in his room in his fever dream. You can send riders out tomorrow; I'd like to see what the morning brings."

Nichal saluted and left.

"What are you not telling us?" Gallahan asked.

"I'm leaving in pursuit of them right now."

"You cannot afford to endanger yourself," Gallahan said.

"I'm an old man. If something befalls me, Nichal will tear the country apart."

"He is not vengeful. He never has been. That was why he was made Segundus; because he has a level head."

"Not vengeful, no," Dorian said, "but he is thorough. We ought to have shared with him our knowledge of the Moteans long ago, to allow him to be tempered before this day."

"So you mean to willingly endanger yourself."

"I mean to ride and save my wife. Do you not think Grissone will protect me?"

"At least take Jurgon."

"Jurgon," Dorian said, "ready our sleipnirs after the last bell. We'll ride out before midnight."

"Yes, Prima Pater."

27

Wings of Faith

Raise thy voice with zeal, and speak words that shall carry you wither and hither.

A known verse may draw thy faith out. Or a quiet prayer. But always with courage.

—from Pater Solivan's *Treatise on Miracles*

The following day Katiam was left to herself, save for food brought to her, and, at her request, she was taken back to the Matriarch, to see that her cares were being met. Maeda slept soundly, and her attendants had followed Katiam's instructions to the letter.

On the second morning, she felt nearly normal again, and at each meal joined the drowsing Matriarch as she recovered her strength.

"It is rather impressive that someone her age made the ascent," one of her attendants said as Katiam check the Matriarch over.

"She has been driving herself hard across the continent to reach this destination," Katiam said. "I doubt anything could have stopped her."

"When last she was awake, she did say that she wishes to gather those who journeyed with her tomorrow morning."

"Then I'd suggest you do as she asks and gather us."

"Her assistant, Sister Upona, said as much."

"How does she fare?"

"She doesn't appreciate our taking over her role. Perhaps you feel the same?"

"The rest you've afforded me has been welcome," Katiam smiled.

When she arrived back at her room, she splashed water over the small tendrils peeking out of the dirt in the satchel, and smiled to herself as it soaked in.

The following morning, she was summoned to attend the Matriarch Superioris, who, like Katiam, wore a veil to protect her from the light of torches, or from what little sunlight reached down through the shaft of the center of the Fortress. After Katiam had given the old woman her medicine, they proceeded arm-in-arm to the throng of sisters waiting in a chapel meant to hold half as many.

"My little sisters," the Matriarch Superioris said, "we come now to the crux of our time on this journey. I have not been to this temple since I was a young woman. It was coming here that led me to become a Paladame in the first place. So, I hope you will all feel the closeness to Crysania that I felt when I came here so many years ago.

"As you know, this is a temple that directly connects to the Dweol, the World Rose. We stand in this holy place, where one of few blooms grow, connected to the others by a single root. And yet we know little of this creation of Crysania.

"Today you shall prepare yourself with the usual rites of purity. Tomorrow at dawn we shall visit the oracle at the Rosebloom. There we shall commune with Crysania, and pull back the veil on the future."

They concluded with a song together, and then returned to their rooms. A pitcher of pungent rose water was left for Katiam, as well as a basin of rose-scented purification water. She would receive no food. She would drink the water from the pitcher and clean herself with the water in the basin. The Rotha appeared unperturbed by the journey, and she gave it a portion of the water from the basin before taking up a cloth and wiping herself down. A phial of rose oil sat under the towel on the stand, and she knew to anoint herself with it as dawn came.

A sister somewhere in the cavernous monastery began a song. The solemn chorus echoed with resting breaks between each line. As it concluded another song began, this time joined with the haunting harmonies of another. Katiam hummed along, not courageous enough to offer her pitchy voice to the choral voices.

Instead, she occupied herself with busy work. She opened up her apothecary kit and checked the volumes remaining, making notes in a ledger. She knelt before her bed and prayed, asking Crysania to reveal something to her in the morning, or to provide the opportunity to attend the college in Thementhu. She prayed that the Rotha would continue to grow.

That took her attention to the satchel hanging from her bed. She opened the top. The journey had loosened the dirt, revealing the five tendrils and the very top of the pod, now split open to set free the five tendrils. She tentatively touched the hard woody edge, only to have it react by closing ever so slightly, like some seaside pool-dwelling creature.

She reached for the pitcher of rosewater, pouring herself a chalice. Then she tipped some of it onto the top of the pod, which responded by opening up to accept more. Katiam could see the largest tendril swelling near it's base. It was the first real change she had seen in the Rotha since they had arrived at Mahn Fulhar, and she wondered whether Esenath would consider it a good thing.

Katiam turned to polishing her armor, humming along with the voices as she did so. A nearly imperceptible whistle joined her, stopping whenever she ceased.

The cycle from washing and anointing herself to praying and keeping herself occupied continued on for countless hours until finally a gong pealed in the heart of the monastery, signaling dawn.

She had already donned her ceremonial armor. She took up the apothecary chest, stepped out into the empty hall, and hurried along to the Matriarch's room.

The old lady knelt before a small shrine, muttering to herself. Katiam opened up the kit and quickly prepared the medicine, putting it into a goblet with some of the rosewater, then offered it to her.

"Here you go, Auntie."

"Thank you, dear," she said, taking it and drinking deeply of the cup. "You are a good girl."

She was visibly tired. Katiam helped her to her feet, and then helped her out of an older smock and into a new one before Sabine Upona appeared to help her into her ceremonial garb. Katiam took out the rose oil and anointed the Matriarch as Sabine dressed her. Finally, she emptied the phial onto her hands and ran it through the Matriarch's hair before the headdress went on.

"You know that the Abbess here did the same before I visited the Dweol as a young girl? I thought it was normal. I was surprised at how conservative the sisters at Pariantür were with the oil when I arrived. I only discovered years later her hand had slipped. She hadn't meant to put so much on me."

"And now you've made it a tradition," Sabine said.

"That I have. Why should we skimp on a sacred ceremony? The oil marks us as ready. Pungent it may be, but our attention is drawn to it. There was a time I grew to hate the smell. Now, it always reminds me of time spent in the presence of my goddess."

The din began to peal at a regular pace, and the three of them turned to the door. Astrid came to open the door for the Matriarch, giving her a reverent nod. Maeda smiled at her, and stepped out into the hall to lead the procession, her closest companions directly behind her. Katiam felt Sabine's hand go into hers for a moment to give a comforting squeeze.

Katiam gave the older middle-aged woman a smile, and they walked hand-in-hand through the door.

* * *

By prayer their sleipnirs flew along the road.

Scenarios wracked Dorian's mind. Two hundred women frozen to death in a windstorm. Hostages of the Motean cult. Every mile that flew beneath him brought another terrible thought.

"Faster!" Dorian called out in the biting cold.

"Prima Pater!" Jurgon called back. "My wife is with them, too. My worry is your worry."

Dorian pulled back on his reins, and they slowed to a stop.

"Jurgon," Dorian said, "I'm sorry."

"No need to apologize, Prima Pater. We've known each other long enough that I know when you're ornery. I just wanted to remind you that I am with you, seneschal or not, because my wife may also be in danger."

As dawn came, they saw the Massif on the horizon.

"To the left and the Green Bastion?" Jurgon offered.

"The way is too treacherous," Dorian said, "and they'll have gone right, to the Trials."

"And we will bypass them?"

"We are not allowed. It will be a slow and enforced three days to the top. Perhaps we'll still beat them there."

"Unless they too flew on the Wings of Faith."

"If the Paladins who led them are heretics, then I doubt that," Dorian said.

"I'm ready," Jurgon said.

Together they sang the hymn to swiften their steeds, and together they flew.

> "Grissone-Anka lift us up.
> Our faith lies in you.
> Give us our wings.
> We shall fly.
> We shall fly.
> We shall fly."

By evening they arrived at the Bastion at the foot of the Massif. Paladins there informed them that their escort, Pater Minoris Gladen, had arrived two days prior, and accompanied the Crysalas to the top.

"Then they've not reached the top yet," Dorian said. "They must be preparing to take the final step."

"The Crysalas shall not allow you to hurry the Trials," the Paladin there said.

"Regardless," Dorian said, "I start the ascent at dawn."

It was with surety and faith-led steps that Dorian bounded through the first stage, the Burden. Jurgon lagged only a few paces behind, and they both came to the end of the long day's ascent panting, and happy to partake in the bread left for them there. The second day they walked the Silence, but at a pace none could deny was determined. When they came to the final way-stop, they took a private room and prepared to rest, yet no rest came. They stayed awake through the long night, praying Grissone guard their eyes and ears from the effects of the Brilliance.

The morning brought dark clouds overhead. Dorian smiled and thanked his god even as heavy rain began to fall on them in torrents.

"Not the answer I thought we'd get!" Jurgon shouted over the downpour. Yet the sheets of rain muffled the pealing bells that would deafen them, and they walked in resolute misery up the final stage, albeit with unblinded eyes and their ears in working order.

It was as they neared the top that the rain relented. The path behind shone with light from the afternoon sun. Those atop the paladinial Fortress watched them approach in astonishment and opened the gate to allow their Prima Pater entrance.

No sooner had they come into the vestibule, casting off sodden cloaks, when a hulk of a Paladin approached, open arms and smiling.

"Prima Pater!" Pater Minoris Jakis Gladen called. He gave a deep bow.

"What is the meaning of this?" Dorian said, looking up at the man.

"What do you mean?"

"Taking my wife and her followers without warning."

"Prima Pater, I don't understand."

"How is it you are here, when, four days ago, the same day the Crysalas emptied their convent and journeyed here, you were with our company. Now you're here."

"I think there has been a misunderstanding," Gladen said. "Four nights ago, I had left to ride south with my men to a Bastion, and came upon the company of Crysalas. Your wife, the Matriarch Superioris told me she was on pilgrimage to the Oracle below. We've been here but a day; the doors to the Oracle below are locked. We've watched to see what they do, and now only singing and hymns rise from below."

"Then you did not take them from Mahn Fulhar?"

"No," Gladen said, holding both hands up. "We sang the hymn of the wings, and arrived here in short time, and began the Trials."

Dorian sighed. "Then why did they not send message to me?"

"That I cannot say," Gladen said, "but one of the Paladins stationed here said they fast and sing as they are doing now before visiting the Oracle in the morning."

"Very well. See I am awakened before dawn," Dorian said. "I shall observe from above."

"And I shall join you, if you'll allow."

Dorian nodded. "Jurgon? Let's find some rest."

Dawn came too early, but Jurgon was about his business. He prepared the Prima Pater and helped him don his armor. They came out of the room provided them and came to look down into the heart of the Oracular monastery below. Gladen came to stand next to them, his own Paladins nearby, their armor freshly polished.

"To our left," Gladen said, "are the gates, barred from the inside. It begins a long circumferential ramp that goes down those five levels to the very bottom, where you'll just make out a stone archway leading into the depths of the earth, where the World Rose sits."

"Where one bloom of the Dweol sits," Dorian said.

"Of course," Gladen said. "I've read that some scholars say they are all interconnected, and one thing."

"This is true," Dorian said.

The sound of singing rose, and women appeared in white robes.

Dorian saw his wife at the head of the parade. Her assistant, Jurgon's wife, as well as Katiam, Dorian's great-niece, were at her sides.

Jurgon sighed relief.

The Matriarch stopped before the portal and made a motion with her staff of office, then disappeared into the dark. The throng of women followed her.

"And now what?" Jurgon asked.

"We wait to see what the World Bloom prophecies," Dorian said.

A long hour later, Gladen fidgeted impatiently.

"It could be hours before anything happens, Pater Gladen," Dorian said, scowling.

"My apologies, Prima Pater," he said.

Dorian felt something in his chest begin to hum. A pink plume of faint smoke wafted out of the hole. He peered with old eyes down into the depths.

He turned to the sound of Gladen rummaging through his satchel at his side. He pulled out a fist-sized orb of twisted metal. The veins a blood red.

"What are you..." he said as the arms of Paladins came from behind him, holding him in place.

Gladen gave a look first of regret, then stoic determination. He took up his hammer in one hand and then tapped the orb in his other. He let it fall from his hand down into the depths, tumbling through the air. Dorian watched as it struck the pavement below and then rolled into the dark portal. A few moments later and the earth gave a quick and sudden lurch.

Then the screaming began.

28

Worldrose

Patterns in prophecy are like the petals of a rose. They each are unique, and fit within one another, yet each contributes to the beauty as a whole. From the outside in, both past, present, and future are seen, and reflected upon.

—CRYSALAS PRIMER ON PROPHECY

They came to the large atrium-amphitheater-like space, built in a spiral, made to look like they were inside of a large rose. The walkway spiraled down, while other sisters, who lived there day-to-day looked on. All was lit by a single chandelier of crystal that hung far above. It looked like a dwov hovering over the space. She could see Paladins watching from the highest levels, where their own outer Bastion protected the temple monastery below, looking down toward the sacred entrance.

At the bottom they came to a black hole that led into the earth. They filed one by one into that hole, leaving the world behind. They stood crammed together in the vestibule, the Matriarch Superioris in the lead. A large door made of solid rose-colored crystal stood in front of her. She reached out with purpose, her scepter, shaped like a rose, in her hand. She tapped the door and it rung with a low crystalline sound, grating out of the way. The Matriarch Superioris entered and disappeared into the dark. One by one they all filed around the circumference of the room within.

It was a dark cave. A walkway of black stone circled the outside. Ruddy red points of light along the walls provided some illumination that took getting used to. As her eyes adjusted, she could see the points of light—little crystals that looked like small rosebuds. They grew out of the wall. The floor of the lower chamber was uneven and dark, like obsidian. Maeda Mür held up her scepter for silence, though none had been talking. The shuffling stopped and they watched the Matriarch take three steps down on stones that jutted from the inside wall of the inner circle. As she touched the floor, her steps left a glow of ruddy pink, the same color as the buds on the wall. She walked in a spiral, drawing closer and closer to the center, lighting up the entire floor. It was a rosebud made of crystal, now glowing a ruddy red, illuminating the entire place in its rosy light.

Maeda Mür knelt before the center and whispered something into the Rosebloom floor. The light then began to grow until soon the entire place was lit brightly in a soft pink luminescence. The rosebuds on the walls began to glow to match it, giving off little puffs of crystalline dust, of which everyone breathed deeply. A cloud of pink filled the space, and everyone began to sway slightly as the Rosebloom's power came over them. It was said the cloud could heal wounds that prayers could not. Soon Katiam felt rejuvenated. Her hearing and sight grew clearer, and she could see everything with a lucidity she could not quite place. The scent that filled the place smelled of roses, but it was only part of the greater whole, which reminded her of the scent of every flower she had ever stopped to breathe in.

The Matriarch began to carefully take her headdress and ceremonial cloth armor off, until she wore only her plain white under-robe.

She breathed deeply of the cloud that continued to fill the place with the crystal mist. It began to obstruct vision, making it hard for Katiam to see even the girl next to her.

They stood watching for over an hour as the Matriarch Superioris knelt, unmoving.

Maeda Mür suddenly fell onto her back. The women collectively gasped as they watched her lie there. A few who knew what was happening held out their arms to stop those who wished to rush to her side. The Matriarch Superioris opened her eyes. They were glowing with an intense pink light.

"The Future Tapestry rolls back before my eyes!" she cried. And then her voice changed. The voice that came out of her mouth was not her own, but a feminine voice filled with the eons of age, rich with wisdom, and deep, as though coming from the bottom of a well, and seemed to come from the entirety of the room rather than just from Maeda Mür's throat.

"Hark! Words from past, truths from present, and visions of the future now unfold. Pay attention, lest ye fall prey. The Seamstress speaks.

"Ominous news cries out unto the stars, whose light grows dim. For all was good, and now is not. Heed fair warning once again, for the first strike has been dealt, and the wilting blight has already begun. Prepare now a hedge of thorns, as was warned. For you shall face trials in years to come, and you shall overcome, yet some shall not.

"A dark thing walks among you and brings its shadow to fall on the believers. Unseen it stalks, and unknown are its ways. A holy one did not succumb, but is visited by death. One walks among you who was cursed, and yet Wisdom seeks them out. For this was his divine purpose. And the War Bane shall be held by one thought accursed.

"The future is dire. Little can be said, for the Tapestry comes to obscurity. It rose to prominence in the frigid lands of apostasy, and yet it was not sundered, for it cannot be destroyed. It is a replica of that made by the Arbiter. And it still has its purpose. And then shall rise another, for the gates are opened and locked. The second sons, abandoners, have chosen their Exemplars, and they begin to move their pieces. Balanced scales become unbalanced, and yet her chooser shall make the decision when the prophecy of the spider comes to pass.

"But now the time for change has come. And these final words she speaks. Proud of you she is, and selects not one to replace her, but all of you shall be a new rosebud. Breathe deep for the fragrance fades and shall not return. For this is the first to fall as the gods reap their actions. Feed these my little roses. Birth and nurture them once again to life."

The Matriarch Superioris fell still. She did not move.

A movement by the door caught Katiam's eye, and a shiny black orb of twisted metal bounced into the door, up over the ledge, and landed on the Rosebloom. A pulse of dust came off it and over the floor below, and a singular sound like a creature choking on a bone shuddered through the room. Suddenly the crystal rose frosted like shattered glass, as the entirety of it cracked into countless pieces.

What little weight Maeda Mür had seemed to crumble the ground underneath her, and she sunk into the newly-formed sand. A Paladame near Katiam gasped and sobbed. Another across the room threw herself over the railing and onto the ground. Where she stepped her legs sank to her knees into the crystal silt. The Paladame was Sabine Upona. She trudged through the coarse sand that was the Rosebloom to the Matriarch, and hollered. "Help me! She's not moving!"

Katiam watched as a blind panic begin to descend on everyone.

Katiam and Astrid leapt over the banister toward the Matriarch's fallen form. It was hard to walk through, and numbed her legs through her clothes and armor as she touched the divine but shattered remnants of Crysania's creation and representation on Kallattai. She pulled herself toward the Matriarch. The three Paladames lifted her up and moved toward the edge. The extra weight pulled them down deeper still. As they reached the edge, they were all chest-deep. They handed the Matriarch to a few of the sisters who stood there. Others had fallen to their knees, sobbing and gibbering incoherencies. Another girl screamed and pointed toward the center. Katiam turned. In the center of the room, the rosy crystals were turning black like an infection quickly taking hold. She saw a couple of the girls on the other side of the room frantically reaching down and grabbing handfuls of the still-rosy glass sand. Others saw it happen and threw themselves in. One tore off her robes and began filling it like a grain sack. Others followed suit.

Two Paladames pulled Katiam and Astrid up onto the side. Sabine was still down in the sand. She was shouting instructions to others, who began hauling up the precious material. The blackness crept across the floor. One girl, closer to the center, did not notice as the blackness crept up behind her. It touched her robe, and she suddenly began screaming. In an instant, her screaming stopped, her face looking up at the ceiling in a panicked rictus as her body froze, turned gray as ash, and suddenly exploded as though a wind had hit a pollen-laden tree. There was nothing left of her.

The other girls collecting the crystals saw this and began scrambling toward the edge, fighting against the sand and the weight they carried in their robes. Some dropped their loads. Others handed their collection up, looking back over their shoulders as the blackness crept toward them. Sabine Upona continued issuing orders, while backing away toward the edge herself. A girl near her held a large quantity of the sand in her robe. They both pushed toward the edge, and Sabine helped her lift the burden. Then she pushed the girl up over the edge.

Sabine had sunk up to her neck as the black crept ever closer. She was looking Astrid Glass in the eyes as she said, "Tell my husband I..."

Her face turned suddenly gray with ash and collapsed into the now-blackened crystal that sat in a shallow pit. The Worldrose died and took its protectors with it. A faint heartbeat moved in the Matriarch's chest, but Katiam could tell from the way her face looked—melted and lifeless—that she would not ever be her old self. The Church of Crysania had been dealt a mortal blow, and Katiam knew that this would only be the beginning of the end of all things.

29

Face of Defeat

Hammer and Forge, Rose and Thorn,
Together they rise and together they fall.
No blood is shed, no tunic torn,
As long as in buttress together stand all.

—WORKER'S POEM FROM THE PROTECTORATE OF THE
HAMMER

"He took Jurgon with him," Gallahan said.

"How is that any better, Gallahan?!" Nichal roared. "Jurgon is no guard. It would have been better if he had taken you, or Queton!"

"If he had taken either of us," Gallahan said, "pacifists as we are, he might have flown even faster. Though, given they both ride toward their wives, I doubt it."

"Jined," Nichal said, turning to the larger Paladin next to him, "see the entourage readied."

"The entire entourage?" Jined replied.

"We've already determined we're surrounded by heretics. That firstly means the Prima Pater may be in danger, and we'll all need to ride to him. Secondly, I'll not leave defenseless scribes here if we're entering a time of war."

"What of the Moteans imprisoned in the holding cells?" Gallahan asked.

"We'll take the keys with us, but ask Abecinian Monks to feed them."

Within the hour, the guards had assembled and readied the six-legged sleipnirs for the ride.

Jined had already been armored in his full regalia. The others knew their business, and had taken little time to don breastplates and gorgets over the metal straps that hung tightly over their robes and leather skirts.

Jined approached the twins, his closest friends, Loïc and Cävian.

"Your prayers will be most welcome today," Jined said.

Cävian cocked an eyebrow.

Why is that? Loïc asked, signing the words with his hands.

"The Prima Pater left last night to ride for the Oracle. He believes the Crysalas, three days ride ahead of him, are endangered."

Swift wings of faith, Cävian said.

His brother nodded agreement.

By faith they traveled, their prayers to their god, Grissone, answered, and they moved faster than the wind. By morning, the mountains of the Massif were approaching undeniably fast. By nightfall, they could see the Bastion at the bottom of the canyon that began a three-day journey to the top.

Despite the warnings to the contrary, they did not wait until morning, but began their march through the Burden, forging ahead by miracle or sheer will. They took a short rest awaiting dawn before they began the Silence. They did not let this slow them, and they came to the beginning of the third stage by midday. Some succumbed to their weariness and begged respite. Those were given permission to sleep. When nightfall came, any who were willing to press on began the final climb by night, to avoid the blinding brilliance that would have slowed them in the day.

The eastern horizon was lightening as they neared the summit. The guards under Nichal, as well as Gallahan, elderly as he was, were all who had not fallen behind. They came to the gate, which sat open and unguarded.

Within, a line of Paladins stood at rails, looking down into a cavity as a wail rose from the choir of women below.

Nichal rushed forward, the Prima Pater revealing his face as he turned with a look of despair to rush to the gate that separated the fortress above from the oracle below.

"Prima Pater!" Nichal shouted.

"My wife!" Dorian replied. The Paladins from the fortress entered their own milling panic and shoved past the Prima Pater's guards, while Jined and the twins approached the gate, which was barred from the inside.

"What has happened, Prima Pater?" Nichal asked.

"Open this gate!" Dorian shouted, pounding on the reinforced wood.

"Does this emergency warrant this gate coming down?" Jined asked.

"Yes!" Dorian shouted.

"Grissone," Jined muttered, "hear my prayer, and let this gate come down."

He raised his hammer to smite open the gate, but the bar lifted, and a face he recognized stood within.

"Brother Hammer," Jined said.

The Paladin smiled, but disappeared into the rushing crowd of Paladins as they surged through the gap and ran the ramping circumference of the holy place, arriving at the bottom.

* * *

Chaos reigned. There was a blind panic for an hour as sisters surged out of the Dweol chambers against others trying to press back in, to gather up the sconces off the wall. A Paladin or two pressed in as well, trying to command the women to calm themselves.

A hand took hold of Katiam's and she turned to see the weeping face of Dorian Mür looking at her.

"What happened, child?" he pleaded.

"How are you here?" she asked.

"Where is my wife?"

"I don't know!" she cried out. "Did Gladen bring message to you? And how so quickly?"

Dorian looked at her with eyes full of horror. "I saw her carried out of the chamber along with the screams. What happened?"

"The Dweol shattered. It died."

What felt like moments and an eternity passed, and they were in a quiet room of an infirmary. People rushed without. Dorian sat by the bed, the hand of his wife in his.

Abbess Foi, along with the abbess of the Oracle, stood across from him.

"We did not call for an evacuation of your Convent," Dorian stated solemnly, "and we did not know you had gone until five days ago."

"We left almost a week ago," Abbess Foi said. "How could you not have known?"

"I have little explanation. We sent a message across the green when Jined Brazstein returned, only to find that the gates were barred for a day to observe the Purification Rites of St. Umatt. We did not suspect a ruse until the following morning, and we only knew you had traveled to the Oracle by means of the city's stables providing note that you had taken the sleipnirs south."

"And now you are here."

"I arrived through the Trials as your company entered the Sanctum. And then, after that long silence, the panic began."

"Gladen lied to us," Abbess Foi said.

"Pater Minoris Gladen?"

Abbess Foi explained what had sent them traveling to the Oracle in the first place.

"He is right," Dorian responded. "It appears there is a sect of Paladins bent on the destruction of the order. I suspect that is what contributed to the lost messages to Citadels and Bastions this entire journey. To think that he is one of them is hard to stomach, but not out of the realm of possibility."

"And, through his treachery, we'll lose the Matriarch," Abbess Foi responded.

"She is not dead yet," Dorian said matter-of-factly.

"Uncle Dorian," Katiam said, placing a hand on his shoulder.

He looked up from his seat to her and shook his head, his eyes brimming with tears. "Don't say it, Katiam. I'll not hear the words to dash my hope."

Katiam nodded. She turned to several infirmarians. "Please gather down pillows to make the Matriarch comfortable, and bring a second bed in here to place alongside it for our guest."

"Sister Borreau," Abbess Foi opened her mouth to protest.

"Abbess Foi," Katiam said, looking up into the older woman's eyes with both command and pleading, "are you of the Aspect of Dignity?"

The Abbess shook her head in resignation and left the room. Katiam followed her out into the hall.

"Abbess Foi," Katiam said to the woman, who was walking down the hall in a hurry.

The woman stopped, hesitating before turning back. When she did, Katiam saw hot tears running down her face.

"You said you wanted pillows to make her comfortable," the Abbess said. "Those are words said only for the dying."

"We do not yet know," Katiam said.

"We cannot lose our Matriarch Superioris."

"And I cannot lose my Auntie. Dorian cannot lose his wife. I will do anything and everything to ensure that she stays."

"The Dweol…"

"Focus on that," Katiam said, "and give me the chance to try and bring my Auntie back to the land of the living."

Foi nodded, stiffening her lips. She turned and left, a quiet resolve in her steps.

Katiam returned to see the Matriarch propped up with pillows. She asked the Infirmarians to prepare a breakfast for her to feed the sleeping woman in an hour, and then turned and walked out into the hall herself. A wave of sadness confronted her as the shock of the day settled upon her. Long moments later she found herself standing outside the portal to the Dweol. Only blackness remained within.

She took a deep breath and entered.

Someone else stood there at the rails across the room. Katiam came and stood at the edge, looking down into the colorless pit.

"Is there bliss found there?" the other figure spoke. It was Astrid.

"Bliss?" Katiam replied.

"Those that disappeared, that the Dweol took with itself when it died."

"Best not to dwell on such things," Katiam said, moving around the circumference to Astrid's side.

"Why not?" Astrid asked. "What point is there if what we guard has gone?"

"Those are dark thoughts," Katiam said. "Are there still women with breath on this world?"

Astrid did not reply.

"Your service is not done," Katiam said, "and while the Matriarch still lives, so do I."

"Then she has not died?" Astrid said with a hint of hope in her voice.

Katiam shook her head.

Astrid sighed. "Then I shall continue my vigil."

"What do you mean?"

"The night after Killian...at the Gold Bastion. I was visited by a figure in my dreams. I was told that I was to give my life for the Rose. For the purpose of the Rose."

"And you feel it was a prophecy meant for you?"

"I have no other reason to think otherwise. If the Dweol and Matriarch were both dead, then I would have thought I had failed. Your words... they give me hope. I will continue to serve."

She turned and left the sanctum.

Katiam stood for a long while in silence. The door to the sanctum filled with the form of a tall man. A Paladin.

"This is a holy place," she said. "You may not enter."

"From what I gather," he replied—it was Jined Brazstein, "this place is no longer holy, and needs to be looked over. Pardon me, sister, but I need to see for myself."

"Please don't touch anything. Several of the sisters were killed by touching the ash below."

They both stood across the room for a time.

Katiam sighed. "I should be with the Matriarch."

She approached the Paladin.

"I understand," Jined said. "Sister Borreau, I will heed your warning, but please tell me what happened."

"The Matriarch Superioris delivered a prophecy. Then an odd black object rolled across the floor and into the black sand you see before you, which usually looks like a rose made of crystal. It shattered and began turning black. Those that the blackness touched turned to ash."

"I think I've seen enough. Let us seal this room; it is not safe."

He took Katiam by the shoulders and led her out.

* * *

Over the course of the rest of the day it became apparent that while the Matriarch Superioris was not dead, she would never be able to leave. The Prima Pater sat by her bed the rest of the day and into the evening. Nichal held a meeting and requested Jined bring the Prima Pater to join them.

When Jined entered the infirmary, the Prima Pater, aged beyond years with his grief, did not look up from his wife's face.

"Nichal would like me to come for a meeting, no doubt."

"Yes, Prima Pater."

"Very well."

He rose and kissed his wife on the forehead. "I will return, my love. And if you should pass, know I will be with you soon."

They walked silently to the office provided for them. Nichal sat behind the table, but stood as they entered. Five others turned and rose.

Gallahan Pír was positioned near Nichal as scribe, with his own right-hand man, Primus Aeger, next to him. Adjutant Amal Yollis and the older Standard Bearer Primus Valér Queton sat on the other side of Nichal. Jurgon Upona sat in a corner, haunted by the loss of his own wife.

"Prima Pater, thank you for stepping away so we can speak."

The Prima Pater left Jined's side and went to sit next to Jurgon, putting a hand on his seneschal's own.

After an awkward moment, Nichal took his seat again.

"It appears the World-Rose has died, or is dying. That leaves the church of Crysania with an unforeseeable future. It leaves us all unable to know what lies ahead. Regardless, we have much to go over. I believe we need to fall back to Mahn Fulhar and speak with the other churches, perhaps end our journey, and proceed back to Pariantür. Prima Pater? Do you have anything to say on the matter?"

Dorian remained silent.

"What of the paladames?" the old standard bearer asked in a thick Œronzi accent.

"They will travel with us to Mahn Fulhar."

"And the rest of the Crysalas who journeyed from their convent to here?"

"To ask them all to leave would be too sudden a move," Amal Yollis said. "It would be better to take those who are willing to go with us, and leave the rest here to prepare for the journey come spring. Some of the local Paladins expect a storm to be rolling in from the west, which will blanket Mahndür by morning."

"You speak well, Brother Yollis," Nichal said. "Prima Pater? Dorian?"

The Prima Pater stood up. "I will not be returning to Mahn Fulhar," he said. "You will go without me. I shall be staying here with my wife."

He left the room.

Nichal stood in silence for some time. He eventually took a deep breath and then spoke with more authority than usual. Gallahan was sent to speak with the paladames, who made it clear that they would be staying longer, and would send a message when they sought to return to Mahn Fulhar.

30

Unseen Shadow

Speak for those who have no justice. You may not see them, but Nifara sees your actions. Stay true. Bring truth.

—ARCHIMANDRITE BARUT

The Nifaran monks had been provided decent quarters within the confines of the Abecinian complex. Each monk had their own room, spartan and easy to navigate. As a whole, they shared a room for meeting with each other or for accepting guests, while a separate dining hall, with a cook provided by the king himself, kept them fed.

Seriah had stayed occupied since the Solstice ceremony, but had not found the time nor the opportunity to leave the complex, keeping busy with those who sought out the judgments of the Nifaran Order. While life on the road was preferred, this winter of work, balanced with solitude, was a welcome respite. People from the city, and even priests of the other faiths, came to visit the monks, who each took turns sitting in judgment.

The still very sickly Pell Maran saw only a guest or two each day before falling once more into a deep sleep, but he was happy to see visitors, legitimizing the rest of them when the visitor came after his rest had begun, and they resorted to making their claim with another monk. Giving was never required, nor forced. But most paid alms, since it always cost more to have lawyers and courts involved in any decision, petty or otherwise.

Five days prior, in the pre-dawn, the Prima Pater sent a messenge that the Paladins were leaving for Precipice Fortress ahead of the planned early spring trip, to join the Matriarch Superioris on her pilgrimage to visit their orphic shrine, located in the fortress.

Kerei Lant, along with Pell Maran and the aging Cräg Narn, while surprised at such a sudden departure, offered their blessing. The messenger, Pater Segundus Gallahan Pír, emphasized that while sudden, important news had come to light and demanded a swift reaction.

The Paladin then became very vague and told the collected monks and assistants to be on their guard. When the monks pressed the issue, the Paladin only said that change was coming, and that the Prima Pater would meet with them when he returned.

To Seriah, not much had changed. People seeking justice came and went, monks took turns sitting with Pell Maran while awake or asleep, and they spent time fellowshipping with one another. Seriah had felt fortunate to spend so much time with the heads of her order, receiving lessons on the faith found in Nifara. It made all the trouble they had gone through to reach Mahn Fulhar worth it.

If there was a change, it was the frequency in which the Black Sentinels made their appearance with the Paladins gone. The head of the Sentinels in particular, Searn VeTurres, came by daily. He checked on the monks, reminding them of the Black Sentinels' intent to escort the monks back to their Templum in Birin when the winter had broken.

On this particular day Seriah prepared to leave the complex for the first time since the Solstice. The assistant Ensayez dela Neitha would travel as her eyes as they visited an orphanage that was said to have taken in many children as of late, suffering from a blinding malady that had fallen upon the local populace.

They came out into the frigid air at midday. While the wind was biting, the direct sunlight made a counteroffer of warmth. Once they left the upper city and entered the long canyon that housed the city, the wind stilled and the sun disappeared, leaving a damp cold over the place.

Ensayez was a quiet girl, and always spoke with hesitation. Seriah understood that she had been abandoned on the streets of Morriego at a very young age.

"When did you come to join an orphanage of Nifara?" Seriah asked.

"I was, perhaps, ten?" she said demurely.

"And you will take your Vows soon?"

"I will be sight bound when I am allowed."

"I was orphaned at eleven," Seriah said. "Redot is plagued with vendettas, so when my parents were murdered, I was quick to desire revenge. Had I not been taken in by a monk, who found me in a tavern plotting the destruction of their killers across the room, I would be dead today. The peace I found in Nifara is more than I can express."

Ensayez laughed a light bubbly laugh.

"What is so funny?"

"I don't think I've ever heard you raise your voice at anyone. I can't imagine you as a little girl plotting to murder."

"Well, it's true. And I have plenty of temper; I just keep it to myself."

"We are coming to where I am told the orphanage is."

"Very well. Let us remember what Nifara has done for us as orphans when we speak. There is a reason you and I were sent here to negotiate with them."

The place they entered smelled musty and close. Old meat sat out somewhere. There was quiet coughing of children elsewhere.

"Good day to you?" Seriah called out.

She heard someone rise.

"It is an elderly lady rising from a chair, but it's hard to see in the dark. There are no candles lit," Ensayez said. "She looks like she's half-blind herself."

"Welcome," the old lady croaked. "Where are you?"

The person shuffled about. Ensayez guided Seriah's hand out to take the hand offered by the woman. The lady began to feel Seriah's arm and robe, and then she found the staff, feeling up its length to the standing ring atop it.

"Ah. Holy Nefers. I have been expecting you. I am Loranne. Welcome to my home."

She did not offer them any food, but they found a place to sit and talk. Loranne, it seemed, had been taking on children all of her life, just never formally. The winter before a malady had befallen the city, and several children had been struck blind and were then quickly abandoned by their families. At the same time, Loranne had begun to lose her own sight to the malady. She continued to find ways to feed the children, but it had become too much with the onset of winter.

"That is why I have asked you here. I understand you help orphans."

"Yes, and more so when they are blind," Seriah said.

"Then please take them. These children are hopeless, and I am old."

"We shall," Seriah said. "Ensayez here shall help to ensure all is completed with the authorities. These children shall never go hungry again. Nor shall you," she added.

The old lady began to cry, and she fell into Seriah's arms.

Seriah could feel the exhaustion rolling off the little old lady's shoulders as she cried. Soon, Seriah, holding the old lady, began to cry softly to herself, soaking her blindfold with warm tears.

Ensayez straightened the place up while Seriah held Loranne, who eventually fell asleep leaning against her. An hour later, the old lady gave a deep sigh and sat up. She became what Seriah deemed her normal, cheerful self, giving kind orders to the children and searching about for bread in her cupboards.

She saw them off with a bottle of wine she had been saving, and sent several children out with her last saved coins to buy some fresh meat for their dinner.

As they walked back to the complex, Seriah said, "Ensayez, when we return, please immediately speak with the Abecinian temple. They are to commission their kitchen to go and restock Loranne's food supplies, and also send carpenters to fix the place up. Have the other monks help you draft up a charter for the orphanage as quickly as possible. I will speak with Kerei Lant about the finances."

Seriah found the Archimandrite in her room. Seriah told Loranne's tale, to the approval of Kerei. But the journey and explanation to the Archimandrite took Seriah longer than she had expected, and her hour to sit with Pell Maran had already passed. She rushed down the hall, hoping someone else had taken the opportunity and not left the old man alone.

As she approached, muffled voices came from within.

"I told you it was not necessary for you to do that to her." The voice of Pell Maran was soft and weak, as though he had just awoken.

"Everything I do is necessary. The gods have too long bandied we mortals against each other, and against opposing gods." The voice was like a hoarse whisper, and it was filled with darkness that froze Seriah in her place.

"You have made yourself clear why you have long sought my life. But why her? Why Rystan?"

Rystan was a sweet girl, and had no doubt gone to take Seriah's place when Seriah had been unable to.

"She was pure of heart. Her blood was just as good for creating the bond. It is almost complete. But I also need yours. It is time."

"The gods will not stand for it. Your crimes will be paid for by your own soul."

"I am untouched because they cannot see me. It is too late. Your life completes the shroud. Two heads of religion. A champion of the Mad Gift Giver. It should be more than enough. Fitting that they should be from the two gods of death—those who will never have the opportunity to weigh my soul on their scales. And if, through my actions, I shall also claim the life of another? All the better. The gods will fall because I will kill them one by one."

"You will not find me willing, even if I am too weak to fight you."

"I know. Your courage will be remembered. You understand I don't do this out of selfishness; I do this for everyone. The gods failed when she birthed the Deceiver through doubt and greed. The gods chose their own destiny when they did not take care of their own house. We could still be in times of great peace had they not abandoned us to him."

"You are wrong. The gods did not know his nature until it was too late, and now they work to unravel what he has wrought."

"And thus you declare the gods flawed."

"That I did not. I declared the gods limited. They were created by the Existence, just as we were created by them. They are creations, just as we are. They are simply greater than we."

"And yet I walk unseen by them. Who is greater, now? It is time now, Archimandrite."

There was a soft sound, a gasp, and silence.

She heard a thrum that rose, and then suddenly quenched itself in utter silence, deeper than the one before.

In the blackness behind the blind across her eyes she saw a blue streak, like a ribbon flying toward the room. The walls that stood between them did not matter; they were not there. Seriah could see her plainly as though she had no blind on. A figure stood there, visible only because of the shadow he cast in her light. Seriah wanted to cry out, but could not. She stood there, witness to Nifara arriving to take Pell Maran away.

There were stories of those who saw Nifara in the moments after a loved one died. And here Seriah stood. The goddess's light began to shift as she turned to go, holding in her hands two balls of light.

The black shadow turned toward the side door and did not see Seriah as he passed. She would have breathed a heavy sigh of relief if she had any air in her lungs.

Suddenly, the air cleared, and Seriah began to take deep painful breaths as panic settled over her. She sought frantically to escape from the place, lest the shadow of the gods find her—a dark figure intent on killing the innocent for an imperceivable aim. The blind panic of a blind monk took her far away and well into the night.

31

Awakening

Little Rose, Little Rose, where have you gone?
I've sought a pretty land to put my feet upon.
Little Flower, Little Flower, what do you see?
Your nose upon my face is how I come to breathe.

— VARIATION OF AN AGE-OLD RHYME

They ignored protocol and left at nightfall, quickly moving along the three stages of the descent. Nichal was terse and agitated when the Paladames informed them of their intent to stay, and it didn't look like his attitude would be changing anytime soon.

Even on campaign against raiding parties of T'Akai, Nichal was always easygoing and quick to make concessions as needed. Now, he walked with a tense authority.

They rode from the stable Bastion at the foot of the mountains at a slow trot, too sad and distracted to properly pray their speedy haste. Jined rode beside Nichal, who read the prophecy transcribed by Gallahan from the sisters' final meeting with the World-Rose.

"The Moteans have something up their sleeve," Nichal said. "We have remained quiet for too long. I think we need to strike hard."

"But we don't know who is Motean and who is not," Jined offered.

"The Prima Pater's inquest didn't reveal any secret members among our own company."

"Then we'll conduct a deeper hunt for them. I want every Paladin to prove they aren't."

"We can't do that," Jined said hesitantly.

"We will do what we deem necessary," Nichal said darkly.

"Pater Segundus," Jined said calmly, "why the sudden change?"

"Sudden change? The Prima Pater is a father to me, to all of us—his wife, a mother. I will not stand idly by and allow them to fall and not provide a rebuttal."

"And what makes you think this was caused by the Moteans? Besides that, the Prima Pater hasn't fallen; he has simply stayed behind. We will see him again."

"Gladen. Dorian said he dropped something down into the Dweol—a metal orb of some sort. In the chaos that ensued, Gladen left before anyone could question him. The Prima Pater had hoped to seek them out, to open a civil discourse with them—but I will root them out."

"That is not necessary," another Paladin said. He rode on the other side of Nichal. The Pater Segundus did not recognize the Paladin, but also did not seem surprised at him suddenly speaking up.

"Brother Hammer," Jined said.

The Paladin nodded. "Do not conduct a witch hunt. Wait. The answer will come to you as needed. Just because the mother goddess's means to connect with her followers has been severed does not mean she is gone. Precisely the opposite. Never has she been more active."

Nichal opened his mouth to speak, but the Paladin was suddenly gone.

"Where did he...?"

Jined smiled.

"Who was that?"

"Pater Segundus, you ought to heed what he said. That was your god."

Nichal almost fell from his sleipnir.

"That was Grissone? But..."

"He often speaks with that familiar tone."

"He saw me at my worst—willing to hunt down members of our own church. I have failed."

"You have not failed," Jined said. "You've simply been given a diverting set of instructions."

He did not cease to talk about Grissone's appearance the rest of the day. His countenance changed, and when they set up camp, he led the hymns with a fervor.

The next day, Jined rose early and scouted ahead. They were nearing the St. Nonn Bastion, and Nichal had asked that he make sure no one had taken up residence.

He neared the hill and could see smoke coming from the chimney. He rode back to Nichal, who watched over the breaking down of camp.

"The fire is lit at St. Nonn. Perhaps the Moteans have taken it back?"

"We ride to take it, then," Nichal said, a twinge of anger in his voice.

The scribes promised to wait an hour before coming up behind them. Nichal led from the front, with the rest of the guards behind him.

The destriers' hooves pounded the frozen ground as they approached St. Nonn. No one came out to greet them, and so Nichal dismounted and marched up to the door, pounding on it with his hammer.

"In the name of Grissone, open up!"

There was a sound of scrambling. Nichal signaled and the twins dismounted and opened the doors. A single figure stood inside, approaching the door to open it. It was one of the Black Sentinels that had joined them on the road, Rallia Clouw.

"Brother Paladins," she said, "I am glad to see welcome faces."

"Arrest and shackle her," Nichal said.

The Sentinel looked shocked as the twins approached. When she realized they were serious, she turned and ran toward the back. Loïc and Cävian went after her and brought her out kicking and struggling.

She was forced to her knees before the company. Jined looked uncomfortably on.

"So, you must be the messenger for the Moteans," Nichal said.

"They call us Coin Cloaks sometimes, but never Moteans. I don't even know what that means. And no, I'm no messenger. I'm on a mission, searching for something. I came upon this Bastion, and some-one had vandalized the eagle. I stayed to scrub it clean."

"More like a spy, I think. She can walk behind us. Etienne, make sure there are no other compatriots here."

Etienne nodded and quickly moved through the bastion. He came back within a few minutes.

"There is nothing," he said.

The Sentinel was put in chains behind Dane's sleipnir.

"I do not understand why you've arrested me," Rallia said calmly, so all could hear.

"You were found," Dane said, "as the sole individual in a paladinial Bastion that was a base for Paladins who had fallen from the faith. Why you, of all people, already in close circles with us, would take up residence here is suspect."

"I don't know what you're talking about. Fallen paladins? I didn't even know that was possible."

"I think that she lies," Dane said. "Her grandfather was a Paladin. I've heard her say so on our journeys. Perhaps her grandfather was a member of the heretical sect."

"That will need to be looked into," Nichal said. "What was your grandfather's name?"

"My grandfather was the kindest man I've ever known. He was faithful to the Hammer. I have no doubt about that."

"His name, girl!" Dane shouted.

"Jadsen Brathe."

Dane made a note to himself, and they rode on. Once they met up with the scribes, Rallia was given a sleipnir to sit upon, though uncomfortably tied to prevent escape.

It took three days to reach Mahn Fulhar. By then all were weary of the road.

"I wish to send a message to my brother," Rallia said.

"In due time," Dane said, escorting her away from the rest.

No one was awake in the Abecinian compound, so they found their beds and slept well into the next day.

* * *

Jined awoke to a light tap on his door. He grunted, and heard the muffled *jin, jin, jin* of a monk's staff outside.

"Just a moment," he said as he readied himself.

When he opened the door, a monk stood before him. She was pressed into the doorframe, trying to make herself hidden from the view of the hall.

"Nefer?" he asked.

"Are you Jined Brazstein?" she asked.

"I am. You are Nefer Seriah Yaledít."

"Please, will you walk with me? I must speak with you, and I feel you are the only one I can trust. I have heard of the miracle your god performed on you on the road."

Jined came out into the hall, and they made their way to the gardens. He offered his arm to the small woman, but it did not reduce the obvious stress and paranoia that seemed to bleed off her.

Once outside, they found a bench against a wall, and he offered her a seat.

She was breathing heavily, and the slightest sound seemed to startle her.

"Nefer, please explain the meaning of this."

"I will. Please allow me time to gather my breath. I have held a secret since not long after you and the other Paladins left, and it has tortured my soul. I have heard you are close to your god, perhaps even chosen by him. I discovered this morning that the Prima Pater did not return with you, and I feared the worst. You see, I am the only witness to the death of our Archimandrite. He was murdered along with another. And it was done by a great source of evil. I fear for my life."

She related what she heard. How she had felt unable to move. The conversation Pell Maran had with the dark voice. How Nifara had appeared and did not see the figure, and how she had stayed hidden while the king's Voktorra came to identify the bodies of Pell Maran and the young monk Rystan Amiré.

"That is dire news," Jined said.

"And now you return without the Prima Pater. Has something befallen him as well?"

"No. He is alive. His wife, however, is comatose."

"What is happening, brother paladin?"

"The world is shifting toward something. Neither you nor I, nor even the gods, it seems, know what it is."

"And now I cannot sleep for fear that I am next. It would have been me, rather than Rystan. I was to sit with the Archimandrite, but I arrived late from an errand."

"It seems the gods have other intentions for you. Call it fate, if you will, but nonetheless you were spared. Do not throw it away to fear."

"I will try."

"Let me escort you back to the monk's quarters. I have some thinking and praying to do to decide what will happen next."

He walked her back and left, though not before Dane Marric saw him.

"Brother Brazstein," he said, "I have been looking for you all morning."

"What is it, Marric?"

"I found something in the possession of the Clouw. I think it important for you to see."

"Why me? Why not Nichal?"

"It was a note written in the blind alphabet you've been studying."

They moved quickly to Dane's room. There, on the table, sat the letter. Jined ran his hands over it, with Dane nearby.

"What does it say?" Dane asked.

"It is addressed to a person known as the Slate. It says it lies in wait in the possession of the Anchor."

"What does?"

"I have no idea. But it does mention its use may be all it takes to break the back of the enemy. It's a short message, but conveys enough."

"Slate," Dane said. "Could that refer to Pater Minoris Gladen's second? Primus Slate?"

"It may. It also may be intentionally incriminating."

"We ought to question this Clouw again; she must know more."

"We bring this to Nichal."

"I will go and begin questioning this Clouw," Dane said, "to see if I can draw anything out before you arrive with Nichal."

He disappeared from the room before Jined had a chance to say anything.

Jined left and promptly found Nichal in the library with Gallahan.

"What is it, Brazstein?"

He put the letter in front of them. Gallahan read it aloud.

"Well, Pír?" Nichal asked.

"Riddles. Obviously Slate and Anchor are members of this secret society. It would seem the Moteans are making use of the blind script, and perhaps have for some time. But what was this Sentinel doing working with them?"

"Dane left to begin questioning her again. I came to show you this."

"Dane swears oaths to not speak to any woman," Gallahan said, "does he not?"

Jined looked at Nichal, a sinking feeling in his gut. "Why this one, then?"

Nichal nodded, and the three of them rushed to the holding cells.

As they approached, they heard chains rattling. The thud of fists on flesh sounded out all too loudly.

Nichal and Jined both rushed forward and pushed open the doorway. As they entered, they saw a gloved fist strike against the shoulder of the woman in the chair, her arms chained behind her.

Her eye was already swollen, and there was a red welt on both her shoulders.

"What have you done, Marric?!" Nichal screamed, rushing to shove him out of the way.

"She refused to answer any of my questions. She insulted me."

"You insolent fool," Gallahan said, examining the young woman.

Nichal took in the sight and turned full onto Dane, grabbing him by the gorget and throwing him out into the hall. "How dare you do this?! We can't imprison and beat a woman, for any reason. The Crysalas will have your head."

"The actions of the heretics have compromised the Crysalas, and they are gone."

"And you," Jined said, "have never cared for the Crysalas in the first place."

"You will repeat what she has said to you," Nichal said to Dane, "verbatim, and then you'll face the consequences of your actions."

"I came here to question her," Dane began. "She stated to me that she was sent on a mission to find someone, though she refuses to acknowledge whom. It seems she was then sent to the bastion of St. Nonn to meet someone. No doubt a traitor, who would understand the message and instruct her on the next stage of her journey."

"But what did she say to you that caused you to strike her?"

"She told me she was bound by her oath as a Sentinel Runner to divulge no more. And I told her I was bound by greater oaths to a god. She told me that it was no greater thing to be loyal to a god than to an ideal."

"And that's what you beat her for? For saying her oath was just as important?"

"I will not have someone question my faith."

"Dane?" Jined said. "I offer you my an insult of my own. You're a fool. I've never met someone so touchy yet uninformed in their knowledge of the divine."

Dane scoffed.

"Did she mention where she had come from?" Nichal asked.

"Something regarding a lighthouse against the coast to the west."

"Jined?" Nichal asked. "Take the twins and go west. Tracking the steps of a Black Sentinel in the middle of winter shouldn't be difficult. Do not waste your time. And you, Dane. You are to go to your cell. There you will stay until I say otherwise. Effective immediately, you are to be given bread and water only, and speak only when I speak to you."

Dane left, not saying another word.

"Jined, be careful. I suspect the Moteans are moving soon. Watch out for them. They could be any Paladin."

"Yes, Pater Segundus. I offer the same warning to you. Be careful."

"I will. Now, Gallahan and I have apologies to make to the Sentinel."

* * *

Katiam watched the slow, far-too-shallow breaths of her great aunt rise and fall. The blanket across her elderly frame was tucked in, her arms lying at her sides. Katiam hoped to see a twitch of her fingers. Every movement and sound startled Katiam, yet nothing came from the body of her Auntie.

She had not stirred in the past five days. Two days after the incident the Paladins had left with Nichal Guess at their head. A week later Dorian himself left, leaving Abbess Foi with the suggestion that she make preparations to leave when the weather turned, perhaps even retreating to Pariantür, if they did not feel anywhere else safe.

Two sisters came in with soup prepared for the Matriarch Superioris. Together they, along with Katiam, sat the limp body of Maeda Mür up and tilted open her mouth. They slowly worked it open and put a funnel in place, then gently poured trickles of the broth down into the hole, taking breaks for her weak breathing to resume. Their chore finished, the ladies left her alone once more.

Katiam took the bony hand of the woman before her and softly began to cry. She was surprised to still find tears within her.

"We need you, Auntie," she said. As the last word left her mouth, her heart cracked, and she began to sob, as she often did. Fewer visitors came. Some came in groups, standing at the back of the room, watching, while others requested time alone with Maeda. It broke Katiam's heart to know that most had given up, but it also gave Katiam the time she felt she deserved alone.

She took a deep breath, choking down her tears. "Maeda Mür. We need you to come back to us," she said. "The Crysalas need you. I need you here."

The old woman simply continued to breathe. Her mouth opened wider than usual, and she took a deep breath. Katiam saw a glint of crystalline pink inside the Matriarch's mouth as she closed it once more.

"What is that?" she thought out loud. She gently opened the Matriarch's mouth and took a look. There, a pink stone was lodged in the old lady's back molar. Katiam put her finger into Maeda's mouth and tried to dislodge it.

As she touched it, she suddenly saw a flash of light, and she was standing once more at the Dweol, surrounded by her sisters, Maeda in the middle of the room, as the Matriarch Superioris said, "Feed these my little roses. Birth and nurture them once again to life."

Light flashed and she found herself in her own room, the Rotha pod had spilled out from the dirt-filled satchel. A root now grew from the bottom, but the five tendrils reached out across the desk to a satchel of glass dust from the World Bloom.

The flash pulsed again, and she pulled herself from the crashing surf and onto a sandy beach. She rose to stare at a wall of vegetation standing before her, the hand of her daughter wrapped around her own. Together they stared toward the impassable wall.

Katiam was back in the room with her great aunt. The Matriarch's breathing was once more regular now. The shard of pink glass was now in Katiam's hand, a slight glow from it now fading. "What just happened?"

She held up the pink glass in her hand and examined it.

"How did you get in Auntie's mouth?"

She thought through the vision. Visions were always said to include moments from past, present, and future.

The collapse of the World Rose was obvious. She had left the Rotha in its satchel on her desk. But that wall of vegetation... she knew it. She felt she should. She could still feel the brush of the little hand holding hers. Her daughter's hand.

Maeda took a deep gasp. Katiam spun her head around and rose to stand over her. The Matriarch's eyes bulged as she looked around.

"Where... Where am I?" she rasped.

"Shh now," Katiam said. "I am here Auntie. I'm here."

Maeda looked up at Katiam and her body calmed, though in her eyes a look of fear haunted her.

"I should not be here. I should have gone."

"You are still alive," Katiam said. "I am so glad you heard me and returned."

The old lady reached up and grasped blindly at Katiam's robes. She took hold and pulled the girl down to her.

"I am only here to come for you," she said.

"Come for me?"

"You must heed the words I spoke. You're the only one I trust to do what was commanded. Birth and nurture them once again to life."

"Those were your final words at the Dweol."

"Then it is gone? Truly gone?"

Katiam nodded.

"Heed my words. If you took the prophecy from my mouth, the one meant for you, then you know what you must do."

"I don't know."

Maeda had fallen to her pillow, exhausted. Her eyes were closed. Katiam rose to get another blanket to cover her cold arms.

"Dorian," Maeda whispered.

"Your husband?"

"Yes. I know he left to attend to matters. You must tell him something for me."

"Of course, Auntie."

"Charge him to complete what he never finished. And to seek what he should have sought on his own."

"I will. Now please try to rest."

"No. The time for resting...is done."

"What do you mean?" she said, laying the blanket under her chin.

Maeda's mouth was open. Katiam took the mirror next to the bed and held it under her Auntie's chin. No breath fogged the glass. She set it down, walked to the door, and stepped out into the hall, then walked back to her room. She heard two women who had stood guard outside the room say something and then step in themselves. It took several seconds before the wail went out.

It was a long walk back to her cell but the wail seemed to race ahead of her, flooding the halls from every room as each began their cry of mourning. The waiting was over. The time for rest was done. The Matriarch Superioris had passed from them.

She stood in front of the door to her cell for some time, staring vacantly at the woodgrain. People rushed past her. One of them might have called her name, but she didn't hear. She touched the handle and it swung open on easy hinges. Within the cell, her desk sat opposite the door. The candle had snuffed out next to her bed, and so she took a spare candle from one of the nooks in the hall and lit it by the one long guttering candle in the alcove and stepped back into her room.

She could see a smear of some sort spilled across the desk, with a ruddy hue to it. She hoped it was only a goblet of wine she had perhaps spilled in her haste to leave that morning. She held the candle and walked forward. A small sack of glass beads had spilled across the desk. She rushed forward, fearing perhaps that someone had stolen something from her room. There were only a few of the beads left across the desk, and the satchel was empty. They each had the dull color of the glass bead she had pulled out of the Matriarch's mouth. She looked under the desk. None had fallen on the floor, but the Rotha's satchel lay spilled across the floor by the wall.

A panic rose in her as she turned and looked around the room for the Rotha, hoping beyond hope that it had not been stolen.

Something gleamed on the floor. Another bead. She walked forward and picked it up. Another one was near the edge of the bed. She looked under the bed to see nothing.

The sound of a whistling breeze seemed to prick at her ears, and she looked up on the bed. Her pillow seemed oddly formed, sitting propped against the headboard. She reached out and took hold of the pillow, pulling it away quickly. The whistling rose to almost a scream in her ears. The Rotha sat there on the mattress, in a nest of crystals. The pod had split open fully, and five vines had unfurled, one sat up in the air taller than the others, while the other four seemed to retreat from Katiam's candle, pulling the nest of crystals in around itself.

The screaming whisper wasn't nearly as loud as Katiam thought as she took a step back. She placed the candle on the side table, and the screaming turned back to a whisper.

"What are you?" Katiam asked.

The pod just sat there.

She reached out to touch the one vine reaching to the sky. It almost deftly dodged her touch at first and then coiled and snapped out, curling around her finger tightly.

"What are you doing?" she said. She pulled on it, but it felt so weak that she feared breaking the little vine. Another vine took hold of one of the crystals and held it up. It still glowed. It touched it to Katiam's palm, and the world disappeared.

32

Interlude

Pater Koel rose from his bed, a chain trailing from his wrists and legs to an anchor in the wall. The ringing in his mind was gone, and he was once again himself. He reached up to touch the healed burns on his neck, shoulder, and heart. The last one was still tender. He did not know what day it was, nor how long he had been in this living prison.

The door swung open and two Paladins entered. Their own eyes had that same look of abject horror in them, but they roughly hoisted him onto his feet. Hunger gnawed at his gut.

Another entered, unhooked the chains from the wall, and came to look Koel in the eye.

"Cast off the harness again?" he said, his eyes dark with anger. "Slate has asked for you to be broken once more."

He turned and stalked out of the small cell, and the two Paladins holding Koel up dragged him forward.

He recognized one of them as a member of his own fortress.

"Brother Namab," he said from a parched mouth, "continue to fight against it. You can break free."

Namab didn't respond. They passed a window, and Koel saw past the white landscape and pine-covered hills to the sea.

A door opened into a central chapel, revealing to Koel that they were in a bastion. A fire roared in the mantle. A Paladin, wearing boots that lifted his height several inches, stood before it. He poked at a coal-filled brazier. Another Paladin held tongs over the glowing embers. As the tall Paladin turned, Koel recognized his face—he was the silent seneschal to the Pater Minoris of the Aerie. He did not recall his name, but the nightmare of past meetings such as this came to mind. The man wore an oversized black gauntlet.

Koel's heart began pounding painfully in his chest.

"Perhaps one of these days, we'll see you permanently under our influence," the Paladin said.

Koel opened his mouth to speak.

"You're going to ask me what's going on, and I'll explain once more what I'm about to do, which won't matter, because it has been done—you'll be broken and forget. So this time, I'm not going to bother. Vanguard ought to order you killed, but he finds it interesting that someone can cast off the shackles time and again, and wants it recorded how many times it takes before you're completely broken."

The man made a motion with the gauntlet, and the two Paladins at Koel's side forced him to his knees. Then he held the gauntlet out for the man with the tongs to place a red-hot coin into his palm. Turning, he walked toward Koel.

"Now, let's try this again."

"Grissone will grant me strength to oppose evil." He quoted Hamul's words, and recalled that he had every time. "Their victory is only temporary."

He silently prayed; he never forgot to.

"Brave words." The man smiled, although Koel thought he saw a hint of fear, or perhaps guilt, in his eyes.

The heretic pressed the coin into Koel's right shoulder and received a scream in response. Then the screaming suddenly stopped. Koel rose to his feet, his face passive and his eyes, like those of the two men next to him, filled with horror.

"How many times has he been put under your control?" another Paladin asked.

"This is the tenth," Slate said, turning to speak. "As you can see, it's a simple process."

"How did you discover it?"

"Vanguard locked me in a room and gave me little more than bread and water, and told me to solve the puzzle."

"The ascetic mind can be a strong one."

"You said you could offer me a secret of your own, if I showed you this."

"In good time."

"Cup," Slate said, "for me to have shared these secrets with you betrays Vanguard's trust in me. But to have someone so influential from the Order of the Feather willing to share the secret of making a shade?"

"A time is coming," Cup said, "where those who have risen to rank by their ability to convince others to follow, will be replaced by those of us who have done the research and solved the riddles in the shadows. You solved a seventy-year old mystery, and have unlocked the Plate. I have taken the creation of shades to the next level."

"What are you proposing?"

"I'm proposing we work together. We take these secrets we know, and travel to Piedala."

"Why Piedala?"

"It's where the Order of the Anvil hides."

"They barely hide; their bells are in plain sight there."

"Yes, but their leader is up north here, in Mahn Fulhar."

"Is he?"

"Yes," Cup said. "So if we take this gauntlet of yours, my knowledge of the Feather, and go together, we can either convince—or, with your gauntlet, dominate—whoever was left in power. We'll have the power of all three Orders, united."

"But that's all the plan you have?"

"For now."

"Then for now I will stay here."

"Why?"

"Because Vanguard has a plan. And if I play my part, I've been promised a great deal of power."

"But subservient to him."

"Voluntary subservience."

"What could he do if we left now?"

"You do not know Vanguard as I do. I've never met a more vindictive man than he. If I betrayed him, he'd turn the world upside down to see me exposed in a field, and then watch as I was devoured by whatever creature caught my scent."

"That's rather specific."

"Because he's done it before. He used a man as bait to rope a griffin and put it under the same influence these Paladins are."

"He tamed a griffin?"

"He dominated its mind. It killed itself in madness."

"And what if Vanguard was no longer in charge?"

"That would change things, I think. Now, the secret you offered?"

"I'll be sending you instructions."

"Why won't you tell me now?"

"How do I know you won't just hear me out and then have me killed?"

"I could put a hot coin to you and force you to tell me."

"I have already made allowances for that. You cannot break a spirit that is not in a body."

"What is that supposed to mean?"

"Await my instructions, and perhaps you'll understand."

PART 5

33

Heresy

"Hark! Hammer rings.
On anvil of the wicked it swings."

—CHILDREN'S VERSE SPOKEN AS
PALADINS OF THE HAMMER APPROACH

Jined and the twins rode together once more. A storm had blown in from the north, dropping wet, heavy snow. Were it not for a bush or two barely peeking up out of the white, they would not have known where the road was. A few farms dotted the landscape. Come summer, these farms might stretch for miles, made arable by the black soil and snow from the winter. For now, it was a canvas of white.

They rode far into the night—too late to stop at a farm. A stand of trees acted as the only shelter they could find, and so they huddled together with their sleipnirs, the wind making a fire out of the question. The next morning, they came to a small village and stopped at the tavern. Two older men mentioned a woman in a black cloak moving through a few days earlier.

It took the third full day to reach the coast, and the small town of Verír. Fortunately, Rallia Clouw had moved with purpose, and it was easy to follow her footsteps. Before nightfall, they were instructed that she had visited the lighthouse a short ride to the north of town. They came to the lighthouse looking toward the Isle of Meldun across the Shallow Channel. Night was falling, and they could see the glow of the fire within, though the lighthouse tower was not lit.

As they came to the door, Jined turned. "Loïc, Cävian, do not say anything. Let me do all the talking." The two silent brothers grinned.

After knocking on the door for some time, it creaked open to reveal the face of a grizzled fisherman.

"What do you want?"

"We seek shelter for the night. Will you allow us to take it here?"

"It's only a mile or so to town. Go find yourself an inn."

"Smells like you're cooking some fish. I know I'd be very thankful to get a bite from you. I'm willing to share some of my purse."

The man hesitated for a moment before opening the door for them.

Jined stepped into the single room, where two other men sat before a fire, frying fish on a pan. A set of stairs led up into the tower. The wind blew against the walls outside, and the floor of the upper levels creaked. It was warm, sheltered from the wind. The Paladins shook the snow off their shoulders.

"Thank you for your hospitality," Jined said. "I am Brother Brazstein, and these two silent ones are Brother Loïc and Brother Cävian."

"Have a seat," one of the others said. "You three out looking for something?"

"What makes you ask that?" Jined asked. "You'd be right, but still, I ask."

"Paladins never come out here. Especially in this weather."

"I understand a woman in a black cloak came through this area a few days ago."

"What about it?" the first man asked.

"Do you know where we might find her?"

"You seem pretty intent on seeking her out, huh?"

"We do."

326 - ANDREW MEREDITH

"Why?"

"We understand she's seeking out one of our number. And we wish to meet her."

"You're not likely to find the girl."

"Well, we're going to try."

The three men sat in silence, glancing at one another.

"There was a Paladin who came through, not too long ago. Haughty fellow. Acted like he owned the world. He gave me something for safe-keeping. Told me someone would come who I was supposed to give the thing to, and then a message for that person to go to St. Nonn and wait there."

"So we've found the right place," Jined said over his shoulder to the brothers.

"There was more to the instructions," the man said. "We were told someone might come looking. And then he paid me some gold to make sure that I stayed put here and did what I could to waylay anyone who came around asking after the Coin Cloak. So when you started asking around town earlier today, I'll admit, I was starting to wonder if you'd come around."

The floorboards above creaked again. Jined looked at the twins, and they quickly scrambled to the door. It opened from without, revealing cloak-covered forms of other Paladins. Down the wooden stairs others clomped on steel-studded boots. They wore black cloaks over their armor, cut in a stylized shape like black wings. They shoved into the space without a word, pressing Jined and the twins back-to-back, hammers held at the ready.

"Greetings, Brother Brazstein," a man said as he pressed through those from outside and entering the light of the fire.

"Pater Gladen," Jined said, "what are you doing here?"

"Doing? I'm continuing my work. After the Solstice Ceremony, I continued on, conducting inspections of my holdings near Mahn Ful-har. Kept an ear on what you've done in particular. The incident at St. Nonn was rather exciting, especially since you were given that mote of power by Grissone. Apparently, the World-Rose has died?"

"And what did you have to do with that?"

"What do you mean?"

"That you're here while I seek out members of the Motean sect speaks volumes. Add to that your sudden departure from the Oracle after escorting the Crysalas there, and greeting the Prima Pater before the incident, and it tells me that you're a Motean."

"Do continue," Gladen said.

"I would also suspect that your excuse to travel north, to report to the King on a supposed rebellion, was pretense. If I had to guess further, I'd guess that the rebellion is your own. Under your own banner."

"I'll admit," Gladen said, "when I first met you, I made poor assumptions. You're a warrior, certainly, but I had no idea you were also intelligent. What I would give to see you voluntarily join my cause."

"I would die first."

"That won't be necessary," Gladen said. "You'll join, regardless. I have means to ensure that you come to my side of thinking, even if it takes trial upon trial."

"Just what do you expect to establish?"

"Oh, as things continue to develop, it appears it'll go by the name of New Varea," Gladen said. "But it'll be an Empire of Man, led by the warrior priests we Paladins ought to have become long ago."

"Pariantür will not stand for it."

"Pariantür will fall. If not by my own hand, then by the discovery of just how deep our Motean faith runs."

"A faith with no god," Jined said.

"No god? What makes you say that?" Gladen said.

"Your pawn in Mahn Fulhar, Primus Melit, he spat on the gods."

"Primus Melit was a scholar, but an overzealous lunatic at times. I am the head priest of a new religion—one that follows all, and follows none. From them we'll draw our strength. From them we'll provide humanity the opportunity to escape the gutter we've been placed in by the other races."

"You mean to dominate."

"Yes!" Gladen said, smiling broadly. "Now you understand. You can join, and give freely that mote of power Grissone has given you, or you can join by the Gauntlet's dominion."

Jined glanced at Loïc and Cävian.

"Together?" Jined said.

They nodded.

"A poor decision," Gladen said.

Jined and the twins both dove backward, lashing at the legs of those on the stairs. The knees of two of them buckled, and they fell from the stairs, clattering across the floor.

Two fell in surprise at the sudden assault. Several others leapt down and landed nearby. Cävian kicked one in the head, while Loïc's hammer crushed the face of another. Jined swung his hammer around, and it came at full impact across the haft of a younger Paladin. He cried out, and dropped his hammer, taking hold of his wrist. He continued to scream in pain.

"I forgot the three of you served under Nichal," Gladen said. "As Pariantür's champion, I'm sure you've learned much from him. Perhaps I'll trade Nichal to the T'Akai as a peace offering."

Jined glanced back to see Gladen close his eyes and take a deep breath. Jined swore he saw the man expand to stand a few inches taller, his muscles growing to match.

Gladen gave a signal. Two Motean heretics stepped forward. Their hammers hung from their wrists by leather thongs, and they began to swing them round and round, spinning faster until they moved in a whirl. A droning buzz grew from the hammers in an unnatural cacophony.

"They may have forsaken Grissone," Jined said, blocking the downward strike of another on the stairs as the remaining three advanced down the incline. "But they still have some sort of prayer of their own."

Cävian forced his way sideways and into the three sailors, still crouched by the fire and watching everything with a look of horror on their faces. They stood and drew their knives. Cävian gave them a push and then kicked at their fire, dimming the light in the room.

"Grissone," Jined muttered, "grant us protection. Grant me speed."

He rushed towards Gladen, who moved as through water in the dimming light. Jined swung his hammer around, and Gladen stepped away, allowing the hammer to hit the man behind him. Jined brought his hammer back around, striking the back of one of the heretics. The sound of the Motean's hammer died with a clatter as it hit the ground. The three off the stairs rushed Loïc, their hammers falling in tandem, again and again as their strikes glanced off an invisible barrier.

"Thank you, my god," Jined whispered. He spun on his heel and swung his hammer across the back of the head of one of the heretics behind him.

"Why would you betray your god?" Jined shouted at Gladen.

"I do not betray him. I do now what we always should have done, whether by his will or not—we take matters into our own hands."

Gladen closed his eyes for a second, taking a deep breath, and as he exhaled he closed the distance to Jined, a backhanded swing of his hammer throwing Jined across the room and into the arms of the three Moteans waiting there. They turned him around, two holding his arms, and the other keeping Loïc at hammer's distance.

The two Paladins still by the door rushed forwards and tackled Loïc from behind, while the three fishermen suddenly made their move and took hold of Cävian.

"I think your companions will go first. I can afford to kill them."

The fire was nothing but embers, but another light now glowed coolly across the room. The second spinning hammer gave off a whine and glow that illuminated Loïc and Cävian. One of the Moteans approached Cävian and touched the back of his knee with his hammer, bringing him to a kneel. Loïc was goaded next to his brother.

"I know you pray to your god for strength. Perhaps he is even here with us. Speak no more words, or I give the order to kill them."

"And you don't fear Grissone's wrath?"

"I said no more words. That was your final warning. If you'd like me to increase the threat, another word, and I'll see the Prima Pater at Precipice smothered in his sleep."

Jined gritted his teeth.

"What?" Gladen said. "Don't you care to take the risk?"

He turned and made a signal and one of the Paladins behind Jined produced shackles.

"I had hoped for a bit more fight from you—an excuse to kill these two."

"They'd be a lot harder to kill than you think," Jined said.

"There," Gladen said. "There's the chosen of Grissone I thought had given up so easily."

Two Paladins raised their hammers over the heads of Loïc and Cävian without warning. Both twins smiled as they made tiny gestures with their hands between their legs.

Loïc took a quick step forward, under the swing of the hammer which struck the tiles with a clang. Loïc continued to rush directly toward Jined and then leapt up over him and crashed into the two Moteans behind. The violent impact threw them through the stone wall behind them. The whole tower shook.

Cävian rose to his feet at the same time, each stride forward seemed to carry him significantly farther and faster than the last. He shot across the room and slammed into the Paladin swinging the glowing hammer. His weapon flew from his hand, and in response Gladen raised his hands to his ears. As the hammer head struck the stone it flashed, and a pulse of power flooded the room, laying everyone out flat. Only Jined remained standing, but his body ached as the pulse threw him against the wall behind him.

In the dim light, Jined made out three figures fleeing out into the cold winter night.

Jined felt around in the dark with his foot. He found Cävian and helped him to his feet, and together they found Loïc, who groggily worked with his brother to get the fire started again. Nearly everyone else was either unconscious or addled. Gladen had been thrown against a wall. His head had a nasty-looking gash that would require attention. One of the fishermen had escaped with two of the heretics, and another had died along with another Paladin. Together, they moved the living to one side of the room, totaling seven, and the dead numbering as many.

The fire roared, and the remaining fisherman had been charged with keeping it going. Cävian moved two of the dead heretics to the front of the door to keep anyone from returning, and to encourage anyone else from running.

I count three missing, Loïc said. *Shall we pursue?*

"We have their leader," Jined said. "Tomorrow we'll ride back to Mahn Fulhar with him. That's more important."

They know where we're going, Cävian motioned.

"Then we'll take an alternate road. Help me take the armor off the survivors."

We're not going to lug all that metal back with us, are we? Loïc asked.

I'd say it's been defiled now, with their heresy, Cävian signed.

"In Verír there was a smithy large enough to handle melting the metal. We can get some coin for it. Will that make you feel better, Cävian? Knowing fire cleansed it?"

Cävian gave Jined a look. *I'm not suggesting I'm feeling vengeful, if that's what you're getting at.*

Jined smiled.

I'm saying if I was given this armor to wear, and I knew someone who had fallen from the faith had worn it, I'd be hesitant.

You know what I think? Loïc asked. *I think our brother Adjutant Brazstein here worries that with his new Vow of Poverty, he'd be the one who ended up having to work the rust and heresy out of each and every set of armor.*

Jined turned and gave them both a wink, which gave way to their silent laughter, and turned back to working the straps of the armor off the dead heretic before him.

After St. Nonn, those who survived had been well enough to travel. Jined worried about how he would get those who survived this fight back to Mahn Fulhar. The two remaining Moteans sat together, sullenly licking minor wounds, and grumbling.

"Care to share anything?" Jined asked.

One of them turned and faced the wall. The other looked at Jined hesitantly. "I will not speak to you," he said. "I cannot."

"What is your name?"

The Paladin was young. Likely had not taken his Vows before turning to this fallen faith. He looked at Jined, and then to the twins, who were attending to Gladen and cleaning the gash on his head.

"You'll mislead me. I won't be led astray."

"Listen," Jined said, hoisting the boy to his feet and taking him to the other side of the tower, away from his companion, "have you ever met the Prima Pater?"

The young man shook his head.

"I have. He's a good man. Have you ever met Grissone?"

The young man now looked more sullen, and shook his head again.

"I have. And he's a good god. And one of forgiveness. You left the faith, but you can return to it as well."

"They'll kill me," the heretic said, sinking to his knees.

"But if you don't turn back to the right way—to Grissone—you'll follow them all to destruction. To Noccitan."

The Paladin sat down and put his head between his legs and began to cry quietly to himself.

"Do you want to be free of them?"

"I... Yes."

"There are only three of us," Jined said, "and seven of you. Even with sleipnirs underneath all of us, I expect Gladen and the rest of them will give us trouble. Will you make it more difficult? Or will you help me? In return, I'll try to see that any Pillory you're brought before is lenient."

"We have sleipnir too," the young heretic sobbed.

"That changes things," Jined said. "Very well. Cävian, go with our young prisoner here. Bring back their mounts. They all come inside tonight. We can't afford to have them stolen out from under us."

Take a look at this, Loïc said, holding out a hammer. It wasn't a paladinial hammer but had a single sledge-style head. The metal wasn't solid, either, but looked folded on itself, with gaps between each layer.

"Weren't there two?" Jined asked. "Isn't this what those two Moteans were swinging round their wrists?"

Loïc nodded. *I found this one over by the fire. But the one who dropped his? He fell over there.* He pointed over to the stone shattered in concentric circles.

"I've never heard of something like this," Jined said. "Have you?"

Loïc shook his head.

"Maybe it's another Motean tool. Perhaps Gallahan will have insight. When your brother returns, we all ought to get some shuteye. I'll take first watch. We'll leave as soon as we're able in the morning."

34

Back Upon the Path

None are lost while they still hold breath.

—HRELGREN PROVERB

Loïc returned from town shortly after dawn with heavy ropes bought from a fisherman, coming in from a night of fishing. Jined worked with the young Paladin, who revealed his name as Gervaine, having given up his second name when he took the Vow of Silence. The twins refused to come near the younger man, since he had broken the Vow they shared with him.

Using the ropes, the two pairs of men tied the heretics into their saddles. Gladen gave them little trouble, as he stared into nothingness, although Jined thought he caught a stubborn glance from the man as he tied the tight knot around his wrists and proceeded to tie the reins of the sleipnir under him to the next beast.

Jined took hold of the front heretic's mount, led it out to his own sleipnir, and took to the saddle. The twins took up the rear, while Gervaine, under the constant poisonous stares from the other heretics, as well as from Loïc and Cävian, acted as outrider.

A lone traveler walking to town for business gave them directions to a northern road that would skirt the smaller mountains of the northern tip of Mahndür, and then along the coast before cutting down to the capital.

As they continued away, Gervaine came to ride alongside Jined.

"We will be riding directly toward one of Vanguard's holdings," Gervaine said.

"Vanguard?" Jined asked.

Gervaine glanced back at the line of sullen prisoners.

"It's what our leader goes by. A chosen name from the brotherhood."

"A chosen name?"

"We are given names when we're initiated into the sect," Gervaine said. "Some inherit names from dead members. That's what I understand."

"How long have you been a Motean?" Jined asked.

"My mentor told me, shortly after I took my Vow, that I had been one since a year into my testing period."

Jined gave the younger man a look of confusion.

"He had already been guiding me, and told me of the theory of the motes of power, and I lapped it up like a thirsty dog. Before I could even begin to question it, I was sent off to serve at the Aerie. And then, under Vanguard's leadership, I could not escape."

"And how many more of you are there? Those stuck under the thumb of this sect, that wish to leave, I mean."

"I do not know. If we were ever to show a questioning...things happen to those that do."

"I need to know more. About the Motean sect," Jined said, "if I'm to battle it."

"I will tell you what I know, but I'm afraid I know little."

"You know more than I do," Jined replied, "and that is enough."

The sun set, and they continued to ride on until the waxing silver light of Umay started to rise. The little light it offered led them to a small copse of trees. They pushed their way in and built a fire against a large boulder to mask themselves from the road. The twins slept first, while Jined kept the fire fed. The heretics grumbled to each other, and Gervaine slept fitfully next to the fire. After several hours the muttering stopped, and Jined found himself staring at the only other soul awake.

"What do you imagine is going to happen now?" Jakis Gladen asked.

"I'd imagine that you're going to tell me," Jined said. "You'll offer some long speech you've been silently preparing all day, in hopes that I'll turn to your cause."

"That would be the culmination of what I had to say, true."

Gladen scooted across the ground into the warmth of the fire.

"Am I truly that transparent? Others have told me as much. Said that I'm too passionate, while they sit coolly gathering power, and assuming they were superior."

"You're a soldier," Jined said. "One who gets things accomplished, I'd imagine."

"But not always," Gladen said. "I was studying to be a chaplain. A theologian. But one of the brothers suggested that we needed a soldier to rise through the ranks, and so I took that responsibility, while the others amassed their own forms of power."

"You could go back to that," Jined said. "Return to the light of Grissone. Be a scholar again."

"Go back? From a penitent's cell in Durance Fortress?" Gladen laughed. "Not after what I've done."

"Grissone is merciful. He will forgive."

Gladen gave Jined a look, confusion across his face. "Oh, you think I meant I couldn't return after the things I've done? That the things I've done make me unforgivable? No, Jined. I'm saying I will not return after the power I've tasted—after the souls I've bound to my will, by my will alone."

"What does that mean?" Jined asked.

"When my men ride to my rescue, I'll show you personally. I'll force you onto our side."

"What makes you think you can do that?"

"What makes you think you can resist?" Gladen asked.

"You keep skirting around saying anything," Jined said. "So let me make the first move, and show you."

Jined rose to his feet, and dropped another log into the fire.

"Grissone," he muttered under his breath. "I need you."

Gladen cocked an eyebrow. "Were you expecting something to happen?"

"Can he not see you?" Jined asked over his shoulder to the glow emanating there.

"He can't," Grissone said.

"See what?" Gladen asked.

"You know of the Moteans?" Jined asked.

"There are misguided sects within my own church, yes."

"Then you understand that they seek to unwind everything."

"There must be freedom in faith," Grissone said.

"They act against you, though," Jined said.

"They are free to do so," Grissone said.

"Except when they endanger others," Jined replied.

"Do you think talking to yourself is going to somehow convince me of something?" Gladen asked.

"If I opened his eyes, he would see," Grissone offered.

"Open your eyes," Jined said to Gladen, "to see the truth."

"I know the truth," Gladen said. "The gods, powerful as they may be, are but pawns in the greater story of the world."

"And just what do you mean by that?" Grissone asked.

Jined thought he saw a glint of anger flash in his god's eyes.

"Go on," Jined said to Gladen.

"The gods were created by the Existence, can we agree upon that?"

Grissone and Jined both nodded.

"But then, if all was good, why did the Deceiver come into being?"

"Sakharn wanted another child," Jined offered. "At least, that is what I've understood of the old myths."

"The Deceiver was planted as a mote in her heart," Gladen said. "A desire for something else. What if the Existence planted that thought in her heart? What if the mother of the Black Coterie was led to do so by a pre-existing Deceiver? What if the plan all along was to sow the artistic flaw in the whole of the universe, for the sole purpose of watching his creations toy with one another?"

"Do you imply that the Deceiver is part of the Existence?" Grissone asked.

"Well, yes," Gladen replied, and then he gave Jined a look. "You didn't ask that question."

Jined shook his head.

"Then who?"

"As I said, open your eyes and see, and you can ask him yourself."

"No," Gladen said. "I won't."

"Why not?" Grissone asked.

"Why after all these years, after abandoning me to those who initiated me into the Motean Faith? Why visit now?"

"Your prayer that day," Grissone said, "it was not for deliverance. You prayed for the strength to infiltrate and destroy them from within."

Gladen toppled from the log he sat on and came to his knees.

"You know my prayer," Gladen said, his eyes shooting left and right. "Yet you did not give me what I asked."

"You always had the strength to fight, but you gave into the temptation of power."

"The power they gave," Gladen said to the voice, "it was real. But where were you?"

"Here," Grissone said. He stepped forward, and touched the man's chest with a finger.

There was a flash of light and Gladen cried out. He stared into the face of the god before him.

"Grissone!" he cried.

Grissone turned and gave Jined a smile.

"Now do you believe?"

"What must I do to be forgiven?" Gladen sobbed.

"You tell me," Grissone said.

"Grissone, I have lost my faith," Gladen said. "Forgive me so I may start again. Forgive me and I will live out the rest of my days tearing down the Moteans—seeking out those who would harm your church."

"Jakis Gladen," Grissone said, "once of the Vow of Poverty, you shall rededicate yourself. You shall not harm another soul as long as you live, for you are now under the Vow of Pacifism. Share all that you know of the Moteans with the Prima Pater and his closest companions. You are forgiven."

Gladen bowed his head, crying.

"That was far too easy," Jined said. "Perhaps you ought to appear to everyone. Then none would deny you and your faith."

"That wouldn't be faith then, would it?"

"No, I supposed not."

"It is not as easy as you think. Gladen's life is now forfeit to the Motean Cult. I abhor witch hunts, but you must remain vigilant, or else this new ally you have gained will not last long."

"What would you have me do?"

"Protect him. Glean from him what you feel you need. And then, sequester him away, I should imagine."

"Will you also protect him?"

"I will keep him as safe as I am able. That he has turned back to me is enough to see him safely on the path of righteousness."

The campfire had died down to embers, and the night plunged into darkness as Grissone left.

"How often does he visit you?" Gladen asked.

"Not as often as I'd like."

"You are chosen by him," Gladen said. "That much is true."

"And you are back among the faithful," Jined said. "You understand how much danger this puts you in?"

"You do not understand how much danger the Grissoni church is in," Gladen replied.

"Then tell me."

* * *

As dawn approached, Gladen had laid out the basics. The primary tenets of the Moteans were praying for miracles and keeping back a portion of the power given to them, letting it grow. He shared, of the branches: those who followed the way of the Feather and its creation of shades, the way of the Bell at Piedala, and the lowest faction—those who had been charged with the unlocking of the Dread Plate—last seen during the Protectorate Wars and now, as Gladen revealed, in the possession of the Paladins at the Aerie.

"And just what does the Dread Plate do?" Jined asked as they rode alongside one another. The other heretics rode in sullen silence, watching their leader betray their secrets.

"We haven't unlocked everything it can do," Gladen said. "But the legends hold that should someone don it, they would be invincible."

"The Prima Pater defeated the Warlord during the Protectorate Wars."

"Because the Apostate betrayed his ally, forcing the man within to become a living shade."

"Then the Apostate knew of all of these."

"I believe," Gladen said, leaning in his saddle towards Jined, "I believe that Moteans were nothing before the Protectorate Wars. They were a philosophy. But after the wars, the Apostate's followers took what he knew, all of the dark magicks he had learned, and disseminated it into various cults and sects."

"To what purpose?"

"To the purpose of one who would regather every tool and trick, and put them back together."

"A new Apostate."

"Shroud," Gladen said.

"Shroud?"

"Each of us takes on descriptive names within the Motean sect. There is one who went by the name Shroud. I thought him dead, but I believe he is still alive. And he intends to do just that—unite the tools once held by one man, the Apostate, and turn them back to the end goal."

"And that is?"

"The destruction of the gods."

"You can't kill the gods," Jined said.

"You do not know that," Gladen said. "But even if Shroud does not accomplish that goal, what damage will be done to the world by his trying?"

"And who was this Shroud, before he supposedly died?"

Loïc came up alongside Jined and waved for his attention. They pulled up short, as Loïc pointed down the road.

Ahead, twenty Paladins, black cloaks draped over their shoulders, stood abreast.

"It seems that those I once called brothers have come to my supposed rescue," Gladen said.

"What should I know?"

"Very likely, all of those are true Moteans. I doubt Slate has brought those under the sway of the Gauntlet."

"What does that mean?"

"I will tell you when we survive this. But, in short, we have unlocked one secret tool of the Dread Plate, and you'll be horrified to learn what it does."

The black-cloaked Paladin in the center of the line kicked his sleipnir and pulled out from the others. As he came within one hundred yards, one of the heretics behind Jined began shouting.

"Vanguard has betrayed us! He has compromised his belief!"

The others started shouting as well, until it grew into a unified chant.

"Betrayer Vanguard!"

The man riding toward them stopped short at twenty yards.

"He expects one of you to ride out to speak to him," Gladen said.

"You don't fear him?" Jined asked. "You're very calm."

"First off," Gladen said, looking at Jined sternly, "you have little to fear from Slate. He's a spineless sycophant. Secondly, I have seen the face of my god. I fear nothing now."

"I will go," Gervaine said, riding forward. Jined caught a hesitance in his voice. "You must get Gladen to Mahn Fulhar. Let me go and speak with Slate. It will be my penance."

No, Loïc said, *it should be me. I am still faithful.*

"I think not," Jined said. "I'll speak with him. You see that Gladen is taken to Nichal Guess. Don't stop until you reach the gates of the city."

Loïc nodded and turned to speak with his brother.

"Gladen," Jined said, "you and I shared a moment with our god last night. And you have taught me much on our ride today. I believe you when you say you have found forgiveness."

"But?" Gladen said.

"If I discover you are lying, even if I should die, I'll hunt you down in Noccitan if I have to, and see that you come to justice."

Gladen laughed. "I understand, Brazstein. But my betrayal of these men, the Moteans, is sincere."

Jined nudged his mount forward, toward Gladen's second-in-command.

"Captured our leader, and then drove right into our hands?" the man asked. It was the thin man with wooden lifts built into his boots that Jined had seen at Gladen's side in Mahn Fulhar. "What is this our men cry? Vanguard betrayed?"

"The opposite, I'm afraid."

"What is that supposed to mean?"

"Your Vanguard," Jined said, "Pater Minoris Gladen? He returned to the faith. Met Grissone himself."

Slate scoffed.

"I'm afraid your leader has turned against you. He's shared more about your Motean Cult since last night than I've learned in the past few weeks, since your ally, Primus Melit, took his own life before my eyes."

"Then you'll have to join our cause, by choice or by force, or you'll need to die."

"I've fought T'Akai near Pariantür," Jined said. "I've faced not one champion of the Cursed Gift-Giver, but two, and lived. I don't fear you."

"If only you knew what powers I can bring to bear," Slate said, although a note of panic shook in his voice.

"You mean the Plate? I've heard what it can do," Jined bluffed. "I don't fear it."

"Then let us make a compromise," Slate said.

"What do you propose?"

"You give us either Vanguard, or the seven other Moteans, and we let the rest of you go."

"Six."

"What do you mean?"

"Gervaine has also come back over to the side of the light."

"There is no light," Slate hissed, "and that young boy means nothing. He knows nothing. You may have him, too."

"Very well. Then I will take Gladen and Gervaine. You take the rest of them back to whatever hole you crawled out of."

The heretic turned his sleipnir around and began to ride back toward the others. Jined followed suit.

Take Gervaine and Gladen, he signed. *Leave the others and start riding.*

Loïc and Cävian immediately leapt from their mounts and un-hooked Gladen's sleipnir from the chain of prisoners, then remounted. The four broke away as the other prisoners stood there, still roped together, hollering to be let free.

Jined rode to meet them in the middle of the snowy field. Gervaine looked back over his shoulder and shouted, causing the other three to pause and join him. Jined glanced back over his shoulder to see fifteen of the Moteans riding at him at a full gallop. Jined urged his mount forward toward the four Paladins slowing to wait for him.

Suddenly Gervaine broke from the other three, passing Jined at a full gallop.

"Gervaine!" Jined shouted. "Stop!"

"For Penitence!" he shouted, ignoring Jined.

He took that odd, twisted hammer, Cävian signed.

"What?" Jined shouted. He turned his sleipnir to watch as the young Paladin charged forward, swinging the hammer round and round, and let it fly ahead of him. It arced through the air and came down before the opposing Moteans counter-charging.

As the cursed hammer hit the ground five feet in front of the Moteans, a pulse emanated out, throwing five Moteans and their mounts up and into the air like rag dolls and crashing into the riders behind them. The last five fought to bring their own mounts back under control. They circled round the fallen Moteans, bearing down on Gervaine.

"Protect him as long as you can," Jined prayed.

Hammers rained down on the young Paladin, as he fought back against the heretics. Flashes of light glanced off of him with each strike that fell.

"He gave himself to buy us time," Gladen said. "We ought to go."

"Very well," Jined sighed as he turn to the others.

May Grissone continue to protect him, Loïc said.

He already protects him, Cävian replied, smiling as the four of them kicked their six-legged sleipnirs into a gallop. They rode hard for Mahn Fulhar.

35

Testimony

Let broken stick, rent in half, and given to each party, be testimony to the decision made. It was made in the presence of Nifara's representative. And the Virgin goddess shall stand behind and by the decisions it shall remain, until the stick has been put back together as though it never had been broken.

— **LONGER VERSION OF THE MONK'S CLOSING JUDGMENT**

Her breath caught at the top of her lungs and hung there painfully. The alcove closed around her, just as the one outside Pell Maran's room had. She heard the muffled voice of someone speaking within the chamber, and the shuffling of two guards nearby, ensuring no one came too close.

Another voice rose, distinctively oratory. Seriah soon recognized it was the High Priest of Aben, Klent Rigal.

"If what this heretic says is correct, then your order has been compromised, and you stand in Schism. Perhaps it might be better if you returned to your Fortress-Monastery and got your house in order."

"You will accept my apology that this occurred in the city of your throne of power," a deep voice said. "But if we were to leave, who would act as protectors, especially if there are those of our order who have turned against us?"

"The Praetors of the Church of the Common Chalice could be asked to come under my direct authority."

"The enforcers of the most violent arm of your church?"

"As I said, I would bring them under my direct authority, and they could not lift a finger except by my hand."

"The Paladins of the Hammer are the protectors of man," the Paladin said. "To what aim would the Praetors, under your authority, act?"

"In Œron they are already their own branch of the church—their own order of Paladins. Why they could not do the same in Mahn Fulhar is beyond me."

"Another order? Their actions would be in conflict with our own."

"If to the same purpose, to protection man, and the instilling of doctrine to the people, then they are not at odds."

"That hints at authoritarianism," an old man said. "I thought only the Church of the Common Chalice subscribed to those doctrines."

"Our church's obsession, regardless of sect," the High Priest said, "is to see our flock safely through and past Noccitan, to the arable fields of Lömin, where they can tend to the gardens of Truth."

"You have said what you have to say on the matter," the drier voice of Pater Segundus Pír said, changing the subject. "Let us discuss things not pertaining to this trial later. There is another testimony we have agreed to hear."

The heavy wooden door creaked open and the quiet murmuring of those within broke out into the hall.

"Holy Nefer," the deep voice of Jined Brazstein said, "thank you for agreeing to come and give your testimony."

"It is my honor," Seriah lied.

"May I walk you in?"

She stood and took his arm. He was strong, and the desire to pull back and flee wilted as he drew her forward.

They walked into the room. She could feel the anger of the men around her.

"How many are here?" she whispered.

"Nichal Guess and Gallahan Pír sit at the front, along with the two remaining leaders of your order, as well at the High Priest of Aben. Seven other Paladins, including myself, sit as witness to the testimony just given by Pater Minoris Gladen of the Aerie."

The day before had been filled with long discussions of the monks of Nifara, when word came from the Paladins that Jined Brazstein and his two silent companions had ridden near to death with a captured prisoner, a Paladin of their own order, turned at one time against them, and now back into their order.

Pater Gladen had been respected and charged by the Prima Pater to seek out an ancient relic, only to succumb to the whims of dark philosophies. To find that one Paladin had turned from the faith had been enough to anger the acting Archimandrite, but to find out that not only was there an entire sect of disloyal Paladins, but that for over a week now the two Pater Segundii had been keeping it secret from Kerei Lant and Cräg Narn had sent her into a boiling tirade that lasted hours.

"Nefer Seriah Yaledít," Jined announced.

"Thank you for agreeing to speak to us," someone said. Seriah recognized the kind voice of the old scribe Gallahan Pír. "We understand that you have a testimony to give. Our fellow Paladin, Adjutant Brazstein, has told us what you said, but perhaps you could do the same for us."

Seriah nodded, bowing her head.

"Before I speak," Seriah said, her voice, quavering, "I wish first to apologize to the leaders of my order, for not sharing this with them. Many secrets have remained so over the past weeks, and I fear their anger for adding this secret to the long list. But I would hope that when they hear what I have to say, they will understand why I remained silent."

Seriah took a deep breath and felt the long years of practice in speech-making fill her spine with some bit of courage.

"You will recall the testimony of the Watchers, who appeared before the council on the Solstice. They warned of some dark thing, walking unseen and taking people's lives, that even Wyv-Thüm could not account for. I have seen, or rather, through a vision, I have observed the shadow left by this thing. I was there when Pell Maran died, and saw the appearance of our goddess as she came to take him on to the afterlife."

"How did you see through the blind of your eyes?" the stern voice of Kerei Lant asked.

"Through blind and through stone, I saw the bright blue light of our goddess, and heard as she spoke to Pell Maran. I cannot explain how I saw her, but perhaps divinity can be seen, when allowed, despite ailment or fetter."

"Very well," she said, "continue."

"As the Archimandrite died, he asked her if she saw the figure who had killed him, and she dismissed his claim. Yet the figure that took his life, whose voice dripped with shadow and poison, moved between me and the goddess, and cast a shadow of deepest black, blocking her light to me. That could not be dismissed. The light of the goddess left, and my breath was caught in my lungs, and I could not speak. I could not breathe. It is all that saved me, for whoever it was passed me, and I felt the wisps of the cloak he wore brush my feet and plunge me deeper and deeper into sadness, misery, and fear."

Seriah stood tall, taking a deep breath, courage flooding through her.

"To speak this living nightmare to you now almost seems to banish it. But know that whatever it was, it is everything the followers of Wyv-Thüm feared."

"Thank you, Nefer Yaledít," Pater Segundus Pír said.

"Gladen," Pater Segundus Guess said, "does what the Holy Nefer said mean anything to you?"

"It is not something I know," another voice, Gladen's, said.

Seriah feared that when she heard his voice, she might discover that it was he who had killed Pell Maran, but there was no cunning wryness in the way he spoke, and Seriah sighed.

"What is it?" Jined asked.

"I feared that he might be the dark murderer," Seriah answered.

"And is he?"

"He is not."

"However," Gladen continued, "you will recall my description of the shadebooks. While I am not privy to the secrets of their creation, I have used them, and conversed with those trapped within. And I confess to you that the feeling that washes over you when a shade speaks is similar."

"Very well," Pater Segundus Guess said. "Jined, will you please see Nefer Yaledít to her cell for rest?"

"Yes, Pater Segundus."

"We thank you once more for your testimony, Nefer," Guess continued.

She walked arm-in-arm with the Paladin, who saw her to her room, and asked an attendant to bring food to her.

The calm that sat on her shoulders was the first she had felt since that day. She startled out of her reverie as a knock came to the door, and Archimandrite Lant entered.

"Seriah," Kerei said, taking a seat beside her on the bed.

"You are angry with me," Seriah said.

"No, child," the woman said wearily, "I am irritated I did not know of your story before today. I am sad I could not help you through this beforehand. But I am not angry with you."

"What was determined?" Seriah asked. "With the paladin?"

"The heretic returned to the order?" Kerei asked. "We determined through his confession, and the secrets he shared, that he is telling the truth. He means to give up his compatriots. He has been given pen and paper in his cell, to write out a full confession, and give them the names of those he knows, so that the sickness may be removed."

"Does heresy such as this cause fear that the same may be so within our order?"

"If there was such a problem, we would know."

"How is that?" Seriah said.

Kerei chuckled. "I am not at liberty to say, but I can say this. Every act of judgment is recorded by our scribes when each monk returns to give testimony. And there has never been given a reason to doubt.

Adding to that, think what should happen if someone was to betray our order. What does that person know of the afterlife? They know our goddess speaks on their behalf, or against them. Imagine the wrath she might have if one of her own turned on her order."

"I'd imagine they'd be forever on the run, in hopes they never face her, nor the Judge."

"Precisely. Now," she rose, "get some rest. For as long as you'd like. I'd imagine that what Gladen has to tell the Paladins of the Hammer will dispel much of the cloud of fear and distrust that seems to have settled over us all."

36

Dream

Where to walk when all paths diverge?
Seek the lights upon the stone.
For that which on our coast submerged,
Are living free in air and loam.

—UNKNOWN

A beach of shattered glass framed a river of finer sand, stretched from east to west. A light from nowhere cast stars upon the pink-hued surface, standing out against the lilac sky overhead. A massive creature walked past. It was hundreds of feet tall, and, like a sleipnir, or perhaps a capricör, yet from its forehead rose a long, sickle-like horn the shape of a crescent moon. It snuffled at a copse of trees and then tore it up by the roots, dirt hanging from the rootball, and falling to impact nearby, almost raining down upon Katiam.

It paid her little attention and moved on past to find some other forest to rob food from. The young kid that frolicked behind her, gamboling over mountains and trampling dew-covered trees of mauve, seemed to consider Katiam for a moment and raced toward her. She turned and ran, trying to get away, her feet refusing to do as she asked.

She saw the crevasse between two rocks almost too late, and made a dive into it as the nose of the great creature's offspring snuffled around like a sleipnir does for grain. Then, losing interest, it moved along.

"This is a dream. It's a nightmare," she said as she peeked out of her hole.

She sat down against the rock that formed the cave entrance and pulled her knees up. "I'll awaken back at the Oracle. It will have been a dream."

A few hours later, the light of the world dimmed but did not fade to black. Stars came out across the sky, more like gold dust on rocks than actual points of light. Katiam's heart slowed, and she curled up to sleep under the sparkling sea of lights.

***

The sound of a flock of birds nearby startled her awake. She lay on a bed of waist-high grass, the blades wide and stiff. The birds had come down around her, their feathers a sleek black that hinted at purple. And yet, they also shone like metal, and from within their mouths the glows of a furnace took the fallen seeds from the grass and ground them up with the sound of some great grain mill.

Katiam stood and yawned, wondering how she had come to move. She froze as she realized she slept in a field filled with the great creatures she had seen the day before. And yet, they did not tower hundreds of feet above her. The creatures, still as massive as an auroch, filled the field. One nearby considered her and rose, its tread impacting the ground. It approached her, and in its quaking steps she felt like a small child being considered by a war sleipnir. Upon its neck it wore a bell.

"You have an owner," she said, putting out a hand cautiously. It sniffed at her hand, but when the bellwether found no treat, it became disinterested and sat back down, taking a clump of grass and chewing it.

The grass kept Katiam from seeing far. She looked in all directions to see if she could find a shepherd, but saw nothing but grass and the single-horned creatures in all directions.

She wandered for hours in one direction before giving up and turning to walk back to the side of the stream of glass that still remained as far across as it had the day before, and, somehow, only twenty feet from her, despite her having walked away from it for so long.

Exhaustion overtook her, and she curled up to sleep. The bellwether found her again and joined her, adding its heat to hers.

* * *

The sound of the herd bleating woke her, and she turned over to see the face of the bellwether staring at her. She sat up and placed her hand on him. He was now a normal size, and as she rose, she realized he came up to her hip. He wasn't the great creature of the day before, nor the titan of the first morning. She stood in a field of grass no higher than her calves, and the herd of white single-horned creatures all walked along the banks of the stream of glass toward the call of a figure in a purple robe a long ways off.

She placed a hand on the bellwether's back and followed the rest of them. Beside them, the stream, still as wide across as it had been, tinkled and sung as it shifted its way down the hill.

The shepherdess sung a haunting kulning song, calling her herd to her side. She turned and saw Katiam, a smile splitting her weathered face and adding ten-fold to the wrinkles around her eyes.

"Another Dreamer in such a short time," she said as Katiam approached.

"Am I dreaming then?"

"In a way," she said. "It shall make more sense the longer you're here. Though few ever come to truly understand the nature of the Veld."

Katiam's heart began to beat rapidly.

"The Veld? The realm of nightmares?"

"The Veld is what you make of it. My own meadow shows nothing to fear, guarded as it is by my reyem."

"Is that what they're called?" Katiam asked. "I thought them reminiscent of the ancient tales of unicorns."

"They go by many names of those who have seen them and return to their world. It is one of them."

The bellwether nuzzled at Katiam's hand.

"I see that Derioth has taken to you," the old woman said. "Come, let us get you fed. I suppose you must be hungry after all that growing."

"Growing?" Katiam replied. "How did you know?"

"Everyone who has ever visited the Veld, all who are called first to my pasture, must develop. I thought I heard your snoring as you slept the days away."

"Days?" Katiam replied. "I've been here only three."

"You've been awake for three," the woman said, "but it takes weeks to reach the size you wish to be."

She turned and began to walk away. Derioth followed after her, bleating to call the others to his side. The flock began following the shepherdess, who moved through the grass with slow purpose to the top of a hill. The pasture ahead stretched on for miles in all directions, with separate flocks of the reyem scattered here and there. To Katiam's right, the stream of broken glass flowed endlessly on.

"What is this river, and where does it lead?"

"I had hoped to ask you the same thing," the woman said. "It seems you brought it with you, and it's cut me off from the flocks on the other side."

Katiam turned to look out over the stream, and saw that across its expanse more pasture lay, the reyem on the other side considering whether to brave its depths. The river, she realized, though it flowed in one direction, did not fall, but sat as a ribbon upon the rise and fall of the land.

"I don't know what it is," Katiam said.

"Perhaps your friend shall know," the old woman said, and she began to walk down the hill toward the house that sat there.

It was a simple building of timber-framed stone. There were no out-buildings, and it had windows on each face. The shepherdess stepped up into the door—wool hanging from pegs as a curtain.

"It must get not get cold here in the evenings."

"Cold would not dare approach my home," the old woman said. "The stern scolding he'd get might shame him too much."

There was a single room within. Though from without the windows had been open, they proved to be closed by shutters now. A table sat by the hearth, and someone sat with their back to them, wearing a gossamer gown over their thin frame. Katiam was suddenly aware that she was clothed in the same lilac fabric.

"How did I come to be dressed like this?"

"Each comes clothed in their own modesty," the old woman said, and then smirked. "Some in less modesty than the Crysalas."

"How did you know I was Crysalas?"

"I make it a point to know of all in my pasture," the old woman said.

The woman at the table turned her head, and then rose.

Katiam gasped as a face she recognized stared blankly at her.

"Sabine!" she cried, and ran across the room, taking the woman up in her arms.

Sabine Upona did not return the hug, but looked at her with bare interest.

"Sabine?" Katiam said, holding her at arm's length to consider her.

"Jurgon...."

"What is wrong with her?" Katiam asked the older woman.

"I had hoped you might tell me. She showed up in the pasture like this. At her full size, and wandering aimlessly, saying that name over and over."

"Jurgon is her husband," Katiam said. "The last words she said before she died were 'Tell my husband I...' and did not finish the thought."

"Died?" the old woman said. "Then why has she come here? Why has Nifara not collected her?"

"Have I died?" Katiam asked. "How did I come to be here?"

"I do not think you did. You have arrived as many others do."

"Others? I'm very confused."

"The pasture. Within it are many sleepers such as yourself. Some take years. Some never come to full size, as their mind rectifies where they are, and prepares them for their great journey. Others come to the Veld in their sleep, and return when they awaken each day. But all start here in my pasture—a place set aside under guard and protection by the reyem flock from the rest of the Veld and the dangers and wonders that lurk there."

She led the two of them to the table to sit. Sabine sat without awareness of the two of them next to her.

"Now, tell me of how this woman might have come to my pasture without dying, yet by leaving the land of the living, and I shall tell you more of the Veld."

"We were in communion with the Dweol's Rosebloom, and something happened. I saw an orb of metal roll into the room, and then fall into the bloom's surface. There was a pulse that emanated from it, and then the surface shattered into untold pieces, like glass. From the center there spread a blackness as each piece of the glass went dull, and those who were caught wading in the pool of glass, those who were touched by the blackness, were themselves turned instantly to dust. As wind caught them, they blew away."

"And Sabine here was one of them?"

Katiam nodded.

"Then she must have followed the Dweol as it retreated."

"Retreated?" Katiam said. "I thought it destroyed."

"That may be true," the old woman said. "But the Dweol is one and many. One bloom being destroyed sent a ripple of damage through itself to the other blooms. It may have taken those who touched with it. It would mean the woman's body is destroyed, but perhaps the Dweol gave a portion of energy to preserve her."

"Can it do that?"

"Of course it can. It was not long after the creation of the four worlds that the Dweol were born, and began their long journey to tie themselves together."

"You're speaking in riddles."

"It is my right," the old woman said. "Now, the Veld. It is one of the four, along with Lomïn, Noccitan, and Kallattai. It is the only world into which the other three can easily flow, for all dreams are had and created here."

"It was made by the sisters, Crysania and Sakharn," Katiam said. "Although it is the realm of the latter, the goddess of the Impossible."

"It became such," the old woman said, "but it was first a place for the sisters to convene, as bosom friends. Aben and Wyv made Kallattai as their co-creation, and then Aben made Lomïn as a home and throne to share with his wife, and Wyv made the depths of Noccitan as a residence for himself and his bride. The Veld was intended to be a twilight space, between them, and yet in the same space as Kallattai."

"Is that why there is no sun? No light by which to mark the hours?"

"It is ever illuminated by Lomïn and ever darkened by its opposite."

"We are taught to fear this place, even as children."

"It is a place to fear," the old woman said. "As one should fear and respect the edge of a blade. It can cut just as well as it can be a tool."

The old woman produced a small tray. On it, dunes of purple sand undulated on its surface.

"Most of the Veld is covered in this sand, called Oneirion. From it the crystal trees grow, and the rocky scapes rise. Touch it."

Katiam reached out and placed a tentative finger in it. It was only purple sand.

"Place your hand over it, and ask it to rise."

Katiam gave the woman a look of confusion, but she did as she was asked, holding her hand over the tray. The dunes on the surface fell flat and motionless.

"You feared it might do as you asked, and like a sleipnir who knows an inexperienced rider, it fell from your grasp."

Katiam looked to her left as Sabine stretched her own hand out to hover over the sand. The dunes returned to their shape, and then undulated and moved, seemingly of their own accord. A face appeared in the sand. The face of a sleeping man. The face grimaced in despair.

"This must be the husband she left behind," the old woman said. "Never have I seen someone take to the Oneirion so easily. She is unattached to the world save for her memories of this Jurgon."

There came a bleating outside the house. The old woman rose and walked to one of the windows. She opened the shutters, and without there was only an inky blackness, with pinpoints of light too few to be stars. She shook her head and walked past a window, the edges of the shutters lit by bright light, and to the next window. Opening it, it looked out upon a larger sea of dunes. Upon the face of one wall of sand stood a face to match the one upon the tray before Sabine. It spoke silent words. Sabine's chair clattered to the ground as she rose and rushed to the window.

"Jurgon!" she cried out. She reached over the lintel of the window, and the image blew away like smoke. Sabine fell to the ground in a heap, sobbing uncontrollably. The old woman stared at her, seemingly unfamiliar with how to deal with grief like this. Katiam sighed and crossed the room to crouch next to Sabine. She held the woman as she sobbed for a long time, until her cries turned to exhausted shudders.

"The two of you shall rest for a time," the old woman said. "But then you must leave. If Sabine can move Oneirion so easily, she would only invite trouble to my meadow. It would be no danger to me, but the sleepers might be perturbed. You must go and discover what you would of the Veld."

"But it is dangerous out there?"

"It will be. I think you'll take Derioth with you; he'll act as a protector as you sleep. But when you are awake, it will be only by your own imagination that you'll survive."

"I do not know your name," Katiam said. "As my hostess, I should like to know you."

"I am known by many names. Zanghard is one I'm rather fond of. If you tell those you encounter that the Shepherdess of Minds has provided you with the Reyem as your compass, then they shall not give issue."

"And how shall we find you to return Derioth?"

"He knows his own way."

"Thank you for your hospitality, Zanghard," Katiam said.

"Ah! What hospitality? I forgot to feed you."

Upon the table sat loaves of bread that were not there before.

Katiam took one and tore it open, smelling the warm butter melted within. She ate pieces of it, not realizing how hungry she had grown, and tore pieces for Sabine, convincing the woman to take bites and swallow them. The old woman watched them both with interest, and then, as they finished, walked them to her door.

Derioth looked up as Katiam stepped down to the grass, a more vivid hue of purple than it was before, and wagged his bobbed tail. He gave a friendly bleat as Sabine came out onto the turf beside Katiam, her eyes vacantly taking in the surroundings.

"It seems the shard river follows you," the Shepherdess said, pointing to the ribbon that stood twenty feet from the door. "But perhaps it beckons you to follow it. If it leads where I suspect, you have a long journey ahead of you."

"Thank you for your hospitality."

"Another warning," the old woman said. "Do you know the sight of a clam or oyster?"

"Yes."

"You'll may see creatures like that, clinging to rocks. Carbuncles. Their flesh within glows. They only open when they feel safe, and thus can be walked toward if you seek safety, though if they see you, they will shut."

"I will keep my eyes open."

"There are creatures, though, that use that same method to lure you in. And the carbuncles near such a creature shall remain closed, for fear of their own safety."

Katiam gave a curtsy and turned. Derioth now had a fine chain of silk around his neck to replace the bell that had hung there before. She took it up, and then took Sabine's hand in her other hand, and began walking. Derioth amiably followed, though Sabine trudged as a sleepwalker.

No less than a hundred yards later, and they came to the edge of the meadow. The same meadow that, on approach, appeared to stretch on for miles in every direction from the small house. The meadow grass ended and gave way to rocks and fine sand, all various forms of purple. Trees grew with translucent pine needles that shimmered and whispered as they passed. After a while, Katiam thought it wise to stop and forage for wood and perhaps food.

Selecting a safe space amidst a small copse of trees, she left Sabine and Derioth and poked around, finding tree fall for the fire, and then found a bush covered in pink berries. She picked a handful and brought them back to the other two, holding a berry out to Derioth. The reyem sniffed at it, and then nipped it out of her hand, bleating for more.

"I assume they're safe to eat, if he has no trouble doing so," she said. She bit one in half, spurting the pink juice over her hand. It tasted sharp and sweet, and went down easily. "I'll wait a bit before picking more for the three of us," Katiam said. "In case our stomachs cannot handle it. Until then, we'll try to make a fire."

She took up the straightest stick and prepared to spin it on another larger stick, when it snapped far too easily.

"This is no good," Katiam said. "I can't start a fire without a tinderbox."

Sabine touched something to Katiam's arm, and she looked over to see a tinderbox in the woman's hand.

"Where did you get that?" Katiam asked.

"I made it," Sabine replied, "in my dream."

"What do you mean?"

She stared vacantly forward. Sabine took up a handful of sand, and cupped it in her hands. She opened her palm to reveal only sand. Then the sand trickled away between her fingers to reveal a small knife, the color of the sand.

"I don't understand," Katiam said.

Sabine said nothing more.

Katiam took it from her and used it with the flint within the box to set a piece of tinder to light, and then the wood.

She handed the box and knife back to Sabine. "Thank you, we don't need those anymore."

With those words, the two objects became sand in Sabine's hands and fell to the earth.

Sabine's eyes turned and focused on Katiam's look of astonishment. "Am I dreaming? Or are you real?" Sabine asked. "Or am I dead?"

"I don't know," Katiam said. "I think the answer to all three is yes."

Sabine suddenly threw her arms around Katiam's shoulders and began to sob openly.

37

River of Glass

Blackened covetousness gives way to dawn.
And night falls on those hearts that give up hope.

—HRYLIAN POEM

"I made a study of the Veld in my younger years," Sabine explained as they walked over ruins of black glass stones. "I was a Paladame guard to a Vault in Ormach, near the border by the Oruche Marches. So many believe them a godless people, and uncivilized. But that comes of ignorance to their true knowledge. The Veld is home to many of them. I became fascinated.

"There were few books on the subject, even at the library of Ammar Citadel. And so I found a woman through the Vaults, an Oruche named Yashi. She shared the tradition of her people with me, having run from the Marches, from a cruel husband, the head of their tribe. She shared of the means to enter the Veld in your mind as you slept. Even while awake. She even shared that there were those who pushed off death a little longer by translating their bodies into the Veld when they were on death's door. Whether that was true or not, I did not know.

"One day I sat on a solitary hill overlooking the sea, and, following the instructions I had learned, I did it. I entered the Veld. And it was a place of nightmare. I got lost in a cavernous tunnel full of massive vermin. I awoke in a downpour of rain, but the fear that filled me was companion to the dread that caused me to lose sleep every night hence, else I return."

"And did you?" Katiam asked.

"Every night," Sabine replied, "for two years. Until the day I met Jurgon. I had journeyed to Pariantür, seeking solace in the Aspects. But nothing seemed to work. Jurgon ran the woodshop in those days. He had just made the rank of Excelsior, and had taken on a project to replace older doorframes throughout the monastery.

"He came to replace mine, and I was returning to the room to find time to sleep. My eyes were sallow holes in my head. He smiled at me, and had just finished putting the door into place. It bore a carving of the Anka upon it, and as I approached, I asked him what he was doing. He muttered a prayer over it. He turned and looked at me with a caring smile.

"'I have prayed a prayer of protection over the sleep of any who rest within,' he said. 'This is my cell,' I replied.

"'Then may your dreams be watched over by the Anka, and Nightmare flee from his sight.'

Sabine stared silently into the flames of the fire they had prepared atop the ruins, in a small room from which the light wouldn't act as a beacon for wild creatures.

"And did you sleep well that night?" Katiam asked.

Sabine smiled. "I've never had a bad night's sleep since."

"How long after did the two of you marry?"

"It took him five years to ask. I was forty years old, and he was three years my junior at the time. I had expected my time for love had passed. Fifteen happy years we had together. And now, I've been taken."

"Yet here you are," Katiam said.

"Alive, yet not alive. In a world I hoped never to see again. How many others?"

"Others?"

"How many Crysalas were taken as I was?"

"The one girl from Precipice. They held a memorial for her, too."

"Tereh Illimander," Sabine said. "The look on her face as she turned to ash—did I look like that?"

Katiam nodded.

"Perhaps she is here too, and I can find her."

"I don't understand," Katiam said, "how you came here."

"The Dweol runs through the four worlds. As you know, there are several Roseblooms. The one in Precipice, the one in the mountains by Pariantür, and one south in the Republic, in Sanae. But there are others too. We communicate with the ones to the east occasionally, and even less so with the Roseblooms found here in the Veld and beyond."

"Beyond?" Katiam asked.

"As real as the Veld is, so too is Noccitan and Lomïn. They bear blooms."

"And so, you think that when the Dweol shattered, it took what it could with it, retracting in on itself?"

"I think that is very likely," Sabine said.

"Then this river of glass, that the old woman didn't recognize?"

"I think it's what remains of the Dweol's world-crossing vine."

Katiam looked out the stone door to the river that sat there. Derioth curled up just outside.

"Now, how did you get here?" Sabine asked Katiam.

"The Rotha," Katiam said. "It somehow found itself in a nest of Dweol bud glass beads. It touched one of them to me, and I found myself here."

"To what purpose does a flower send you to the realm of Dreams?" Sabine asked. "What is it?"

"If I can find my way back, I mean to find out."

"Then let us see if following the river of glass leads us both home."

The ribbon of glass took them into mountains made of clouds, as easy to walk upon as a hill of tilled earth, and Katiam found herself panting for breath as they climbed higher. Sabine did not seem as hard for breath, and Derioth gamboled from cloud to fluffy cloud.

"How," Katiam said, panting, "are you not dying? For breath?"

"There is no air here," Sabine said.

"What?" Katiam replied.

"What food have we eaten?"

"Those berries. And the bread that the old woman gave us."

"And how many days have we been walking?"

Katiam thought back. "I don't know."

"Time doesn't mean much in the Veld. Nor food. Nor even breathing."

"How are we not starving, then?"

"If you think about starving, then you will," Sabine said.

To that, Katiam's belly began to rumble.

"And you don't need to eat," Sabine said.

The feeling in her stomach subsided, and the burning in her lungs ceased.

"How?"

"This is dream. If you truly want to, you could fly."

"But in dreams," Katiam said, "you fall to earth after a time."

"Something to consider, though," Sabine said.

A breeze began to blow, and the river began to sing as the glass shifted. The clouds under their feet began to move too, as the wind picked up, and then in a burst of energy became a sudden gale, sheering the clouds away.

Derioth came and stood between them, and the two women placed a hand on his horn and back. The three stood against the wind.

"What is happening?" Katiam shouted over the wind.

She couldn't even hear Sabine's reply, but felt the woman's head shaking.

A minute later, the wind stopped, leaving the world around them calm, and revealing the new landscape. They stood upon a long stone walkway, over a bottomless gorge of blackness. The river of glass had been reduced to a small brook that ran along the bridge that went on for miles, further out over the abyss.

"Is that what we walked on?" Katiam asked. "Were we this close to falling to our death the entire time?"

"I don't know," Sabine said. "But I imagine we're about to find out."

She pointed to a figure standing one hundred yards away. He wore a robe of purple sand that fell from him in an endless cascade. His hood concealed his face in shadow, but Katiam could make out a black halo of whiskers around his mouth.

"Your names," he called out to them in a thick accent Katiam did not recognize.

"We are only two travelers," Sabine replied.

"From where do you come from, and to where do you go?"

"From the Meadow of the Shepherdess of Minds," Sabine called out. "And we travel in this direction, to a destination not yet known."

"If the Witch sent you, then you are interlopers."

"We simply pass through," Sabine said. "If you'll allow us to do so."

"Only by way of Toll paid to the Amethyst Council."

"And by what means would you have us pay this toll?" Sabine asked.

"Show me something I have never seen, and I shall let you pass."

"And should we fail?"

"Then you'll be cast into Labyrinth."

"Your name, that we may know who we entertain?"

"Meresmand the Tollkeeper."

"I thought as much," Sabine muttered to Katiam.

"What does that mean?"

"Apparently, we've journeyed into one of the domains of the Amethyst Council. There are countless myths and legends of each one. Meresmand captures people and places them in an endless labyrinth, in which they do his bidding, solving puzzles he has created. Few have passed his test."

"And we have to show him something he has never seen?" Katiam said. "How can we know whether he has or not?"

"One legend tells of a man who showed Meresmand wind. Another man, a sailor, had once fallen overboard, and seen creatures from the bottom of the ocean. He showed him that."

"So it could be something unseen, shown for what it is, or something that he has not conceived of?"

Sabine nodded and closed her eyes for a moment. When she opened them, Katiam saw the resolve she had come to know well in the other woman. She turned to Meresmand.

"What shall you show me?" the man asked.

"We show you nothing," Sabine said.

"Sabine!" Katiam cried.

The man laughed. "No one has ever refused. Such hubris from a woman! I admire it, of course, but you forfeit your lives to me with that answer."

"The hubris is yours, Meresmand. We have shown you nothing, and you have revealed that by that we have won."

"I do not understand."

"We have shown you something you have never seen. No thing. You have never seen nothing. And no one has ever shown it to you."

The wicked smile that spread across the man's face melted away.

"We have defeated you in your mind puzzle. And thus we have won."

"What will you take as a trophy?" he asked.

"What does he mean?" Katiam said. "Our freedom is not our trophy?"

"I'll explain later," Sabine muttered and turned back to the man.

"Along with our passage through your domain unharmed, you shall grant us the means to map our course."

Meresmand nodded and raised his arms. The world exploded in a shower of color, leaving Katiam blinking away the flashes that persisted in her vision.

They stood on a cliff overlooking a wide basin filled with empty ravines. The skies overhead were filled with the same.

Meresmand stood beside them, his hood pulled back onto his shoulders, revealing his bald head. He appeared young, but his eyes spoke of years of loneliness.

"This is the edge of my domain."

"Those ravines are the Labyrinth?" Sabine asked.

Meresmand nodded. "The arrival of your little river has cost me ten people so far. I finally caught on. They were throwing themselves in to escape me."

"Can you blame them?" Sabine said. "I should do all I could to leave, if I was under your command."

"They trespassed, and those are the rules I set."

"Show me the means to navigate the domains," Sabine said.

He took out a fold of parchment and laid it on a rock.

"Take up Oneirion and pour it out on this."

Sabine took up a handful and threw it at the parchment. The sand stuck in places, and revealed lines and rivers. Names and mountain ranges.

"This shows all that you can see for one hundred miles in each direction."

"And the names?" Sabine asked, pointing to the name to the north.

"Every Amethyst mage shall require a different price."

"And how shall we know that price before we enter their domain?"

"If you wish to know that secret, you must give me a truth in trade."

Sabine walked to the edge of the shattered glass ribbon and took out a single piece of glass, rounded like a bead, and turned to face the man. She placed it on her tongue. Her eyes began to glow a soft pink.

"The Amethyst Council is cracked, and by her hand shall it shatter. Upon the back of the reyem she rides. And she brings hope to the darkness, and dims the false light."

"What is this? Prophecy? By what means?"

"A truth for a truth," Sabine replied.

"I..." he looked at the map and then to the river, and then to Sabine. "A whisper of hot breath upon the name will reveal many secrets known to those who seek them."

He seemed to lose interest in the two of them, a glint of greed in his eyes, as he considered the river of glass. He walked to its edge and stared down into its depths.

Sabine took Katiam's hand, and the collar of Derioth, and pulled them along. Katiam took hold of the map. The sand fell from the paper, leaving it blank.

"What happened?" Katiam asked.

"He is considering taking a bead himself."

"A bead?" Katiam asked.

"They have been tumbling on themselves for many days," Sabine said. "Look at the river now."

Katiam noticed that the river was no longer made up of shattered glass, but polished beads that looked like the beads of rosy colored glass the Crysalas used in their silvered bowls.

"Then, it is from the Dweol?" Katiam said.

"It is the Dweol. Only, rather than the small sconces, the vine shattered, and has now beaten itself down into the something more manageable. Now, we must hurry."

"Why?"

"Because there is also a blackness that pursues us down the vine."

Katiam turned to look back up where they came from and saw the river miles off turning from the rosy purple to a dark black. Then she heard the screams of Meresmand.

"Apparently, he has seen the future tapestry," Sabine said, "and did not enjoy what he saw."

"What was the prophecy you spoke?"

"It revealed something to me that I suspected, but did not dare wish to face."

"What was that?"

"When we reach the far edge of Meresmand's domains, I'll tell you. But let's get clear of his power first, in case he decides to break the trust and betray us."

They followed the lay of the land, the Dweol river now roaring like a rushing river alongside them. They came after a day to an escarpment, a winding path leading up the cliff face. Where Katiam's footing failed, Derioth provided the help she needed, and they came up the other side to a plain as flat as a pane of glass, that stretched on for countless miles.

"We are free from him now," Sabine said.

"Now what did you learn?" Katiam said.

"That our journey ends in a forest on the other side of this plain. But we shall only succeed if you bathe within the pool found there before the blackness takes it, and you'll reach the arms of one you love."

"What is the catch?"

"The blackness that killed the Rosebloom fast approaches, and we have little time."

It seemed like days they walked. For it had been. Yet only a few moments seemed to pass as the ever-creeping blackness that sought to consume the river of rose-glass beads moved in a swift and inexorable pace.

The edge of the forest that loomed before them stood as black as the death that pursued them. Derioth bleated a warning as the two women approached its edge.

"I don't think that forest is safe," Katiam said.

"It's not," Sabine said. "The Dweol revealed to me that it is no safer out here, either. The plain we crossed is going to be consumed by the blackness and Meremand's realm will share a border with the forest before this day has passed."

"Who is the owner of the forest?"

"Nobody. It is unclaimed."

"How do you know all this?"

"Because that river," Sabine said, pointing to the rose glass, "that vine has always been here, below the surface, and knows more of the realm than any other."

She walked to the edge and crafted a bowl of Oneirion with one hand, and a satchel in the other. She drew beads from it and filled the bag, and then threw it over her shoulder.

"Why do that?"

"Because I'll need it to do what I've been shown I must."

Sabine turned and marched into the forest. Katiam, and finally Derioth, followed behind.

There were no leaves, fruit, nor the sound of any creature within the wood. Their steps echoed off the trees. Katiam tripped and kicked a rock into one, and it reverberated like hollow metal.

"Who crafted this forest?" Katiam asked.

"Who knows?" Sabine said. "It's ancient."

The river made popping sounds far behind them, as glass beads shattered to blackened ash. The blackness did not try to race them, but almost seemed to watch them moving, and allow them passage.

Derioth eyed the water cautiously, taking up the rear.

The sound of a gurgling brook ahead filled Katiam with a sudden thirst, and she rushed forward, Sabine beside her, to look up over the lip and down to the pool revealed below. There water stood, and, at the bottom, a pink hue glow emanating from an undamaged Dweol Rosebloom. On the walls of the pool the pink lights of sconce buds glowed.

"There it is," Sabine said. She took up the Oneirion and formed an axe in her hand.

"Are you going to cut that back edge? Drain the pool?" Katiam asked.

"No," Sabine said, and began chopping at a tree. The iron crumbled from rust and fell across the Dweolvine River. Sabine dropped another, and then another. Soon a dam stood, and the beads began to pile up, just as the black overtook the pile, and turned it to black ash.

"We haven't time," Sabine said.

"For what?"

"For you to go," Sabine said.

"Go?"

"You have to dive to the bloom. It has revealed to me it will take you to your destination."

"So let's go!" Katiam said.

"I am not leaving," Sabine said.

"What?"

"I have no body to return to," Sabine said. "And my purpose was revealed here."

"What do you mean?"

"The Prophecy I spoke. It was about me. And I intend to fulfill it."

"I don't understand."

"Sakharn was once a part of the Black Coterie. Under her tutelage, the Amethyst Council learned the dark ways, and have since continued to hold so beautiful a place as the Veld under their sway. But their infighting has cracked their resolve."

"And you mean to take them down."

"She has given us Derioth. There are few she lets take the reyem from her pasture."

"Why is that important?"

"Because Zanghard is known by other names. And what she gives cannot be taken away. I intend to take the gift she has given me, and the prophecy her sister has granted, and bring hope."

"Jurgon..." Katiam said.

"He has his own purpose to follow. He ought to do so. But tell him, when his purpose is fulfilled, if he seeks me, he will find me."

The rusted trees began to crack under the pressure of the blackness pushing against them.

Katiam threw her arms around Sabine. "Thank you," Katiam said.

"No," Sabine replied. "Thank you for finding me, and rescuing me from my despair. Now I have purpose."

Katiam turned and gave Derioth a scratch behind the horn to stifle the tears that streamed down her face. She turned to the pool and leapt feet-first, plunging as deep as she could. Then, turning downward, she began to crawl through the water warmed by the light of the Dweol. As she touched the Rosebloom, the petals contracted, closing around her as she turned to look up out of the water. Sabine stood above, axe in one hand and Derioth under the other. The trees began to pop and bloom to life, even as the blackness poured over and into the pool. The pink rose petals closed around Katiam and her chest screamed in pain for air, but then she remembered she needed none here. And she took deep mouthfuls of the blessed water. And suddenly, she was a seed in soil, awaiting her birth.

38

Root

Flower grow, leaf climb.
Thorn protect, vine bind.

Her body became tree sap, slowly oozing through the tight confines of a tree trunk. There was the smell of a new garden, and she began to grow. Finally, she felt herself fall to the ground ever slowly, settling into a bed of leaves dying around her.

Katiam was standing at the foot of a grassy knoll. A dead tree stood at the top. It had no leaves upon it, and looked ancient and withered. The black rot was crawling its way up the side. A figure stood at the top of the hill, looking up at the tree.

She began walking uphill. The tree almost seemed to grow the closer she got to it. The other woman standing there turned to watch her with curiosity.

"Who are you?" she asked. The other one had her hair cropped short in the Crysalas custom.

"I should ask you the same. I'm Katiam Borreau."

"I thought I recognized you, though I couldn't place your face at first. You're one of the Matriarch Superioris's attendants."

Katiam nodded.

"I'm Zarra Ferluça. I'm the Sister Superior of the Dweol Chapter at Ikhail's Oracle. How does the Matriarch fare? We were gathered, expecting to speak with her when she visited the Oracle. But then the collapse happened."

"It happened at your Worldbloom too?" Katiam asked.

Zarra nodded and spun, looking down the hill. Another had arrived. She was tall and elegant, with flesh-covered knobs rising from her head. A long tail followed behind her. It was a qavyl. She flowed up the hill toward them, smiling demurely.

"I did not expect that to occur," the qavyl said.

"You come from the Sanae Massif?" Zarra asked. "I recognize your voice. I think perhaps we've spoken before."

"Yes. You must be Zarra. I am the Matriarch Minoris of the qavylli republic, Thillanis Dellitoss."

Katiam turned, feeling someone else had arrived. This proved to be a green-skinned hrelmaiden. She walked up the hill with a broad smile upon her face, her overly wide hips swinging as she did so. She barely stood as high as Katiam's elbow. Before they could question where she came from others quickly began to appear. Soon there were ten of them, politely chatting, and discovering that their order had people in countries they did not know existed from continents the others had not yet discovered, and yet they were all drawn to this place by their worship of Crysania.

One of the women turned and looked down the hill. A figure stood alone at the bottom, looking up at their group. They all started to stare. The figure was taller than the rest, even taller than the qavyl, due to two long, black horns that rose from the top of her head. From her cheeks two more horns curled, the tips curving under and then out from her face. The sharp ridge of her beak-like mouth was not long, but short like the face of a hrelgren. She had the hands of a hrelgren as well, with a thumb on each side of the two central fingers, though instead of toes she had two sleek, black hooves. Katiam took a step forward first and walked down the hill. A thrill and fear filled her as she approached the T'Akah.

This was the enemy of all, a T'Akah. Member of that godforsaken race that was a scourge to men, hrelgrens, qavylli. But Katiam felt they had been assembled for a reason. She would not question the will of her goddess.

Katiam held out her hand. "Come. Join us, sister."

The T'Akah held out her hand and spoke. "Why are we here?" Somehow Katiam knew her words, even if the T'Akah was speaking words she should not understand.

"I don't know. But I imagine we shall find out."

The two of them walked to the top of the knoll together. They stood in a circle and looked at one another. There was hesitance, but acceptance of the T'Akah.

"I realize you never answered my question," Zarra said toward Katiam. "How fares the Matriarch?"

Katiam sighed. "She is gone from us. I was taken through the Veld to reach this place"

The others let out a collective gasp.

"I am here," Katiam heard a familiar voice. She turned and saw the old Matriarch step out from behind the tree. She was no longer old, but looked as she described herself in her youth, with a mess of red curls, some of which bunched upon her head in swirls, like roses. She was as small as she was in life.

The others smiled when they saw her and gathered around her.

She held up her hands and indicated they listen.

"You all must do as I say. The Mother is approaching. You must all gather near me. We must keep the root of the Dweol between us and her, or you will be struck down and join me here in Lomïn."

A bright light, cast in a rosy hue, suddenly flashed. Only the shade of the tree kept the fullness of the light from washing over them. Even so, Katiam found herself blinking her eyes clear.

There was a sound that was more a feeling that filled the place. It pressed heavily against her chest, and held her shoulders like a warm embrace.

She found herself falling to her knees, along with everyone, as they bowed. Above the Dweol, they could just see the tips of the headdress Crysania wore, or perhaps the headdress was part of her. It looked like the ceremonial chasubles the Matriarch Superioris wore. From around the Dweol root, Crysania's wings, like six large rose leaves, expanded. They glimmered with life.

"My children," the voice said, filling the whole of Katiam's being. "I welcome you here, if only for a time."

Katiam felt a smile grow across her face. Her own goddess was speaking to her directly.

"You stand now at what remains of the Dweol. This is its root, and even now it is blighted, but not gone. Another must now take its place."

She was silent.

"There is another?" one voice asked.

"There is. Do you not know of the Warotha?"

There was a general murmur of voices not understanding.

"Of course. There are three. And only three of you have found one. One of them has awoken. You must see them all delivered to their homeland. The worlds will die without them.

"I cannot help you," Crysania continued. "It would draw the attention of those who would see the Warotha destroyed. And thus I must leave it in your hands. The entire Crysalas was founded for this very day. I pray you are strong enough to stand against the trials you will face."

"What trials?" It was Maeda Mür herself that asked.

"Trials greater than the pogroms that tried to hunt the Crysalas down to extinction to get to my little roses."

"Were we not founded to seek your purity?"

The mother goddess laughed. "No. How little you seem to know. The seeking of purity was an allowance to accept you as followers, to sanctify you for joining me in my own garden in Lomïn. The Crysalas was founded to protect the Dweol until the coming of the lost generation of Warotha."

"What is a Warotha?" another asked.

"Iwarat." It was the T'Akah next to her that spoke. She was whispering to Katiam. "I know of the Iwarat."

"Why us... Why us?" Katiam felt her own voice ask the question before she could stop herself.

"Do not ask why. It is not your business to know why. Only ask how you will fulfill the destiny set before you."

"How then?"

"You must take my Warotha home."

"Where is home?"

"You must seek it out yourself. I cannot reveal it to you. The Deceiver will wish to stop you, and I shall do all in my power to ensure that his attention is distracted elsewhere, though I cannot control him. He fulfills his own destiny."

A gong sounded.

"It is time for me to leave you. And it is time for you to leave. Maeda, you shall see them away."

"Yes, my goddess," the Matriarch Superioris said.

There was a vast emptiness that fell upon each of them as Crysania moved away. They were left gasping for breath.

"We have only a short moment," the Matriarch said. "You must find one another. Assist one another. Protect the Warotha."

"And how will we know what we seek?" Zarra asked.

"Our goddess already said. Three of you have one in your possession already. If you do not know, then you do not have one. Protect those who do."

"I shall endeavor to cross borders formerly disallowed by my people," the T'Akah said. "Speak to those I send by the word 'kaigal-onti'. None would harm those that speak words of peace."

"What is your name?" Katiam asked.

"I am Vuduin eb'Gatha."

The hrelmaidens gasped.

"What does this mean to you?" Katiam asked.

There was a sudden strong power that seemed to pull at Katiam.

The others quickly pulled away from the group, disappearing in an instant. Maeda's hand reached out and took hold of Katiam to stop her from going.

"Please do not let go," Katiam pleaded.

"You must go, soon."

"I cannot leave you."

"But you have the Rotha. It has awoken."

"I cannot leave without you. I already left Sabine behind."

"You must, child. But what of Sabine?"

"She was taken to the Veld. And she has chosen to stay, to fulfill a prophecy revealed to her. She aims to disassemble the Amethyst Council."

"A dire quest," Maeda said. "Be sure to give that word of hope to her husband. Now go. Return to the Monastery at Precipice. My body is already gone to ash. You must protect the Rotha. But take this."

She placed something in her hand. "Keep this flower from the Rotha. Give it to her when you know the time is right, but not before."

"What is it?" Katiam asked.

She was sitting in her cell on the floor, cold and naked. Her clothes were laid upon the bed, folded, and the room had been tidied. Tears streamed down her face. She stood up, pulled her robe over her head, and looked to the desk where she usually kept the seed pod. It was gone. She remembered it had somehow moved to her bed. She tore back the covers. It was not there, either. The Rotha seed, Warotha as Crysania had called it, or in the T'Akai tongue Iwarat, was gone. She had been charged with protecting it, and she had already lost it.

39

Face of Death

The blind shall determine the fate of the world. In ten-fold ways shall they lead. The blind who have no vision shall bestow vision on those fully blinded in their cowardice.

—*STAFF OF ORDER*, RELIC OF THE NIFARAN MONKS

Seriah woke to the clacker of the monk assigned to wake the others. She sat up in bed and readjusted the blindfold over her eyes before putting her feet on the floor. She pulled her robe over her frame and then wrapped the sash around her waist before pulling the cowl over her shoulders. Her sandals and staff were by the door. As she opened the door and stepped out, she ran directly into Ensayez de la Neitha.

"I am very sorry, Nefer!" Ensayez said breathlessly, helping Seriah to her feet. "I don't know what to do, and I didn't want to wake you."

"What is the problem?" Seriah asked.

"Loranne, the old lady from the children's home. She is sick."

"She is well cared for now by you and the Abecinians, isn't she?"

"The changes made to improve her situation have been just fine, but after a week her health began to fail. She's been four days in the Abecinian infirmary. I don't know what else to do. The children are distraught, and I haven't seen you in days."

"Let us eat and take some food to the old lady," Seriah said.

Seriah didn't mention why she had been scarce over the past ten days. The relief that had washed over her after her confession to the Paladin, Jined Brazstein, had finally given her the courage to find her own bed rather than the hidden closet that hid her from the nightmare in the corners of her mind. It was a surprise even to her that they had found her for the trial of their fellow Paladin, to give her testimony before the paladinial leadership.

Ensayez served food quickly to Seriah, hovering over her the entire time.

Seriah didn't have much appetite, so she pushed her plate back. Ensayez cleared it and returned to stand next to her.

"Tell me what happened as we walk," Seriah said, taking Ensayez's arm.

"At first Loranne was very amiable to the changes we made. The monks of Aben were quick to lend a hand, scouring the place clean. We were able to purchase the surrounding homes. We converted one of the homes into a place for servants and the kitchen. Another one was turned into beds and playrooms for the children. But then things quickly got out of hand."

"How so?"

"People with Day-Blind began flocking to the place. Children, women, the elderly. Loranne didn't know what to do. She took them all in. A family came who had been struck by the malady arrived with a newborn child. Loranne took them in and the next day the parents disappeared, leaving her with the babe and the two older children. I had been away for three days going over paperwork on the charter, and returned to chaos and shouting from the children, blind adults, Abecinians. I couldn't find Loranne. She had gone out into the streets, having not slept for two days, with the baby in her arms, seeking a wet nurse."

"You found her, though?"

"Yes. And we found the baby a wet nurse. But Loranne is not doing well. She has a fever and a deep cough. The Abecinians at the home wouldn't dare go near her for fear of catching the same. So I brought her up to the complex and got her situated here in the infirmary."

Seriah could smell the room as they approached. The quiet coughs and soft shuffles of monks of Aben filled the large space. Her staff lightly tapped the flagstones, and she could sense the beds as she passed. A monk sat beside one bed, calmly shushing the patient there. From another she heard the muttering of a monk who had complained of a broken leg he had suffered.

Ensayez pulled her close. "Keep to the right here. On the opposite side they have hung sheets to keep a few patients segregated from us."

Seriah nodded. She could perceive the smell of greater sickness wafting from within.

"They are left in here alone?"

"They are given food, and made comfortable," a monk of Aben said from nearby. "There is little our medicine can do. They have an infection of the limbs."

"A leprosy?" Seriah asked.

"Their feet are infected with a sickly disease. It will soon overtake them and Nifara will deal with them. Who are you here to visit?"

"Hello Brother Garmon." Ensayez tugged on Seriah's arm. "Brother Garmon runs the infirmary."

"Greetings, Brother Garmon," Seriah said.

"Welcome, Nefer," Garmon said.

"Brother Garmon, this is Nefer Seriah Yaledít," Ensayez said.

"You're here to visit Loranne?"

"Yes. I sat with her last night," Ensayez said. "She did not wake all night."

"I'll have the kitchen send more soup."

They walked the rest of the long hall and came to stand at the end of Loranne's bed. As she slept, the old lady took long, deep breaths that shuddered as they left her. Ensayez offered Seriah a seat.

"What have the infirmarians said?" Seriah asked.

"They don't know. They attribute most of it to exhaustion, and say she just needs rest."

"And what do you think?" Seriah asked.

"I agree. I think she's tired. She has spent so much of her energy on the orphans. The changes, perhaps, were too fast and her health gave in."

A monk came with the bowl of broth. They propped the woman up and Ensayez worked to feed the feverish woman. Seriah sat next to them for several hours. She felt a hand on hers and reached out. Loranne had awoken.

"Who is there?" she asked.

"Seriah. The monk who came to visit you. And Ensayez is here too."

"Why do you sit with a dying woman? Leave me be."

"Her fever has reduced," Ensayez whispered.

"We fear we brought you to this," Seriah admitted. "Now you have more to care for than you ever intended."

"Child," the woman said, "you gave me a gift. I know now Nifara can take me, and I need not worry about the children. You will care for them."

"Of course we will."

"Where am I?" Loranne asked.

"The infirmary in the Abecinian complex," Ensayez said.

"And the baby? Little Œsley?"

"He is cared for now. We found a wet nurse."

"Very good. I'm hungry now."

"I'll fetch more broth," Ensayez said.

"Bah. No broth. Bread and meat. I need a full belly if I'm to journey with the goddess."

Ensayez left, while Loranne and Seriah sat in silence.

"What is she like?" Loranne eventually asked.

"Ensayez?"

"No, girl. Nifara. What should I expect? I'm ready, mind you. But I want to know what I must steel myself for."

"I...don't know," Seriah said.

"You're a monk of Nifara. Don't you know last rites?"

"Of course, I..."

"Tell me what will happen."

"Nifara is said to come and take you to Noccitan. There you'll stand before the Judge, and he'll decide if you are to stay in Noccitan, or continue on to Lomïn."

"What happens in Noccitan?"

"I don't honestly know."

"Your goddess delivers souls to the afterlife and you don't know?"

"My studies have been in the here and now. I understand the law pertaining to the acquisition of orphanages, and judging between two people."

"You're not much use then, are you?"

"No."

Seriah fell silent.

"Girl. I'm sorry. I didn't mean to insult you."

"But you're right," Seriah said, "and it scares me."

"What does?"

"Death."

"Why be afraid? It happens to us all."

"I fear it, because it was supposed to be me a week ago. I was slated to die, and someone else died in my place. I saw Nifara. And I saw death, too. He came for me, and I wasn't there."

"Death? He's a person?"

"No, but I saw a man who was death."

"You're speaking in riddles."

"Because I don't know what I'm saying," Seriah nervously giggled.

"Well, why don't you sit here with me for a while. Perhaps we can ask the goddess together."

"You don't sound like you're dying."

"Bah. What do you know? I know I'm at death's door."

Ensayez returned with the food. Loranne devoured the bread, and complained that Ensayez had brought no meat. After another hour, Ensayez rose.

"I haven't slept since yesterday."

"I'll sit with her," Seriah said.

Ensayez excused herself, leaving the two of them to wait the evening out. The light cough of the sick and the moans of suffering cast a dark shadow over the place.

There came a moment, perhaps an hour later, when all fell silent. It took Seriah back to the cold chill that fell over her by the Judgment Tree, the figure visiting her. She listened hard, wondering if she once more might encounter that chill. Instead, a long sigh of a mourning world seemed to come upon her.

She caught herself gasping for breath several times, having somehow forgotten to draw air into her lungs. It enraptured her until she found a peace, but only for a moment. It was then a sharp staccato of a sound tore the peace from her forcefully, replacing it with irritation. The harsh *tap, tap, tap* came first, followed by the familiar sound of a monk's staff.

"Are you leaving?" she heard Loranne ask, half-rousing from her sleep.

"No," she whispered.

The sound of the approaching monk seemed to last as long as the silence had, until finally the monk entered the long infirmary. She listened as the monk walked from bed to bed, pausing at each one. She sat silent, knowing they would not even know she was there if she did not speak up.

The monk's cracked, old voice whispered to each patient, and he moved on. She could not place who it was until he came to the bed before reaching them. It was the elderly Cräg Narn. He shuffled along and came to stand at the foot of Loranne's bed.

"Holy Nefer," Seriah said. Her own voice startled her, but seemed to come as no surprise to the elderly man.

"Greetings, Nefer Yaledit," he said. "Who have we here?"

"This is Loranne," Seriah responded.

"I can speak for myself, thank you," Loranne interrupted. "I'm Loranne. Who are you?"

"Cräg Narn, an old monk and follower of our lady Nifara."

"Well, take a seat, you old Nefer. Because I have questions, and this young one here needs an education."

The old monk shuffled around to sit in Ensayez's empty chair.

"I shall answer as best I can, Loranne."

"Good. Tell me about Nifara."

"Our beloved goddess, is..."

"No. Tell me about her."

"She is... holy."

Loranne made a sound of disgust.

"Please. Hear me," Cräg said. "Nifara can only be described as holy. To stand in her presence reminds you of your littleness, yet encourages you to be more."

"You sound as though you've met her," Loranne said.

"I have."

Seriah's heart skipped a beat.

"Then what shall I fear when I meet her?"

"Have you anything to fear?" Cräg asked.

"No, I don't think so. I'm ready to settle my debt with the Judge."

"Then you are ready. Good. I will come by and visit you again. You should sleep."

Loranne didn't need any encouragement. She rolled over and began breathing steadily. The old monk rose.

"Walk with me, Nefer," he said.

She followed in silence behind him for some time, her steps hesitant.

"Why do you dawdle?" he asked, pausing.

"I fear she'll die while I'm not there."

"Why should it matter?" he asked.

"She should not be alone."

"I think she's made it clear she was ready. And she will not be alone. She will hold the hand of the goddess into the afterlife. That is not why you wish to sit with her."

"Yes. I fear I may have caused her to kneel on death's door. I took on her orphanage, and the pressure caused by such a drastic change overwhelmed her."

"Tear down your webs, you're not the child of the Deceiver."

"Pardon me?"

"I said, speak plainly. Admit to me why you sat with her."

During their entire trip the old monk had spoken kindly, plainly. But that seemed to melt into an authority she could not deny.

"I wish to see the Lady."

"I thought as much. Many of us have done the same, in our old age, most usually. Why?"

"I... I was meant to die last week."

"You feel guilty for the deaths of the Archimandrite and for young Rystan."

"I was supposed to be with Archimandrite Maran that night."

The old monk began to laugh. "You do not understand the ways of the gods at all, do you? You think death came for you? And that Nifara took someone else in your place? Rystan no longer has any fears. Taken ahead of her time, yes, but to a place that is better than here."

"What are you saying?"

"I am saying why do you skulk about and look for death? Your goddess has other things planned for you."

"Are you in the infirmary to seek out Nifara?" Seriah asked.

"No. I have no need for that. Do you recall the great decision that was made by Nefer Koragh Neyarn?"

"The Seventh? He broke his staff so that the kings assembled at the council of Morriego would promise to care for the elderly and ailing. Infirmaries were set up in Morriego, Setera, Düran, and Mahndür. Other nations less so, but the elderly travel to these places to die, in dignity."

"Yes. The staff was broken. And now many of us elderly monks, perhaps also ready to go, and no longer with enough faculty to ad-minister judgment for people, spend our days delivering last rites and comforting those who fear the Judgment of Wyv-Thüm."

"So you are here to do that?"

"I am here for more of a reason than that. Yes. And I have done it for many, many years."

"What reason more could there be?"

"Young monk, that is a secret I'm not sure I am willing to part with just yet."

"I have wondered these last several months what our purpose is. A question was raised to me shortly after we arrived in Mahn Fulhar, and it nags at me."

"And what question is that?"

"Does our goddess perform miracles? And if not, why not? And if so, why do we not hear of them?"

"What do you think?"

"I wondered if perhaps her delivery of souls to the Judge was a miracle, and her power is thus spent doing that."

"So you propose that her power can be spent, or perhaps diminished by the power she exerts by traveling from world to world?"

"Is that not so?"

"Does your walking from town to town diminish you?"

"It tires me, certainly."

"But does it diminish you? Or, perhaps, does it make you stronger?"

"Stronger, I suppose. The more I travel."

"She has taken almost every soul that has ever passed on to their destination to the gates of Noccitan. It does not diminish her. She performed miracles. Nine to be exact."

"Only nine?"

"Yes. Nine great decisions. Nine staves broken. And there will come a day when she performs many more. I have spoken with her on the subject."

"What miracle is there in a broken staff?" Seriah asked.

The old monk paused and waited for something.

"What do you mean you have spoken to her on the subject?" Seriah asked.

"Perhaps we shall speak more on this later. The sun is rising. I must away to my cell."

"I suppose I must sleep. I understand."

"Were that the case..." Cräg Narn shuffled away. Seriah heard the sounds of coughing, and realized they had walked a full circle back to the infirmary. She came and sat next to Loranne, who did not fully wake, but instead spent the morning in and out of consciousness, muttering unintelligible phrases.

Ensayez returned before the midday and sat across from her.

"I'm sorry I was away for so long. I received a message and had to go to the orphanage."

"Oh? What news?"

"The Abecinians are bringing the orphans up to visit. I wanted to come ahead and make sure she was presentable, and to ready you to step away with me so that they may have their privacy."

Before the orphans arrived, they tried to feed Loranne another bowl of soup. The sound of feet pattered on the flagstones, and Loranne suddenly awoke and sat upright.

"My children are here," she said.

"Yes, Loranne," Ensayez said. "Come, Seriah, let us leave them to their peace."

They stepped away as the children gathered near Loranne. There was a cacophony of voices, crowding over one another to speak. Eventually they all settled down. One of the older children spoke up first.

"Mamma-Lor, are you well?"

"I will be better soon. Now each of you tell me what you have done."

They each took their turn, adding to stories others told, of arguments they had had with one another, food they had eaten, and adventures they had imagined. The smallest ones climbed up into her arms, while others stayed quiet. The little ones laughed, or chattered, and some just let her hold them in silence. Seriah could hear the squeak of a little one ask her when she would return to their home.

"I shall not be returning," Loranne said matter-of-factly.

"But who shall tuck us in at night?" the little girl's voice implored.

"I will," the voice of an older girl said.

"Alright," the little girl agreed.

After a few long minutes, the younger children became antsy and were escorted away to allow the older children to gather around.

They stood around Loranne for a long time in utter silence. It snapped as one child let free a sob, then choked it down.

"Oh Mezz," Loranne said. "Come here."

Seriah could hear the creak of the bed as the girl climbed up onto the bed and cried for a long time. Loranne shushed her, both knowing it might be the last time she would comfort her. The children excused themselves one by one. Eventually only one remained.

He sniffed every once in a while. It was the only way Seriah knew anyone still sat there.

"Why?" he croaked.

"Why what, Koril?"

"You can't leave us."

"Yes, I can. I'm old. And I'm tired."

"What do I have to do to stop you from leaving?"

"There is nothing you can do to stop death."

"Why must you leave?"

"I had to die so that babe could live. It took me two days to find the wet nurse."

"You should have sent for someone."

"No. I had to do that myself. But now you have a job to do."

"What?"

"I know you've been healed from your blindness. The light from the forge did not leave you forever blinded."

He whimpered his acknowledgement.

"How long have you been able to see?"

"Six months now."

"Very well. Then you must take care of the children. Show them I love them."

"I will. Because I love you."

"I know child, I know."

The boy softly sobbed for some time before he stood. "Goodbye, Mamma-Lor."

"You will see me again when your final day comes. But you must make the best of your life until then."

"Yes Momma-Lor."

Koril left and joined the other children out in the hall. The patter of feet subsided. The hall was quiet once more.

"Please make every effort to leave the responsibility of the home to him," Loranne said.

"Of course," Ensayez responded. "He's been very helpful this last week."

"Then I am ready."

The tap of another staff drew slowly closer.

"Nefers," the voice of Cräg Narn said.

They both acknowledged him.

"Ensayez," he said, "please allow me to take your place. Seriah and I shall sit with Loranne."

"I have much to do at the orphanage, anyway," Ensayez responded.

Loranne promptly fell asleep, worn out by her visit.

"Shall we continue our conversation?" Cräg asked.

"I'm not sure where to pick the conversation up," Seriah said.

"The Nine. What do you understand of them?"

"I'm going to guess that you're going to tell me, regardless."

"Very well. You likely know simply that they each made a world-changing decision and broke their staff over each affair. But there was much more to each of their stories. You see, they knew their decision would be world changing. And so they beseeched Nifara before making it, to have her blessing, to ensure that their decision would be protected. As compensation for this blessing, they were asked to make a sacrifice. A great sacrifice."

"I'm not sure what you mean."

"Very well. The Third–Belligar Mand. He was the founder of the building of the Templum. He broke his staff and broke the ground where the Templum now stands. He consecrated the land to Nifara. He is a kind man. Always greets me."

"Is a kind man? Don't you mean was a kind man? He lived over a thousand years ago."

"It is true. He sits at the door to the Templum to this day."

"You mean to tell me he is immortal?"

"That is the sacrifice he made. He asked to never leave the Templum. Nifara honored him with that sacrifice. And now he receives each guest as they arrive. He has for one thousand years."

"And what of the Seventh, Koragh Neyarn?" Seriah asked. "The monk who started this ministry to the elderly and dying? What sacrifice did you make?"

Cräg Narn chuckled. "For a blind girl you see much. I gave up sleep. But I, perhaps more than the others, have thus had the opportunity to speak with her more than most. I'm there at many a passing, and can speak a few fleeting words to her each time."

"Will I see her when she takes Loranne?"

"Most don't. Perhaps you will, but I've rarely heard of those who have seen her more than once before their time comes."

"Will you tell me when she is here?"

"You will know."

Loranne woke an hour later. She did not say much more than the repeated words, "I am ready. I am ready. I am ready."

A priest of Aben arrived with oils for last rites. Cräg took them before dismissing the priest, and placed the fragrant oil upon her forehead.

"I anoint thee, servant of the helpless, and caretaker of the fatherless. Speed to you in the arms of Nifara. May the Judge give weight to your goods, and turn blind his third eye upon your wrongs."

A purse was placed in her hand with three coins within. She lightly shook the bag, giggling like a little girl.

"I'll give these to Wyv himself. I'm ready." Her voice was as clear as the day before. She sat up in bed.

"What a beautiful blue dress you wear," she said. The purse of coins fell from her hand and onto the floor.

"My Lady," Cräg said. A moment later, he said, "Yes. This Nefer saw the deaths of Pell Maran and Rystan Amiré. I think perhaps she worries about their fates."

There was a long silence.

"She says they are well," Cräg said. "The Judge ruled in favor of them both."

"I have something else I must say," Seriah said, "if I may."

"*Speak,*" a voice said from all around her.

"I was approached by a figure, and coldness was his companion. He bade me to say something to you, be it on my deathbed or not. He said you would know what it meant."

"*Be quick, for I must go.*"

"He said he wished you had not shunned him. And that things might have been different for all if you hadn't."

The air seemed to suck out of the room and the voice of a young girl sobbed all around them. The cry shook the building. There was a bright flash of blue, and then stillness, and blackness.

"What have you done?" Cräg asked.

"What do you mean?"

"Do you not know whose words you spoke?"

"I..."

"You have just announced the end of an era."

"What? How?"

"One of the first prophecies spoken by Crysania: Their arrangement sundered, they shall not speak to one another. But a messenger shall arrive delivering words one to the other. The gates of Noccitan shall shudder, as one who would open it shall begin his march toward death's door, Judgement Key in hand."

"What do you mean?" Seriah begged. "Have I done something wrong?"

Cräg sighed. "Nifara was the first to shun Achanerüt. She knew something was wrong when he appeared. She vowed never to speak to him, nor to hear words from him. You have delivered a message from the Deceiver to Nifara. You have signaled to us that an end to the way things are has arrived."

40

Interludes

Two Paladins went about their work, applying chains to his wrists. "Those aren't necessary," Jakis Gladen said. "I'm not going anywhere."

"Brother Aeger," the younger of the two said, "Pater Minoris didn't mention chains."

The old Paladin looked at the one speaking and gave him a motion to leave the cell.

He hesitated for a moment, and then turned as Aeger glared at him. After listening to the Paladin's steps leave the holding area, Primus turned to Gladen.

"I am no messenger," Aeger said, "but I did offer to make sure you went nowhere until Slate could decide what to do with you."

"If Slate were able to make a decision on his own, then I might be afraid."

"Nevertheless."

"The Pater Segundii asked that I prepare a list."

"I'm aware of that. It was my suggestion, after all. And I intend to see to it that you create the list."

"After which, you'll make a few editorial changes of your own."

Aeger smiled.

"I could refuse to make the list until after I've given you up."

"I doubt that," Aeger said. "I'll be taking something of yours first, to ensure you don't."

"There is nothing of mine you can take. My dignity is already forfeit."

"I wasn't thinking of your dignity."

"If I'm to make the list, why the chains?"

Aeger had turned to the writing desk. He opened up a small pen box, and took out a quill-tipped rod.

"From what I've gathered," Aeger said, "you tend to think very territorially. You assume that your sect stood alone out here in the west, seeking to answer the questions posed by the Dread Plate. Seeking to establish dominion from the Aerie. You assume, based on the maps I've seen captured by those you had stationed at St. Nonn, that the Order of the Feather tended to run all operations from St. Hamul. That the Order of the Bell issued from Piedala. That may be semi-true, but you and I know it's much more fluid than that. After all, I understand you had tools crafted from skyshards."

"What is your point?"

"I've spoken with Slate, and I understand some of what the Gauntlet does. And while Dusk is the leader of the Order of the Feather, I am the foremost scholar on the ways of the Feather. That being said, I have come to notice similarities in the dominion you're able to establish with your gauntlet, and the stripping bare of the soul through use of the bells, and the separation of it with the shadequills."

"You mean to take my soul from me," Vanguard said. "You'll kill me, and hold my soul hostage in one of your books."

"See, you're basing your assumptions only on common knowledge. You assume that's all my order does. I'll be taking your soul while you live. The discomfort and despair you'll sink into will ensure you do as I ask."

"I'll break free of the chain you're suggesting."

"What makes you think you can do that?"

"It has been done."

"From the dominion the gauntlet has over someone's mind? I met the man who continually casts off your grip. What I'll be doing is very different."

He approached Gladen and held up the stylus. The tip was crafted from the twisted metal Gladen had seen in the orbs and mauls he had requisitioned in his hunt for the Dread Plate. The plate itself had appeared to be forged by the same method.

"The best practice is to sacrifice a bone of your own. I've discovered that's even stronger than the Skyfall metal. I believe it's because then it's fully voluntary commitment. I gave one of my toes to craft my own quill. But the metal works almost as well."

He opened Gladen's robe and found his feather tattoo. He pressed the quill into the flesh on his ribs and let the blood that slowly seeped out siphon into the bone reservoir.

"I'd imagine the coins you minted are also made from the metal. I hope to offer my scholarship to Slate, to see if we can discover a more efficient way. Coins, while small, will use through the stores of Skyfall the brotherhood has collected far too quickly."

He turned to the desk and pulled out a small ledger.

"I suppose the pages of those shadebooks are made from human skin?" Gladen asked.

Aeger laughed. "Nothing so nefarious. That's a thought, though. This is just parchment."

He set the quill to paper and wrote something down.

"How does it feel?" Aeger asked.

"I don't feel anything," he said.

Aeger took up the book and walked toward the door. Each step he took away from Gladen felt like a tiny drum on Gladen's heart. The weight that pulled him down with each of those steps was imperceptible, but nagging.

"The farther I go from you," Aeger said as he walked back toward Gladen, "the more your heart will scream out for the loss of a piece of its companion soul."

"This justified my turning against the Motean Order. That you would wield such power over me without my consent."

"And what do you call the dominion you establish over others with the gauntlet?"

"I thought what I did was justified. I did it to help others find truth. But you've taken a tool that could grant people immortality in books, and weaponized it into something that compromises souls that would willingly go to Noccitan."

"I have to admit," Aeger said, "I didn't expect you to catch on so fast."

He reached up and unlatched one of the shackles. Gladen's hand shot out and took hold of Aeger's throat.

"Give me the book," Gladen said.

"Did you not renew your Vow as one of Pacifism?"

"You are traitor to all mankind," Gladen said.

"I'm also no fool," Aeger said. "This journal? I've rigged an acid into it. If you don't know how to open it, the acid soaks it through. When the chemical is exposed to the air, it will combust, and all of the souls I've collected will burn into nothingness. No Noccitan. No Lomïn. Just destruction."

"You don't know that is what will happen if they are set free," Gladen said. "I can see the doubt in your eyes."

"And I can see the doubt in yours. Will you take the risk to compromise not only your soul, but the dozens of others I've collected here?" he said, holding the leather-bound book up.

Gladen dropped his hand.

"See, that wasn't so hard." He rubbed his throat, and then moved to remove the other shackle.

"Now, write your list, and I'll be back later to collect it. It may take you some time. I'll stay here at the Bastion until tomorrow evening, rather than run the errands I had intended to go on. If I go too far, the distraction of your soul, parted too far from you, might be unbearable."

Gladen stared at the desk, and tried not to think of the sinking feeling that settled in his chest as Aeger turned to lock the door behind him and walk away. Each step sent Jakis Gladen deeper into a depression he identified all too well as what would be the new normal for him—confessed and re-sanctified by the Vow he had taken, yet compromised by the pillaging of his soul.

He took a seat at the table and began writing down the list of names of those who had turned against the Hammer. He tried to think of a way to ensure an untampered list reached Jined Brazstein, since Grissone's chosen champion was the only Paladin he knew he could trust not to be a Motean.

The hammering in his chest continued, and he wondered if he might die of an exploding heart. He had suffered headaches in the past, but the dread and pain that filled him now was worse. If the feeling of hopelessness was anything like what he had visited on countless Paladins put under the dominion of the gauntlet, then he welcomed this feeling, to share in the pain as penance for what he did.

He worked through the initial list, and then folded it up to place in his boot. Then he began again, listing those first in authority, and then those who answered to him. It did not matter what he wrote. Aeger would take off the names of those he wished to protect, and likely add the names of those he hoped to destroy.

The sound of a key in the cell door rattled. He turned to see who had come, hoping it might be Jined.

The door swung open, but he saw only blackness. From that deep shadow a face emerged, and the blackness melted into the color of bone. The man who entered the cell wore a cloak of that same color. It was a face Gladen recognized.

"Roderig?" Gladen said. "But you're dead!"

"You know that's not true," the man said, flashing a smile. "You may have denied to yourself who I was, but you've always known my death was faked."

"So you are Shade."

"You just can't stand that a quiet, younger man would rise to such prominence and become the leader of the Sect, yet apart from it."

"It doesn't matter to me anymore," Gladen said.

"But it does to me." Roderig walked over to the desk and perused the list. "You were kind enough to leave my name off the list. For that I thank you. But given how hastily you wrote the names of the leaders, I'd imagine this is a copy of a list you've already compiled and put in your boot. I'll make sure to take that when I go."

"I won't give you a thing."

"You haven't leapt to try to stop me," the other man said. "You were always the fighter. And now you're just a weakened betrayer."

Gladen stared at the man before him. The pulse of his heart continued to nag at his conscience.

"You seem distracted. Am I boring you?"

Then the other man gave a knowing smirk. "Cup visited you, didn't he? Took something of yours? Well, in that case, I might as well finish what I came to do."

"And what is that?"

"I can't have you providing names from one sect to another sect of Moteans. In fact, I don't even want you to be giving names to Aeger himself. He has more manipulative power than anyone gives him credit for. I imagine I'll need to do something about him. Although I'd like to figure out if he's answering to Dusk in Waglÿsaor, or Fidelity back at Pariantür."

The man in the bone-colored cloak stood considering something for a moment and then turned back to Gladen.

"That's not really a concern of yours, though."

He lifted his arms, and suddenly the cloak turned black, tendrils of darkness seeping off of it like rain dripping down its surface.

"What is that?" Gladen asked.

"Something entirely separate from the plan."

"What plan?"

"You think the Moteans' long history is half-true?" the man said. "It was all a lie made by Master Scholar, put to him by his own master, and given to me. Delving into the knowledge of the Feather? The Bell? Even the recapturing of the Dread Plate. It was all in preparation while I made this cloak over the course of my lifetime, to bring them all together."

"But what is it?"

"A cloak made of chain links of bone, gathered from countless sources and sealed in blood. Invisible to the gods, confusing to the pantheon. It's even picked up a few tricks along the way."

The blackness swirled about the figure. Gladen looked on in horror as the cloud of black souls surged around the room in a maelstrom. As each soul licked across his skin, it lashed away flesh. His pain rose to a crescendo his missing soul left in his heart. He smiled in a grimace as he felt the flesh leave his bones, then he fell to the ground. There was as sudden snap as he collapsed, and the walls of the cell disappeared. He was suddenly in a dark place that smelled of ink and blood and parchment, but he was whole again, his heart and soul once more as one.

* * *

"I admire your character," the Paladin said as he placed bread and soup before the girl. "Especially to a personal affront."

Rallia smiled. "I've had an eventful set of days. That bad followed good is no bother to me."

"Oh?"

"You are personal assistant to the Prima Pater, right?"

"I was, yes. But he commanded I leave. And I couldn't bear to stay any longer at that place, where my wife...."

He sat down across from her, his face going rigid as he fought back tears. He looked up at the young woman across from him.

"If I knew that what happened had been caused through violence, as that black eye you received was, I should act out in a manner not befitting a Paladin."

"I would too," Rallia said. "Jurgon, I'm a hired bodyguard. I'm not paladame, but the Sentinels and the Paladins have that in common. We guard. We protect. A bit of violence goes with the territory."

"You and I both know," Jurgon said, leaning closer and in a whisper said, "that most violence is wrong. It is rarely justified." He glanced over at the Paladin, Silas Merun, sitting by the fire, not much older than Rallia.

"What exactly happened to him?" Rallia asked.

"If you're mixed up in all this, then you know."

Rallia laughed. "As I've told everyone, I don't! Honestly!"

"And we don't know that yet. It must be determined."

"Yes. How is my being found in a bastion, scrubbing clean a desecrated Anka, a problem?"

"You cleaned the Anka? My Anka?" Silas said, turning.

"Someone had painted it black. I felt I had a duty to. My grandfather was a Paladin. To see such a thing perturbed my heart. And after what happened to me on the western coast..."

"What happened?" Jurgon asked.

"I shared a meal with someone on the beach," Rallia said. "I thought perhaps he was a Watcher. But he revealed that he was more than that."

"What is more than a Watcher?" Jurgon asked, looking at the other Paladin as he sat with them.

"I believe I saw Grissone once," Silas said. "He touched the face of a young boy crying on the side of a street. The boy stopped, and immediately walked through the dense crowd to his mother. There was no way he could have known where she was."

"My grandfather used to talk to himself after my father finished clearing things away from the poor kitchen," Rallia replied. "He would come through and pray a blessing over those that had come and gone— he'd pray over the place to ensure it continued to do its blessed duty. But I swore at times the prayer was a conversation and I only heard half of it."

"The Prima Pater often talks of the gods as walking among us," Jurgon said. "And not as a trite aside, but indicating they always are."

"And this meeting you had," the young Paladin said, "it changed you, didn't it?"

Rallia nodded. "Even before that Paladin came and gave me this," she pointed to the black eye, "I knew he was a troubled soul. When he spoke so unkindly at the bastion. As he dragged me behind his sleipnir.

There was a feeling coming from him that I can't describe. It surpassed hatred."

"It is not my place to say," Jurgon said, "but due to events in his childhood, Dane Marric has a particular dislike for women. And I think the only thing he hates more is heresy."

"That is a dangerous combination," Rallia said.

"It is."

Rallia took a bite of bread and offered a piece to Silas.

"What happened to him in his childhood?" Silas asked Jurgon.

"As I said," Jurgon replied, "it is not my place to say. I was made Prima Pater's seneschal for my ability to keep my mouth shut, and I'd prefer to keep that honor."

"Admirable," Rallia said.

"Your own actions are admirable," Jurgon said. "You've not tried to run from the imprisonment we've placed on you. And you brush off the offense Dane gave you by my simply telling you his childhood was rough."

"I do not leave because I think, due to my encounter on the coast, all things that happen after are divinely intentioned."

"Providence?" Silas said.

"Yes," Rallia replied. "I am angry that I was mistreated. But you two are not treating me unkindly. I know where I am and that I am safe. And if your leadership, a higher authority than I care to question, would prefer for a time that I remain in the bastion, then I'll remain. I'd like to tell my brother where I am, but I am safe. And I expect he'd only get angry. He doesn't care much for the holy orders."

"Why is that?" Jurgon asked.

"I don't know. I'm trying to figure that out."

"I'll speak with Nichal about getting a message to your brother," Jurgon said. "I'll not go behind his back, but I can press on him the honor in it. That ought to tug at his heart a bit."

"Thank you, Jurgon," Rallia said. "I'm sure your wife would be proud to know that you continue to do your duty in the face of grief."

Jurgon gave Rallia a look.

"I've never said that she..."

"You didn't need to," Rallia replied. "You have the same look my father had when my mother passed."

"How old were you?" Silas asked.

"Twelve. That was a rough year. But the three of us made it through. Not a day goes by where I don't think of her, though."

Jurgon stood and excused himself, leaving the room.

"I was orphaned," Silas said, "and left as a boy at the local bastion. So I've been with the Paladins since I can remember. I don't know that I can fully understand the depths of your sadness caused by that loss."

"Perhaps not," Rallia said, "but, given that admittance, I'm sure you have an idea."

Silas smiled and took another piece of bread from the basket, tore it in two and shared the other half with the woman next to him.

PART 6

41

Bitter Reunion

The elder sat upon the stoop,
Gave wisdom as he went.
The man he stopped and drew near,
     Heard words that wisdom meant,
          Struck down by sage words sent.

—*THE TRAVELER*

Over the following week, one quarter of the Sentinels had made excuses to leave town, or disappeared entirely. Hanen tried to keep the remainder of them happy by giving out additional work—work he had intended to do himself, which kept him at Blackiron alone, with his coin purse quickly dwindling. The time wasn't wasted; the caravan-planning quickly concluded three days prior. Every time Hanen thought of something else and then shuffled the timetables around, it all amounted to the same thing. It was done. Whisper, bored with him sitting and doing nothing, wandered off at random times, returning as restless as before.

With the remaining Sentinels they could run a caravan of merchants all the way to the south end of Œron that would be double to triple the size of caravans that were running from Edi. A few merchants were already showing interest in joining, too. In a few week's time they would press as many merchants into joining as possible and begin collecting fees.

One of Rallia's Runners arrived, presented two letters, and took payment from Hanen. One was sealed with gray sealing wax and addressed to him. The other smelled of perfume and was addressed to Blackiron Guildhall. Neither appeared to be from Rallia, which was starting to worry him.

He opened the latter first. Inside was a request for a bodyguard, more specifically, Ophedia del Ishé. It was signed by Lady Dathab. Hanen pulled out a book he and others had been compiling of the gentry in town. Lady Dathab was the sole heir of a shipping magnate who had gone missing at sea a year earlier. The magnate's fortune was caught up in legal matters.

Ophedia entered Blackiron. She was eating an apple that still had a bit of crunch left, despite the lateness of winter.

"What kind of contracts do you have right now?" Hanen asked.

"Nothing important," she said.

"I just got a request for you as bodyguard."

"It better not be another handsy idiot. I'm not going through that again."

"Doesn't sound like it. This request comes from Lady Dathab."

He handed her the request. Ophedia sniffed the paper and grimaced. "Even I know that perfume is cheap. I suppose I could teach her some of the finer points of perfumery." She tossed the apple over her shoulder into the bin kept by the door.

"And manners too, I'm sure," Hanen said.

"That goes without saying," she said, licking her fingers. She opened the letter and then handed it back to Hanen. "What does it say? I don't have time to sound the whole thing out and look stupid."

"She heard what you did to Lord Lümboch. She says it's been all the talk among the noble ladies. She wants you as her personal bodyguard and agrees to pay handsomely."

"And you want me to take it?"

"Her father was a shipping magnate. That kind of connection could help us in our own work."

"Fine. The other contracts were dailies. I'll give those back to you and start right away."

"Really? No further thoughts?"

"Should I have some? She's got money. I plan on taking my share of that. You get a connection to improve your little empire you're trying to build here. Searn will be happy. I'm happy. We're all happy."

"In that case, have a seat and I'll draft up a contract."

Ophedia had already poured herself a beer and sat on one of the seats nearby.

"Diben Laur left yesterday," Ophedia said.

"He was a local," Hanen said. "Or at least he had lived here long enough to be so. You and Aurín never found anything out about him."

"True, but I still think he was probably doing something he ought not to have. Or else why leave? Especially in this weather."

Hanen finished up filling out the pre-made contract and invited Ophedia over to sign her name.

"It starts tomorrow night," he said, and then gave her instructions to the contract's estate.

"Thanks, Hanen. I won't be late."

Ophedia left and Hanen turned to the other message. He broke the wax and opened the letter, revealing a small gold coin minted with a lantern on one side, and one of Aben's Watchers on the other. The writer, a monk from the Abecinian complex, name unsigned, requested that Hanen visit. He was asked to come at his earliest convenience, without his Sentinel cloak, in order to avoid harassment by monk, priest, or Paladin. The coin was to be presented at the Guesthouse doorman.

Hanen left Blackiron after the sun set and crossed the green. He wore only his black tunic. He had no doubt anyone who had seen the Sentinels would notice him, but wasn't going to make any big show of it. He walked toward the Abecinian complex and through the front gates. To the left he came to a second gate, a heavy oak door set into brown stone, and knocked.

A small view port opened and a priest's face appeared.

"I have an appointment. I'm to show you this," Hanen said, not waiting for the priest to ask him his business.

The priest nodded and opened the door. The place was stark, and the paths were straight, every wall built to draw the eye forward. A large entry to a smaller chapel drew Hanen and his guide into it. It was easily three times as large as the one attended by Father Diono in Düran.

Walking down the aisle, he could feel eyes on him. He knelt before the altar, going through the motions he knew were required. He stood and exited the door to the right, into the north annex.

The directions in the letter had been clear and easy to follow as he weaved through the complex and came to a final hall. There were no windows, merely torches guttering on the walls. He walked the long hallway, and could hear the prayers of the faithful in several of the rooms he passed.

He came to the last door and raised his hand to knock when the door opened, and a tall figure in a robe, and carrying a tall leather-covered staff, stepped out and nearly ran into him. The figure closed the door behind him and dropped his hood back.

"Greetings, Hanen," Ymbrys Veronia said.

"You summoned me here?" Hanen asked, surprised to see the qavyl in a human monastery.

"I do not think so, no. The monk within likely did that."

"Why are you here then? We keep running into one another."

"Ah, yes. In short, we do not simply run into one another, I can admit that much. You see, I sought you out, even in Edi, because it was the only way I could find the person I have been seeking for well over fifty years now."

"And now you've found them?"

"I have, but I have also said too much. And I have much to consider now, so if you'll excuse me, I shall dismiss myself, and allow you to go in."

The qavyl walked down the hall, his staff tapping on the floor at the long intervals of an equally long stride. Hanen took a deep breath and tapped on the door.

"Come in," the voice said. It was vaguely familiar.

He turned the latch and pushed in on the door. It was a larger room than he thought it would be. An ornate wall hanging, made of fisherman's knots, hung from the wall. The bed was spartan, though the rug on the floor was thick and made from knotted rags. A single bookshelf hung on one side, with a writing desk underneath. A man sat at the desk with his back turned. He wore the gray robe of a monk of Aben, and his head had a strip of hair shaved away down the middle. The hair he had was short, but thick, blonde, and turning ashy.

The monk turned around, revealing a face similar to what Rallia would look like in twenty years. Marn Clouw still had the heavy look of a worried man, continually struggling against all the odds to keep afloat. The answer to where he had disappeared to for the past seven years answered itself in that moment.

"Hello Hanen," Marn said. He took a deep breath and rose. He came and stood near his son. "It never ceases to amaze me how much you look like your mother."

"Father," Hanen acknowledged the man standing before him, "you're a monk now?"

"Yes, a loyal follower of Aben. The years have changed you; you look like an adult now. Have you found success?"

"Yes, we have."

"And where is Rallia?"

"She is off on an errand out of the city, but when she comes back I will make sure she visits."

"It pleases me greatly you are here," Marn said. He continued to consider Hanen, examining him for trouble, for changes, for his son. "I only just learned you were in Mahn Fulhar yesterday. We have so much to speak about."

He indicated for Hanen to sit down on the edge of the bed. Marn brought his stool over and perched upon it.

"Tell me all of what happened after you left Garrou."

"Master Verith took us up and down the road from Bortali to Edi. We helped him smuggle the goods, and I learned to run his books quickly."

"You were always good with numbers. I'm sorry, smuggle?"

"Yes. He wasn't just a cheesemonger, father. He moved luxury goods for the rich as well. It was all perfectly legal, but smuggling kept bandits from targeting us until the end."

"The end?"

"We were attacked by bandits. They killed Taben Verith. That was five years ago. Now I've shared the first part of my story. Where did you disappear to?"

"I will tell you, but first, finish your story."

Hanen sighed.

"We took the last load of goods to their owners. Our master left us his savings, and we set about to find our fortune. We ran across a group of outlaws in an inn. We waylaid them from attacking a duke. His bodyguard, named Searn VeTurres, is a member of the Black Sentinels. He offered us a position, and we became Black Sentinels in Edi City. We quickly built up a protected caravan for merchants traveling north from Edi, and it's been bringing in a great deal of money ever since."

"Why, then, are you in Mahn Fulhar?"

"Searn requested we join him in escorting a group of Nifaran monks from Birin to here. We've been here since the beginning of winter, setting up a new trade route from here to the Marches."

"And tell me," he said, his voice turning from excitement to a genuine warmth, "of Rallia."

"Rallia is well. Ever the organized and consistent soldier. She is constantly requested for guard work, and she's good at it. She's also the best barber I've ever known. The others love her."

"And you?"

"They could care less for me."

"I'm sorry to hear that. But I meant what do you do with the Black Sentinels?"

"Well, I organize the contracts and I've been arranging another caravan."

Hanen felt hurt that Marn skipped over his not being liked or appreciated.

"You are both successful though, right?"

"Yes."

Marn heaved a sigh of relief. "Then my curse perhaps did not pass down to you."

"Don't start talking like that again, father."

"No. You don't understand. And it's something I have only learned since you left. I summoned you here to explain."

"Explain what?"

"My curse. The bad luck I've always had. I know now why I have it."

"Did some priest try to drag you into taking the cloth with some tall tale?"

"No. Now you keep quiet and listen, Hanen. I know you did not enjoy your childhood. You've always resented my marrying Rallia's mother, but I think we were the better for it."

"Very well. I'm sorry, please proceed."

"A month after you left, I was finding a bit of work as a net mender. It was keeping me fed. It was enough. An old woman came to me and begged me to let her buy me a meal. She persisted for a week before I relented. The years had been unkind to her, and so of course I did not even recognize my own mother. Your grandmother, Thanessa Clouw, had been seeking me out ever since I left the port town in Morraine, which I had left before ending in Garrou. But I will get to that."

Hanen sat listening intently. He had never heard his father so much as speak more than how to tie a knot correctly, or to make their beds, or serve food. To hear him say anything of his own past was out of character.

"Your grandmother then began to tell her story. You see, her two parents, it seems, had fled from some odd history to the Isles of Bronue Jinre. My mother had me at a young age, and she said something ominous happened after my birth. I will explain that shortly. Her own father, who I knew as Nethen, had been a Paladin of the Hammer. He fought in the Protectorate Wars. It seems that he fled with his wife from the citadel monastery of the Paladins because she was the daughter of the instigator of the wars. They fled from her past in hopes to escape it."

Hanen held up a hand to request a pause.

"The instigator of the Protectorate Wars? You mean the Apostate of Ikhala?"

Marn nodded. "He was a servant of the dark god Achanerüt. When I was born, in Bronue Jinre I am told, it seems in the middle of the night a zvölder bit my infant leg. It took priests and doctors to save me from the poison, and it left my leg shriveled. It was a message from Achanerüt. I was marked by him, and the family of the Apostate would never escape his control. So, you understand, this is why I have always been unlucky, and why life has always seemed to try to take away from me whatever I touch. That is why I glory in your success; because perhaps it means the Deceiver has not claimed you, nor Rallia. It is why I fled to become a priest—to pray for the two of you. To perhaps counteract the control he wishes to put upon us."

Hanen began laughing.

"Why do you laugh?" Marn said, hurt.

"Because of this story. It's foolishness. You actually sat and listened to an old lady you didn't even recognize, who claimed she was your mother, who bought you a meal, and told you a tale worthy of the skalds of Bortali, and you believed her. You actually think the gods care about us? About you? You're a cripple, father. A luckless cripple. I can't imagine how many people you've told this story to. I'm sure if I go down to a nearby tavern they'll be telling the tale too."

"I have told no one. Only you, and the qavyl."

"You told Ymbrys?"

"Yes. He asked."

"Why would you tell that sort of story? Why would he even care? Father, you're insane!"

"He sought me out. It was he who told me you were in the city.

He claimed he had been searching for our family since the end of the Protectorate Wars."

"And because someone showed you kindness you just believed him? Took him at his word? Shared a tale that would put any family to shame, if only because now I have an unlucky cripple for a father who fled his life to hide in a warm chapel under the cover of piety?"

"Hanen," Marn said, his eyes welling with tears, "you cut me deeply. I am sharing this with you because I have spent my time here researching our history, for your sake, so you can escape your past and be something more."

"I will not be telling Rallia you are here. If you feel the need to share this disgusting lie with her, you can do that yourself. You should have stayed dead like we thought you were. Now I have to live with the knowledge that you're spreading such an ugly story about me, and it will follow me wherever I go. I'm leaving."

"Hanen, please."

Hanen stepped out of the room and closed it gently. He wasn't going to draw attention to himself. He felt the eyes of his father on his back as he marched down the hall and back to Blackiron.

By the time he came to the open air he was breathing heavily and his heart was pounding. Whisper was waiting there patiently. Hanen didn't recall him following him from Blackiron, but he reached out and touched the ynfald and continued to walk. He marched toward town, stalking the streets as anger consumed his mind.

The story Marn had told was madness. Gods didn't become zvölders and bite people. Gods didn't curse and mark people. It was pure insanity. That people would believe such falsehoods showed just how unintelligent they were and made Hanen feel as though he was the only person with a shred of sanity left.

42

Remember

What loss was suffered by the Protectorate Wars? For many died, and many remain unborn for the men that did not return. What good do we have to show for it? Would that we had stayed away, and left those heathen Ikhalans to their own self-made fate.

— **EZIRI OF CASTENARD**

He did not need to guess where his legs blindly led him. The Grotto was still alive, the black sky of the evening holding no power over people's need for social interaction. He had come almost daily, staying well out of view of the tailor and wishing he had the courage to close the distance. Whisper stayed put next to him, bristling at passing cörs and rustling at other ynfalds. When he nudged Hanen, he received a morsel or scrap.

Within the shop, the women shuffled about, straightening their wares, or showing a customer a bolt of cloth.

"You could have just come to the shop and said hello," a voice behind him said.

Alodda was picking over a stall selling small toys. Hanen suspected she wasn't actually considering them. She placed the last one down and looked up at him.

"I feared you might still be angry with me," Hanen said.

She laughed. It melted away the anxiety that meeting his father had given him.

"It's been a month since we've spoken. You think I would remain angry for that long?"

"After the accusations you laid out on me?" Hanen said. "Yes."

"Well, if you think that, then I can tell you took what I said to heart. Perhaps I did remain angry. But I still hoped you might stop by. Even more so after that Voktorra came into the shop and told me what you did."

"Did he come by, then?"

"A week ago. I could hardly believe it. Then, when Velli came in, I had her confirm that you had come by to question her—then I knew it was true. You really confronted the man who was bullying her husband Goev?"

Hanen nodded. "He almost killed me."

"Hanen!" she said, putting a hand on his arm. "That was so brave of you."

Hanen shook his head. "Foolhardy. My sister is the fighter. I was in over my head."

"But you survived."

"Only because that Voktorra, Captain Navien, put a bolt through the man's throat."

Alodda gasped and covered her mouth.

"Alodda," Hanen said leaning forward. "I'm sorry. I'm sorry that the actions of Black Sentinels, who ought to have been better than they were, darkened your thoughts of me."

She took his hand in hers, and leaned forward.

"I forgive you," she said, stretching up to kiss his cheek.

As she came back to her heels, he gawked down at her. She looked around, blushing.

"Better not let your father know you did that, Alodda," the merchant behind the nearest counter said.

"Yes, Lar," Alodda said, her face blushing red.

"He actually might leave his window seat and come have words with that young man."

"Thank you, Lar," she said, taking Hanen's arm and pulling him away. "Will you take me for a walk?" she asked.

Hanen let her guide him forward, the scent of her lingering on his cheek and now following him in her presence at his side.

They moved through the market, stopping at one stall or another, and Alodda introduced him to the vendors. They came by the stretch of hrelgren merchants. They all gave their greetings of *azho*, and Hanen replied with his own *ashini*.

Zhag *rm* Tellis had somehow scrounged up new goods to sell, and smiled broadly as Hanen approached.

"Azho," the hrelgren said, giving a polite bow. He gave Alodda an even deeper one.

"Ashini! Eti-bo-sha'shina-zidil-palitan," Hanen replied.

"You speak Hrelgren?" Alodda asked, looked at Hanen in astonishment.

"Not as much as I would like," Hanen said. "Enough to negotiate and show my respect."

"But what does it mean?" Alodda asked.

"The Hrelgren greeting," the merchant said, "is a blessing. It means..." he looked at Hanen in embarrassment, "but perhaps I have stolen from you the opportunity to explain."

"No offense taken, Zhag," Hanen said. "Whomever first greets the other in Hrelgren says, 'Azho. Sint-hati-oi-zidil-moni-palitan.' It means 'May the grass grow where your feet tread'."

"Or," the merchant said, "if you're familiar with the other, saying simple 'azho' is enough. Which means greetings."

"And the response," Hanen continued, "'Ashini! Eti-bo-sha'shina-zidil-palitan,' means, 'And greetings returned. The grass grows only by your blessing'."

"How much more do you know?" Alodda asked.

"The Hrelgren alphabet, and a few more phrases, but not much."

"I shall assume you know the bookseller on the other side of this market?" Zhag asked.

Alodda nodded, looking up at Hanen. "He's only a few doors down from me."

"He has many books, from learned books on history, modern events such as the Protectorate Wars, and, most importantly, an extensive collection of books on the Hrelgren Language. If you sought him out, I'm sure he'd part with them for less than they are worth, as you're the only man in this city who shows interest in our culture."

"Master merchant," Alodda said. "Please let me apologize for the entire market, if you've not been shown respect. My father owns the tailor near the bookseller. How many Hrelgrens are here with you?"

"The five of us."

"Stop by and view our wares, and I'll see to it my mother invites you into our home for dinner sometime. We'd welcome you, and perhaps others seeing you will generate a bit of interest in you and what you have to sell."

"You do me a great honor," Zhag said. "I would ask your name."

"Alodda Dülar."

"A very humbled ashini to you then, Alodda Dülar."

They continued on and came to a side street. The smell of food and sounds of quiet chatter came from a small inn at the back end. Alodda drew Hanen toward it, and they found a table near the rear. Alodda chattered on about wool and linens from the south, and asked about Hanen's life on the road. The Œronzi wine they drank was sweet and warmed with spices, and the lean meat went well with the rich flax bread.

"Have you lived your whole life in Mahndür?"

"I've lived my whole life here in Mahn Fulhar."

"You've never left the city?"

"I mean, my father and mother took me on a trip to Alnír when I was very young, but I don't remember it."

"So you don't have family elsewhere?"

"My mother is from here, but my father never really talks about where he came from before the war. His family is probably all gone now."

"I'm sorry if that is a sore subject," Hanen apologized.

"It's not, really," Alodda said. "He's happy. I'm sure the memories of the war are painful, but they are far away and long ago."

Hanen stood, pulled out her chair for her, her arm going into his.

"So you'll be leaving with the coming spring, then?" she asked as they came back out onto the street. The market had grown quiet, and most merchants had closed up their wares to take home with them.

"As long as the roads look clear, we'll leave as soon as we can. Merchants who travel with us will want to be at market towns like Sal-du-Markt before the year grows too late. And it sounds like the water lanes don't become easy for ships from the Lupinfang to travel for an additional month."

"Just the one trip, then?"

"For the first journey. And we'll have to arrange return merchants from our destination. Once we've made the full round-trip we can plan multiple caravans going at once, and we'll probably have to set up an office in Aunté, maybe Nor-Vio."

"I hear it's a lot warmer there. Would you stay and administrate from one of those cities?"

"I'm not sure. I doubt I could stay put in one place. I like to travel."

She came to a stop, pulling back on his arm.

"Hanen?" she said.

He turned and faced her.

"Will you remember me?" she asked.

"How could I forget you?" Hanen said. "You've shown me kindness as a stranger in your city. And you've shown me forgiveness when I still feel to blame for the Sentinels abusing people...your friends. I can't think of a time when someone showed me that sort of kindness."

"I mean," Alodda said, blushing, and looking down at Whisper, who sat considering the two of them, "will you remember me on the road? Maybe stop by my shop again when you return?"

"Of course," Hanen said.

"Even if..." she hesitated, and gave a resigned sigh. "I'm sure you'll meet others."

"I meet plenty of people on the road."

"Other girls? I'm sure you do. I'm sure they have no problem meeting you."

"What do you mean?" Hanen asked.

"I'm sure the women you meet on the road are quick to make friends with you."

"Alodda," Hanen said, "women don't find me interesting. I'm a dry humored, bookkeeping planner."

"I don't think so," she said.

She reached to her shoulders, lifted off the blue embroidered ribbon, and then reached up and draped it over Hanen's own shoulders.

"If you'd keep this, and perhaps return it to me, I'd be grateful."

Her hands hadn't come off the ribbon, but tugged down on it, gently. Hanen fought back the urge to lean down.

Whisper circled up against the back of Hanen's legs and sighed. It pushed Hanen forward an inch. It was enough. Alodda met him halfway, their lips brushing, and the cedar and porumarian oil in her hair flooded his senses. He fell into her embrace. He breathed deeply, trying to take the gaze of her eyes into his, the taste of her lips that still had the southern summer wine upon them. She pulled down on the ribbon, and he pulled on her back, drawing her as close as he could. His hand reached up and took the nape of her neck and tried to draw her closer. Her tightly braided hair plaits were smooth on his fingers. They each took a deep breath, and then sighed as they broke contact.

"I won't forget you," Hanen said. "How could I? I will think of you often."

She smiled. "I hope you visit me just as often as you think of me. Even before you leave town."

He nodded dumbly.

He leaned in for another kiss, but she placed a hand on his chest.

"I think perhaps you ought to walk me home now," she said. "My mother will be worried."

"Alright."

She took his offered arm again, but leaned even closer than before as they wound their way through the stalls toward the tailor.

A single candle was lit in the window, with more burning in the windows up above.

"I should go," she said.

"I know," he said, "me too."

She parted from his arm awkwardly, walked to the door, and put her key in. She turned back and giggled.

"Good night, Hanen," she said.

"Good night, Alodda," he said, and watched her disappear into the shop. She lifted the candle and looked out the window, giving him a wave before turning and disappearing into the depths of the shop.

43

Confrontations

They speak but you do not listen. They prophesy yet you take no heed. Let the embers of wrath fall upon your head. For you shall hide in the darkest of shadows, and be seen by the light of your doom.

—ABECENNA VEGOLL, PROPHET OF MORRIEGO

Hanen walked toward the back of the Grotto, to take the stairs to the upper district. His heart pounded in his chest, and a smile lit his face. The bookstore still had candles lit within as he passed. The pounding in his chest turned suddenly from giddiness to dread as he recalled first the story his father had told him only a few short hours before, and then what Zhag had mentioned. The bookstore, with books on history.

An old man came out of the shop and put a key in the hole before turning to consider Hanen.

"You're looking for something?"

Hanen shook his head, began to leave, and then turned back.

"The Protectorate Wars," he said.

The old man nodded, indicating he follow him inside. He came back from the stacks with a book.

"You want the story of the Protectorate Wars? This is your book."

"Is the source a good one?" Hanen asked.

"The greatest. Written by General Donskarl of Ikhala. At the end he turned against Ollistan Gœrnstadt and sided with the Pariantür to vanquish the Apostate and his followers."

"How much?"

"I'll sell it for a gold Royal. And if you bring it back I'll buy it back for half that."

Hanen nodded, pulled out a Royal and handed it to him, taking the book.

On the street he glanced back at Alodda's shop, and then down at the ynfald.

"Too much is happening," Hanen said, and then chuckled. "Thanks to you and your little nudge." He knelt down and gave the ynfald a scratch. "Let's go home and see if we can figure out if what my father said was true or some lie."

Returning to Blackiron, he found a quiet corner, lit a tall candle, and began to read the history of the Protectorate Wars.

The General wrote from a very Ikahalan point of view, which considered the rest of the world below them. As Hanen understood it, they had a very different view on the pantheon of gods, and it showed. The author continually invoked the names of saints Hanen hadn't even heard of.

It spoke of the Hrelgren envoy who appeared in the capital to arrange trade, speaking at first of their deceitful ways, and how they were seeking to start a war—in the same breath speaking of the monarch's confidant, Ollistan Gœrnstadt, secretly planning the outcome of the whole thing, including the murder of the envoy and declaring war on the Empire.

The Paladins of the Hammer, whom Ikhala looked down on as a group of oppressive arbiters, declared their land between Ikhala and the Hrelgren Empire a neutral zone. Yet Paladins set themselves upon a battalion of Hrelgrens, murdering all but one survivor.

From there the story became convoluted as armies from across the world heeded calls from various factions and the war grew out of control.

One major turning point, early in the campaign, came when seemingly unrelated raids by both T'Akai and vül began striking in tandem against supply lines. Units of fallen Ikhalans rose again to fight alongside the living.

Hanen found himself surprised as he read not of lifeless bodies rising to fight, barely able to hold onto a sword, but instead soldiers, grievously wounded, rising with a spiteful anger. The author wrote of how appalled he became at his own soldiers coming back to life. His own troops began to fear death more than before, for fear that they too would rise as these revenants.

It was shortly after this the Prima Pater of the Paladins, Galen Rond, died, leaving a vacancy in the leadership. The very young but rising star, Dorian Mür, became Prima Pater. The entire nature of the war changed as the Paladins brought their hammers down on the enemy. The author, General Donskarl, quickly lost control of his army as the vizier flexed his power and brought in the help of three dark figures—a vül of some standing, a man who was said to be made of bronze, and a giant of a man who wore large black armor, referenced to simply as the Warlord.

These five brought their alliance against the Hrelgrens and the Paladins. In an act of betrayal, the General turned on the Vizier, and it cost General Donskarl both of his legs. Soon after, in single combat, the new Prima Pater slew the Apostate and ended the war.

The Prima Pater then turned all of his attention to seeking out Gœrnstadt's daughter. Despite having allies in all of the countries of Ganthic, she was never found. Thus, the Protectorate Wars came to an end not quickly, but with slow resolution as all the nations resettled.

Hanen finished the book as the sun rose the following day. He returned to the bookstore, waiting for it to open, hoping to catch a glimpse of Alodda. The old man had two books in Hanen's hand in trade for keeping the gold Royal—one on the beliefs of the Ikhalans, and another on mythologies of heroes.

"The Ikhalans are simply a very mystical people, much like the Oruche are said to be," Hanen read to the ynfald who sat with him silently. He closed the book and thought out loud. "It seems more like these Protectorate Wars were a cultural conflict, and the Paladins of the Hammer were just the formal wing of religion seeking to suppress the beliefs of the people." He felt fatigue starting to scratch at the edge of his awareness and knew he'd need to fight to stay awake the rest of the day, or else his sleep would be thrown off.

He set the books down and went for a walk. It was midday and the markets were busy under the sun that had broken out in the clear sky. It was not hard to spot who he was looking for. Ymbrys Veronia stood taller than everyone else.

Hanen stayed near, but didn't reveal himself until Ymbrys wasn't speaking with a merchant.

"I'd like to speak with you," Hanen said, approaching from behind.

"Ah, Master Clouw," he said, turning. "I have been expecting you to seek me out."

"Can we find some place quiet to talk?"

The qavyl smiled.

They walked in silence until they found a very small beer room with only a passed-out drunk sitting on a stool. They took a table at the back. Whisper slunk under the table to Hanen's feet, and Ymbrys leaned his covered staff up against the wall.

"What may I do for you, Hanen?"

"You spoke with my father. I'd like to know what you spoke about."

"I expected you to ask me about that. And I've spent more time than you know compiling an answer."

"You have very obviously run into me and my family multiple times now. I think I'm owed an explanation."

"Yes. Very well. Short version then?"

Hanen nodded as he sipped on the ale the barkeep brought to them.

"What do you know of the Protectorate Wars?"

"I have a cursory knowledge."

"Then you know of Ollistan Gœrnstadt? Very well. You see, his appearance was a rather important event. Never had Achanerüt, more often known simply as The Deceiver, shown himself through a specific follower, and certainly never so publicly. When that occurred, human, as well as many qavylli scholars, knew that it meant the darkest of gods was showing his hand and making a play.

"When the Protectorate Wars ended, I began seeking to know what could connect the Deceiver to a single follower. But to know that I needed to seek out the family of the Apostate. And thus, after over sixty years of seeking, I found your father, who, according to his story, was indeed marked by the Deceiver himself."

"You speak of the Deceiver as though he is real."

"Because he is. Do you truly not believe in the gods?"

"I do not think they matter to me. And that there should be good gods and dark gods makes me wish them away all the more."

"The gods are very real, Hanen, I can assure you. As real as you, and certainly as real as I. Once they were a single family. You understand that things can go wrong. Things can turn good people bad and split brother from friend."

"Of course. But we're people. We go bad because of circumstances."

"Yes. And thusly, a god can fall because of a circumstance considerably greater. Does that make sense?"

"I suppose."

"Then you must simply believe, or take my word for it, for the sake of the story, that this is true. This Apostate-Necromancer, your own great-great grandfather was this man."

"And so you believe this curse falls on me as well?"

"That remains to be seen. Perhaps you should seek to curry the favor of another god? Perhaps they will mark you with their own greatness, and you can avoid this curse falling on you. I see you as very fortunate, unlike your father. Change your fate, Hanen."

"I don't understand how I can listen to you spout what I still feel is untruth and be calm about it, but find myself so very angry when the same words come from my father's mouth."

"My own father," Ymbrys said, "explained something just as dark to me one time. A friend of mine fell away. The very truth of it broke me. But once I had the chance to hear it from another's mouth, I came to accept the facts, and have ever since resolved to remedy the situation. It has been a long road."

"I am sorry for your friend."

"Well, I am sorry for your father. I think, though, that his choice to take up the cloth was a wise one. He will live a happy life now."

Hanen rose. "I have a lot to think about. I think this is goodbye, Ymbrys."

"Goodbye, Hanen Clouw."

Hanen began to walk back to Blackiron and thought on the boneshroud that Searn was still seeking—a mantle that would allow him to shrug off the influence of gods. Hanen would change his own fate and seek out the boneshroud for himself. Perhaps then he wouldn't need to curry any favor, as Ymbrys had suggested.

Blackiron was deserted, and a note sat on Hanen's table from Searn, to meet the other Sentinels at the Dark Stave Inn. He walked over to the bed he had put together by the wall and sat on it to consider just what had happened over the course of the last day. As he put his chin down on his fist, Alodda's aroma wafted over him again and he smiled.

The door to Blackiron opened and two men walked in, whispering to one another. They looked around, their eyes passing over Hanen, and they walked through the hall toward Searn's area. A shadow passed by a single candle Searn left standing, and Hanen realized that Searn had been in the back sitting in silence himself. His form filled the door, and he gave a quiet greeting to the two, then invited them in.

Hanen quietly got up and circled the room to approach the back office, the thin walls easy to hear through, as one of the mysterious figures spoke.

"And they are all away?" a voice was saying. It was a reedy voice that held contempt for everyone.

"They will be away long enough for us to talk," said a voice that belonged to Searn. "Your message said you would be coming alone. I feel a bit outmatched now, with two of you here." The way he spoke, Hanen knew Searn had flashed a smile.

"I shall remain quiet. I did not know I was joining Cup to meet with someone else." The third voice sounded confused.

"I asked to meet so I could share news. Vanguard was captured and lies in a prison cell at the paladinial bastion."

Searn did not respond.

"Dusk has sent word that he believes war between Bortali and Boroni will begin with the coming of spring, and his city is positioned to be a linchpin."

Again, Searn did not reply. The awkward silence hung in the air for a long time.

"Dusk has asked that you assist us to break Vanguard free from his cell, and that you and whichever Sentinels you choose escort Vanguard to Waglÿsaor."

"And why, my friend," Searn said, "would I help you in this way?"

"With Vanguard now imprisoned, it is feared he'll reveal some of us. Perhaps he even reveals you."

"I don't go by the name Roderig anymore. I don't fear implication. But you do."

"I would be eternally grateful if you did this."

"I have my own agendas here, and I don't intend to leave them behind for some internecine politicos of one Motean Sect and the other. It will not be long before we're once again under the same roof."

"And that is what Dusk hopes for."

"Ah. Now I see. He hopes to establish something even greater in the midst of that war. He seeks an empire drawn from the ashes of two fallen nations, rather than the violent takeover Vanguard has planned here."

"His plan has merit," the other voice said.

"Cup," Searn said, "it is time for you to make your own educated decision. I think, perhaps, that you ought to take him yourself."

"And abandon what I have here?"

"Well, yes."

"I can do so much more to send others to the cause, such as our newest recruit, young Etienne."

"I recall you from the road," Searn said. "Where is Vanguard held?"

"When you go through the stables," Cup said excitedly, "take the left and go down the hall. Three cells stand there. One stands empty. The middle one holds Vanguard."

"And the other?"

"A young woman we caught sneaking around St. Nonn. One of your Black Sentinels, in fact."

"And what did you want with her?"

"I have not taken the time to question her myself. In fact, I wondered if she had been sent by you. She claims to have a badge issued by the King to deliver messages. She sought refuge in St. Nonn, but since Nonn was where the first Moteans were captured, it is assumed she was somehow mixed up in all of this."

"She didn't know anything. I sent her to search, and she ended up crossing your path. I was preparing her. If you've sullied her and she is not keen to join the cause now, I'll hold you personally responsible."

"Sullied? What are you implying?"

"If you have harmed her, if you have made it more difficult for me to bring her into my good graces, then I will hold you accountable. What we work toward is not just some random goal. We work to bring change. To pull the stone out from under the pedestal. I need her as a leader for what I have planned. Rallia is ripe to be one of the best."

At hearing Rallia's name Hanen's heart began to pound in his chest.

"Nice speech, but I'm just the messenger. Will you release Sentinels to us?"

"How many will you need?"

"Six. Including yourself."

"Why myself? Oh. I understand now."

"What is that supposed to mean?" Cup said.

"It means I know now you're playing too many sides. Dusk thinks I'll have the boneshroud back by now, and will deliver it to him. I won't be doing that. I have my own agenda."

"If you take a step out of line, we will kill your daughter."

There was silence.

"What do you mean?" Searn asked.

"Dusk is not a fool. He has known she was your daughter since before you did. He kept a watchful eye on her and says he will kill her if you take a step out of line."

"Because you bear this message, I want you to know how serious I can be," Searn's voice was full of cold malice. Hanen heard a twang and the deep thump of metal being pierced. A body hit the floor.

"You fool! He didn't do anything to you."

"I told you to come alone. You brought him. That alone was reason enough. Second, if I had killed you first, he would have run."

"But now your crossbow is empty."

Hanen heard chairs clatter as both men rose and threw themselves at each other. Hanen raced into the room, drawing an ax. He saw the form of a fully-armored Paladin crouched over Searn, attempting to throttle him with gloved hands.

Hanen came up alongside the two. Searn looked up and saw Hanen. He nodded through gritted teeth.

"Stand down," Hanen said.

The Paladin paused and looked sideways and then swung wildly with a ham-sized fist. Hanen jumped back out of reach and then took a step in and swung down with both hands on the axe. He glanced off the top of the paladin's gorget and gouged flesh off his scalp. The Paladin screeched and grabbed his head, rolling over. Searn was on top of him how, and drew a stiletto, plunging it into the Paladin's eye. He stood quickly, leaving the knife where it lay, and turned to Hanen.

"You did well, Hanen."

"You just killed two men. Paladins."

"Barely. They were traitors."

"What about you?" Hanen said. His blood was pumping hot. "You were a Paladin."

"Yes. And I left them behind long ago. This man was a spineless traitor. Perhaps you recognize him. He traveled with us. He was known as Aeger—the self-serving fool."

"Where is Rallia?"

"The Paladins arrested her a few days ago, it seems."

"And how long have you known?"

"This Aeger only just told me. And now I have to leave."

"Leave? To where?"

"It seems I have unfinished business with an old friend."

"This Dusk?"

"So you heard that. Yes. Dusk and I were Paladins together. I left when I discovered just how dark their intentions were. I left and decided to go on my own path."

"For the boneshroud?"

"Yes."

"How do I make one?"

Searn stopped placing random objects into his pockets and looked up.

"Why would you want to?"

"I want to release the power the gods would exert over me."

"I remember that tone. I had it when I was your age. Good. You are ready then. Seek out your sister, and then seek me out. I will tell you how to make one."

"You know where to find it, then?"

"Yes. I think perhaps this Vanguard has it. To think that this Dusk would have me deliver my own treasure to him. You had best go find your sister. We both have reckonings to attend to."

44

Complicit

Darkness walks, and Shadow lies.
Beauty kills, War cuts ties.

—QAVYLLI PROVERB

"What happened?" Ophedia asked. Blankets lay over the two bodies. Searn had a blood-covered metal spike lying on a cloth on top of his desk.

"They came and threatened me," Searn said. "I got one shot off with my crossbow, and the second lunged at me. I dropped the spike into his eye. He died instantly."

"Are you going to..." Ophedia asked hesitatingly.

"No. It won't help. I think it's too late anyway. Their soul has already been taken off to the Judge."

"I don't like this," Ophedia said.

"I don't either. If you'll help me, though, I'll pay you for your trouble."

"I'm not sure how we're going to get the bodies out of here."

"I'll continue straightening up here. You see if you can get a drover."

An hour later she returned. Searn had rolled out two empty ale casks near the door.

"You didn't..." she indicated to the barrels.

"No, they're empty. They wouldn't fit without a lot of work."

Together they moved the two bodies into the cart and then placed the casks overtop of them.

"It was hard to find a drover in the middle of the night," Ophedia said.

"Where is he?"

"Outside the gates. The Voktorra there were not being helpful. I offered to pay the drover extra to let me drive it up here and do the work of loading it. He was hesitant, but liked the idea of not having to work for his coin."

"That's helpful."

The Voktorra at the gate was nearing the end of her shift, and didn't bother much with the inspection. Searn and Ophedia squatted in the back while the drover took the long meandering route to the sea.

"Do you know anything about your parents?" Searn asked.

"I've always been told I looked Macenan, but that hardly means anything. It's a new country, so they don't have much of a look, if I'm being honest."

"It's the red in your dark hair," Searn said. "Macena was established with nearly half the population coming from Ikhala, the rest from the darker hair of Morriego, mostly. So after only a couple generations, everyone there has some red in their hair."

"I figured as much. It's why you found me there. I was looking to see if I could find anything about my parents."

"Macena would be a much easier place to look than among the countless red-headed people of Ikhala."

"That," she smiled, "and I didn't want to spend too much time looking in Temblin."

"You going to go looking again?" Searn asked.

"No need. I have better things to do now," she said.

There was an old sea-hand buying up empty barrels. Searn gave half the money he paid for the barrels to the drover, and suggested he ought to go to the nearby inn and quench his morning headache while they unloaded. The man obliged.

Ophedia and Searn lifted the rigid bodies of the two Paladins off the back of the cart.

"I expected them to be a lot heavier," Ophedia said, "with their armor."

"I stripped them of their armor. I'll take care of that later."

"They might have sunk better with the armor on."

"I'm kind of hoping they're found," Searn winked, "and cause a bit of a stir."

The second one went off into the water. The sea-hand twenty yards down the pier gave them a look.

"Garbage," Searn called to him. The sailor turned back to his work.

He turned to Ophedia.

"Maybe you ought to go find Hanen once the sun is up," he said.

"Why is that?" Ophedia asked.

"These two," he shrugged toward the water, "they said Rallia is in a cell in the paladinial Bastion. Hanen is thinking through how to break her out."

"He's going to get himself in trouble."

"Then maybe you see to it that he doesn't."

She nodded, considered the sea, and then turned to leave.

"I left a pouch with some silver on your bed at Blackiron."

"Thanks," she said. "I'd prefer if you'd stop asking me to help you do things like this, though."

"You keep saying yes."

"It's not because I trust you."

"Then why?"

"Because... I fear you a bit," she said. "If I said no, I might end up like these two."

"You don't have to fear me," Searn said. "What I'm doing, I'm doing for the good of all."

"Then why doesn't it feel like that?" she said as she turned and walked away.

Searn spent the rest of the night walking the dark alleys. A cold washed over his frame he couldn't explain. He pulled the inner cloak up from inside his Sentinel cloak, and over his head. The bone-colored mail cast a deep shadow over his face. Two figures rounded the corner. The damp breeze off the sea struck the street and walls around them and turned immediately to frost.

Searn stepped into a shadow and watched them approach. They were muttering to each other and suddenly stopped, three feet from Searn.

"What was that," the shorter of the two asked. His voice was ragged.

"What was what?" the other said. From under the figure's hood, Searn could see a mouth full of large teeth.

"I felt something," the first said. "Or, perhaps I felt a nothingness."

"Mmm," the second said. "I feel it, too. It feels like..."

"The moment between Noccitan and the Veld. When you think you won't make the leap."

"Yes. That is what it feels like. Then why can't I put a hand on it?"

The figure looked around. It lowered its hood and peered into the blackness that hid Searn. Thirteen black eyes stared into Searn's two. They all moved in different directions, trying to pinpoint what they couldn't see.

"More like a deception I can't root out," the tooth-filled mouth said. The breath that washed over Searn smelled like moldy dust.

"If it is meant for us," the shorter said, "then I don't doubt we'll feel it again. If not, then let the chaos it brings do its own thing, and we can manipulate it to the plan."

"Wise. Ever wiser."

They both turned and continued their walk down the lane.

Searn waited a long time to breathe. He stepped out of the shadow and lowered the hood of the boneshroud.

"It worked," Searn giggled in slight hysteria. "They couldn't see me. I'm invisible to the gods."

He laughed out loud, and then threw a hand over his mouth.

He marched up the hill to Blackiron. Ophedia had come and gone. The bloody metal spike still lay on the desk, though she had covered it with a white handkerchief. He unfolded the cloth and took it up. He sat at his desk and pulled out a black leather journal.

Searn took up the pen, and scratched his wrist, to draw a little blood.

He held it hovering over the paper and let the pen move of its own accord.

So, words appeared on the page. *This is how this is.*

This is how it is, Searn wrote.

Kill me, and then entrap me.

No need for offense, Aeger, Searn wrote. *You knew as I drove the Shade Spike into you that you'd end up in someone's library.*

You'll put me with others, then?

I'll have to, Searn wrote, *I'll need your exquisite scholarship to solve the problem that stands before me.*

Why would I help you? You betrayed me. Killed me.

This is true, Searn wrote, *but you were going to betray me to Dusk. I'm not demanding that you help; the other Shades will help. I'm offering you the chance to work with them. I could just cast you into the fire—see how you fair standing before the Judge.*

No words appeared.

I'll even let you be the one who leads the discussion.

What problem needs to be addressed?

Searn tapped the pen to his lip and thought.

If one could approach a god, unseen and unknown, how would you kill them?

You want to kill a god? The bloody words bloomed.

I want to kill them all.

45

Infestation

Lo, I beheld a visage, and he was my god, and he spoke unto me:
My child you shall be mine, and I shall be yours.
You shall be my Hammer.
And many will follow after you, though you be split in twain.
Go therefore into the forests, and go farther still,
For there I shall guide you, and bring you up to be my Paladin,
My champion. And you shall be the first of many heroes to come.

— GOSPEL OF ST. IKHAIL 8:1-6

It was a still, small voice that led him to walk the upper walls. At least, Jined felt that way, since he usually took the lower walkways on his solitary morning walks. The wall that circled the Abecinian complex obscured the view of the city, but to the south it opened up to look at the farmlands that covered the landscape as far as the eye could see.

It was mostly a whitewashed landscape of long-fallen snow, swept into heaps by wind long since dead. This early in the morning nothing moved. The sun would not dawn for some time. Yet on this cloudless winter night it used the snow as a blank canvas to spread a soft orange glow in the east and all upon the ground.

A traveler as solitary as Jined traveled on the road. Jined knew it was a figure on sleipnir by the way it swayed. The mount was tired, and the rider, too. They rode slowly toward the walls, knowing full well they would not gain entry this early in the morning. The figure wore a black robe and hood pulled down over their face, and had a thin, frail frame. They were hunched over, as though they carried the weight of the world upon their shoulders. As the figure rode within a hundred yards of the wall, they looked up toward Jined and then, keeping their cloak-shaded eyes on him, they dismounted and began walking toward the wall. There was no gate, simply a wall, and, on the other side, the gardens.

The figure continued to walk toward him and then disappeared. Jined blinked, wondering whether he was dreaming—still warm in his bed. The frosty morning on his breath and burning cold air in his lungs told him otherwise. He ran to the other side of the wall and saw the figure now walking in the garden, shuffling toward the door into the complex. Jined moved to shout but found he could not. He said a quick prayer and leapt down into the garden, fifteen feet below, hitting hard dirt.

He walked up to the figure shuffling slowly along, and reached out to touch their shoulder. The figure spun and caught his wrist with a bony, gnarled hand. The robe fell from his face, and the gaunt, haunted face of Dorian Mür, Prima Pater of the Paladins of the Hammer, stared back at him. Dorian's mouth turned to the broad smile Jined had come to know and love.

"Brother Adjutant," Dorian said, breathing out a long sigh of relief. "I am glad it is you who has found me. Please escort me to my study quietly, then summon Nichal and Gallahan. We have much to discuss."

The old man was devouring a large loaf of bread as though he had not eaten in days. Nichal, Gallahan, and Jined waited for him to finish. He had changed into the simple brown robe of a Paladin, though he wore no gorget. He did not have his immaculate armor, though he had brought his four-winged scepter.

"Do you have a copy of the prophecy my wife delivered?" Dorian asked.

Nichal nodded. "How does the Matriarch Superioris fare?"

"She lives, though she does not understand anything that goes on around her. She recognized me once," he said, with almost no emotion in his voice. "That was enough for the two of us to say goodbye."

He grew quiet.

"Prima Pater," Gallahan said, "there must be a reason why you pulled yourself away from Maeda. And, more importantly, why you are not wearing your armor."

"Yes," Dorian said, refocusing his eyes on them, drawing himself back into the conversation. "For now, all shall think me still at Precipice; it is best this way. I have been studying this prophecy, and was able to study the references it made. I believe I've come to a conclusion. I believe the Moteans are in possession of the armor of the Warlord."

"This is true," Jined said.

"What do I not know yet?" Dorian said, blinking in surprise.

"I will not interrupt you and your message," Nichal said, "but, suffice to say, we have taken confession from the leader of the sect of Moteans here in the west, Jakis Gladen. And he has told us much of what his sect has accomplished in the past decade."

"Very well," Dorian said. "I feared Gladen was part of this, for the actions he took, unexplained, at Precipice. Now, what have you learned of the armor?"

"That the Apostate betrayed the warlord in his invincible armor, called the Dread Plate," Jined said. "And because of that, you struck him down."

"It is said that the armor was unbreakable," Gallahan offered.

"Yes," Dorian said, "it was unbreakable. What is more important, though, is that my wife's prophecy reveals an even more important fact of the armor we only speculated at until now. Its origins go back to antiquity. This is the first I've heard it called by the name Dread Plate. I suppose that is something."

"Which passage of the prophecy do you refer to?" Gallahan asked, poring over the document himself.

"This one here," Dorian pointed to the middle.

Gallahan read out loud, "It rose to prominence in the frigid lands of apostasy, and yet it was not sundered, for it cannot be destroyed. It is a replica of that made by the Arbiter."

"You understand who the Arbiter is?" Dorian asked.

"We can only assume it is meant literally, referring to Rionne," Gallahan responded.

"Yes. Rionne, first son of Wyv, and god of civilization."

"How is he the god of civilization?" Jined asked. "He is one of the dark gods of the Black Coterie."

"But was he always?" Dorian asked. "Before the betrayal and destruction, it was he who taught all people civilization and founded the first cities."

"But why is he referred to here as the Arbiter?"

"When the Deceiver came into being, Rionne, known at the time as the Arbiter, saw him for what he was and challenged him to a duel. The duel was intended to sentence Achanerüt to destruction."

"But he failed," Nichal added.

"He did not fail," Dorian corrected him. "He defeated Achanerüt. Or at least, he had seemed to. But he was deceived. Rionne held the Deceiver at the point of his sword, the Judgment Blade, and so Achanerüt begged for his life, begging him not to destroy him. It is said in one way or another he hinted that Rionne might even go so far as to slay Achanerüt with his own weapon.

"Rionne thought it a fitting punishment to do so, and reached out and took the Deceiver's axe, which lay nearby. Immediately, it is said, Rionne's hand withered away, becoming naught but bone. He was driven mad. In his madness, the Arbiter fled, and began destroying his own creations. He murdered several dragons, and from their bones, blood, and leather skin, crafted an armor that would be impenetrable. Then he laid siege to the greatest city of the world—his own city. This was the beginning of the destruction."

"What does that have to do with the Warlord's armor?" Nichal asked.

"When we defeated the Necromancer, the hold he had over the revenant Warlord broke, and the armor collapsed. But shortly thereafter it disappeared. It was said it was stolen by someone. I commissioned a council of Paladins to hunt it down and seek out its secrets. I believe this prophecy confirms what they discovered: that the armor reenacts the Arbiter's creation of his own armor. Perhaps it is related to the deaths the Pontifex of Wyv-Thüm spoke of. I do not know."

"And you think the Moteans are behind this?"

"Yes, I believe so. I returned without my armor to remain hidden. The prophecy suggests that the dark one will seek out a holy one. He has killed the Pontifex of Wyv-Thüm, and I suspect the dark one will attempt to kill another head of church. I'd rather not draw special attention to myself, but I fear for the lives of the Archimandrite of the Nifarans or Klint Rigal of the Abecinian church."

The other three remained silent.

"What else was I not aware of?"

"Pell Maran," Nichal offered softly.

"He is dead, then?"

"He is. And we have a witness. A holy Nefer. What shall we do then, Prima Pater?" Nichal asked.

"That is why I have asked you here, Nichal. I am stepping down as Prima Pater. I move to make you the acting Prima Pater until you can return to Pariantür and have the congregation elect you officially."

"You are not dead yet, Prima Pater. And I am not worthy."

"No. I am not. However, I wish to flush out the Moteans without conducting a witch hunt. I believe that when your promotion to Prima Pater is put to a vote at Pariantür, those who adamantly oppose you will be showing their true colors. In the end, I am still alive, and can return if needed."

"Prima Pater..." Nichal began to protest.

"I second the plan," Gallahan said. "We've all suspected you had Nichal in mind. And he's a young enough man to take the responsibility on his shoulders and follow through for years to come."

"He will not be alone," Dorian said. "He'll have Jined beside him."

"Me?" Jined asked

"Jined seems to be mentioned in the prophecy too. 'The second sons, abandoners, have chosen their Exemplars.' We must make sure we stand out of the way of Grissone and his plans, but also keep an eye out for the opposing side of that line. Grissone was second son to Aben. Kea'Rinoul is second-son of Wyv. The T'Akai may themselves begin to move, too."

"This is going to cause problems across the entirety of the order," Gallahan said.

"Problems we already have."

"But Prima Pa... what do we call you?" Nichal asked.

"Call me Brother Unteel. It's the name of a friend of mine I lost in the Protectorate Wars—Maeda's brother."

"Now, about Jakis Gladen," Jined said.

"Please," Dorian replied with a wave of his hand.

Jined described the incident at the lighthouse.

"And he is in our prison now?"

Nichal shook his head. "He is dead. Someone broke into the cell and left him as a pile of bones."

"How?" Jined started. "I had not heard that."

"We do not know. He was discovered by Aeger as he went to feed him and the others."

"The others meaning those captured at St. Nonn?" Dorian asked.

"And the Clouw," Nichal said.

"The Black Sentinel?"

"Yes, the sister, Rallia."

"Why do we have a Sentinel in our holding cells?"

"Prima Pater," Gallahan said. "As we returned to Mahn Fulhar we traveled past St. Nonn. The Sentinel had taken refuge there. While she claims innocence, and had even begun the process of restoring the vandalism done there by the Moteans, she carried a note implicating her in association with the Moteans."

"This saddens me," Dorian said. "I believe I heard her to be the granddaughter of a Paladin."

"Jadsen Brathe, in fact," Gallahan said.

"Dane Marric has complicated things further," Nichal said.

"What did he do?" Dorian asked.

"Attempted to question her, and in a fit of righteous anger, caused some harm."

Dorian pinched the bridge of his nose. "What have we done to make up for it?"

"Dane has been locked up. And we've provided some comfortable accommodations for the Clouw girl. She stays in the guest house with Jurgon, and the young Paladin from St. Nonn, Silas Merun."

"And what does she say?"

"Very little."

Dorian sat back and took a sip of the goblet before him.

"What news of the Crysalas at Precipice?" Nichal asked.

"I issued orders to the Paladames before I left. They are to leave everything and send a message to all of the Crysalas Integritas across the continent to retreat back to Pariantür, under our protection."

"And what of the bastions?" Gallahan asked.

"While I leave the final decision to Nichal as acting Prima Pater, I'd advise all Paladins to return to Pariantür."

"That seems an act of defeat," Gallahan said. "And drastic."

"And yet, it is what High Priest Rigal suggested we do," Nichal said. "Although his suggestion had, as Gallahan and I have discussed, apparent ulterior motives."

"What do you mean by that?" Dorian asked.

"He was at the trial of Gladen. He suggested that, since our church is apparently entering a schism, we ought to recall all Paladins to Pariantür and get our house in order.

"And when we suggested that to take all Paladins from Ganthic it would leave a hole, he suggested that he would work with the Church of the Common Chalice in Œron. He believes that if he can bring them under his direct authority, he could undermine the Common Chalice, and at the same time enable the Praetors to take the place of the Paladins of the Hammer in the lands owing allegiant worship to Aben."

"He is declaring theocratic dominion," Dorian said. "I did not think him to be so power hungry."

They fell silent as Dorian contemplated this.

"Nevertheless," he said, looked at each with a smile. "I am no longer Prima Pater. I leave the decision to you, Nichal."

"I agree with what Doria... Brother Unteel says. We ought to retreat to Pariantür. If we are not welcome here in Mahndür, or anywhere else in the west, we can avoid needless bloodshed if our order is at war. And through this act, we need continually remember that we shall not conduct a witch-hunt, just as Grissone commanded."

"What is this?" Dorian asked.

"It was only for a moment, but Grissone visited me as we rode to Mahn Fulhar, and commanded that we not tear apart the order to look for Moteans. Thus, we will give every Paladin a choice. How will we send out messages when we don't know who to trust?"

"We can take volunteers to act as messengers," Gallahan said. "But each must know that they are risking their lives."

"This will cause a panic in the city. In every city," Nichal replied.

"Open war between Paladins, and potentially a third faction in the Praetors, will cause more," Dorian said.

"That is why we retreat to Pariantür," Nichal said in resolve. "We choose where we take our stand."

"We have much to think about, then," Gallahan said. "And I have no doubt you are very tired, Dorian."

Dorian rose, nodding. He shuffled to the cell in the back of the office to find a bed, looking his age for the first time.

"We should prepare to leave in the next three days. And we move by cover of night," Nichal said.

"This is going to leave everyone with a sour taste in their mouths," Gallahan said. "Both ours and the people."

"I don't doubt this," Nichal said. "But if the Abecinian church plans to found their own Order, I expect the Moteans will have their hands full as that church establishes itself." He shook his head. "This is against everything our order stands for."

"Yes," Gallahan said, "but we cannot stand here and fight against

Moteans, an Abecinian Order, and continue to do our job. The retreat is a tactful one."

"I think we all have things to ponder," Nichal said. "Jined, you're our direct connection to Grissone, it seems. We need to know this is his will."

Jined left by the side door and turned the corner to see Dane standing guard outside the main door to the office.

"What are you doing?" Jined asked.

"My job," Dane said. "Standing guard."

"You weren't here earlier."

"I took my position after my morning prayers."

"Have you been listening?"

"As guard, it is my duty to keep secret what I hear."

"You have been listening."

"I heard voices speaking, but I am not at liberty to say what I heard."

"Dane, I shouldn't have to threaten you with Nichal's authority."

"No," Dane said. "You shouldn't have to. Why you continually question my loyalty is beyond me."

"Perhaps I turn your volleys back against you," Jined sighed.

He came and stood directly in front of the other man.

"I want to trust you, Dane," Jined said. "After all, if Grissone continues to allow you membership in our brotherhood, he has a reason."

"Do not speak to me as though you have the ear of our god. That is blasphemy."

"How so?"

"That he would seek personal conversation with a criminal such as yourself over the contrite heart of one with the purification of all heavy upon their soul..."

"Minu the Gentle Giant was more a criminal than I."

"Minu was purified by the Vow of Pacifism."

"From what life did your own Vow of Chastity purify you from, then?" Jined asked.

Dane's eyes darkened. "Do not judge me, nor dig into the life I have forgotten."

"Nor should you," Jined said, turning to leave.

As Jined arrived at his own cell he found Loïc and Cävian waiting outside.

"What is the trouble?" he asked as he approached.

Follow us. And stay quiet. Loïc signed, motioning for him to follow. They exited through the stables and out to the green in front of the palace. They moved slowly, but with purpose, directly toward the Crysalas complex. They turned to the right and skirted the main building, inside the convent walls, to the stables, now devoid of people and animals. They had passed a few servants who were maintaining the place, though all Crysalas had gone, still at Precipice with the ailing Matriarch.

Cävian walked ahead to the back of the stables and into a smaller servant's quarters, while Loïc dropped the bolt on the stable door.

Within, two figures lay on separate beds, sheets pulled over their faces.

Cävian pulled a sheet back. Underneath lay Etienne, stripped bare, with a hole in the center of his chest.

Brother and I were on guard duty early this morning, Loïc said. *A sailor came knocking at the front door, and asked us to come with him. They were found at low tide, their hammers chained to their legs out front of his fishing pier. We brought them here, knowing if we took them to the Bastion it would draw attention.*

"Who is under the other sheet?" Jined asked.

The second figure had a gash across the back of his head, and one eye socket was empty. It was Aeger, Gallahan Pír's personal assistant.

Look here, too, Cävian motioned, pulling back both sheets to reveal their hips. There they had a tattoo of a feather. While Etienne's was new, Aeger's was well faded.

"This will be the first strike," Jined said.

Both looked on quizzically.

"I trust you both," Jined said, "and so you need to hear this from me. But you are sworn not to mention it to another."

Both nodded.

"We are pulling out of the continent and returning to Pariantür."

We? Loïc asked.

"All Paladins of the Hammer are being recalled to Pariantür. The Prima Pater is gone, and has asked that Nichal Guess take his place. I aim to go with him."

Then we will follow, Cävian said.

"Thank you. I hoped you would say that. I need the two of you by my side."

What should we do with the bodies? Loïc asked.

"I will speak with Nichal. Until then, leave them here. And I want the two of you to be looking out for anything suspicious. If they are targeting Paladins, or each other, we need to know. The Moteans already killed Gladen."

How? Cävian asked.

"I'm not sure of all the details myself, but nothing was left but a pile of bones."

That wasn't something Gladen said the Dread Plate could do, Loïc said.

"Then perhaps the Moteans have unlocked another ability since Gladen was captured."

They left the room together, and locked it behind them. As they came around the bend, a group of ten Paladins, each wearing black capes, quickly marched into the complex and toward the front door of the Crysalas temple. Jined motioned the brothers back.

Those were Moteans, Cävian motioned.

"Let's find a back way in. If they feel they can march around in broad daylight, how many are there?"

And how long have they been here? Loïc asked.

They found their way back to the stables and took an entrance into the serving halls. A woman walked by with buckets of soapy water. She moved quickly out of their way, a look of fear and suspicion in her eyes.

"Which way to the kitchen?" Jined asked.

She indicated which way they should go, but said nothing. Coming to the kitchen, a matronly woman was standing with her arms crossed as a Paladin shouted orders at her.

"You'll prepare beef and bread for us tonight. The Prima Pater demands it."

"Then you tell your Prima Pater to take a look at his records. We don't cook on Umay. It's forbidden. You'll have raw and preserved veggies like everyone else."

Jined peeked around the corner. The Paladin who stood there had his arms folded to match the cook and a black cape hanging from his back. His cordons displayed a bead of the Vow of Silence.

"Why is it you've been sent to deliver the message? Didn't you take the Vow of Silence?" Jined said, walking quickly up to him. Before the Paladin could even act surprised, Jined swung with his fist and knocked him out flat, his nose bleeding profusely.

"Loïc, take his cape." Jined turned to the cook. "How long have these criminals been here pushing their weight around?"

She looked shocked. "Criminals? I thought they were Paladins. Three days ago, a few of them came in. He just asked me to serve cooked meat, and on Umay. When are the sisters returning?"

"When all this blows over, you find me and ask again. Do you have somewhere we can keep this man?"

She nodded and showed them to a cellar off the kitchen. They tied up the heretic to a post and stepped out into the hallway. Two Paladins walked along with black capes on their backs.

"Did you find where they are keeping Vanguard?" one asked.

"No. And Slate is becoming agitated. I was able to get close to the prisons, but no one responded when I gave the signal. I don't think he's in there. Perhaps they moved him?"

"Or sent him to Pariantür," the first one said.

"I just wish it wasn't Slate in charge now, but don't be repeating that."

"I won't. I don't like him either."

As they walked by the door to the kitchen, Jined dove out, shoving one of them against the opposite wall. The other was pulled into the kitchen by the twins. They didn't have time to struggle before they had shoved rags into their mouths and were dragged toward the cellar, kicking and fighting. They came back with the three black cloaks. The cook stared in surprise.

"They should stay down there," Jined said. "Will they be heard?"

"I should hope not. I'll keep them fed and quiet as long as needed."

"Thank you."

46

Perfidy

Stray not in your dreams, lest the Queen seek out your fears.

Submit not to wrath, lest the Destructor maim and destroy.

Seek not after vanity, lest the Scarred-One take your best.

Wish not for treasures, lest the Gift-Giver curse you thrice.

Give not of yourselves to witchcraft, lest you compromise your souls, and be delivered unto the Deceiver.

—*BEATUS GRISSONI 5:32-36*

Jined and the twins came to a balcony overlooking the throne room. It was similar to the Prima Pater's own throne room of judgment at Pariantür, where many decisions were made for the order. The tiles that covered the floor were large slabs of both white and rose marble.

At least a dozen black-cloaked Paladins stood around, speaking in hushed tones with one another, standing away from the throne, upon which sat a Paladin with his back to Jined and the twins.

He wore his black cloak over his armored shoulders, which made his frame appear bulkier than it was. Though his thin neck, visible from above within his gorget, revealed that he was a gaunt, slight man.

Most paid him little attention. If the way the Paladins in the hall had spoken of him was any indication, not many cared for him.

In the center of the room stood a small pedestal. On it rested a blood red pillow. On the pillow was a heavy gauntlet of black metal.

A bell tolled. The man on the dais stood. He had built tall wooden heels into his boots, which clacked on the marble tile and provided him height.

"It is time to commune," he stated in a thin voice. "Have we a new disciple?"

A Paladin who was stationed near the door knocked twice on the wood with his hammer.

Four Paladins entered, dragging a fifth, who wore no black cloak, kicking and screaming. Cävian put a hand on Jined's shoulder, and Jined then realized it was the herald, Amal Yollis. He was forced to his knees in front of the pedestal in the center of the room.

"He was found sneaking around near the front gate."

"You ought not to have," the tenor-voiced Slate said to Amal. "But you will add to our numbers just as well. We welcome you to the Brotherhood of the Gauntlet."

"Who are you? In the name of all that's holy, what are you doing?!"

"We're going to set you free from the constraints that have been put upon you."

He came up to stand before Amal.

"What is your name, paladin?"

"I will not give you my name. I am a faithful servant of Grissone. I defy you, apostate."

"You defy me for now. But like it or not, you'll be joining our brotherhood."

He turned around, took up the Gauntlet, and put it on. It looked like it weighed more than he could bear.

"Bring the brazier."

A hot brazier of coals was wheeled out. Slate took a coin from a purse and gave it to the brazier keeper, who used tongs to place it into the hot coals.

"I want you to understand what is happening," Slate said. "This gauntlet is our benefactor, so to speak. With it, I will break your will to mine, by attaching your will to mine."

"Beatus Grissoni 5:36," Amal said. "Give not of yourself to witchcraft, lest you compromise your soul, and be delivered unto the Deceiver."

"Do not quote your scriptures at me. I have left that far behind. And now, so shall you."

Then the leader took out a coin on a leather strap around his neck and tore it off.

The Paladins surrounding Amal forced his mouth open. The leader placed the coin onto his tongue. Amal shuddered as it slid down his throat.

"Now, what is your name?"

"Brother Amal Yollis." Amal's eyes looked horrified that he had given the name up so easily.

"Very well. You will now take the Vows of the Brotherhood."

By instruction he could not seem to resist, he stripped his own armor and robes down to his bare chest. The tongs were pulled from the brazier holding the now red-hot coin. The leader held out the Gauntlet, and the coin was dropped, red hot, into his palm. He did not wince. He approached Amal, who shook visibly. The leader took the coin in his gauntleted hand and pressed it into Amal's chest. Amal began to scream. The gauntlet was pulled away, but the coin remained. It cooled on his flesh as he continued to scream.

"It will fall out eventually, as your tissue scars. But you are now a member of the Brotherhood, and answer to the bearer of the Gauntlet, until your dying day."

"Why?" Amal muttered.

"Because the time of turning has begun. Pariantür has had power for far too long. It is time to return the power to the people. It is time to tip the scales away from the gods."

The gauntlet was placed again on the pedestal, and the leader walked back toward his throne.

Brotherhood? Cävian signed. *I thought they were Moteans.*

I think they are Moteans. Jined replied. *But it appears Slate is taking it to the next level.*

Down below, Amal had risen to his feet, though he was still panting, bearing through the pain, and following two other heretics toward the main doors. A figure appeared before them in the doorway.

He wore a mantle over his shoulders with a matching hood. It was the color of dirty bones, but undulated with smoky wisps of black that curled across its surface. The face of the man was imperceptible within the shadow of the hood. Below it, smoke began to seep onto the floor.

"That was an interesting trick," the figure said. The voice sounded ancient and deep. The cloak wavered on unseen winds. "How does it work?"

"What in Noccitan are you?" the leader upon the throne asked.

"You must be Slate. Vanguard spoke of you." The deep voice seemed to break character. It now spoke jovially, yet still full of dark hatred.

The leader sneered. "What do you know of Vanguard? Who sent you? Dusk? Bell?"

"I don't answer to anyone. They all answer to me. You answer to me. You may call me Shroud. Has Vanguard never told you this?"

"I don't answer to you. We hold the relic."

"Thank you for confirming that. I came to understand it was in the city."

The figure had begun creeping slowly forward. He stood halfway to the pedestal displaying the gauntlet.

"You," the figure said, pointing a hand at Amal. "You did not choose to join us."

Amal shook his head.

"Then I shall make an example of you, and free you from your bond."

"No!" Slate shouted. "Attack."

Like a puppet on a string Amal leapt up at the dark figure of Shroud. The figure's cloak went suddenly black and seemed to flare open of its own accord, flaying out in all directions and exploding into hundreds of dark shades. The whirlwind of spectral wisps flooded toward Amal, who waded into them. They swirled around him, and he fell to his knees into the black fog that spun along the floor. As the shadows swirled, the blackness drained from Shroud's form, leaving the chain mail cloak of bone hanging limply from his frame. When the black fog coursed back toward the cloaked figure, all that was left on the floor was Amal's robe, now full of bones.

He is at least put out of his misery before he could be forced to do something he would come to regret, Loïc signed to Jined, who nodded solemnly.

"Now," the figure said, his black cloak of shades wrapped once more about him. "I have come to collect what is due me."

He walked up to the leader, Slate, who dropped to his knees in cowardice.

"What shall we do for you? What is our debt?"

"First, you can tell me how you came to power?"

"Vanguard is gone. Captured. I took his place well over a week ago."

"And so these actions committed by this 'Brotherhood of the Gauntlet' are on your orders?"

"Vanguard has long waited for a time to exert his dominion over all of Mahn Fulhar. We've been actively recruiting for over a year now."

"Has the armor been unlocked?"

"No. It remains in the sarcophagi."

"And where is it now?"

"In the south in the Aerie, where it belongs."

"Very well. You will swear fealty to me. And you will give me the Gauntlet. It is mine by right."

"Who...whose right?"

"I am the heir of the Black Warlord. And I claim the Dread Plate for myself, starting with the Gauntlet."

He reached out and picked up the Gauntlet and placed it on his hand. Then he walked over to the throne and sat down.

"You shall each swear fealty or die. And then we shall discuss the destruction of the Paladins of the Hammer, which begins tonight."

One by one the Paladins gathered together and dropped coins from around their necks into the brazier, and they were rebranded one at a time—consecrating their fealty to their new leader.

What is happening? Cävian asked, looking on in horror. *They took control of Amal with a coin? How is that possible?*

"I suspect dark magicks at play, just as Amal said," Jined replied

There is no such thing as magic, Loïc signed.

"What do you call our prayers?"

Gifts from Grissone. What the multitudes consider magic is simply that, gifts from the gods.

"Continue to think on that line of thought. It may be that is exactly what this was."

They moved from the balcony, stepping into the side hall. Jined turned the corner and ran squarely into another Paladin. He wore the gold cordons of a Pater Minoris.

"You are to come with me," the Pater said. His words were vacant as he said so. "Together we'll swear fealty."

"We're not going anywhere," Jined said, placing a hand on the Paladin's chest.

"We've all been summoned to swear fealty to the new leader of our order."

Loïc placed a hand on Jined's shoulder. Jined glanced over.

That is Pater Didus Koel of the Bulwark in Birin.

"Pater Koel?" Jined asked.

A flash of recognition came over the Pater's face, and then disappeared again.

"We must go," he said flatly, turning.

"He thinks we're members," Jined said.

Cävian rolled his eyes, indicating to the black capes they still wore. Jined nodded, realizing his stupidity.

"Pater Koel," Jined said, walking behind him. "Remind me when you joined the Brotherhood."

"I...don't remember," Koel said.

Jined whispered a prayer. "Grissone. Did he go willingly?"

Koel's head began to shake a resounding no.

Grab him, Jined signed.

The three of them jumped forward, tackling the man to the ground. Cävian held his mouth with his leather glove, and Jined unfastened the breastplate from the man, who struggled to free himself. He tore open his robe, to reveal coin-shaped scars on his chest.

"Grissone, make him clean," Jined said, holding out his palm. The skin began to sizzle and bubble around the scar. Koel began to whimper, and then scream as his chest began to burn.

"I'm sorry to do this," Jined said. "But you need to be quiet."

He fist shot out, hitting him on the forehead. Koel's head bounced against the stone ground. He stopped moving. The skin continued to bubble and burn until only a scar shaped like a hammer remained.

"Bring him with us," Jined said, "but we need to be quick. He's probably just alerted the entire complex."

They lifted the man. Jined unfastened his armor as they went, leaving it behind. They came to the top of the stairs leading toward the servant's hall. Behind them he heard a shout and looked back. Three Paladins at the far end began to race toward them.

"Down!" Jined barked.

A figure stood at the bottom, washing the floor with soap and water.

"Fastest way to the stables!" Jined shouted, tearing off the cape on his back.

"Through the third door down," she said.

Their pursuers could be heard at the top of the stairs.

"Thank you."

"You're the first to say thank you since you and your brothers took over."

"They are not our brothers. They are fallen."

The servant nodded, stepped aside from the stairway and kicked her bucket over, spilling the soapy water in front of the landing. The three pursuers came to the bottom just as Jined went through the indicated escape route. They slipped and fell, slamming into the opposing wall.

They had entered a leather shop. The musky smell of tannery and leather oils hung in the air. There was no light but the door behind them. Jined pushed forward past the twins and their prisoner, and felt for the exit. He found the latch and opened it up, letting in light from outside. They were deeper into the complex, and could see the stables between them and the exit.

"Let's get to the stables," Jined said.

He pushed ahead and came to the back door. Opening it, he saw a tight set of stairs up to the hay loft. Jined ascended first and reached down to pull Pater Koel up into the loft. They propped the man against a bale of hay, and sat in silence. They heard a rush of activity as several others entered the stables and began looking through the space. They could hear them move into the back room, where they had kept the bodies of Etienne and Aeger. The people below soon began shouting, and then rushed out, looking for those who had invaded their space.

"Thank you," a voice cracked. Jined snapped his head to look at Pater Koel, who was now awake. He was examining the scar on his chest. He looked up at Jined. "I don't know how you broke it, but thank you."

"I am hoping you can explain to me how it happened in the first place."

"I'm not sure," he said. "Where are we?"

"We're in the cathedral complex of the Crysalas Integritas in Mahn Fulhar."

"Mahn Fulhar? What day is it?"

"The 8th of Kashi," Jined replied.

"Six months. I feel like you raised me from Noccitan."

"What happened, Pater?"

"We received orders to rush to the aid of the Aerie in Haven. The situation was vague, but seemed dire enough that I took the entire fortress with me, and then Pater Minoris Gladen did something, but I can't seem to recall what it was. There was a loud noise, and later a hot searing pain. Everything since then is a blur. And now I'm here. Who are you?"

"I am Brother Adjutant Jined Brazstein. These two Excelsiors are Loïc and Cävian. They're bodyguards of Prima Pater D... bodyguards of the acting Prima Pater Nichal Guess."

"Dorian Mür is dead?!" Koel tried to stand, his face covered in genuine shock.

Jined pursed his lips. "His wife is on the verge of death. He has relinquished his authority."

"What do we do now?" Koel asked.

"We have to escape the complex and return to the Bastion in the Abecinian complex."

"But now our enemies know we're here."

"Correct."

"Get me a hammer," Koel said. "They'll wish they had never betrayed me."

The twins nodded.

Cävian snuck down in the stables below to look outside and make sure they were clear. His head popped up through the door, and he offered up a heavy awl he'd found below. Koel smiled as he took it.

"This will do."

There are two guards posted outside, Cävian signed. *One at the entrance to the tannery. One further along as we head toward the entrance.*

"But there are four of us," Jined said.

And we've taken on ten, Loïc added. *And then, only the three of us.*

"The three of you have taken on ten paladins?" Koel asked, astonished.

Cävian held up two fingers.

"Twice?!"

Jined nodded. "I've seen these two take on five T'Akai by themselves before."

Koel walked to the doorway and began to head down. "I'll do my best, then."

Cävian still had his black cape on his back. He walked out of the stables, looking toward the tannery. Cävian held three fingers behind his back.

There are three coming, Loïc responded.

Cävian indicated the figures outside follow him, and held the door as they entered the stables. They had no time to respond as Jined and the others fell on them. Koel took one down, and then set upon a second.

They put them into a stall and went to the door. Cävian indicated that no one outside had reacted.

"We need to make our break," Jined said.

The twins nodded, and Pater Koel clenched his fists on the awl in his hand.

Jined walked to the door and peered out. He stepped out in the light of day, his hammer held down to his side. He walked confidently toward the front, and came out into the front courtyard. Far across the way a group of five Paladins stood, black cloaks hanging from their backs. Jined made a hand signal to the twins, *Stately*.

They walked with confidence. One of the Paladins broke away from the group opposite them and approached.

"Pater Koel," Jined said lowly. "Command them to stand down. Use your rank."

Koel held up a hand, and the Paladin paused. It seemed to work. They walked out onto the capital green. When they reached the green they broke into a sprint and ran toward the Abecinian complex, shedding the black cloaks off their backs, and didn't stop until they had entered the paladinial bastion, safe, if only for a few short moments.

47

First Strike

Forgiveness is easier given than sought.

Indeed penance seems easier than looking in the eye of he whom you have betrayed.

— *HAMULEON 45*

Jined marched through the Bastion with the twins and Pater Koel on his heels. When he arrived at the office, he walked in without a knock. Nichal was seated behind the desk with Gallahan across from him. Dorian Mür sat in a comfortable chair by the wall.

"I apologize for the intrusion," Jined said, "but we have a serious problem."

"Who is this?" Nichal asked, pointing toward Pater Koel.

"This is Pater Minoris Didus Koel, of the Bulwark."

Nichal stood up, his chair loudly scooting backwards across the stone. "You have much to answer for, Koel," he said.

"I do," Koel said.

"Where have you been? Why was the Bulwark emptied?"

"I..."

"Nichal," Jined said, holding up a hand. "Please allow me to explain."

Jined then told the story, starting with the bodies of Etienne and Aeger, the loss of Amal Yollis, and their saving of Koel.

"Aeger?" Gallahan said. He leaned forward in his chair, his hands on the sides of his head. "I don't understand? He was like a son to me."

"That leaves us with little time to prepare," Nichal said, glancing sideways at Dorian in the corner. "The three of you," he said, indicating to Jined and the twins, "are to spread the word to everyone to meet in the chapel, during the Abecinian High Mass, fully armed and ready. I wish to speak more with Pater Koel."

Gallahan looked up, tears streaming down his face. "I cannot believe Aeger was a Motean. He should have known better. I've known him since he was a boy. How did he go undiscovered for so long? And how did he die?"

"There is, of course," Dorian said, "an even more pressing question. How did the Moteans sneak into the Crysalas Convent, and why are we only just noticing this today?"

"Amal was growing suspicious," Jined said.

And it cost him his life, Loïc signed.

"I should like to discover a way to free those of my own Fortress from this curse," Koel offered.

Jined bowed, to provide the leaders some privacy. The twins followed him out into the hall.

"I expect things are going to move quickly now," Jined said. "If we don't strike first, then we're leaving ourselves out in the open for an attack."

Nichal did say that everyone was to appear armed, Loïc said.

Cävian held his hammer up. *We're always armed.*

"But there are those who haven't worn armor since the Solstice," Jined said. "As Nichal said. Everyone is to be armed."

The Pacifists, too? Cävian asked.

"Just because they won't raise their hammer against someone else doesn't mean they shouldn't be protected."

Nor that they shouldn't march alongside us, Loïc said.

Jined journeyed through the back gardens and then through the shared hallway with the Abecinian monastery to see if any of the Paladins were visiting friends they had made there.

"Brother?" a monk of Aben said as he walked by.

"Brother," Jined acknowledged, as he continued on his way.

"I understand you arrived with the Prima Pater's entourage," the monk said as their arms brushed.

"I did," Jined said. "I apologize that I cannot stop and chat, but I'm afraid the errand I'm on has a great deal of urgency."

"Of course. Matters of church urgency take precedence," the other man said. His face became crestfallen. Jined turned to go, and then sighed.

"I have a moment," Jined said.

The man looked back up, smiling. He was vaguely familiar.

"I understand the entourage traveled through Garrou."

"It did," Jined answered distractedly.

"Before I became a monk here, I was, for many years, in charge of the kitchen there that fed the poor. Financed by the paladinial bastion. Does it still stand?"

"I'd imagine, given the war that's brewing, that it will certainly be busy during and after the conflict," Jined said.

"And you met up with the monks of Nifara, and, with them, the Black Sentinels who escorted them?"

"Yes."

"My children were among their number."

"Your children?" Jined said.

"Hanen and Rallia Clouw."

"The two Clouws who acted as second to the Sentinel leader?"

The monk nodded, a smile growing across his face. "And did they perform their duty well?"

"I can't say I paid them much mind. But I can say that one of them was very comfortable among us. She spent much time alongside the Paladins, chatting and speaking fondly of her time in Garrou."

"That would be Rallia," the monk said.

It pained Jined to think of the harm caused to the girl, now sequestered with the Prima Pater.

"She is a good girl," the monk said. "I pray for her daily. And what of Hanen?"

"As I said," Jined replied, "I did not pay as much attention as I probably ought to have."

"What do you mean?" Concern washed over the monk's face.

"I do not trust Sentinels," Jined said, "especially their leader, Searn."

"Then I shall pray that they earn your trust."

"You ought to pray for the safety of the city this night," Jined said. "Now, if you would excuse me."

The monk gave a bow and turned, humming softly to himself.

As Jined re-entered the Paladinial bastion, he walked the hall to observe Paladins readying themselves—whispering prayers to their gods, kneeling beside their beds, polishing their hammers. The bells for High Mass began to toll, marking the hour. Jined knelt down in his room; Etienne's empty bed stared at the back of his head like a tombstone.

Nothing happened.

Jined rose, disappointment playing across the back of his mind, and marched to the chapel.

There were thirty Paladins in full regalia there. Nichal stood at the front of the room, the morose Gallahan Pír on his right. Both stood, their hands lifted to silence all.

"Everyone, please calm down. We have much to say in very little time," Nichal put both hands to his side. "This morning, we received a message from the Prima Pater at Precipice."

A general murmur rose.

"He is not returning. He has asked that I take up the role of interim Prima Pater, to be voted upon by the Order at Pariantür."

The Paladins began suddenly talking to one another.

"Please," Gallahan said, "there will be time to discuss this later."

"Do not think I take this announcement lightly," Nichal continued. "I will do everything in my power to lead with diligence, and if the congregation at Pariantür decides that I am to take on the full role, then so be it. However, first, we must attend to a matter of utmost urgency."

Jined noticed movement out of the corner of his eye. Brother Hammer walked around the periphery, unseen. He looked Jined in the eyes, and motioned that he follow him into the outer hall.

Jined stepped out as Nichal said, "Our order has been infiltrated by a great heresy, and members of that sect have invaded the complex of the Crysalas today."

They stood out in the hall. The voices on the other side of the door went silent.

"You stand here now before me in a hallway that does not exist," Grissone said. "The Paladins on the other side of the door are about to find themselves in a quick and grizzly battle. As you gathered, ten members of the Motean sect entered the Bastion. The moment you rejoin, they will attack. But I need to speak with you first."

"Whatever you would have of me," Jined said, but his attention was now drawn to those within, unaware that their deaths may be falling on them momentarily.

"Tell me what happened when you went to the convent," Grissone said. "I was watching when the twins showed you the bodies of Aeger and Etienne. But then things grew dim, and I was unable to continue observing."

"What do you mean?"

"I don't know," Grissone said. "But I should like to. Please, tell me what happened."

Jined explained what they observed, with Amal's will shattered by the gauntlet, and then the appearance of the man in the black cloak of bone and shadowy ghosts.

"I think it was the same figure I saw leaving the Green Bastion glade," Jined said, "when I fought and destroyed the accursed creature that controlled the furies."

"Then something about that cloak he wears blinds me. Blinds us all."

"What do you mean?" Jined asked.

"The Nifaran said that Nifara herself did not see him as he murdered the Archimandrite. The deaths he causes go ignored by Wyv, or at least unrecorded as such. And I cannot draw near to him."

"How can we stop him if the gods cannot see him, nor approach him?"

"I cannot see the man in the shroud," Grissone said. "But you can. I cannot do anything to him, for whatever reason. But you can."

Jined shook his head. "I don't know if I can even reach him, if he releases his cloak of shades upon me."

"But he cannot attack me," Grissone said.

"We do not know that."

"No god can be harmed by mere mortal. Therefore, take up your hammer and hold it out."

Jined lifted the hammer.

Grissone approached and touched the weapon. Grissone became like smoke in the wind, but instead of dissipating, his form entered the hammer. Jined imagined this must have been what it had looked like for him when he felt himself melt away into Grissone's own Not-Hammer.

A small voice crept into his mind. *Go. I am with you.*

The sounds from within the room returned, joined by the sound of a door exploding off its frame. Jined threw himself back into the room. Ten Paladins came rushing in the opposite door, brandishing their hammers, and wearing the capes of the Brotherhood of the Gauntlet. One struck out and hit Loïc across the breastplate. It glanced off, but still threw him crashing against a wall. Cävian rushed at the one that hit his brother, and the press of the attackers shoved him into the arms of several others. The press of the ten, though outnumbered three-to-one, forced everyone into an outright brawl.

Nichal lifted his hammer as one of the heretics rushed the dais. He swung, taking the man across the top of the head. Nichal stepped off the dais and into the fray, swinging this way and that, as everyone stepped back to give him a berth. Three more came at him. With one long swing he brought one down, shoulder rushed the second, knocking the enemy into the third. The Paladins rallied and rushed the others.

One of the Moteans held up an orb of metal.

"Stop him!" Jined cried out, pointing his hammer across the mass of bodies.

The orb fell as Loïc and Cävian both tackled him to the ground. But nothing happened. Loïc rose from the ground, his brother still atop the Motean. He held the orb aloft in his hand. Jined sighed a relief.

The fighting ceased. Seven Moteans lay motionless. Three had fled. The seven heretics had given their lives to kill half their number. But the energy of the room had left, and the Paladins, though still strong in number, nursed minor injuries and bruises.

"Gallahan," Nichal said, "see to it that the Abecinians are safe. And have them bar their doors until you or I have come to release them."

Gallahan nodded and left the room. The older standard bearer, Valér Queton, joined him.

"The rest of you," Nichal said, "take up your hammers, and shake free any doubt you had."

Paladins rose from their seats, shocked that they had been attacked by their brothers.

"Brothers," Nichal said, "can you hold your hammer?"

They looked to their leader, nursing their minor wounds, nodding, or grunting their determined acknowledgment.

"Then rise up," Nichal said. "Rise and ready yourself. We march on the Moteans. We march to save our order from internal destruction."

48

Interlude

"Apparently they discovered it when they found the breastplate five years ago," the man said, taking the glass of wine offered to him. He did not drink from it, but stared at the bone-colored cloak, thrown over the bed so casually.

"Go on," the other man said. He filled his own glass and took a deep breath.

"I'm sorry, I am just in awe that you accomplished what you said you would. But also, I fear it."

"Why is that?"

"You used it to destroy Vanguard. You've killed Cup. How do I know you won't eventually decide to kill me as well?"

"Pellian, you're my dearest friend. As long as you don't give me a reason to do the same to you, then I won't."

"That's comforting," Pellian said wryly.

"I also value your scholarship. Even after I faked my death, you continued to go where I could not. It was your scholarship that discovered the replication of the bells you use in Piedala."

"What's humorous," Pellian said, taking a sip of the wine and suddenly turned back to his story, "is I discovered how to do it when I

465

found the breastplate myself, twelve years ago. I hadn't realized it at the time, only that the blacksmith had discovered how to forge with Skyfall metal."

"You didn't think to take the man's forge from him?"

"He was already years ahead of me. I wasn't going to take that from him, when I knew he'd continue to excel and learn without my tampering."

"But Vanguard found out too and took him."

"And he's still working at the Aerie for all I know. It's for the best; the man was using it to mint the coins, and had an entire village wrapped around his little finger. They all wore them on leather thongs, and basically treated the man like a king."

"How was the breastplate being used?"

"Interestingly enough, it was the forge."

"What do you mean?"

"Vanguard discovered the man and his use of Skyfall, so he conscripted the man, who brought the forge with him. Slate helped him move in and watched as the man took the final piece of the Dread Plate from his cart, put it into his forge, and covered it over with coal. It had been in the family since his grandfather had been the village blacksmith.

"And what happened then? He started forging. Vanguard's supply of Skyfall gave the man all he needed. They actually have an anvil of the stuff there. They replaced the breastplate with a flat plate of Skyfall metal, and it's been used to make the thrumming hammers, based on the principles of my bells."

"You said the villagers were wearing them around their necks. I had wondered why those here were both wearing them and burning each other with them."

"Well, I think it goes without saying that the heating and burning of the coin on flesh is a very strong dominion. Wearing them is similar to what the bells of Piedala do. It's a weaker but perhaps more permanent bond, and a symbol of membership."

"This is why I enjoy talking to you. You see things that I sometimes miss."

"But now you're going to send me on my way, back to Piedala."

"I am."

"Even after all I told you? About the high Priest of Aben effectively declaring himself a theocratic ruler of the west? That he's going to found his own paladinial order?"

"Yes. Because I have a very important plan for you."

Pellian sat back, sipping at the cup in his hand.

"I want you to return to Piedala. When you receive the call to return to Pariantür, I want you instead to march on the Aerie. When you arrive, I want you to use all of your cunning, all of your administrative skills, all of your diplomacy, and bind the Moteans into a single order."

"Do you not expect to be there?"

"When I am finished with the Paladins here in the northwest, I'm going to first go to the Aerie and take the plate; then I'll go to Bortali and bring Dusk to heel."

"And if he doesn't join you willingly?"

"I am already deeper in the knowledge of the Feather than he is. If he doesn't join, I'll take his soul from him, and he can come as a book in my library."

"Remind me never to cross you," Pellian said.

"Never cross me, Pellian Noss."

"You have my friendship, and my allegiance, Shroud."

"I believe you," Shroud said. "I've had allies. I've had people I work with only as colleagues, but I have always been able to call you my friend, since the day we joined the Paladins those eighteen years ago."

"And look where we are now," Pellian said, raising his glass.

"Look where we are now," Shroud repeated.

PART 7

49

Messages Received

What proof do we have that Nifara speaks on our behalf? We need not her approval to arrive wholly pure at the gates of Lomïn. Our path speaks for itself. So says the sages. So says the histories. We need no monk of the Staff, where our holy priests of Aben intercede.

—DISCIPLE VERD OF THE OUIQUIMON DUOMO

Cräg Narn, or Koragh Neyarn, as he should be called, aimed to avoid Seriah now. Or perhaps it was the other way around.

To keep herself busy, Seriah helped Ensayez organize the orphanage. The boy, Koril, a young man really, was a great help. Seriah never mentioned to him that she knew he could see. She felt no reason to bring his guilt out in the open while sitting under her own, as an unwitting messenger of a dark god.

She often ran out of excuses to avoid the other monks shortly before Archimandrite Lant called for a meeting, forcing her to make an appearance and sit in the same room as one of Nifara's saints.

"Seriah?" Kerei asked. "Are you paying attention?"

"I apologize," Seriah said, blushing, "I was not. My mind was on other things."

"Care to share with us?"

"I'm sure young Yaledít was considering the orphanage she took on." Koragh was quick to jump in.

"Yes." Seriah paused, "though it is more a project of Ensayaz's than mine."

"That is what we shall discuss next," Kerei said. "But first, will you agree to take a message to the Paladins for us?"

"Of course. When you ask I shall deliver it."

"We just did," Kerei said sternly.

"I apologize," Seriah said. "My mind, as I said, was on other things."

"I'd appreciate if you would stay focused on the present, Nefer Yaledít."

"Yes, Archimandrite."

"Now," Kerei continued, "as we were discussing, you are to deliver the message we are leaving Mahn Fulhar within the week to return to Birin. Our time here is done, and I'd rather not wait until Spring. We can make our way south through Varea to Redot, and we can cross through the mountains at the Castenard Pass. It will be a longer road, but far more pleasant than trying to force our way through in the middle of winter."

"What about the Sentinels?" another asked.

"They'll be informed that we're leaving. If they wish to fulfill their promise, they'll join us. If not, then we shall proceed without them."

"Ensayaz," Kerei said, changing the subject, "I believe you have something to share."

"Yes," the young woman said. "I wish to stay here to administrate the orphanage. But I need to have my sight bound to do so."

"You are ready to take your Vows?"

"I am."

"Very well. We will conduct a ceremony in three days. You'll confine yourself to your cell to make ready after dinner tomorrow night."

Kerei stood.

"That concludes our meeting. Seriah, please go to the Paladin leadership at your earliest convenience."

Seriah took up her staff and moved toward the door.

"Nefer," the voice of Koragh Neyarn said. "I need to speak to you."

Seriah stopped and turned.

"Let us find a place to sit and speak."

She sighed and followed him. The sharp rap of his staff on the flag-stone shocked her with new waves of guilt. He found a bench on the wall and took a seat.

"Please join me," he said.

They sat in awkward silence for some time.

"I believe that it is safe to say that we've both been avoiding each other."

"Yes," Seriah said.

"Two hundred years, and I still avoid conflict."

"It is hard to believe that you are that old."

"Don't I look it?" he asked.

"I wouldn't know," Seriah said. "I don't believe we had the chance to meet before I took my Vows."

"Well, I feel it. Especially after that evening."

"I never meant to hurt anyone. Certainly not our goddess."

"You cannot hurt Nifara," Koragh said. "But you have caused her distress, I don't doubt."

"I should have known better," Seriah said.

"Tell me what happened," Koragh said, "when you were given the message."

"I had spent the day sitting at the Judgment tree, down in the city."

"When?"

"The day after the Solstice."

"And what happened?"

"A Paladin, the Pater Minoris of the Piedala Fortress happened upon me, and we walked through the city, with people following us for me to sit in judgment."

"Piedala?" Koragh said. "He was far from his station."

"I imagine he was here to visit the Prima Pater."

"The paladinial leadership has constantly spoken of messages gone awry. How then would a Paladin from the far southeast know to come here? Nevertheless, continue."

"After I sat in judgment, I stayed and sat in the silence of the side street. It felt like the first moment I had found for myself since we had arrived. But then something happened."

"What?"

"A coldness washed over me. I thought that someone had come to do something...wrong to me. But then another presence approached, and admonished the coldness."

"And did coldness listen?"

"It did. It did not leave, but seemed to pull back when the second one spoke to me and asked me to deliver a message to Nifara if I met her, even if it was on my deathbed."

"Why did you give the message, after an event like that?"

"I don't know."

"Why didn't you ask one of us about the visitation?"

"I don't know."

"You were visited by not one but two gods, Seriah."

"Two?"

"There are times—times before events that shape the course of history—during which the Mad Gift Giver and the Deceiver walk together, plotting and prodding at mortal wills to make way for their plans. And it seems you were an unwitting asset. They very likely bent their wills against you. I'd say you had little choice whether you'd deliver the message or not."

"How can we hope, if we are at the will of the gods?"

"That is a foolish thing to ask," Koragh said. "I am at the will of the Lady. I do as she wills, whether she forces me to do her bidding unconsciously, or willingly."

"And if the dark gods should bend us to their wills?"

"You may have unwittingly done so," Koragh said. "But you have not done so willingly. Should they visit you again, what would you do?"

"I should hope I would deny them."

"And if they should threaten you? Or perhaps even offer to reward you?"

"Then I would rather they end my life, if only for the hope that I find favor in the eyes of Nifara once more."

"Then I do not fear for your soul," Koragh said as he rose. "Deliver your message to the Paladins. You and I will have much to discuss on the road south."

Then he left the room. Seriah rose and made her way from the room. She passed the Abecinians quarters and took the side hall that led toward the paladinial bastion. There was no guard at the door, so she slipped in and walked down the hall toward the Prima Pater's office. She passed by cells with doors cracked open. She heard Paladins within, donning armor, and others in muffled prayers of supplication to their god. She thought to whisper a prayer to Nifara, but feared her goddess might this time answer back.

She came to the door of the Prima Pater's office and knocked. No one answered. She put her hand up to knock again and the door opened. Someone stood on the other side.

"It is a Nifaran," the voice of one man said.

"Her name is Seriah Yaledít," a woman's voice said. She recognized it as the Black Sentinel, Rallia Clouw, whom she had met those months ago at the chapel in Düran.

"Let her in," an elderly voice said. "But continue to be reserved."

"Of course, Brother Unteel."

Seriah stepped into the room.

"I am Seriah Yaledít. I come bearing a message for the Prima Pater, for our order."

"The message shall be delivered to him," the voice of the elderly Paladin said.

"The message..." Seriah said, and then paused. "I cannot give the message to you. I must give the message to the Prima Pater himself. I have recently learned that I must be more aware of who I give information to, and from whom I receive it."

"Very well. Take a seat, child. Tea?"

She nodded.

"Are you well?" Rallia asked.

"Yes," Seriah said. "Why are you among the paladins?"

"Rallia is a guest of mine," the older Paladin said. "Jurgon, please see to the tea."

"What are the Paladins preparing for?" Seriah asked.

"It is not something I am able to share," the old Paladin said, "nor will Pater Koel here."

"Pater Koel? From the Bulwark?" Seriah asked.

"Indeed."

"Where have you been?" Seriah asked. "What might have happened if you had been there to escort the Archimandrite?"

"Pell Maran?" the other Paladin asked. "What of him?"

"Have you not heard?" Seriah asked. "He is dead."

"I... did not know."

"I imagine there is much you still do not know," the older Paladin said.

"Your voice," Seriah said. "It is very familiar. You traveled with us from the Green Bastion?"

"I did."

The bells chimed the beginning of the High Mass to Aben.

"It will happen soon," Jurgon said.

"Yes. I expect as much," the old Paladin replied.

Someone else placed tea in Seriah's hands. She took a sip, and held it in her lap.

"Will the Prima Pater be long?"

There was a commotion from somewhere nearby. A group of people rushed by the door. Seriah opened her mouth to speak.

"Rallia," the old man said. "Our time together tells me you are innocent. Under all this commotion, it is an ample time to escape."

Rallia touched Seriah's shoulder. "I hope your goddess blesses and protects you."

She moved across the room and out another door. At the same time, there was a loud crash in the distance. Shouts began to ring out. Then the door near Seriah creaked open. She felt the presence of several men walking in.

The youngest of her companions rushed at them, but was quickly subdued.

"He told us we'd find you here, traitor," one of them said.

They proceeded to beat Pater Koel to the ground and kick at him until he stopped moving.

Leather-gloved hands took hold of her and she made to cry out before one leather glove went over her mouth and dragged her away. She began to cry.

"Do not cry, young one," the elderly Paladin said, being dragged alongside her. "The gods are near, and hope is not lost."

50

Jail Break

I smote him in the blackness, enemy none sought.
For who doth think that man could e'er dress him.
> Did not we craft him in our lies,
> Did not we make him in our sleep.
Is he not us, and we not him?
Forsooth he is our dream. He is our heart.
> He is our seeking answers for what was
> And that which is to be.
He is our strife.
Our heroism, our tales told 'fore hearth and home.
> And he can only be brought low in blackness.
> When we look inward on our own deceits.

— **FROM THE BRONUAN TRAGEDY,** *DHAGG VENONN,*
BY ELLAM GAVALIN, DÜRANI PLAYWRIGHT

H anen and Ophedia stood in the shadows of a massive oak tree on the green, watching as members of the cloth moved toward the great cathedral to hold their long service before retiring for the evening. The Paladins in the Bastion within the Abecinian complex would be holding their own meeting soon. The bells from the cathedral also marked the changing of the guard, as Voktorra switched out at the gates to the Stone.

"Thank you for coming with me," Hanen said to the girl next to him as she gave Whisper a scratch behind the ears.

"I had nothing better to do," Ophedia said. "And I certainly wasn't going to let you go alone. You'd just end up getting caught, and then I'd have to put up with Searn giving the rest of us all of your responsibilities."

Another bell rang from across the green, the crystalline sound of a massive gong. The door to the Crysalas convent opened, but instead of white-robed women, out strode a compliment of Paladins, each wearing black cloaks over their shoulders. The light of the nearly-full silver moon, Umay, illuminated everything. A single figure led the Paladins in a long black robe.

"Let's move," Hanen said, "before those Paladins see us."

They stepped out of the shadows of the trees and quickly walked into the complex, taking a right toward the paladinial bastion. They came to the stables, and behind them came the footsteps of the group of Paladins. Hanen tensed. He was not expecting to be surrounded by Paladins so quickly in his plan.

Ophedia practically pranced at the thrill of being chased, while Whisper agreeably kept to Hanen's side.

"Find an empty stall," Hanen whispered hoarsely.

Six-footed sleipnirs snorted in the cold. One of them whinnied, and Ophedia leapt into the air.

"Here!" she shouted as she came down. She slunk into a clean stall used for keeping fresh hay. Hanen and Whisper followed and together they crouched down.

A miserable cold seemed to sweep over them as figures entered the stable area. A raspy voice spoke that sent shivers up and down Hanen's spine. Ophedia's own eyes filled with dread. The rustle of Whisper's scales would have given them away had the sleipnirs' snorts not covered the sound.

"I have selected you ten to make the initial attack. You shall not flee. You will give your lives to make the first strike. Make them wish they had known the truth we know now. I will shake hands with you again in Noccitan."

The sound of their boots echoed as they marched away, leaving only a cold in the room, which soon left in the other direction, back the way it came, letting Hanen breathe again.

"What was that?" Ophedia asked.

"It felt like that thing that saved us at the Green Bastion," Hanen said.

Ophedia gave him a furtive look.

"It spoke with the same voice, too," Hanen added.

"Whatever it was," Ophedia said, "it's gone."

"Let's go find Rallia."

Hanen snuck ahead, every sound startling him. They walked in the wake of the Paladins that had come before, each door kicked open, Some exploding off hinges. There was no one in any of the paladins' private cells.

They came to a juncture. The signs of the invading force continued ahead. Hanen took a right. Up ahead torches guttered. A single guard stood leaning against a wall with his back to them. Hanen approached softly, and then suddenly Whisper bolted on ahead into the firelight. Hanen's stomach leapt. He feared the creature had given them away, and yet the guard did not move. Hanen reached out and touched the shoulder of the Paladin, who slumped and fell over onto the ground. The inside of the Paladin's gorget was filled with blood from a slit throat. The doors of all but the last cell had been opened. The keys had been tossed to the ground nearby.

"Rallia?" Hanen whispered.

There was no answer.

"Rallia!" He called out louder.

"She's not here," Ophedia said.

"Maybe they moved her," Hanen said.

"Back to the stables?" she asked.

They moved through the corridor and came back to the stables, where they could hear bells pealing from all directions, sounding an alarm.

"I hope that's not for us," Ophedia said.

They came to the entrance to the stables and saw out in the courtyard a Paladin standing before the priests of Aben outside their cathedral doors, commanding them to return to their own cells. This one wore no cloak. Now there were other Paladins standing at the gate, looking out across the green.

"Let's see if we can find a back way out," Hanen offered.

Whisper suddenly took off running down a side corridor and turned a corner.

"That ynfald is going to get us in trouble," Hanen groaned as he went after him.

As they turned the corner Whisper was slinking through a door as it closed.

Hanen walked to the door and opened it quietly to peer into the darkness of a garden.

Archways led between various sections, and each had been swept clean of life for the winter. One garden door led into the Abecinian monastery. Ophedia peeked in a door and immediately shut it quietly.

"The halls are filled with monks," she said.

"Back the way we came," Hanen sighed. "Again."

"I think we're trapped," Ophedia said.

"Tell me something I don't know," Hanen replied.

"Don't get smart with me," Ophedia huffed. "I am just as stuck as you are."

"Don't fight," someone said from the shadows of a tree. Whisper shot out of the shadows to Hanen, and the figure of Rallia stepped out to give Hanen a smile. "Hello, brother," she said. She had a brown Paladin's robe on, and a black eye.

"What happened to you?" Hanen said, rushing forward.

"I had a mix up with a Paladin."

"The Paladins beat you?"

"One of them did. Yes."

Whisper was sniffing at a leafless rosebush. In the winter cold, with no leaves to block the view, a small door could be seen. Ophedia walked up to it and tried the latch. It opened easily and she stuck her head in.

"It's a tunnel. Maybe this'll lead us to the channels that run to the canal or something."

She slipped in, followed by Hanen. Whisper refused to enter at first, but Hanen lifted the smaller creature down. Rallia came last so the others could help her down as she still moved stiffly. Ophedia took out a candle from her satchel and struck tinder with her flint and steel to light it. She pressed down the tunnel and stopped.

"There's a set of five stairs," she said, disappearing for a few moments before she came back up out of the darkness.

"Looks like a long straight tunnel."

Hanen, Rallia, and Whisper followed, and they continued together. Ophedia found a torch mounted in a ring on the wall and it lit easily. She let the others pass her, and backlit them as they continued on.

How long they walked, they did not know. But they came to the end. As at the Abecinian garden, five stairs rose, and a short hall led to a door, this one not opening to the touch, as something leaned against the outside pushing back against Hanen as he gave it a shove.

Voices suddenly echoed from back down the tunnel. Ophedia lit her candle again, and then beat the torch against the ground to extinguish it. She gave the candle to Rallia, and then crept back down the stairs to have a look. She reemerged.

"A whole group of people heading this way," Ophedia said. "And they're marching like they know where they're going."

She joined Hanen as they pressed against the debris on the other side, which clattered as it fell around the door, opening inch by inch.

They piled into a storeroom beyond, and then shoved the debris back in front of the door as Rallia tried the door out into the hall.

"This one is locked," she said.

"Give me an axe," Ophedia said, and she took it as Hanen held his out. She placed the head under a hinge and hit the butt with a club.

The hinge popped up and out. Then she did the same to the second hinge. The door fell off the wall, making a great clatter. They all froze, but no sound of alarm came.

The hall outside was lined with whitewashed stone. The windows looked out into the cold dark night. Snow had blown away in drifts, revealing the landscape of a massive estate and garden.

"It faces north," Ophedia said, pressing close to the glass. "And I can see some glow from the city to the east. I think we're in the Crysalas convent."

"Did you see any rope in the storeroom?" Hanen asked.

"Why?" Ophedia asked.

"We could climb down out this window and escape."

"Because *that* won't sound an alarm." Ophedia rolled her eyes.

"I don't thinks it's a good idea," Rallia said, pulling up the arm of her robe to reveal welts. "It still hurts to even lift my arms."

"Shall we at least go and see if we really are stuck in here?" Ophedia asked. She took off down the eerily silent halls.

Given that none of them had ever been there, it was too easy to get lost. They heard voices and snuck toward them.

They came to a stairwell.

"Up," Rallia muttered. "Let's get our bearings."

They came to a long, round hallway with arches at regular breaks. Ophedia ranged ahead to one and looked in. She came back out and motioned that they follow. They came to the break and walked down the short hallway to a bright light. From within the balcony, they looked down into a huge hall.

Groups of Paladins with black cloaks over their shoulders stood chatting, though all seemed tense, keeping one eye on the raised platform just below where they hid in the shadow of the arch.

The door opened and a single Paladin entered, his black cloak trailing behind him. There was a limp in his step.

"You survived," a raspy voice announced from the dais. Hanen recognized it as the cold voice that spoke at the stables.

"No doubt you expected otherwise."

"You swore your loyalty without the coin upon your breast. For that, you were asked to pay dearly."

"And so I have."

"How so?"

"The payment," the Paladin said, "comes. He was given into the hands of the Coin Cloaks. They bring the captives by the passage you spoke of."

"No one calls us Coin Cloak in Mahn Fulhar with that kind of contempt," Hanen said.

"He's a Paladin from Haven, in Limae," Ophedia said.

"How do you know that?" Rallia asked.

"Searn and I were walking through the city a while back, and we saw him. Searn pointed him out, and said he's from there."

"I suppose everyone in Haven would call us that, then," Rallia replied.

"What does he mean, captives?"

"Whoever it was coming up behind us in the tunnel perhaps?"

"The Paladins," the unseen voice spoke. "Did our attack mean nothing?"

"We killed three, and of our number I remained."

"Ten of us for three of them."

"Only nine," the Paladin standing before the dais said.

"No, your own life was meant to be forfeit. I cannot afford you always dogging me and plotting some sort of betrayal."

From the dais, black tendrils of smoke reached out and sought their way toward the Paladin, who immediately dropped to his knees, his hands held up in supplication.

"Please! Don't do this. I am loyal! What more must I do to prove that to you?"

The doors at the end of the room burst open and Paladins poured in. At their lead were three paladins: Jined Brazstein, and the two Pater

Segundii. One of the Paladins carried the standard of Grissone, and all held their hammers ready for battle.

"I expected you sooner," the dark voice said, turning his attention from the Paladin groveling before him. "But I suppose you had to make sure everything was in order first."

51

Solitude

Silence reigns in the Kingdom of the Three-Eyed Judge.
—COMMON EPITAPH ON TRAITORS' GRAVES.

The scrape of her own boot startled her in the silence of the cavernous monastery. She swallowed as her heart leapt in her chest, taking a moment to breathe before continuing on. The emptiness was palpable, and she continued opening door after door, hoping to find she was not alone.

The kitchens proved to be not only cold and empty, but stripped bare of all supplies. A table near the hearth showed some signs that someone had eaten there, but the crumbs on the plate looked stale.

She came to a back hall that led to the monastery library. The shelves sat bare. The place did not look ransacked, but systematically emptied, as though it had been abandoned years ago. Katiam wondered if that were true.

Natural light lit the halls ahead. Katiam blew out her candle and walked towards it. She came out to the central hall, opened to the cloudy sky above.

The long stairs curved up and around the place, leading to the Paladinial Bastion above. No one stared down into the void below.

A wind whistled, and Katiam pulled her robe tighter around her. She walked to the foot of the stairs and prepared to climb. Perhaps she could see down the Fated Path and find that she had just missed the sisters. She knew it to be an empty hope, but a hope nonetheless.

Something caught her eye, upon a landing overlooking the chasm below, where the shattered Dweol lay. She turned and approached, not daring to let hope rise in her chest.

A beam of light broke out across the five vines, leaves budding on the ends of each. Two groups of roots lay over the edge, propping up the pod, faced downward like a skirt, as though it sat pondering the hole below. The vines, once just tendrils, rose up and around the open box. They had swollen, and were beginning to close around the cavity from which they had grown.

A sixth and central vine had formed, more stalk than vine, and was mostly hidden from view by the banister column. Katiam circled closer and saw the stalk had at its top a pink bud forming, like an unopened tulip or rose. It turned towards her, as though seeking out a presence and gave a breathy, whistling sigh. Katiam stepped out carefully into the light, while the little Rotha held up the five vines to the light, to capture diffused sunlight.

"Little Rose," Katiam said, thinking of the Matriarch's prophecy. "Do not be afraid." She laughed in relief to have found it. She reached out and took hold of the pod which already seemed larger and heavier. The roots held firm to the ground.

"Come with me, Little Rose," she said again. "We'll find you a better place to take in the sun."

At that, the little Rotha let go with its roots and came free. Katiam held it up to examine it. The whistling came from a single thorn that had formed just below the head-like bud. The five vine-like arms, with leaf-like hands, wrapped themselves around Katiam's own arm and nestled in. It seemed to sniff at Katiam constantly, taking her in as best it could.

"What is it?" a voice said. Katiam startled. Astrid Glass stepped out into the light.

"The flower?" Katiam replied. She ought to have been surprised to see the other woman, but was too taken in by the creature in her arms.

"Yes. I have been watching it for three days, unable to decide whether I should approach it."

"This is the Rotha."

"If I had realized that," Astrid said, "I might have left days ago and caught up with the others. But then, I might not have found you either."

"What do you mean?" Katiam asked.

"When the Matriarch..."

"I know that she passed," Katiam said. "I was with her when she went."

Astrid nodded. "When she passed, you disappeared entirely. We found only your clothes on the floor of your cell. It was thought that you had perhaps stolen away with the Rotha, to answer the prophecy. And so, Abbess Superioris Foi and the other leaders decided that we would abandon Precipice. Some were assigned to go to each of the Vaults, but most began the journey toward Nemen and Setera, since they are still allied with our church."

"And you?" Katiam asked.

"I agreed to stay here, as the sole guard of the dead Dweol."

"I'm glad you're here," Katiam said.

She looked down at the Rotha that continued to sniff about Katiam like a small animal, taking her in, and then breathing out through the tiny holes in the thorn.

"Where were you?" Astrid asked.

"When the Matriarch passed, I returned to my room. The Rotha here had somehow gathered up a nest of Dweol crystals around it on my bed, absorbing the energy, and growing. It touched one of them against me and I was transported to the Veld, where I journeyed for days or weeks with Sabine."

"Sabine is alive?!" Astrid gasped.

"In spirit and mind," Katiam said. "In the Veld. We traveled together to another Rosebloom, not yet tainted, which took me to the root of the Worldrose in Lomïn, where I met others who had been summoned, and Crysania herself."

Astrid gasped.

"She charged us all to continue on, and then shared something that will sound like heresy, had it not come from anyone but our goddess. The Worldrose lives, but more so lives on in the Rotha, and two others like it. The entirety of the church of Crysania was founded not for any other reason than to prepare for this day."

"Sabine lives?" Astrid said again, hardly able to believe it.

"In Dream. She has taken upon herself the mantle of protector there."

"And Crysania sent you back?"

"The Matriarch, my auntie Maeda, was there. She sent me back. To find the Rotha. And to seek its home."

"What does that mean?"

"I don't know. But I've spent the last several hours wandering and worrying that perhaps I had already failed, with everyone gone, and the Rotha stolen."

"We all thought you had stolen off with it. Esenath most particularly. She was livid. But we were told we were tearing the monastery apart for a pod with five small tendrils coming from it. Once we couldn't find it, Esenath finally agreed to leave with the others. The day after they left, I came across the Rotha down by the dead Worldrose Bloom, sitting over its remains and whistling mournfully. I didn't know what it was, and I picked it up as an act of cleaning the place of a weed. But it got rigid and began to scream in a piercing whistle. I flung it away and it almost rolled into the remains of the Worldrose. I can't imagine what would have happened if it had."

"I imagine Crysania would not have let that happen," Katiam said.

"The next day, after my ears had stopped ringing, I returned to find it had crawled up from the Worldrose and made its way like some sewer gloth, inch by inch, to where we are now."

"My understanding," Katiam said, "is this is the heir to the Worldrose. Crysania called it a Warotha. The T'Akai call it the Iwarat."

"T'Akai?"

"I met one. At the Root. She is a keeper of the Worldbloom in their lands, I think. Apparently she has the knowledge of the Warotha. I think I need to seek her out."

"That will be very dangerous," Astrid said.

"It will be," Katiam said.

"I'm the sworn guard and keeper of the Worldrose," Astrid said.

"Which means nothing now. Only the Rotha matters."

"Then I am sworn to protect the Rotha, and you, its Keeper."

"I'm glad to hear that," Katiam said.

"Let's go gather up some of the supplies the others left for me. And I bet the Paladins who had left the Bastion above will have left their own Bastion in disarray. We'll find more there."

"Where did they go?"

"I don't know," Astrid said. "We performed the cremation of the Matriarch the day after she died. When it was decided to leave two days later, the Paladins had completely abandoned the Bastion—there was not even a note left by them."

"So they left three days ago?"

"Closer to four," Astrid said. "But all in different directions."

Katiam nodded and followed Astrid to the room she had set up for herself, and together they packed up her things in a bundle to take up the Bastion and find a means of carrying it all. The light whisper of the Rotha nestled in her arms gave her hope against the equally desperate feeling that tried to overwhelm her.

Astrid put a hand on Katiam's shoulder, giving her a smile. It was, Katiam realized, the first genuine smile she had seen on Astrid since her brother had died.

"All is not lost," Astrid said. "Let's go see if we can catch up with the others."

52

Enshrouding

Does not all heresy, all treachery, have its root in deceit? Our very gods have spoken to us. This we can attest to. That the thirteen-legged god is known as, and indeed declares himself, the Deceiver, why then do we take his words as truth? That which speaks against that which has been established is suspect. Indeed, all thought since those days in which the gods passed down their lore is suspect. Instead, seek the words of the gods themselves, and deny yourself the whispers from the Deceiver.

—ST. RÄMMON, THE SAILOR PALADIN

As Jined exited the Bastion door, he saw the two Pater Segundii speaking to a ranking priest. Valér Quéton stood nearby, the standard of Grissone once more out, and polished to a shine. The brass hammer and eagle displayed atop the heavy beam of a staff flashed in the torchlight. The monk before the three of them bowed, and then disappeared into the monastery door.

"They've agreed to stay out of sight," Gallahan said to Jined. "They will only unbar their door to one who quotes *Beatus Instructi 6:7*."

"I think he just left off to look that one up," Nichal chuckled. He turned to the Paladins gathering nearby.

"Before we march off across the green," he announced, "we're to determine formation. While there are thirty of us, nearly a third of you are pacifists. You'll be taking up the rear, with Gallahan. Loïc, Cävian?"

The twins stepped forward. Cävian now had an arm in a sling, but his good arm was still free, and held his hammer.

"You two are to stand guard for the pacifists."

Both gave Nichal a look.

"I'd point out," Jined said, "the prayers that come from the two of you always seem to hold weight. You'll still be by our side, if only in spirit and prayer."

Loïc smiled.

"Where is Etienne?" someone said.

Jined turned as Dane pushed his way through the others.

"Where, I said, is Etienne?"

"Why do you ask?" Jined replied.

"What is that supposed to mean?"

"Brother Marric," Nichal said, walking up and putting a hand on Dane's shoulder plate. "Etienne Oren has fallen."

"No," Dane said, "his faith was strong. What a loss that he should die. Heretics will fall for taking him."

"They did not take him," Jined said.

Dane sneered.

"Etienne Oren," Gallahan Pír announced, "along with my own right-hand man, Aeger, have both gone over to the heretical sect we stand against. They were both Moteans."

"Then we tear down their falsehood for leading the weak-minded astray," Dane growled.

"If you are to fight for anyone," Nichal said, "fight for those who stood strong."

"Fight for Amal Yollis," Jined said.

"Amal?" Standard Bearer Quéton said.

"He gave his life," Jined said. "Never faltering. Let us fight not to tear down the falsehood, but to the protect the faithful."

A cheer went up from those around him.

"What is this you're speaking of?" a voice said from the entrance to the courtyard. The High Priest of Aben stood there in only a white robe. The head monk came scrambling out from behind him, carrying his mitre and chasubles, handing them to the younger man.

"High Priest Rigal," Nichal said.

"Pater Segundus," Rigal replied.

"In fact," Gallahan said, "Nichal Guess is acting Prima Pater."

"Acting?" Rigal said.

"Until a vote can be made at Pariantür."

"Very well," Rigal said. "Prima Pater Guess. I'd like to ask what is going on."

From around the corner, the sound of sleipnirs pounded the dirt, and ten riders entered the courtyard. The grey-clad Voktorra surrounded the King atop his own white stallion.

"Rigal," the King said, "I heard a war cheer from across the green as we rode."

"It appears," Rigal said, "that the Paladins of the Hammer, under the authority of a new Prima Pater, seek to march to battle."

The king urged his sleipnir forward to stand above the Paladin leadership.

"I'll not have fighting in my kingdom," King Erdthal said. "Most certainly not in my city."

"Whether you like it or not," Nichal said, "you have fighting on your hands."

"Explain."

"Our order has experienced a rift," Nichal said. "Members of our brotherhood have given way to a heretical teaching, and left the faith. Some even sought to use you and your own connections to betray our own. Pater Gladen of the Aerie was one of them."

"Gladen was not of your order then?"

"He practiced his treachery in secret," Nichal said. "This has been dealt with."

"Then the problem has been taken care of," the King said.

"No," Nichal said. "With the Crysalas no longer in residence at their own convent, Moteans, these heretics, have moved in under our noses, and hold the place as a bulwark against us. We prepare to march to take what does not belong to them."

"That is all well and good," the King said, "but as I said, I will not have fighting in my land, and in my city."

"Your majesty," Gallahan said, stepping forward to interrupt Nichal before he could speak. "The Abecinian Complex, and, by the same right, the Crysalas Convent, are independent states, not beholden to your laws. Thus, if battle occurs within their grounds, it is not in your country."

"Tell that to the people," the King flipped his hand, looking over at Rigal. "Will you stand for this? This complex here is yours. Will the Church of Aben stand for such?"

"There is little I can do to dissuade the Paladins from fighting here. They will need to cross your green to reach the Crysalas Convent, though. You could bar them."

"Why are we arguing over this?" Nichal said, turning to speak to Gallahan.

"What are your terms?" Gallahan asked. "If we choose to break our friendship with you, and march across the city, albeit a mere few hundred yards across an open field of grass, what are the consequences of our actions?"

The king pulled his leg over his mount, dropped to the ground, and approached the High Priest. They whispered to each other for a long while.

"What trust I have for these two men," Nichal muttered to Gallahan, "is gone."

"Do you want to finish what we set about to do?" Gallahan asked.

"Yes."

"Let me negotiate. You run the battle."

"If I don't negotiate," Nichal said, "any authority I have as Prima Pater will be pointless. And what is the point in me even being Prima Pater if I can't lead?"

"Prima Pater," Jined said, "I think they no longer respect our authority here, regardless. We need to stand together as an order. That is something they cannot deny, even if they cannot respect us."

The two men opposite turned and approached.

"Prima Pater Guess," High Priest Rigal said, "if you will recall, I mentioned I would be taking the authority of the Praetors of the Chalice under my wing. Indeed, I sent word for them to send delegates. They are expected to arrive by Spring. I am asking you to hand over the keys to your Bastion, as it will be theirs when they arrive, and the Paladins of the Hammer will be allowing them to restore the order your brotherhood has failed to keep.

"This is the first act of the military arm of the Abecinian Church. Until such a time as they arrive, you continue to hold the authority you once had within the borders of Mahndür. However, as you and the heresies within your order have failed to heal, we must ask you and your entire order to leave the countries of Mahndür, Varea, Redot, and Œron. These four countries have agreed to declare the Church of Aben as their one and only religion."

"You no longer recognize the Grissoni church?" Nichal said.

"As foreign authorities? Yes. As a religion whose schisms threaten the livelihood of everyone around them? No. We ask you take your squabbling home."

"And the Crysalas?" Gallahan added.

"I have it from a good source that the Matriarch is dead. As no one sister has returned to take command of the convent, be that from those who left with you, or from one of their secret covens, the king and I consider them and their convent forfeit."

"Forfeit?!" Nichal shouted.

The Voktorra urged their own mounts forward a step.

Nichal took a step back.

"You speak of this singular schism as threatening to all," Gallahan said. "Then you know what danger it possesses, somehow better than we understand, it would seem. But what of the four branches of your own religion?"

"Three," Rigal said. "By allying myself with the Church of the

Common Chalice in Œron, we unify two branches. Add to that, all branches have co-existed alongside each other peacefully for some time."

"And the Nifarans?"

"What of them?"

"Will you no longer recognize them?"

"I have no quarrel with them," Rigal said. "Nor do most monarchs, if we're honest. We'll be making some theological changes to the tenets of the Common Chalice, but I think that the Rose and Hammer ought to return to the east, where they came from, and let the kings of the west run their own houses."

"And you have nothing to say to this?" Nichal said, turning to the King.

The King shook his head. "I follow the path of Aben. And the High Priest is my confessor, after all. I follow his wisdom."

"His young, arrogant wisdom," Nichal muttered.

"So," Gallahan said, "if we march across the green, we forfeit our holdings?"

"You forfeit them anyway," the King chuckled. "Yes, High Priest Rigal and I have just been looking for a good opportunity to see you on your way. You'll be out by week's end, regardless of the outcome of this night."

"Then let us pass," Nichal said, and took a step forward.

The king made a motion, and the Voktorra parted

The standard bearer immediately followed, and then Gallahan, and soon every Paladin moved. Jined took up the rear, watching the smug look on the High Priest's face turn to victory.

"I doubt," Jined said, approaching the High Priest, "that your god is looking on this with favor."

The smugness faded.

"And given you've now seen Watchers come from Noccitan to address you in particular, I would have thought you'd seek to ensure your acts were that of a faithful servant, rather than one intent on ending up in the Ever-Dark."

"How dare you?" Rigal said, gripping his mitre tightly.

"No," Jined said, "how dare *you*."

The other Paladins marched on ahead of Jined, and he wondered what would become of the Paladinial Bastion, or what the King and priest would do with the convent, if they survived this night.

"You witnessed that?" Jined muttered under his breath.

Every word. Grissone said as a voice in his head.

"And do you agree with me?"

Certainly.

"Then what will Aben do about it?"

Very likely, my father will do nothing. His tenets are clear. Follow the path, and the destination will be its own reward. Humans are more than capable of discerning right from wrong. If this new unified church of Aben is rife with heresies, people will choose to follow the path laid before them, or they will not. The question is, what will you do to ensure the safety of the Order of the Hammer? Will you kill tonight?

"I will protect the faithful. I will do as you ask."

The voice in his mind did not respond.

The thorns that grew up the walls of the convent opposite the cathedral were black in the night, and the open gate to the courtyard stood as an open maw, inviting the Paladins to enter.

They moved alongside one another without words. The pacifists fell back, and the twins gave Jined a look as they passed one another—the look they had given each other plenty of times on the fields east of Pariantür, preparing to meet what may be their final fate against an enemy. They came to the main doors to the convent. Jined stepped forward alongside Nichal, and they both pushed in on oiled hinges.

"Thank you for standing alongside me," Nichal said. "We've lost too many along the way."

"You are my Prima Pater now, and you have for many years now been my commander on the field. Of course I stand by you."

"And why do you stand by me?" Nichal said, turning to the older standard bearer. "You are standard bearer, but you are pacifist."

The old Paladin gave them both a look.

"I don't stand by you, Prima Pater Guess," he smiled. "I stand by the champion of Grissone, chosen by divine ordination."

Nichal glanced over at Jined. "Then let's stand together."

The long hall sat empty. Tapestries had been removed from their places, and flowers lay dead in vases.

"They've neglected and ransacked the place," Nichal said. "They've broken their Vows, and bear no resemblance to our order."

"Then we'll reorder them," Jined said.

The door to the throne room was guarded by only two Paladins, who watched them approach with glazed eyes.

Suddenly, the two of them lunged out and toward them, closing the gap in a few strides. They did not cry out in alarm nor battlecry, but they charged Nichal with their hammers.

Nichal thrust his own out and struck the face of one, sidestepped, and hit the other from behind. They both fell.

From a side door, five more Paladins came running out and placed themselves in front of the door.

"Open the door, Jined," Nichal said.

Jined felt a hand on his shoulder and turned to see Cävian. He winced as he lifted the hand in the brace. He still held the orb of twisted metal.

"Turn their own weapon against them?" Jined asked.

Cävian nodded.

Jined took it up and turned toward the black-clad Paladins. These did not have the dead look of those under sway from the gauntlet. These were brothers turned traitor by choice.

"Jined," Nichal said. "The door."

Jined gritted his teeth, lifted the Hammer-that-was-Grissone, and tapped the orb. It began to thrum with power. He tossed it in a long arc toward the door. Their opponents watched it come down in their midst. One looked up at Jined for a split second, horror across his face. The explosion threw the men in every direction, and the door swung open violently into the great hall beyond.

Gallahan Pír stepped up next to the two of them. "My prayers will support you."

Nichal nodded.

As they entered, forty Paladins wearing black cloaks stood about in small groups, looking on in shock. The dais on the far end was filled with shadow, and nothing could be seen within the inky blackness.

A voice of pure malevolence spoke from the far end.

"I expected you sooner, but I suppose you had to make sure everything was in order first."

"We're now well-outnumbered," Jined muttered.

"But not outclassed," Nichal added.

And not alone, Grissone said, alongside the pounding of his heart.

* * *

Panic settled over Seriah as they handed her down the stairs. The place smelled damp, and the cold of the tunnel ate at the clammy sweat of fear that clung to the insides of her robe.

"Now the old man," a voice ahead said, reverberating down the length of the space.

"Would you explain the meaning of this?" the old man next to her said calmly.

"Why would we do that?"

"You enter a paladinial Bastion and kidnap an older Paladin and a blind monk. You all are companions to a traitor. I think we deserve to know why we're being handled so."

"We owe you no explanation."

Seriah heard struggling as they fought to bring down the limp form of the third victim.

"No need to be cruel," the older man said.

"He's a traitor," one of them said.

"I should imagine the same can be said for the four of you."

Seriah felt one of their captors rush forward, and then stop before her companion.

"Stop, Scribe," another said, "the bearer said no harm was to come to him."

"I heard a rumor that each of you took names as part of the brotherhood," the older man said. "Why is that?"

"We're not going to answer you," Scribe said.

"Very well."

"Foresworn," Scribe hissed, "a light up ahead."

"Maybe someone was sent to meet us at the other end."

"Only the four of us know of this tunnel."

"It went out," another said.

"Someone is down here who ought not to be."

The four captors goaded them along for what felt like an eternity. The old man started humming a hymn, ignoring the protests of the man shoving him along.

"Go up and check and see if whoever held the light is still there."

She heard steps as someone went on ahead and ascended stairs.

"Something is in the way," a voice called back down from a tight space above.

"Like the door is locked?"

"No, as in someone has shoved debris in the closet down front of the door."

"So shove through," Scribe called. "Shroud wants them brought before him."

"Why me?" Seriah croaked.

"I would imagine it is because you were with me," the old man said tenderly. "I'm sorry."

They heard the shifting of rubbish, followed by clattering, and then hollering.

"I'm alright," the man called. "Bring them up."

"Go, old man," one of them said. Then another took Seriah's arm and forced her up the stairs.

Behind her, she heard the groans of the third captive coming to.

"Brother Avice," the waking man muttered.

"Silence, Koel," Scribe said.

"I recall," the old man said, "a Brother Avice who was stationed at the Bulwark ten years ago. Sent to audit them, after the Prima Pater visited when he last toured the continent."

"How do you know that?!" Scribe shouted.

"When did you become so angry?" the old man asked. "When did you lose your faith?"

"Be quiet!" Scribe shouted.

"Keep your voice down, and your hands off the old man," Foresworn said. "Shroud wants him unharmed. I think you can control your anger another few minutes, can't you?"

Scribe sighed.

"Bring the monk," Foresworn said.

Rough hands hoisted her up the stairs, through a confined space, and into an echoing hall. They sat her down on cold marble, and then the old man next to her.

"I'm sorry you got mixed up in all this," he said.

"What is all this, though?" Seriah asked.

"We Paladins are going through a schism. And those who oppose Prima Pater Guess have made their first move and taken me, and those near me, hostage."

"Why?"

"We traveled together on the road, if only for a few short weeks. I thought perhaps you might recognize me by my voice."

"Your voice is familiar, but I haven't given it much thought," Seriah said. "But you said Prima Pater Guess, which implies the old Prima Pater is dead."

"Not dead. Only in hidden retirement. But it seems my presence is known by the Moteans, and I'm being summoned."

"Oh no," Seriah said. "It's the dark figure."

"Shroud they called him."

"No," Seriah said, panic welling up again. "He's come for me too, then."

"What do you mean?"

"I can't be here," she said. "I'm not ready."

"Calm, child. The gods protect."

"Not those who have betrayed them, though."

* * *

"You are commanded to stand down, and submit to our authority!" the Paladin at the front of the new arrivals shouted.

Hanen observed as they fell into a semi-formation. At the rear, eleven of the Paladins, including their head scribe, stood close to one another. Their hammers remained at their belt, save for two that stood on either side as guards. The remaining Paladins split into two small squads of six, with the Paladin commanding surrender at the front, with the hulking figure of Jined Brazstein and the elderly Standard Bearer on either side of him.

"And why should we?" the dark unseen voice called.

"You wear paladinial armor. You will submit to the authority of your Prima Pater."

"I see no Prima Pater."

"I am the Prima Pater," the Paladin said.

A general murmur of laughter came from several in the room down below.

"I count thirty of you. A third of you can't fight. Won't fight. It is you who will submit to us."

"If you will not reason," the Prima Pater said. Hanen recognized him now as one of the Prima Pater's right-hand men, the Pater Segundus Nichal Guess. "Then we have no recourse but to drag you back to Pariantür in chains."

"If you value the lives of those you hold dear, you'll stand down."

A door at the side of the room opened, and four Paladins shoved three figures through. They were forced to their knees.

A shadow flooded out from the dais below. It was a figure, wreathed in shadow—the figure from the glade at the Green Bastion—only more so now. He knew now what it was the figure wore. The cloak on the figure's frame was Searn's Bone Shroud.

Whisper whimpered next to him, and Ophedia gasped.

The figure stopped and held up a hand, encased in some oversized gauntlet of black metal.

"What is it I have here?"

The Paladins stood stock still, watching as he stepped toward the three captives.

"A beaten down Paladin. One I even recognize from the days of my youth. Pater Koel of the Bulwark, is it? A traitor to our own cause, and one who has thrown off the dominion of the gauntlet. But, more importantly, a monk of Nifara."

The monk was openly weeping, and recoiled as the figure held out a hand to touch the top of her head.

"In fact, if I didn't know better, I would think this is the one who is rumored to have seen me take the life of her Archimandrite. She dodged death that day."

Then he stood before the brown-robed old man, who looked up at him stoically. Hanen recognized him a second before Rallia did, as his sister touched his shoulder and gripped hard.

"That's..."

"Unhand the Prima Pater," Nichal Guess shouted.

"But," the figure said, "I thought you were the Prima Pater."

There was no dark laughter, only the statement as the black clad figure uncovered the man's lie.

"It appears I hold all the pieces. You are outnumbered, and I offer you the chance to avoid destruction and turn from the Order of the Hammer to that of the Gauntlet."

He held up his gauntleted fist.

"We would rather die," Nichal announced as the Paladins opposing them, each wearing black cloaks, fell into their own formations.

"Four groups of ten," Rallia muttered. "Forty against a smaller force of only twenty fighters."

"Two to one," the figure announced. "That hardly seems fair. Let's tip the scales to a better set of odds."

He waved his hands and two more side doors opened. Peak-hooded figures entered from each side. Each Black Sentinel brandished their clubs and axes.

"Traitors," Rallia hissed.

"No," Hanen said, "following the gold. And, if my guess is right, then one of them is Searn. He's here to reclaim what is his."

"What is that supposed to mean?" Rallia said, looking at him.

"Searn confided in me that years ago, someone, I can only assume that dark figure there, stole something of his. He's been working to get it back. The Black Sentinels are here under his command, to take it."

"What is it?" Rallia asked.

"A Bone Shroud," Hanen said. "I'll explain later."

"But Searn had..." Ophedia said, but then stopped herself.

The sentinels fell into formation, a single line of warriors between the black-clad Paladins and those who stood against them.

Suddenly, the beaten prisoner, Pater Koel, stood and rushed toward the dark figure. The cloak itself suddenly splayed open, whipping out and batting the man aside like a rag doll. He flew twenty feet and fell still.

"First blood is mine," the figure called, turning back to the Paladins before him.

The Paladin Jined Brazstein took a step forward from Nichal Guess and held his hammer up in both hands before him as a holy icon.

"No more pretense. No need for a full battle," he announced. "I banish you and the evils you bear. By the name of Grissone, god of man and faith—I strip you of your power!"

The hammer in his hand began to glow bright white.

Then the light focused and burst forth, scathing the black cloak from the figure, peeling it back layer by layer.

"Can Paladins do that?" Ophedia asked.

It left only a man wearing a long-hooded cloak made of mail the color of bone. As he stood up, his hood fell back from his face, revealing Searn VeTurres, creator and bearer of the Bone Shroud.

53

Prayer

Light dwindled.
The storm raged.
All was changed.
The world crack'd.
His wrath fell.
Havoc sundered all.

—LAST LINES IN THE POEM BY HRYLIAN POET
LORU *TA* ROSHEP, *DESTRUCTION, DESTRUCTION*

Jined ought to have been surprised to see the face of the head of the Sentinels under the black shroud, which was now nothing more than a rag of bone-colored material worn like a tight suit of mail across his frame. The man stood, wiping blood from his nose, and staring at him darkly.

The blackness that had clung to the cloak, the inky evil that had stripped the flesh from Amal Yollis, was now splattered across the walls, dripping like blood in an abattoir.

Searn stood, held up the gauntlet still in his hand, opened the palm, and pressed it toward Jined. The Sentinels in front lurched forward.

"They're under his sway, then," Jined said.

So it would seem. Grissone said.

"Then you can see him now? See what is happening?"

For a time. Although, the shadow seems to be returning. I see metal coins hanging from leather straps on the necks of the black-cloaked Sentinels.

"Perhaps he bought their loyalty."

Perhaps.

"Grissone, be my blessing," Jined stated as he stepped forward and swung the hammer in a wide arc. Without even touching the advancing Sentinels they flew back, each struck across the gut by an invisible hammer. They fell, strewn across the ground as rag dolls. The other line of Sentinels that sought to close around Jined hesitantly backed away.

Their faltering gave the Paladins on each side of Jined's flanks the urging they needed. Rushing from behind, they charged the heretical Moteans headlong.

To his left, they clashed into one another and fell to exchanging brutal blows. On the right, the charging Paladins suddenly lurched forward, backed—Jined could tell—by the supplications of Gallahan and his praying choir.

Jined pressed toward Searn; Nichal rushed to fight alongside him. Another figure came up on the other side. Jined turned to see Dane, a look of earnest hatred plastered across his face.

"To the Prima Pater," Jined said to him.

Dane nodded and took off toward the old man on the ground. The hail of hammer swings from Dane made quick work of those standing guard over Dorian and the monk. Then, he turned and gave those approaching a look that might have withered Jined if he had stood against the arrogant man.

Cries of distress came from the back of the room, and Jined turned to see a group of Sentinels sneaking around toward the choir of pacifist-vowed Paladins. Valér Queton fell back to their rescue, holding his standard high as a rally point. Several other Paladins broke rank and ran alongside him.

"Go," Jined said to Nichal, who nodded and fell back, leaving Jined alone.

Loïc and Cävian were there, standing against fifteen Sentinels who were swinging at them with axe and club. The Sentinel Hanen Clouw, the leader under Searn, was nowhere to be seen, and likely off preparing something even darker. Jined looked around to see if they waited in shadows, crossbows at the ready to assassinate them, and saw a group of figures huddled in an upper balcony, watching the proceedings.

There was a cry of alarm from several, and Jined turned back to see the form of Gallahan Pír crumple as a Sentinel lifted his axe to bring it down on his unmoving form a second time.

The standard bearer, old Valér Queton, screamed in rage and thrust his standard violently past the twins and those who assailed them, into Gallahan's attacker. He pulled it from the body and shoved it into the hands of Cävian.

"You bear this now. My Vow is broken. I die in the service of Grissone!" Valér screamed. He took his hammer from his belt, turned, and rushed headlong through the halls towards Searn, gaining more and more speed, his faith propelling him forward.

As Jined watched, wisps of blackness coalesced back to Searn one by one. Half had already done so. The rate at which they returned to his frame, flying off the walls to rejoin him, increased until, as Valér came within only a few strides, Searn was once more enwreathed in a shroud of evil blackness.

Valér cried in rage and dropped his hammer, taking Searn's throat in his hands, and began to throttle him. Searn laughed, and the blackness about him flayed open in tentacles. Then they whipped around violently before enclosing around Valér and Searn in a storm of shadow.

They both fell to the ground in a heap.

The room stood silent. Jined heard Nichal take a deep breath to give the command to charge, and then faltered as the black cloak rose unnaturally. Searn opened up the front of his cloak to reveal only the armor and bones of Valér Queton, faithful even to death, and now reduced to nothing.

"Let all who dare to oppose me stand this night before the Judge in Noccitan," Searn said. "Tell your god that his end is nearing."

He held the gauntlet pointed at Jined. The shades began to surge forward. He saw faces, screaming behind silken cloths of nothing, surging forward to feed on his soul, begging him to join them.

"Tell him yourself!" Jined cried, holding out his hammer toward the enemy. Bright white light flowed endlessly. Unlike the tenebrous rays that split clouds and illuminated a painter's landscape, this was a pillar of divinity piercing the black flow of souls. The beam met the shades, though they pressed forward like water from a hole in a dam. Try as the pillar of Grissone's divinity might, it gained no more ground, nor did Searn's rush of shades.

The shades began to creep around the horizontal pillar of light, threatening to consume it, nearing Jined, like clawing, scrambling, plague-ridden pests. Their forms were becoming more individual. The shades of thousands and thousands of vermin could be seen in the horde of evil, and not a few faces of people.

"I need something else," Jined whispered to himself, to Grissone. "Faith!" He shouted, and a bubble seemed to pop around him in a sudden relief. Shades pummeled themselves against it, but could not reach their victim. Jined began to trudge forward, his own strength now pressing into the black throng. Each step now harder, and heavier. He saw stars in his vision, and fell to his knees.

He seemed to be in another place. He was looking down at his hammer, held preciously in his hands.

"I do not know what else to do."

You can take deeper faith.

"Can't you smite him? Strike him down?"

Not only would I not do such a thing, it seems I cannot. It falls to you.

"I do not know that I can take on the burden another Vow will require of me."

Is that truly a concern of yours? Here, as you face certain death? This is what faith is. Pressing yourself past what you think you can accomplish, toward that which you believe can be done. Have faith—greater faith than you knew you possessed.

"As you command, my god. I believe you."

He stood still, holding up his hammer high against the darkness. He turned to Nichal and then looked at Dorian, and began a shout of declaration:

"Prima Pater, my words shall hence forth be my prayer! No utterance shall come that bears vulgarity. From this day forth my thoughts shall be prayers, and my words a supplication. I take, therefore, the Vow of Prayer, effective immediately and without end."

As before, his cordons changed color, to the black of a Primus. Three vow beads sat along the cordons: Chastity, Poverty, and now the Anka's wing for the Vow of Prayer.

His vision seemed to fill with newness. He saw the movement of the Paladins and their enemies in slow, exact detail. Dorian was smiling and nodding. Dane's eyes grew in astonishment and a hint of envy. Jined waded directly into the flow of darkness, strode up to the dark figure, and struck Searn down with his hammer. The hammer, glowing brightly, cut through the shades, revealing the mail. Jined struck again, and the figure flew back ten feet and onto his back. As he attempted to stand, the shades hung on him limply, as though he wore a cloak that had been doused in rain.

* * *

"How is that Searn?" Rallia asked. "What is happening?"

"It seems he got back what was his," Hanen said.

"What does that even mean?" Rallia pleaded.

"Searn was a Paladin in his youth. He left their ranks in search of that cloak. To create it. And then it was stolen and turned for evil. Perhaps gaining it back has infected him somehow?"

"It was never stolen," Ophedia said. Hanen and Rallia turned to regard the girl. "He had it at the Bastion in the woods. I know because I caught him working on it, putting the...souls of furies into it, I guess."

"Why didn't you say so before?" Hanen said.

"He asked me not to. Don't you see what it does? How could I and think he would spare me?"

They turned back. The Paladin Jined was staring up at them, and then turned to see one of the older Paladins fall. The standard bearer handed off his icon, and then turned and charged across the room, tackling Searn. There was a storm of black shadow, and Searn revealed what remained of the old Paladin.

"That's why I didn't dare oppose him," Ophedia said. "I didn't want to become that. Why else do you think I spend most of my days away from Blackiron? To stay away from that."

The Paladin Jined cried something, and another beam of light issued from his hammer, and was met by the black shades of Searn. They pushed against one another, and a bubble of light shielded Jined from the assault. It popped, and Jined's armor began to glow white. He charged forward toward Searn and began beating shades from the air with great scything swings. Fragments of shades exploded from the shroud and skittered about, like an ynfald losing his legs to fright. Some of them flew into torches on the wall and dissolved. Then others that remained flew back to the wearer, quickly coalescing.

"Let's leave," Hanen said. His tone was dark.

"What?" Rallia asked.

"I said let's leave. This isn't our fight."

"Not our... Hanen. Do you hear yourself? That's Searn down there, cloaked in some sort of cape of darkness." She motioned rigidly toward the floor below. "He's murdering Paladins. He's stripping them of their flesh. He has Nefer Seriah and that old man, the Prima Pater, captive!"

"We can't take sides. It's time we leave—make a fresh start."

"We can't just leave!" Rallia growled through gritted teeth. She shoved Hanen up against the wall. Whisper skittered away and looked up in shock. "He's turned those Sentinels, those who we would then ask to serve alongside us, against Paladins, who stand for good."

"Do they?"

"Where is this even coming from?"

"You wouldn't understand."

"I'm not an idiot," Rallia said, "I'm your sister. How about you say what you're thinking?"

"We could go down there and side with Searn. If he wins, what will happen? I don't know. But the use of that shroud will be continual trouble as others come to oppose him. If he loses, we lose, because the Paladins will arrest us. Maybe even execute us. But let's say we side with the Paladins. Alright, we win. We have now killed the head of our organization. You don't think we'd be hunted down to the ends of the earth by Sentinels? We would. But let's say we lose. And Searn down there wins. He'll string us up, or worse."

"I can't believe you're even weighing the consequences and trying to decide who you'd side with. Is it even a question?" Rallia implored.

"Who would *you* side with, Rallia?" Hanen asked, seriously curious.

"The Paladins. Of course."

"Why?"

"Searn is wearing a cloak that strips those opposing him to nothing but bones. He's forced the Sentinels to side with him by some other dark means, whether by coin, or by the motions he's been making with that gauntlet. He said so himself." Rallia stood up. "I'm going down there, whether you're with me or not. I will not throw my lot in with a man in collusion with the dark gods. I'd rather die fighting him."

"Fine," Hanen said. If he could take possession of the shroud, he could use it to hide himself from his father's curse. Perhaps use it to protect Rallia, too.

Ophedia sighed and followed them to a set of stairs descending to the room below.

A Black Sentinel came blindly rushing through, saw them, and attacked without thought. Rallia rushed and lifted her leg and stomped him in the chest, throwing him against the wall. They took his hand axes.

"Ophedia," Hanen said, "grab torches from the wall and begin lighting them. As many as you can find. I have an idea."

They walked into the hall. Paladins were pressing hard against their enemies. Searn stood recovered from the blow and now raised his gauntlet. His allies, regardless of whether they were falling back, suddenly lurched forward, stood together, and began to press—moving like puppets on strings.

Jined struck at him again. This time it visibly shook Searn, who fell to a knee. He looked over at the form of a Paladin, crawling to stand up from a blow to his head. Shades coalesced and reached out to enshroud the dying man. He fell in a heap, and the shades returned, glutted with some sustenance, and surrounded Searn once more. He stood, unfazed by Jined's attack.

"Does it tire you, to know that no matter how many times you strike me, I will continue to stand? I cannot be stopped. So long as one shade remains upon me, I will continue. I will march into the throne-room of the gods, and strike each down, one by one."

Searn hesitantly circled away from Jined, putting himself between Jined and Dorian. Dane rushed forward to attack the man from behind. The cloak swung out in a single arm and swatted Dane away, throwing him skidding across the marble. He turned and considered the old Prima Pater and monk.

Seriah was crouched over, holding the sides of her head and screaming uncontrollably.

"You saw?" Rallia cried. "Now do you agree? He just consumed that Paladin and now he's threatening the Prima Pater and Seriah. I have to help."

"I don't disagree," Hanen said. "We need to take him down quickly. You can comfort your friend there when this is over."

A blur moved across the opposite wall. It rammed into a Motean inching up to retake Dorian. The heretic went flying, and the blur stopped. It was one of the silent twins. Then he looked directly at the Clouws, along with Ophedia, gathering up torches. He rushed at them, moving at an inhuman speed. Hanen held up a sign of peace, and the Paladin stopped in front of them.

"We're friends," Hanen said. The Paladin looked at them with suspicion.

Suddenly, a tentacle of blackness shot out from Searn and wrapped around the legs of a now-dead traitor Paladin, swinging the body at the Jined in the center. The large Paladin, Jined, fell as the armored body crashed into him.

"Take these. I think fire might help," Hanen said. Loïc nodded, took two, and stepped away. Hanen walked out toward Searn. He held a blazing torch in each hand.

"Searn!" Hanen said. He could feel the heat of the torches Rallia and Ophedia held behind him.

The man sheathed in black turned to consider them.

"Hanen," he said, "do not interfere. You found your sister, I see. But why did you bring *her*?" he said, looking to Ophedia.

"You need to stand down," Hanen said. "You've done enough damage."

"How little you understand. I hope one day you will."

A Paladin, the other twin, it seemed, had come to the front and was kneeling next to Jined to help him up with the hand that wasn't holding a metal standard.

"What are you doing?" Hanen asked.

"What I always meant to do. Toppling the powers that be. It is my purpose. And it has been since I was a small boy. They must fall if we're to pick up the pieces and move forward."

"You continue to spout lies," Hanen said. "It seems that every time I turn you say something else that contradicts what you said before."

"Like a father teaching a child. You can't explain things as they are. No one is ever ready for it."

"I am not a child," Hanen said.

"Dark One!"

Searn spun to see Jined standing again. The Paladin holding the banner stood next to him. The old man, Dorian, hobbled up to stand with them, Nichal Guess, the new Prima Pater, propping him up.

"You have much to answer for," Jined said.

The Paladin with the standard struck the banner on the flagstone. Those around him took hold of the pole. A light appeared above it, and it grew into the form of an eagle with four wings. It screeched, looked around blindly, unable to see Searn. Searn braced as the screech pushed him back. Jined charged Searn. He swung with the hammer and a great explosion came out from the impact, flashing bright-white. All the light went out of the hammer, and a being seemed to hang there above the two of them, and then float up toward the eagle. The eagle and man faded away from sight, leaving all those watching in awe. Searn collapsed on the ground. The Bone Shroud lay wide open on the ground now, barely clinging to his frame.

"Even the gods flee from what I've made," Searn spat.

"Now!" Hanen shouted. The blur of Loïc appeared with them, and they formed a circle around Searn and Jined with torches in their hands. As shades shot back toward the bone shroud, they swung out with torches, swatting them away like pests. The first ones burnt into nothingness when contacted by the flame. Other shades began to circle, and then more, until the shades swung into a wide vortex, circling the four of them faster and faster, seeking a way into the inner circle of enemies now keeping them from their shroud.

Searn looked up. "What are you doing, Hanen? Have you no loyalty?"

"Why would I have loyalty to you? All you ever did was tell me lies."

"You tell lies to those you love," he said. "To those you see like a son."

Jined stood above him now, his hammer held ready to strike.

Searn spoke through exhausted lungs. "You tell one you want them to be your apprentice, when all you want is a daughter kept close, so she will not be exposed to the darkness that drives you."

Ophedia gasped.

"You tell another they have a purpose, to organize a petty trade route, when you're simply preparing them for a greater service. That of leadership. Inheritance."

"It is time to stop spinning your lies now, Searn. You've done enough harm."

"No. Not enough. I am not done yet."

He took out a four-inch needle of bone.

"I will speak with you soon," Searn said. He drove the spike through his own eye with such force it disappeared entirely.

The surprise of the action caught them all off guard. They ignored the shades as they slipped past them and entered the shroud again. The cloud of black did not reappear. The shroud simply lay there, a mantle of bone, clinging feebly to the body of a dead man.

Hanen turned to Rallia and Ophedia. "There. He's gone. And we're out of work. The Sentinels are finished."

54

Aftermath

And so the path continued,
He bid comp'ny adieu,
Onward, upward, off to find,
Some rest on fields of dew,
On road ever anew.

— *THE TRAVELER*, THE EPIC POEM
BY JUREN LEIFSEN OF MAHNDÜR

The few remaining Sentinels and traitor Paladins fled the hall. Paladins moved to pursue, but their leaders called them back, gathering around Cävian. They were pointing up above the standard and speaking of their god in hushed tones of awe.

They had easily lost half their number in the fight. Hanen focused on counting survivors, rather than focus on the body of his dead mentor lying in front of him. Rallia had gone over and tried to comfort the monk who sat blankly in silence. Her screaming faded away, leaving nothing but weariness.

"You seemed to have arrived out of nowhere," the old man, Dorian Mür, said as he approached. "And with just the right idea."

"We watched the whole thing. It made sense. So I acted."

"You're Sentinels, though, so you'll be needed for questioning."

"How dare you!" A Paladin with a look of disgust approached them, pointing his gloved finger at Rallia. "You were our prisoner."

"An escaped convict, eh?" Dorian said. "What was she meant to have done, Dane?"

"She was arrested by us at St. Nonn. She has been colluding with the heretics."

"I think her actions speak loudly. Let's not be pointing fingers just yet. You may go, Marric."

"He gave me those welts and the black eye," Rallia mentioned quietly to her brother.

Hanen gritted his teeth.

"May I ask a favor of you?" Dorian said to the two Clouws. "Stay your hand. I'll make things right. In the meantime, I'd like your help. I want to move the body of Searn back to the bastion."

"The King and High Priest Rigal may not allow us to move back to the Bastion after this," Nichal Guess said, approaching.

"We know a secret way," Hanen said.

"It was you ahead of us in the tunnel, then?" Dorian asked.

Rallia nodded. "Just trying to find a way out of the Bastion after you told me to go."

The silent twins helped Hanen and Rallia gather up Searn's body and go ahead of the rest of the Paladins through the tunnel.

They laid the body in one of the cells, and then left to return to Blackiron.

None of them said anything as they walked past the Voktorra, eyeing them suspiciously as they passed by. They entered Blackiron and closed the door behind them. Whisper stayed by the door, refusing to go further.

"Ophedia," Hanen said, drawing the three of them around the map and figures Hanen had spent the entire season preparing.

"No. I don't need to hear it from your mouth. I heard what Searn said. It makes sense."

"You should leave," Hanen said.

"And leave you two to have all the fun with these paladins? No. I expect they'll be taking you in chains. If I'm Searn's daughter, they'll want me too. I don't need them chasing me. I'll come willingly. Maybe I'll learn a thing or two about my old man as I go."

She walked off toward her bunk. "I always wondered why he never made a pass at me."

Hanen turned back to Rallia.

"She's right," Rallia said. "We need to go with the Paladins willingly. They're going to have plenty of questions. You have enough information in your figures. Maybe they hold plans Searn had intended to set in motion. You're the only one that can make sense of them."

"I don't know anything," Hanen said.

"I understand. But they think you do, so we oblige them. Maybe we can undo some of the damage he did. If anything, it'll give us some distance from what happened here."

"I need to go to sleep," Hanen said.

"Me too. But I need to walk outside a bit first."

Rallia left. Hanen went to his bunk. A black sentinel cloak was folded up on Hanen's bed. He touched it and felt something within. He opened the folds. Two books, each bound by a buckle, fell out.

One was bound in a freshly-oiled brown leather. He opened the buckle and opened the front page to an inscription, recently written.

Hanen,

This is my journal. It will explain the journey that led me to this day. And it will guide you on the steps you must now take. I leave this to you, and not Ophedia, because I know what you are made of now. I know you will finish what I started. Before you read this journal, though, and before you read the other book I have left here for you, you must obtain the shroud for yourself. Do not read the other book without the shroud upon your shoulders. It will protect you from the gods and from their influence. Only then will you know that the actions you take are your own, and not the will of others.

—Searn VeTurres

Hanen scoffed and took the other book in his hand. It was wrapped in cracked and dusty paper. Tearing open the paper, he held the leather-bound book in his hand. It was well crafted. It bore the leather working of a zvolder's web. He opened the clasp and then the cover. Something fell out onto the floor and clattered. He negligently reached down and picked the object up, and then read the title page.

~ *The Book of Ollistan Gœrnstadt.*

Hanen shut the book quickly, latched the clasp, and threw it onto the bunk. Ollistan Gœrnstadt, his great-great-grandfather, the Apostate, instigator of the Protectorate Wars, Disciple of the Deceiver, Achanerüt. His fingers played with the long slender object in his hand. He looked down at the long needle of bone. The same one Searn had thrust through his own eye. He stood up and let it drop onto his bed.

Words in blood appeared along the length of the bone, which was flat, like a sail-cloth needle. The words read, *Retrieve the Shroud. It's yours.* The words faded into the bone.

*　*　*

"What was it those coins did to us?" Aurín asked.

Ophedia took a long drink of ale and stared at the man across from her. He had a bandage over his head, and one of his arms in a sling. He wore brown travel clothes now, though he still wore an axe hanging from his belt.

"How should I know ?" she said. "Searn asked I give that package to you at the Dark Stave, and then I returned to Blackiron where Hanen asked me to help him break Rallia out of the Paladin prison cells."

"We're making friends on every side, aren't we?"

"So it would seem."

"Where are you going to go?"

"Unlike you, I was left under the paladins' watchful eyes. I can't leave town until they finish questioning me, and I'd imagine the Voktorra will have questions, too. Better to stay and give them what they want. You?"

"I'm going to go to Haven and report to the Sentinel council there of Searn's death. Maybe I can go off and disappear into the East, or stay in Haven. What was the point of all this?"

"I don't know," Ophedia said. "I guess Searn said he wanted to kill the gods or something."

"Sounds like madness to me. But then, the way I had no control over what I was doing when we marched against those paladins?"

Aurín finished off his drink and then started in on the spare the barmaid had left.

"Drink to forget?" Ophedia said, raising her own.

"To forget," Aurín said.

*   *   *

Jined sat on the edge of his bed. The hammer in his hand was dull, made only of metal now. He had held his god a few short hours before. Now the weight of three Vows sat on his shoulders. The Vow of Chastity he was comfortable with; he had lived with it long enough. It would take years to understand the weight of the Vow of Poverty. But now he had the Vow of Prayer. His every word would be directed at his god.

"It is not such a bad thing, the Vow of Prayer." Grissone said from across the room. "I don't understand why more don't take it. It is not my will that I force anyone to take any Vow in particular. Each must make their own decision. But I suspect most do not take it because they fear their solitude would be invaded."

"Will it be any different than the conversations we have now?" Jined asked.

"No. Though for a time, it will be you speaking, and I will not be responding. I can't be in all places at once, you understand."

"You have other things that need attending to."

"Such is my lot."

"It is funny to hear you speak so informally."

They did not speak for a time.

"I am called to take them all, aren't I?"

"As I said, it is not my will to force any particular Vow on anyone."

"Very well. Then what is your will?"

"You have always been direct, Jined Brazstein."

"I think I can safely say you won't smite me down for speaking so. I suspect you have a plan?"

"Yes. You will travel back to Pariantür. You must retrace your steps. There is much happening that you will need to unravel. The Deceiver is playing the strings of his web like a lyre. It is causing great discord."

"Very well. Grissone?"

Grissone looked Jined directly in the eye.

"Thank you. For choosing me. It is an honor to serve you."

He was alone in his cell once more.

* * *

Rallia walked along the street. It was the middle of the night, and though the cold made her wounds ache, she breathed deeply. She was free. She was not locked up in a dungeon, nor under arrest, nor even as guest to the old Prima Pater. She was not being sent on what was obviously a wild mission to get her out of the way.

"The lonely strolls of a Clouw," a voice said. A tall, languid figure stepped out from an alley. He bore a long leather-covered staff, and his tail flipped around behind him.

"Ymbrys?" Rallia said, with a smile that turned into a grimace with the pain of her blackened eye.

"Yes. It is I," the qavyl said.

"What are you doing up here in Mahndür?"

"I have been searching for someone. But I seem to have found them. Now my travels shall take me elsewhere."

"It seems we'll be moving on ourselves."

"Do tell."

"Searn betrayed the Sentinels. As it turns out he's been involved in some dark dealings. It might not be my place to say, though."

"I think you'll find you can trust me," he said.

"I don't know who I can trust anymore."

"Have you ever heard of a qavylli trust pact?"

Rallia shook her head.

"It was given to the qavylli by their god, Lae'zeq. All of the gods have six wings. His were made of the pages of wisdom. He made a trust pact with his people by tearing a page out of the book of wisdom, and smearing his own blood on it. Then, cast to the fire, the pact was made."

"I'm not shedding any more blood this day," Rallia said.

"No. You don't understand. Lae'zeq shed his own divine blood. Only the one making the promise sheds their blood. The one receiving the promise sheds nothing. I would make this pact with you if it meant I would learn this truth you will share. It will help me on my journey. It will tell me what I hope to learn."

"You're speaking in riddles."

"But I do not speak in lies."

"What are you proposing?"

"I want to hear the story of what happened tonight. I will swear a qavylli trust pact with you. If I ever betray you, I give you my life."

Rallia pondered the offer. She got the merest inkling that the words Ymbrys spoke were truer than any words ever spoken.

"That you would stake your life on events of a single night seems odd. But, given what I saw tonight, not so odd."

The qavyl looked at her with his large eyes, waiting.

"I will take your word. I will not ask you to take this oath you offer. My word is itself the greatest thing I can offer, and I expect others to hold to the same level of trust."

"Rallia Clouw, your act of trust does not go unnoticed. May the gods bless you for your trueness."

Rallia described the events of the night as she saw them. From Hanen breaking her free, to watching Searn lead the enemies of the

Paladins against them, to the power held in the hands of Jined Brazstein and the appearance of an eagle.

"Then Grissone and Anka were both present."

"I'm sorry?"

"Grissone, the god of men. Of Paladins, I should say. He is not one, but two. Grissone and Anka, the four-winged eagle, are of one soul but separate. If they were both there, then the full force of Grissone was present. And yet, it was your simple torches that defeated Searn, not a god in the flesh. I find that interesting. And you say the body of Searn is now resting in the hall of the paladins?"

"I also bear a message from an old man I met on a beach near Verír. He implied he was greater than a mere man, though."

"Oh? What did he say?"

"We shared a fish together, and he asked that if I ever were to meet you again, that I tell you the following:

"Tell the War Breaker that Aben speaks: The Father wishes to converse. The Sister fears something that moves. The Mother is half blinded. The Brother has a wound."

Rallia took out the stick she had kept, and presented it to Ymbrys.

"What is this?" he asked.

"It is the stick from which the messenger ate the fish I gave him."

"What more was said?"

"Much. He thanked me for the fish I shared with him. Answered many questions I had. Blessed me."

"Not many who would think to share a fish. But of all people, you are who I would most expect to."

"He said as much," Rallia replied.

"Consider your message delivered," Ymbrys said with a smile and nod. "Let us speak no more of it."

They were approaching the capital green now. Torches were lit, and Paladins seemed once more to be moving to and fro, though there were significantly fewer of them now.

One of them, wearing the red cape of the Prima Pater, saw the two of them walking, and approached. He was certainly larger than the old Dorian Mür, and walked with both a military air and a weight of the responsibilities on his shoulders.

"Rallia Clouw?" he asked. He glanced at the qavyl, and bowed his head in acknowledgment, but paid little attention to him.

"Yes?"

"I believe I owe you an apology for the way my Paladins treated you. But I'm afraid the apology will have to wait. Where is the Shroud?"

"What do you mean? We brought Searn back and left him as he lay. Your own Paladins will attest to this."

"I understand that, but that doesn't explain why the body of Searn no longer has the Shroud upon its shoulders, nor the Gauntlet on its hand."

* * *

Seriah walked along the snow-dusted road in file with the other monks, and yet she felt more alone than she had in months. Rallia Clouw had held her once the battle had subsided, calming her panic and dragging her back from the precipice of madness. She had floated in a haze of shock, washing her mind free of questions she should have asked. Had Rallia known that the head of their organization was the bearer of the dark shroud? That Searn had murdered her Archimandrite?

The saint, Koragh Neyarn, walked along behind her, as though he sensed she might try to flee. He drove her like a shepherding ynfald, meant to keep her on the path before them, returning to the haven of their Templum. Seriah had thought to question the decision. Kashir and Teralyr would be the worst months to travel. Woodsmen in Bremüm could be hired to take them through the mountains, or they could, as monks, risk the travel into Boronii and Bortali without the fear of being molested by brigands.

Seriah no longer cared. She would do as she was told. And as Koragh had informed her, she would speak to the council of Nifara's saints in Birin, to give testimony to what she had experienced, and they would decide her fate.

*   *   *

Astrid blew on the embers and got a meager fire started. An evergreen bower sheltered them from the white that stretched out to the horizon to the north of the Massif. As she fed branches into the flames and goaded it to life, Katiam pulled out the jars of buttered nut paste. And as the air around the fire warmed, she opened up the cloak wrapped tight around her form, revealing the bud of the flower, closed to the cold.

"Care to join us, little rose?" she asked.

The small thorn had been joined by a second one over the past few days skirting the mountains. Both whistled breathily, and the vines and leaves began to unfurl from the makeshift carrier across her center.

The bud opened up, revealing its small, pink petals. The center of it began to sniff and seek, as a leaf-like hand reached up and touched Katiam's face, before returning to the bud, where the flower sniffed at the leaf. The thorns sighed.

"If it's a plant, does it need soil?" Astrid asked.

"All the soil is cold," Katiam said. "But once the fire warms it, we could half bury it."

She offered one of the jars to Astrid, who took out her knife and dug up a smear of the pulsed nuts, licking it off the blade.

"It'll be nice to reach somewhere safe," Astrid said. "I think we're far enough along; we can head northerly towards Zebudé."

"That might be the closest Vault," Katiam said. "From there we can decide how best to go east."

She pulled out a satchel of candied flowers and held it out for Astrid to take one. It was a broad, purple Loosetongue. Astrid took it, placed the morsel on her tongue, and smiled. Katiam felt something pulling down and looked to see the vine-like leaf take hold of the satchel and curiously feel into it, pulling free one of the sugared candies.

"Should it be allowed to do that?" Astrid asked.

"I have no idea," Katiam said.

The Rotha placed the sugared petal into the center of its flower. Petals moved of their own accord, and the sugared treat disappeared into its depths.

"What are you doing, little rose?" Katiam said, giggling.

"Vvvvllaaaaarozzzzz" the two thorns hummed and whistled.

"What was that?" Astrid said, scooting closer.

"I don't know," Katiam said. "Did you say something, little rose?"

"Laaaaroz."

"I think it said 'Little Rose,'" Astrid said.

"Larozh," the Rotha said again, the two thorns situated to vibrate against one another as they whistled.

"It can talk," Astrid said, smiling.

"And I think," Katiam said, her own smile broadening, "it just said its name."

Epilogue

Hanen had found the small door a week before. It was an old wooden closet in the back of Blackiron. It had been cleaned out to use as a vault for their earnings. He opened the door and crouched down, peering in. He took a candle and placed it inside, then crawled in after it, closing the door behind him. The two books sat there beside him, as well as the heavy bundle he had risked his life and limb for. He opened it up and looked at the chain links made from bone. Each link was whole, with no seams. He wore gloves and dared not touch it with his fingers.

He lifted it and pulled it over his shoulders. Nothing happened. The cold of the little room crept around him, and he shivered. The blackness of the room was deep, and a comfort, as he hid this act from the world. He opened Searn's book, assuming that the Bone Shroud was doing its job, and began to read.

There is not much to say about my childhood. The two men who found me and raised me were not kind, nor unkind. But they slowly explained to me over my childhood and into my formative years that I would become an instrument to bring about the death of gods, and bear the responsibility of building their machination, unread of in any text, and unknown to any god. And together we three began the rites it would take to build the Bone Shroud. For with it, we could take up the tools meant to slay gods, and they would never see us coming. We would not be beholden to their prophecies, nor their curses, but be something else entirely. And thus I grew into my destiny as the Precursor to the End.

The End

TO BE CONTINUED IN
BOOK THREE OF THE KALLATTIAN SAGA:
DARK GAUNTLET

Glossary I - Dramatis Personae

Hanen Clouw (HA-NEHN KHL-OW) — A Black Sentinel mercenary and organizer of the Clouw Sentinel Merchant Detail. Hanen is a 1st Lieutenant in the Black Sentinels, and thus has earned his second hand axe.

Rallia Clouw (RAH-LEEAH KHL-OW) — Like her older brother Hanen, Rallia is a 1st Lieutenant in the Black Sentinels, though she prefers to carry a staff she had built with both of her clubs mounted on the ends. Rallia is also deft with a razor, and often shaves the heads and faces of fellow Black Sentinels.

Jined Brazstein (JIH-NED BRADJ-STEEN) — Rank of Brother Excelsior. Vow of Chastity. Son of Jarl Jaegür von Brazstein of Brazh, Jined left home to avoid execution for murdering a fellow prince of Boroni. Jined joined the Paladins of the Hammer as a Penitent, committing his life to Grissone, the god of Faith.

Katiam Borreau (KAH-TEE-UM BURR-OH) — A Paladame of the Rose. Personal physician to the Matriarch Superioris and Prima Pater. Aspects of Peace, St. Klare, and Dignity.

Seriah Yaledít (SUR-EYE-UH YAHL-EH-DEET) — Monk of Nifara. She is known for often establishing orphanages in towns that have none.

———

Abenard Navien (ABB-IH-NARD NAY-VEE-EN) — A ranking member of the Voktorra guard guild in Mahn Fulhar.

Abgenas Dülar (AB-GHEE-NAHS DOO-LARR) — An old tailor who served in the Protectorate Wars.

Aeger (A-GUR) — Paladin of the Hammer. Rank of Brother Primus. Vow of Silence. Scholar and assistant to Pater Segundus Gallahan Pír.

Alodda Dülar (UH-LAW-THUH DOO-LARR) — A seamstress and daughter of Abgenas Dülar.

Amal Yollis (AH-MALL YAH-LISS) — Paladin of the Hammer. Rank of Brother Primus. Vow of Poverty. Herald.

Astrid Glass (ASS-TRID GLASS) — Paladame of the Rose. Aspects of Discretion, Compassion, and Honor.

Aurín Mateau (AH-REEN MA-TOE) — A Black Sentinel from Œron.

Bell (BELL) — A mysterious Paladin, member of the Motean sect.

Brother Hammer (BROTHER HAMM-ERR) — A mysterious Paladin who quotes scripture. Revealed to be the god of Faith, Grissone, in physical form.

Cävian (CAVE-EE-AN) — Paladin of the Hammer. Rank of Brother Excelsior. Vow of Silence. Twin of Loïc.

Cräg Narn (KRAGG NARN) — An old monk of Nifarah, currently acting as advisor on the Archimandrite's council.

Dane Marric (DAEN MARE-IK) — Paladin of the Hammer. Rank of Brother Excelsior. Vow of Chastity.

Derioth (DERR-EE-OTH) — A Reyem.

Diben Laur (DIE-BENN LAOOR) — A Black Sentinel.

Didus Koel (DIE-DUSS COAL) — Pater Minoris of the Paladins of the Hammer. Vow of Prayer.

Dorian Mür (DOOR-EE-AN MEW-R) — Prima Pater of the Paladins of the Hammer. Head of the Church of Grissone. Vow of Prayer. Became the youngest Prima Pater in history, elected almost unanimously during the Protectorate Wars. He still holds the title, seventy-five years later, at the ripe age of 95.

Dusk (DUSK) — A mysterious Paladin, member of the Motean sect.

Eimeé Dülar (AY-MEE DOO-LARR) — Seamstress. Wife of Abgenas Dülar.

Ensayez dela Neitha (EN-SAY-EZZ DELL-UH NEETHAH) — A monk of Nifarah.

Eralt Loth (ERR-ALT LAW-TH) — Paladin of the Hammer. Rank of Primus. A Motean.

Esenath Chloïs (AH-SEN-OTH KHL-OH-EES) — Paladame of the Rose. Botanist. Sidieratan. Aspects of Cleanliness and Charity.

Etienne Oren (EH-TEE-EN OR-EN) — Paladin of the Hammer. Rank of Brother Excelsior. Vow of Poverty. Guard in the Prima Pater's Entourage.

Gallahan Pír (GAL-A-HAN PEER) — Pater Segundus of the Paladins of the Hammer. Chief Librarian of Pariantür. Vow of Pacifism.

Gervaine (JERR-VANE) — A Paladin of the Hammer. A Motean.

Goev Mütse (GO-UV MOO-TSEE) — A buckle-maker.

Jurgon Upona (YOOR-GAHN OO-POH-NA) — Paladin of the Hammer. Rank of Brother Primus. The Prima Pater's Seneschal. Husband of Sabine Upona. Vow of Prayer.

Kadok Galistine (KA-DOCK GAL-IH-STINE) — Pontifex of the Sect of Thüm.

Kalle Bann (KALE BANN) — A Black Sentinel.

Kash (KASH) — A storyteller.

Kerei Lant (KEE-REE LAN-T) — Monk of Nifara. Councillor to the Archimandrite.

Klent Rigal (KHLENT REE-GALL) — High Priest of Aben.

Loïc (LOW-EEK) — Paladin of the Hammer. Rank of Brother Excelsior. Vow of Silence. Twin of Cävian. From Setera.

Loranne (LORE-ANN) — An old blind woman who runs an orphanage in her home.

Maeda Mür (MAY-DAH MEW-R) — Matriarch Superioris of the Paladames of the Rose. Head of the Crysalas Church. Wife to Dorian Mür, Prima Pater of the Paladins.

Melit (MELL-ITT) — A Paladin of the Hammer. Rank of Brother Primus. Ranking Paladin of the Bastion in Mahn Fulhar.

Meresmand the Tollkeeper (MARE-EZ-MAND THE TOLLKEEPER) — A member of the Amethyst Council in the Veld.

Milu Gentry (MEE-LOO GENTRY) — A new Black Sentinel.

Nair (NAY-ER) — A storyteller.

Nichal Guess (NEE-KAHL GESS) — Pater Segundus of the Paladins of the Hammer. Castellan of Pariantür. Vow of Poverty.

Oditte Foi (OH-DIE-TT FOI) — Abbess Superioris of the Crysalas Convent in Mahn Fulhar.

Ophedia del Ishe (OH-FEE-DEE-AH DEL EE-SHAY) — A new Black Sentinel and apprentice to Searn VeTurres.

Pell Maran (PELL MAH-RAN) — Archimandrite of the Monks of Nifara.

Pellian Noss (PELL-EE-AN NAH-SS) — Paladin of the Hammer. Pater Minoris of the Piedala Fortress. Vow of Prayer.

Runah Dülar (ROO-NUH DOO-LARR) — Younger sister of Alodda.

Sabine Upona (SAH-BEEN OO-POH-NAH) — Paladame of the Rose. Assistant to the Matriarch Superioris. Aspects of Humility and Discretion.

Searn VeTurres (SURN VEH-TOOR-EZ) — Captain of the Black Sentinels.

Shroud (SHROUD) — A mysterious disembodied voice who speaks through a Shadebook. Member of the Motean sect.

Silab Rork (SIGH-LAB RORK) — Grandmaster of the Voktorra guard guild.

Silas Merun (SIGH-LUSS MARE-UN) — Paladin of the Hammer. Rank of Brother Paladin.

Sälla Fyfe (SAW-LUH FIE-FF) — A Black Sentinel.

Slate (SLATE) — Paladin of the Hammer. Rank of Primus. Vow of Silence. Motean.

Valér Queton (VAH-LAIR KEH-TAHN) — Pater Minoris of the Paladins of the Hammer. Standard Bearer of Grissone. Vow of Pacifism.

Vanguard (VAN-GARD) — A mysterious Paladin, member of the Motean sect.

Velab Erdthal II (VELL-AB URD-THALL) — King of Mahndür.

Veli Mütse (VELL-EE MOO-TSEE) — Wife of Goev Mütse.

Whisper (WHISPER) — A smaller black ynfald.

Ymbrys Veronia (IM-BREES VER-OH-NEE-AH) — A qavyl spice merchant.

Zanghard (ZANN-GUARD) — The Shepherdess of the Veld.

Zenn Abar (ZENN AH-BARR) — Grandmaster of the flax guild.

Zhag rm Tellis (ZHAW-GH REM TELL-ISS) — A young hrelgren merchant.

Glossary 2 - Pantheon of Kallattai

The Existence — The Maker of All and He That Is, the world of Kallattai came into being at the first word: BEGIN. He made first the two brother gods, and then the two sisters as their wives. Power was granted to them, and through them all was created, and the Existence was worshiped.

Aben (A-BENN) — High King in Lomïn, the Ever-Day. Made from a white star. His way is the Path. His Gray Watchers hold lanterns to guide those that seek the Path. His tenets are an Arrow, pointing the way to the green fields of Lomïn. The Chalice raised symbolizes his first domain, the sea. And from those depths the Ancient Ones sing.

Wyv-Thüm (WIHV THOOM) — The Three-Eyed Judge in Noccitan, the Ever-Night. Brother to Aben, and formed by the Existence from the well of a black star. When he descended to his Realm of Noccitan he donned the title Thüm, or Judge.

Crysania (CRI-SAH-NEE-AH) — Life Mother, Purity Resplendent, and Seamstress of the Future Tapestry is wife to Aben. Only she can untangle the knots caused by time and see what the future holds. Her people are those that seek to protect the Dweol, the World-Roses that speak directly to her and one another, providing the Crysalas Integritas a chance to glance, ever briefly, at the Future.

Sakharn (SA-KAHRN) — Wife to Wyv, Shepherdess of the Veld—the Dreamscape from which the impossible is dreamed and made fact. She is the goddess of the Improbable, for she impossibly birthed the Deceiver without her husband to sire him.

THE CHILDREN OF ABEN AND CRYSANIA

Lae'zeq (LAY-ZEK) — Firstborn of Aben, god of Wisdom, Curious One. His people, the qavylli, follow his path into the depths of knowledge, for upon his own pages he wrote the secrets of life. Long has he now sojourned, seeking an answer to the prophecy that ties his fate to the death of his closest friend.

Grissone-Anka (GRI-ZOHN AHN-KHA) — Twin-Souled, god of Faith. As Grissone came of age his soul was two. The Anka, who soars above all and sees all, is joined to him. He was the creator of man, who abandoned Grissone to worship many. Now his loyal followers are few: the Paladins who seek protection of the people who no longer follow their god.

Nifara (NIH-FA-RAH) — The Virgin of Justice, Soul Messenger, Once-Betrothed, Future Healer. She learned to step between worlds from her once-betrothed, Kos-Yran, before he fell. She bears now the responsibility of that now-mad god, escorting souls between worlds they were never meant to set foot upon. Justice is her only concern, as she attempts to balance the scales perfectly.

Kasne et Terral (KAZ-NEH ET TEH-RAHL) — Prince of the Forest, Toucher of Souls, Youngest of Aben and Crysania, Kasne strode from the forests that he had created, his people, the Minotyr on his heels. And yet it was he who agreed to leave his own people to take the enslaving Gren under his command, and from them came the Hrelgrens, touched by his hand, and blessed with a command of peace.

THE CHILDREN OF WYV AND SAKHARN

Rionne (RYE-OWN) — Firstborn of Wyv and Sakharn, Creator of Civilization, the Arbiter, The Fallen Warrior—fallen to ruin when he was deceived by Achanerüt. Driven mad, he slew his greatest creations, and turned his own people into a scourge of the sky.

Kea'Rinoul (KEE-AH-RIH-NOOL) — The Scarred One, He-Who-Was-Beautiful. Kea'Rinoul abandoned his own people, the Goranc, for he had been a god of beauty, marred by his fallen brothers. It is said he is a god who bathes in the blood of his followers, the T'Akai, wracked with torment by his own visage.

Kos-Yran (KOSS EE-RAHN) — The Mad Gift-Giver, Once-Walker-Between-Worlds, Kashir Two-Gloves, the Walker. Yet now he is banished to wander, gifting curses to those that seek him out. His own people, the vül, though small in number, are an infestation upon the civilized, sowing mayhem and destruction wherever they call home.

Achanerüt (AH-KEN-ER-OOT) — The Deceiver, The Weaver, The Thirteen-Limbed One, Fatherless. His thirteen limbs sow lies and weave dissension. His eyes see far, and bring kings to their knees. All that is in ruin is his attribute. All that is built up fears that he shall tear it down. The machinations of his web cannot be understood, even by the gods.

Glossary 3 - Black Sentinels

The Black Sentinels are a mercenary organization in which each individual seeks out their own bodyguard contracts, and pays dues back to the organization, thus allowing them to wear their trademark black, peak-hooded cloak. They carry various weapons to denote their rank, which equates to their pay grade, hidden under their cloaks to keep their ability concealed.

BANDED CLUB — An initiate with a single club is not yet an official Black Sentinel.

BLACK CLOAK — This marks their joining the organization. They now pay dues back to headquarters.

2ND CLUB — Sergeant rank. Can ask for a full silver Baro a day in pay in the northern nations.

HAND AXE — Lieutenants can negotiate a higher pay, armed with a more lethal weapon.

2ND AXE — 1st Lieutenants have several clients who will give them good reference.

CROSSBOW — Only by being promoted by the upper echelons can a Black Sentinel become a Captain.

BATTLE AXE — Commanders are rarely seen away from the Black Sentinels headquarters in Limae.

Glossary 4 - Paladins of the Hammer

The Paladins are the followers of Grissone, god of Faith. Each Paladin takes on one of the five active Vows. There once were those that took the sixth Vow, that of Introspection, or Blindness. But none have taken it since the last Prima Pater to take the Vow disappeared long ago. The Paladins were founded in the Hrelgren Imperial Year IIII. Just before the T'Akai first appeared, launching attacks into what is now the Protectorate of Pariantür, and simultaneously against the Hrelgren Empire and Qavylli Republic, the seven apostles of Grissone began their work at Pariantür. Heeding the call of the seven, humanity brandished weapons against the invaders. Many of the men who survived the war stayed on at Pariantür, founding the Order.

The Paladins live in communities of two or more brothers and their monasteries are scattered across the world and have different sizes and designations.

BASTIONS
Bastions always have at least two brothers stationed there. There can be as many as twenty-five. Most major cities and towns have a Bastion, and many are raised at intervals along long stretches of road between cities.

FORTRESSES
A Fortress commands local Bastions, and usually has upward of one hundred Paladins stationed there.

CITADELS
There are four Citadels. Each commands a network of Fortresses and Bastions.
PARIANTÜR — Pariantür is the head of the entire order and acts as guardian over the eastern lands known as the Protectorate of the Hammer. Over half of the entire order is stationed there—over seven thousand Paladins. There is enough

space to house over ten thousand Paladins if necessary. The Paladames have over three-thousand sisters stationed at Pariantür.

St. HAMUL — This Citadel holds sway over the Order in the eastern nations of Ganthic. Nearly five hundred brothers are stationed there.

THE AERIE — Located in the country of Limae, the Aerie has almost four hundred brothers stationed there. Northwestern Ganthic is its domain.

AMMAR — Located in Ormach, Ammar Citadel has over one thousand Paladins stationed there. It is a source of great learning and agriculture. While this Citadel controls the fewest Fortresses and Bastions, it is the greatest library in the lands of man outside of Pariantür.

Those seeking admittance to the Order of the Hammer begin as either:

ACOLYTE — Someone who seeks out Pariantür and goes through trials of the soul.

PENITENT — Someone who has chosen servitude over imprisonment.

These lower level Acolytes and Penitents are all grouped together and wear brown robes, shaving their heads. They are for all intents and purposes servants in the Hammer, learning to live the life of a Paladin. Once they have learned the Rule of St. Ikhail, and have served their term they are allowed to join the Order, taking on the entry level of Estudiate.

ESTUDIATE — The Estudiate lives a life of routine and constant change as they are tested in various occupations over the course of a year. During this time they will review each Vow, and come to a decision of which Vow they will take. This decision marks the completion of the Estudiate rank.

NEOPHYTE — The Neophyte takes on their Vow, and begins study under a master in their chosen trade. They are given their hammer, which is chained to their belt by the twenty-two links, and they are given the Vow-Icon which will hang from their belt until they receive cordons, from which it will then hang.

Vow of Chastity — Haloed Hammer
Vow of Poverty — Stylized Pattern
Vow of Silence — Tower
Vow of Pacifism — Shield
Vow of Prayer — Anka's Wing
Vow of Blindness — Band

PALADIN — When the Neophyte is given their armor, they are called a Paladin, but in name only. It is only if they proceed past this level that they will be considered a true Paladin by the Brotherhood. They have a single year to test as a Journeyman in their field if they wish to proceed. If they do not master their chosen profession, they will wait anywhere from five to ten years before being allowed to test once more.

BROTHER PALADIN — If deemed worthy, a Paladin is given the red cordons, marking them both a Master in their trade, and a Brother Paladin—full member of the Brotherhood with full rights to vote on all matters. If leadership requires they take on another trade, they will learn from, and proceed through the same lessons and trials, however, nothing can take their rank of Brother Paladin from them.

BROTHER EXCELSIOR — Brother Excelsiors are the equivalent to a lieutenant, commanding brothers of lower rank, marked by green cordons. These have shown themselves to rise above the rest in an occupation—a senior master that all defer to, including some higher levels. As an example, one Brother Excelsior in the Smithy may be an expert and specialist at inlaying metals and most will defer to their knowledge as needed.

BROTHER ADJUTANT — Marked by white cordons, there is rarely more than a single Brother Adjutant in an occupation at a single location. They often fill administrative roles left vacant by higher- ranking Paladins. This rank is also considered the first "true" leadership rank, although most are administrators. Those with the knack for leadership are only passing through the rank on their way to Primus.

BROTHER PRIMUS — Leaders and masters, the black-cordoned Primus commands both respect and authority. If at a Bastion, they will be the highest- ranked Paladin. While uncommon, Primus can hold the highest rank at some Fortresses.

PATER MINORIS — A Paladin will rarely rise to this rank without there being a vacancy. Each Citadel is led by one, and there is a Pater Minoris from each Vow stationed at Pariantür. Besides wearing gold cordons, their armor is also often adorned with symbology reflective of the long traditions of a Citadel. The five Pater Minorii stationed at Pariantür fill very important roles in the community.

Pater Minoris of Prayer Hiram van Höllebon, Chaplain to Pariantür
Pater Minoris of Poverty Mason Diggle, Keeper of Fealty
Pater Minoris of Chastity Pol Dunkirk, Hospitaliter
Pater Minoris of Silence Daveth, Grandmaster Smith
Pater Minoris of Pacifism Klous Girard, Groundskeeper

PATER SEGUNDUS — Under the Prima Pater there is a council of four Pater Segundii. With the Prima Pater in their lead, each Vow is represented. They are marked by blue cordons and their words hold nearly as much authority at the Prima Pater himself.

Pater Segundus of Poverty Nichal Guess, Pariantür's Castellan
Pater Segundus of Pacifism Gallahan Pír, Master Scribe
Pater Segundus of Silence Athmor, Master Cellarer
Pater Segundus of Chastity Agapius Emiro, Sacrist

PRIMA PATER — There is only one Prima Pater. A Prima Pater's armor is crafted to match the motifs and symbols of the founding saint of their Vow. When a Prima Pater's rank is passed on, one of the Pater Segundii under him will take on the role, donning armor of their own figurehead saint, thus ensuring that another Vow takes dominance.

VOWS OF THE PALADINS OF THE HAMMER

VOW OF PRAYER — Those that adopt this Vow ground themselves in the memorization of scripture, and make the conscious effort to speak all of their inner thoughts directly to their god.

VOW OF POVERTY — Paladins are still supported via family that pay a stipend to Pariantür, or by their own trade practiced at their location. Those that take this Vow are required to do additional duty merely to pay for their food and board. They are never paid a stipend, nor may they keep personal items.

VOW OF CHASTITY — Those that take this Vow are forbidden from marrying. Many avoid contact with members of the opposite sex entirely.

VOW OF PACIFISM — Paladins who take this Vow never raise their hammer against another, seeking peace by any other means.

VOW OF SILENCE — Brothers who take this Vow do not speak another word for the rest of their lives, instead communicating through their hands. These brothers also give up their surnames as their founder, Sternovis did.

VOW OF BLINDNESS — This Vow is no longer taken. Those that did bound their eyes away from the world.

Glossary 5 - Crysalas Societas

Followers of Crysania are known collectively as the Crysalas Societas. This includes women of the secret Vaults, known as the Crysalas Integritas, the Shield-maidens of Boroni and Bronue, as well as qavylli and hrelgrens who have chosen to follow Crysania. They meet in secret Vaults across the world of Kallattai, and guard prophecies shared at the Dweol, as well as each other. They were hunted down by the Church of Aben long ago and went further into hiding. The majority fled to Pariantür, where they took on the new name of Paladame alongside the Paladins, known as the Crysalas Honoris. After they spent time reevaluating their organization, they began to trickle back towards the other countries, and changed the nature of their Vaults to be ones that guarded women from predatory men. Those that hail from Pariantür are still called Paladames, and often wear armor of that namesake.

Across the entire organization, however, members of the Crysalas take on Aspects of purity, rather than Vows. Some of these have been around since the foundation, while others have developed over time. Most sisters take on an average of three Aspects, though some take on more. They are noted publicly by adornments, which creates a general customized look among the sisters who otherwise wear only white robes and headdresses. These Aspects fall into four categories:

Blossom — Purity of Form
Thorn — Purity of Choice
Leaf — Purity of Service
Root — Purity of Function

ASPECTS OF THE BLOSSOM
ASPECT OF CLEANLINESS — (Shaven Head) This Aspect focuses on a ritualistic and meticulous cleaning regimen.
ASPECT OF SILENCE — (Veil) Wears a veil over their face so they cannot be seen. They are not completely silent, talking in quiet whispers, but experience an aloneness that others naturally give them.
ASPECT OF VIRGINITY — (Gilded Rose) Women who select this Aspect are

forbidden to marry. And while most Crysalas do not marry, they are not forbidden from doing so as these sisters are.

ASPECT OF PEACE — (Wooden Mace) Sisters who take this Aspect cause no harm to another.

ASPECT OF STRICTNESS — (Solid Plate on Shoulder) — Sisters who take this Aspect have no choice over their diet. They must eat what they are served, and may not leave any of it untouched, nor ask for more when the meal is concluded.

ASPECTS OF THE THORN

(It is often frowned upon that any sister take more than one Thorn Aspect, as alone they are hard to take upon oneself.)

ASPECT OF SANCTITY — (Gloves) Sisters who take on the Aspect of Sanctity do not feel the touch of another save through a glove.

ASPECT OF SOLITUDE — (Fetter Hat) The fetter hat is a very recognizable adornment. It forces the wearer to look towards their feet at all times.

ASPECT OF SOLEMNITY — (Black Circlet) One of the harder Aspects to master, the Aspect of Solemnity allows no outward show of emotion.

ASPECT OF PRESERVATION — (Leaves—no roses on uniform) Those who take this Aspect may not eat meat of any kind.

ASPECT OF ST. KLARE — (Thorn Necklace) This Aspect was developed when members of the Aspect of Preservation overcame their abstinence from meat by drinking too much. St. Klare developed a variant that was very ascetic, allowing the eating of only breads, insects, water, and certain fruits and vegetables.

ASPECTS OF THE LEAF

ASPECT OF DISCRETION — (Rose Earrings) This Aspect requires a sister to listen intently to others without interrupting.

ASPECT OF CHARITY — (Brown Robe) The Charitable Sisters are very often found matched with the Paladins who take on the Vow of Poverty.

ASPECT OF COMPASSION — (Dwov Elbow Guards) These sisters are required to serve those with needs that can be met.

ASPECT OF OBEDIENCE — (Bell Earrings) The Aspect of Obedience is not a slaving Aspect, but one that allows one to be congenial, and helpful as requested.

ASPECT OF DIGNITY — (Bound Sleeves) — Those sisters who practice this Aspect seek to restore the dignity of those that are ailing or are elderly.

ASPECTS OF THE ROOT

ASPECT OF HUMILITY — (Heavy Boots) — The menial, janitorial tasks of a sister of the Aspect of Humility keep the order continuing as they do what no one else wants.

ASPECT OF CLARITY — (Scroll Front Cloth) Those sisters with a knack for memory, or wish to develop such a gift take on this Aspect. They are constantly testing one another with the recitation of verse.

ASPECT OF HONOR — (Thorn Spiked Mace) Of all the Aspects, this is the most practiced among the Paladames at Pariantür. While they do not go out on patrol against the T'Akai, they do leave Pariantür to act as guards at all the hidden Vaults across Ganthic.

ASPECT OF FORM — (Plain Bracers) The Sisters of Form are capable of besting the largest of men without wearing armor, nor using a weapon.

ASPECT OF FUNCTION — (Utility Belt) Those that seek to master an art or craft will take on this Aspect and delve as deeply as they can into their art.

Glossary 6 - Monks of Nifarah

The Monastic Order of the Staff, or the Monks of Nifara as they are more commonly known, are perhaps the oldest religious organization on Kallattai, and make up the sole followers of Nifara. While the largest community of monks are humans, Nifarans can be found in every race on Kallattai. Their purpose is to offer judgment between two arguing parties. They rule fairly, impartially, and quickly. Some deem their judgments too harsh, but this is tempered by their consistency. When a monk of Nifara is addressed, the correct honorific in the lands of man is Nefer. This is said to be a very old title, dating back to an older name for Nifara, Nefereh. When a judgment is made, a stick is broken, and given to each side of the argument, in memoriam. Nine times a judgment has been made that was deemed world-shifting. When that occurred, the monk broke not a stick, but their staff. These nine are honored above all others, with statuary made in their likeness at the Templum of Nifara in Birin. While there are many myths surrounding the Nine Saints, the most interesting fact is that none of their tales reference how they died.

Afterword

Even authors find unexpected twists in what they write. Whisper has long been planned, written, re-written, pulled, and reintroduced. To finally have our lovable scaled companion brings a certain satisfaction. But the unexpected twist for me was the introduction of Alodda. She just showed up in a one draft, and has made sure to ask me, however politely, for attention and pages. I'm not complaining. She's a joy to write, and she offers yet another hurdle in Hanen's way. Not a hurdle toward accomplishing his goals, but a roadblock to try and prevent him from making mistakes. And oh boy, mistakes Hanen has made, and will make.

Alodda has also provided for me additional opportunities to do something I find a great joy in: moments of normalcy. It is probably these small vignettes, from telling tales, to playing the local game, that a few readers have commented on—tagging my book as a cozy fantasy. I enjoy those moments in a book, show, or movie, that take a second to show the rain, or focus on a small beetle crossing a sidewalk. They remind you that while adventure threatens to change everything, nothing truly changes. The world continues to thrive outside of these characters and our lives.

And so, as you close this book, before you pick up your next one, take some time to yourself. Go for a walk outside. Watch snow fall across your favorite vista. And when you've done that, return to your chosen world of in print.

While you're browsing online for your next book, could you take the time to write a review of the Kallattian Saga books? It is only through your spreading the world that the Kallattian Saga will be discovered. I can shout it from the rooftops until I'm hoarse. But it's your voice that is best heard.

Until next year, when Volume Three comes out, I wish for you success in your own journey, and moments of normalcy that you'll think back on as character defining.

—Andrew D Meredith